HOW TO GET AWAY WITH LYING

ENYA CLANCY

HOW TO GET AWAY WITH LYING.

ISBN 978-1-7383523-3-3

To everyone

who is struggling to find hope,

this is for you.

Playlist

"Still Alive" ~ Demi Lovato

"Who Are You, Really?" ~ Mikky Ekko

"Angel" ~ Kate Voegele

"i can't breathe" ~ Bea Miller

"Help Me Close My Eyes" ~ Those Dancing Days

"We're All Gonna Die" ~ Joy Oladokun and Noah Kahan

"The Night We Met" ~ Lord Huron

"Love Story" ~ Taylor Swift

"Halo" ~ Bethany Joy Lenz

"Exhale" ~ Sabrina Carpenter

"Deja Vu" ~ Olivia Rodrigo

"Tragic" ~ Fleurie and Tommee Profitt

"Afterlife" ~ Hailee Steinfeld

"You Belong With Me" ~ Taylor Swift

"Someday" ~ Bryan Greenberg

You either die a hero or live long enough to see yourself become the villain.

—Batman: The Dark Knight

August 1ˢᵗ, 2015 – 8:00 PM

 T ied!" Adley Morgenstern and I shouted for the fourth time that night, sounding more exhausted than happy.

The stars filled up on the TV screen before announcing my and Adley's scores. We then flopped down on the leather couch behind us, where Jessi Alvarez sat, huddling under a gray wool blanket. I tossed a lock of my golden-blonde hair out of my blue eyes as I smiled over at Jessi, who was twiddling her thumbs and looking out the living room window. She was clearly bored out of her mind.

Once again, I felt bad for crushing her score in Just Dance. So, I tried to find something to say that would boost her mood. "You know, Little J, you were really good at that Britney Spears song."

"I got *two* stars for that dance. *You* guys got *five*," Jessi grumbled. She didn't look away from the darkening sky.

"That doesn't matter," I remarked, brushing the comment off. I now realized that *wasn't* helping — but it wasn't necessarily *my* fault for being so good at something I barely played anymore.

"Why don't we do something else?" Adley offered.

She tossed her white Wii remote dangerously close to Jessi, who flinched as it landed. She scowled at Adley, but Adley didn't seem to realize as she bent down to shut off the Wii.

"I mean," Jessi began slowly as she sat up and unraveled the blanket wrapped around her. "We don't *have* to. You guys can keep playing–"

"Oh, come *on!*" I cheered as I walked over to the coffee table. I filled up the empty, pink bowl with more barbeque-flavored chips. "This is *our* sleepover, which means we decide what to do *together*."

"*Okay.* What did you have in mind?" Jessi asked as she plucked a chip from the bowl.

"What about Truth or Dare?" Adley smirked, and as happy as *I* was about the idea, I caught Jessi's smile drop.

I knew that Jessi hated playing that game with us since Adley and I played at a *way* more extreme level than Jessi. But Adley always reminded me that Jessi needed to get out of her shell once in a while to have a little fun.

"Ooh, a classic slumber party game! I like it," I stated. Without giving Jessi a second to say no, Adley and I sat down on the floor with the chip bowl between us.

"Um, I don't know, guys," Jessi muttered, biting one of her blue, chipped nails. "I-I was actually looking forward to watching *Twilight* for the first time."

"*Nonsense.* I don't even know why Anna suggested we watch *that* film," Adley chuckled, playing with a lock of dark blonde hair. "If you wanted a rom-com, you should have picked *Clueless*. Paul Rudd is so much hotter than sparkly Robert Pattinson–"

"Why don't we just play–"

"Truth or Dare is *just* a game, Jess. Unless, of course, you're hiding something." Adley laughed as Jessi blushed and glanced down at the floor.

"I promise we'll go easy. Right, A?" I looked over at my best friend, as Jessi hesitantly sat down beside me.

"Of course. We'll save the harder levels of this game for the *pros*," Adley promised, irritation lacing her cheerful tone. She glanced at me with a smile that I could tell was forced.

Something inside of me whispered that Adley wouldn't play nice for long. After all, she always enjoyed making these games a *little* messy.

However, this only made me more excited to play.

"Fine," Jessi huffed, pasting on a smile. "Someone, ask me first."

"Wow, I didn't see *that* coming," Adley mused, her eyes widening in surprise.

"Okay, truth or dare?" I asked Jessi, happy to see that she was wanting to play after all.

"Truth," Jessi answered. As confidently as she tried to respond, though, I could see her muscles tense up.

I searched for a question, trying to avoid the many that came to mind that I knew would make Jessi uncomfortable. I soon settled with something that Adley would still approve of. "If you were put in the position to either sacrifice yourself or let someone else die, what would you do?"

"I'd sacrifice myself," Jessi admitted immediately. She didn't even take a second to consider her answer, and my eyes widened in shock. "That's what I'd want someone else to do for me."

I smiled, knowing that Jessi was playing the kindness card.

Adley, on the other hand, rolled her eyes. I could tell that the response was getting on her nerves. "Okay, there, Miss Sappy. It's *your* turn to ask a question. And, please, go harder. This isn't third grade."

I could see the anger boiling inside of Jessi, but she stayed calm and kept a smile on her face. "You want *harder*?" she asked with an unfamiliar, mischievous glint in her brown eyes. "Okay, Adley. Truth or dare?"

"Dare," Adley said confidently as if she wasn't afraid of what Jessi could ask. After all, everyone in Ember Falls, Wisconsin thought she was too innocent and kind to even hurt a fly.

"I dare you to take off your shirt. And you must stay shirtless for the rest of the game," Jessi declared with a smirk.

"*Easy*," Adley purred as she tugged at her gray t-shirt and pulled it over her head. After tossing the shirt aside and fixing her hair, she sat up straighter. She didn't seem to care that she was only wearing her black Victoria Secret bra. "Now, Anna. Your turn. Truth or dare?"

"Truth," I answered, wanting to avoid doing a dare. Knowing Adley, all she wanted now was for somebody else to do something embarrassing so that she wasn't alone.

"Out of the three of us in this room, who do you think would die first in a horror movie?"

Classic Adley and her addiction to slasher films.

"Of course, you would die first, Adley Morgenstern," I teased with a grin, and Adley's jaw dropped as if offended by the remark. "I see you being the character who doesn't look behind themselves before the killer smashes their head with an axe or a shovel."

"*Hey!*" Adley cried in defense. "After all the movies I've watched, I'd *definitely* be a Final Girl." She crossed her arms over her chest, scowling. "And if I *did* die, the murder weapon would *at least* be a knife like in the classics." Adley sighed, shaking her head. "Anyway, it's your turn to ask someone, Anna."

I mentally sighed, feeling divided between having fun or playing things safe. I wanted to loosen Jessi up – she seemed ready for it after daring Adley. But I didn't know what question to ask.

"Truth or dare–" I stopped myself mid sentence as I heard a creak from nearby and caught sight of my annoying twin walking down the main staircase. He passed quickly in front of the living room on his way toward the kitchen. "Ethan!"

My brother rolled his eyes exaggeratedly as he slowly retraced his steps and entered the living room. He poked his head inside, taking a long glance around the room before spotting Adley. For the longest second, I then caught him staring at her chest, his eyes wide in shock, and I had to bite my tongue to stop myself from laughing.

His face turned red before he looked down at the ground, and then up at me as if trying to act cool. "Um, y-yeah?"

"Truth or dare?"

"Ugh," he moaned, glancing between Adley and me as if finally understanding what was going on. He then walked into the room with a horrified expression on his face. "Why am *I* playing?"

"Because it's fun when you play," I laughed, hoping the fact would make him more intrigued. "Come on, it's just a game."

The truth was, though, I just wanted the opportunity to embarrass him in front of his crush. He always acted as if I *didn't* know that he was in love with my best friend, but I had known since the night of the ninth-grade dance – even before he had asked Adley to dance with him. The look that had been on his face when she rejected him made it obvious that he wasn't looking at her as *just* a friend.

"*Fine*, dare," Ethan sighed as he sat down on the couch. His arms were crossed over his chest as he attempted to look cool, though I could see through his façade that he was nervous. "I don't trust you when it comes to dares."

"Okay," I responded with a giggle as I glanced around the room. "I dare you to compliment the prettiest girl in the room."

Ethan shifted uncomfortably as if I had asked him to dance naked in the middle of the road. He cracked his knuckles, and I could see the veins pulse on his neck. "Okay. Um… A-Adley," he began as his face immediately turned as red as a tomato. I watched as he licked his bottom lip slowly before his eyes fell upon Adley's chest. "I, um, like your, um, bra."

The room went silent, and Adley's face flushed crimson before Jessi and I burst into a laughing fit. As we did, though, I noticed how we were the only two who were laughing. Ethan and Adley sat awkwardly, barely moving and avoiding making eye contact with each other.

"*Okay*, so I can tell that the dare was a *little* mean," I concluded as I stopped laughing, and so did Jessi. I didn't regret what I had asked Ethan to do – it had turned out even better than I imagined it would – but I didn't want to seem cruel. "To make it fair, it's your turn to ask, E."

"All right," he replied with a grin on his face. "*Anna, truth or dare?*"

"Dare," I told him right away, having predicted this happening.

"Okay, Miss Confidence. I dare you to kiss a girl in this room." It was now his turn to smirk with satisfaction.

"I have a boyfriend," I reminded Ethan, hoping that bringing Drake up would change his mind. The thought of choosing which friend to kiss made my heartbeat speed up way too fast.

I would do *anything* but that.

Spin the Bottle was one thing, but when it came to picking who was "better," it didn't seem right. *Especially* when my mind always leaned toward one person in particular–

"Since when have *you* backed out of a dare?" Ethan laughed, shaking me from my thoughts. "Remember, it's *just a game*." He was becoming an asshole, and he knew it.

But maybe I *was* just overthinking everything. Maybe I was the only one who believed that choosing between which of my two close friends I should kiss would change things between us. It was just a petty dare, after all. I didn't want to back out – it would go to Ethan's head way too much.

"Fine," I replied as a knot formed in my stomach.

As I was about to lean toward the person that I had chosen, though, Jessi exclaimed, "I'm *really* thirsty. I-I need a glass of water." Before anyone could tell her to wait, she stood up and ducked out of the room.

I caught myself sighing in disappointment.

"And *I* need to change," Adley added, still obviously feeling uncomfortable from Ethan's comment. She stood up slowly, picked up her wrinkled shirt, and marched up the stairs, hugging the shirt to her chest so that the front of her wasn't exposed. A few seconds later, I heard the faint sound of a door slamming shut.

Ethan looked over at me, concern painted all over his face. "I-I should go after her?" he said, though it sounded more like a question than a statement. "I probably just made her feel uncomfortable–"

"No, *stay*," I insisted as I stood up. "*I* will go see if she's okay. No offense, but you'll probably only make it worse." Before Ethan could add anything, I zipped past him and ran up the stairs.

The upstairs hallway was dark and eerie. But I was positive that Adley was inside my bedroom once I found the door closed and heard crying coming from behind it. "A?" I whispered, hoping that she would stop whimpering and answer the door. "*A?*"

Realizing that she wasn't planning on answering me, I took a seat on the beige carpet that covered the hardwood floor like soft grass. I then leaned my back against the cold door–

That was when I heard it.

Whispers.

"Leave me alone. Leave me *alone*! I don't want any part in this fucking plan. Just stop, *please!*" The voice was definitely Adley's, and it sounded as if her sobs were weakening her willpower. I wanted to bust down the door and save her from whoever was hurting her—

Wait… is nobody else in there?

After a moment of silence, just to confirm my revelation, Adley added, "I'm going insane! You're just a *voice*, and there is no way that I'm going to hurt *anyone*."

The remark frightened me, but I knew that she wouldn't do such a thing. Adley could be crazy, but she wouldn't do something like that willingly.

It was just the little voice in her head that was commanding her to do so.

I hadn't wanted her to get involved. I had never wanted her to turn into what she was now becoming. As positively as I tried to think, though, I knew that I was too late to save her.

Even the voice in the back of my head agreed with me as it shouted, *"You've been warned, Annabeth Landers. Watch out!"*

Chapter 1
Jessi

I Wouldn't be Standing Here if it Weren't for You

The last thing I would have expected on October thirty-first was to find Adley Morgenstern dead in a cemetery.

But then again, Adley seemed to have a way of ruining everything.

After all, right when she was going to pay for her crimes, Adley had decided to go and *off herself.* Now, a month after her death, I was forced to sit through her funeral, listening to people praise her as if she hadn't been a cold-blooded *murderer.*

"–and I know that Adley is in a better place now. I bet she and my sister are already up to no good," Ethan Landers laughed softly from his spot behind the podium at the front of the church. I watched as he wiped a hand under his eyes. Anger bubbled inside me rather than sympathy.

Ethan shouldn't have been wasting a *single* tear on

his sister's killer.

No one should have been.

Switching focuses, I looked toward Adley's brother, Caleb – who had been away at college until recently – and Adley's mother, who were standing to Ethan's right. Ms. Morgenstern was leaning against her son's shoulder as if he was the only thing keeping her upright. She sniffled into a light blue handkerchief, while Caleb stared into the distance, his face unreadable.

Would they still feel the same if they knew what Adley was?

I was so caught up in my thoughts that I didn't notice Ms. Morgenstern calling my name until my dad nudged me in the shoulder, gesturing toward the empty podium.

Whatever, I thought, feeling people's eyes on me. I slid out of the pew that I was sitting in, then made my way to the front of the church. *I've got a free pass for being weird. I'm supposed to be devastated and all that.*

Once I made it to the front of the church, I looked out at the sea of people. I suddenly felt a little dizzy as I glanced around the church – the sense of déjà-vu was overwhelming. In place of the red roses that had adorned the building during Anna's funeral, there were now white carnations. Anna's photo had also been swapped out for Adley's so that instead of an angel's face, a *murderer's* stared back.

I looked back at the audience, feeling the familiar urge to chew my nails. But I wasn't about to let a speech at *Adley's* funeral make me nervous.

So, instead, I gripped the edges of the podium and took a deep breath – more to calm my anger than anything else. "What is there to say about Adley Morgenstern?"

Would this be considered "burying my problems?"

I watched as the last shovelful of dirt topped off Adley's grave after we exited the church at the end of the ceremony. I now stood awkwardly, sandwiched between Ivy Blackthorn and Nate Tucker, who kept exchanging these strange, sly glances with each other.

Looks like Karma caught up to you, huh, Adley? I thought as I looked down at Adley's headstone – a light gray stone with a few simple designs chiseled on it.

Adley Sofia Morgenstern
Loving Friend and Daughter
May 13th, 1999 – October 31st, 2015

Slowly, everyone then began to disperse, either staring warily at the gloomy sky or trying to comfort Adley's family. Without trying, I could hear people whispering about "the poor Morgenstern family" who had lost two people in only a few years – both Adley and her father.

"Unfortunate, isn't it?" Ivy asked flatly from beside me. She glanced down at her sharp, black nails.

"Like either of you care," I muttered, continuing to stare at Adley's headstone.

"She *was* our friend," Nate protested from my other side, crossing his arms over his chest. "We cared so much about her."

"Oh, *please*," I laughed sharply, rolling my eyes. "Cut the sappiness. You're gonna make me puke."

Nate shot me a glare as he tugged at his black tie. "It's not like we *wanted* her to die—"

"Well, you don't really *look* too sad about it." A smirk appeared on my face, and I laughed cruelly. "But then again, *did* you ever care about Adley? You two *were* hooking up together before Adley and Nate even broke up. You know I sadly saw you guys together the night of Nate's party."

Ivy narrowed her eyes at me as she stepped closer. She then whispered, "When you confronted us two weeks ago, you said you'd keep your mouth *shut*."

"And I will – it's not like anyone would care now. But I'm also reminding you that *I* have the upper hand now – and that you should really work on your acting skills."

"I could say the same thing about *you*, Short Stack," Ivy responded, leaning away from me and plastering a look of boredom on her face. "You don't look even *close* to sad. Though, if I were you, I would be more worried than anything."

"And why is *that*?" I hissed, putting my hands on my hips.

"Haven't you heard that bad things come in threes?" Ivy asked, a smirk pulling at her glossed lips. "First Annabeth, then Adley…"

"*You* are probably gonna be next," Nate chuckled, filling in the blank as his hazel-green eyes narrowed at me.

I scoffed at his attempt at a warning. "Is that supposed to *scare* me?"

"No," Ivy answered simply, straightening the sleeves of her black blazer. "But it might make you think twice before you do something stupid."

"Adley killed Anna," I whispered to myself, leaning, shell-shocked, against the banister of Adley's staircase on Halloween night. "Adley killed Anna."

Part of me wanted to scream, part of me wanted to pound Adley into the ground, and another part of me wanted to puke.

Adley killed Anna…

But she's not going to get away with it–

Someone sprinted past me, slamming into my shoulder but not stopping to apologize. I looked in their direction and noticed that it was Ethan, who was running so quickly that he was tripping over his feet. He flung open the front door and ran out of Adley's house.

Curious to know what the hell was going on, I followed, my shock-numbed mind seeming to forget that I had more important things to worry about besides Ethan's whereabouts. I trailed behind him as he darted down the dark streets, wishing that my legs were longer so that it wouldn't take so much effort to chase after him.

When Ethan finally slowed his pace, we arrived at the cemetery. Without a moment's hesitation, he shoved his way through the front gate and resumed his insane sprinting.

A graveyard. In the pitch dark. On Halloween.

You've *got* to be kidding me, Ethan.

I could barely make out Ethan's silhouette in the inky darkness, so I focused on following the sounds of his footsteps in the damp grass.

Where in hell is he *going*–?

Ethan's footsteps halted, and I ducked behind a

nearby gravestone. "Adley?" Ethan's voice called. "Adley, it's Ethan!"

He's looking for Adley? Adley's here?

But if Adley was in the graveyard, she clearly hadn't heard Ethan.

"Adley?" Ethan shouted again, his voice sounding slightly more panicked now. "Adley, where are you?"

I saw a flashlight click on, illuminating a small patch of grass—

A horrible choking sound, somewhere between a sob and a scream, sounded, and the flashlight fell from Ethan's hands. "Adley!" he screamed, dropping to the ground. "Adley, answer me!"

In the dim light of Ethan's flashlight, I could make out the horrifying scene in front of us: Adley, in a short red dress, lying crumpled against Anna's gravestone. Her head was surrounded by a pool of blood, and an empty pill bottle lay beside her.

Adley's... dead.

I must have made some sort of sound because Ethan turned his head toward me, tears running down his cheeks. His face twisted into a mess of horror and pain. "Don't just stand there!" he shouted, making me jump back. "Do something!"

I opened my mouth but couldn't seem to form any words. I felt rooted to the spot as if my feet were glued to the ground.

"Do something!" Ethan repeated, his voice breaking. "Please!"

Somewhere in a haze of shock, I called the police.

They showed up a few minutes later, slightly annoyed at first – I seemed to be a well-known pest amongst the Ember Falls Police after being interrogated more than once. But when they spotted the scene in the graveyard, everything escalated.

I mostly remembered bits and pieces from there onward.

How the police tried to pry Ethan off Adley's corpse.

How Adley's dead body looked cast in blue and red lights.

How the little, transparent, orange pill bottle rocked back and forth in the breeze.

How Ethan's flashlight got crushed underneath an officer's leather boot.

Then, there was the news report that aired the next morning, which I couldn't forget, no matter how hard I tried.

"The death of Ember Falls teenager, Adley Morgenstern, was confirmed early this morning, ruled as a probable overdose based on the evidence present at the scene," *a brunette news anchor stated, staring blankly ahead.* "The head injury present on the victim was attributed to the trauma that she would have sustained when she hit her head on a headstone after she collapsed. This event marks the second death in the small town of Ember Falls in less than six months." *The news anchor took a deep breath, then added,* "I'm Rachel Roberts, and you're watching the Channel 8 news."

I hated watching news reports since they made everything feel so real. It was the reason why I had avoided all television screens during the week following Anna's death.

This time, though, the reports only reminded me of the terrible fact that Adley had committed suicide.

God, what has my life become? I wondered as I forced myself out of my riptide of memories. A bitter laugh escaped my lips. *Anna's dead, Adley's dead, and for all I know, I may be next.*

Tired of watching everyone cry about Adley and her devastating death, I took off toward the forested area behind the church, where I fell upon a decent-looking tree to climb. I pushed a few strands of my messy, dark cocoa-brown hair – which I had recently dyed and allowed to grow past my shoulders – out of my face. I then grabbed a branch and tried to find myself a good foothold–

"Ow!"

Alerted, I pulled back my foot, looked at where I had stepped, and found a hand. "Oh, God. I'm so sorry," I apologized, embarrassed. I looked up from my foot, hoping that the person wasn't too mad–

"You *really* need to start being more careful," Ethan groaned, shaking his hand and wincing.

"Ethan?"

"The one and only," he responded, though his joking tone lacked anything remotely happy. He looked at his hand, bending his fingers as if to check that they were all still working.

"What... What are you doing up here?" I asked tentatively, pulling myself up onto a nearby branch and, this time, carefully avoiding Ethan's hands. He and I hadn't spoken much since Halloween — and that conversation wasn't even the friendliest.

Ethan shrugged, looking down at his dangling feet. "It's nice up here — away from everyone."

"I won't argue with that."

Ethan glanced over at me, his face questioning. "No colors today?"

I looked down at my funeral outfit — black blouse, black pants, and black ballet flats — and shrugged. "Didn't feel right."

Ethan didn't say anything back as he stared at his hands. They were — unsurprisingly — slightly stained black with machine grease, meaning that he had been tinkering, once again, as if it would make things better.

I hated how devastated he was over Adley.

She killed your sister! I wanted to scream. *She's the enemy!*

But I couldn't do that.

Ethan probably wouldn't believe me and would assume that I made up a lie about Adley because we had hated each other. He would then hate me even more — if that was still possible.

But if he *did* believe me…

Anger burned in my chest. *Why is this all so complicated?*

"You know," Ethan said, bringing me back to reality, "I'm not sure I believe the news."

My eyes widened in shock, and I almost choked on my saliva. "What do you *mean*?"

"I… I don't think that Adley, you know… *killed*

herself."

"Ethan, you *know* that she did."

Anger blazed in Ethan's eyes, and his hands formed into fists. "Something doesn't make sense, though! *Why* would she *do* that?"

Because she was a murderer, and I caught her.

"I don't know, Ethan," I lied, looking away from his eyes. "But she's gone now."

"No one's even *trying* anymore! There was an investigation for-for Anna–"

"Though it wasn't like they ever brought *that* killer to justice. After Ivy was let out of jail because my father proved that she had nothing to do with the murder" –I tried hard not to roll my eyes– "the police called it an 'unsolved case' since they had no other leads. They closed it to focus on an odd *bear attack.*"

I knew that I could have said *something*. I knew for a fact that Adley had killed Anna since I had overheard Adley state it aloud to Damion on Halloween. But then again, if this Damion guy wasn't insane and what he said about this supernatural world was *true…* the police would definitely think that I was high.

Besides, it wasn't like I had any evidence against Adley. I only had suspicions and a conversation that was heard off the record. It was better to stay quiet until I found more proof.

"Ethan, if they couldn't catch a *killer*, do you think the police would drop everything to investigate something that was clearly a *suicide*?"

Ethan looked at me with wide eyes as if I had slapped

him. "But-but Adley *couldn't* have. We-we were–"

"Ethan, Adley *killed herself*," I snapped, not able to hold it together anymore. "She's *dead,* and she's *never* coming back. You just have to accept that."

Ethan glared at me, his eyes shimmering with tears. Without speaking, he leaped off his tree branch. Before walking away, though, he looked back up at me. "Something else happened that night, and I'm not going to stop searching until I find out the *truth.*"

Chapter 2
Adley
They Both Live in the End

Air filled my lungs as I opened my eyes to see darkness wrapped around me. I tried to feel around, but my arms barely had space to move since walls were surrounding my shaky, cold body. I noticed that the ceiling was rounded like an arch – and so close to my face that I couldn't sit up – and the base that I was lying on was soft like silk.

I started to feel as if the air had gotten heavier and the walls were closing in on me. I wasn't claustrophobic, but I knew that the longer I stayed trapped in the box, the sooner I was going to die.

I tried to remember my last memories so that I could recall where I may have been now, but it was hard since my mind felt fuzzy. I knew that there had been a Halloween party at my house, which involved a bucket of red slime and a heated fight with Nate. I then had to run away for a reason that I couldn't remember, and I decided to visit Anna's grave on my way out of town. I had also been on my phone texting–

"Ethan!" I cried but choked on my words since my

mouth was dry as if I hadn't drank water in weeks. A tear slid down my cheek, and I waited in terrifying silence for a response.

I didn't hear one, though, which worried me.

If Ethan's not here, who was walking into the graveyard when I was at Anna's tombstone–?

A loud sound burst my thoughts, and I covered my ears with my hands. The ringing seemed to only grow louder, and I winced in pain. When I got used to the noise, I uncovered my ears and noticed that something seemed to be digging around me and occasionally hitting the box that I was trapped in.

Shit, I'm buried underground! *Has someone found me?*

"Ethan!" I screamed again as I banged with my fits against the top of the box. "Help me!" I didn't hear a response, but it had to have been him. How long did it take to get to a damn graveyard, anyway?

He said that we would meet up. He said that he would run away with me from this town – from the police who will soon know the truth about that night. He told me that he loves–

I was tossed to one side of the box, then to the other. I realized that the box must have been moving.

He's moving the box. I'm going *to be okay.*

When a shocking vibration rippled through my body as the box hit the ground, I took a few deep breaths, while I heard a lock snap open. I then watched as the box's lid was removed, and cold air poured into the musty-smelling box.

"Damn, the air is chilly," I laughed as I closed my eyes

and a tear of relief slipped down my cheek. I was shaking, but I tried not to show the fear that was in my eyes seconds before. "Ethan, my God, *thank you*–"

"Oh, *please*. Your clueless boyfriend is *far* from saving your ass," I heard a familiar voice snicker, and my smile flipped into a frown.

Confused, I opened my eyes again and sat up, looking around the dark field dotted with headstones and outlined with the familiar, Eastern white pine trees of Ember Falls. But I then spotted the tall girl with olive-toned skin and long, green-streaked, black hair, and my heart dropped. She was dressed, of course, in her usual all-black ensemble and was wearing her trademark smirk that scared every five-year-old in town.

Staring down at me was Ivy, alongside Nate, the tanned boy with the sandy-blond hair and the green-brown eyes that I used to stare at for hours. Of all the people to find me, of course it had to be my ex-friend and, *now*, my ex-boyfriend, and I could tell by the scowls on their faces that they hadn't yet moved on from catching me and Ethan kissing behind Nate's back at the Halloween party that evening.

"Seriously, can you hurry up already? We have *way* better things to do than watch your brain catch up," Nate whined as I climbed out of the box.

"As if we don't have to watch *you* go through that process *daily*," I hissed as I passed a hand through my dark blonde hair, which felt as if it had become a bird's nest. "You know, I was *going* to thank you."

"For what?"

"For *saving* my *life*," I reminded Nate, rolling my eyes. "Stupidity must be a disease since you've clearly caught it. Unless you were just born with it–"

"Adley!" Ivy snapped, huffing at my remark, and I rolled my eyes, glancing down at the ground–

I raised an eyebrow in confusion as I caught sight of myself wearing the long, black cross-neck dress and black heels that I had worn to Anna's funeral a few months ago.

Wait, what happened to my devil Halloween costume? Why do I look as if I just came back from a funeral?

"Guys, it *was* you who opened the..." I trailed off, looking behind myself to see what I had been trapped in.

"*Casket*. Yeah, though you've only been in there for a couple of hours," Ivy said nonchalantly. "We could have left you in there a little longer if tonight wasn't the full moon."

I started laughing, though I stopped abruptly when I noticed that I was the only one reacting to Ivy's unusual humor. "Okay, please, tell me what the hell you are talking about."

"You're acting as if you don't know much about the supernatural world," Ivy stated, tucking a lock of green hair behind her ear. "And here we are thinking a demon like you would be experienced."

"Y-You know a-about... *you-know-what*?"

"Oh, stop with the fucking code words. Yes, we know that Annabeth was an angel, that Jessi was her guardian angel, and how Jessi knows that you were the one who killed Annabeth because you're a demon," Ivy summarized, smiling as my jaw dropped.

That was why I was running away from Ember Falls. Jessi said that she had called the police.

"You mean, *half*-demon," I corrected, though I was still astonished by how much they knew.

"No, we mean *full* demon," Ivy remarked. "You were a half-demon, but then you detached from your 'puppet master' when you died."

"Wait, *what*?" Panic surged through me, and my body numbed at the thought.

But-but that's impossible–

"Oh, stop worrying. We resurrected you – honestly, you should be happy," Ivy exclaimed. "Now you have control over every demonic ability. Of course, that's why we need you."

"Okay, slow down. How do you know about the supernatural world?"

"We're *witches*," Nate stated with a grin, and I could tell that he noticed my jaw drop again. "Ouch, it's like you can't even *imagine* us being similar to your kind."

"That's because I *can't*." I crossed my arms over my chest in annoyance.

So, all along, my friends were hiding the truth from me?

"Well, you think you know someone until they surprise you," Nate confessed, narrowing his hazel eyes at me as if to remind me about what had happened at the party.

I didn't comment. Instead, I changed the subject. "And you also said that you know that I killed Anna?"

Ivy walked up to me and pressed a finger to my lips. "That's a story for another day. The witching hour is going to end in twenty minutes, and we have a *lot* to do tonight."

"The *witching* hour?"

"The most powerful spells must be performed between midnight and one o'clock under a full moon," Ivy explained in a know-it-all tone that I had never heard before from her. "Now, stop asking questions. We'll get to everything after we perform the ritual."

Tugging my arm, Nate led me down the graveyard aisles until we came upon the L section – *Annabeth's headstone.* As I looked down at the gravestone, which was now covered in what looked to be dried blood, the seconds before my blackout began to resurface.

Talking to Anna's ghost, texting Ethan, hearing the gate creak open, feeling something smack my head, a lock of green–

"*You* killed me?" I screamed, flicking my eyes over to Ivy. "And then, you *resurrected* me? What is wrong with you?"

"You don't understand," Ivy responded in a soft voice, trying to calm me down but failing. "We *needed* you dead. People were going to find out about your killing Annabeth, and with you *dead*, the cops would be off your back. Plus, now, you're a full demon, which means that you can help us out with many rituals, including one that will bring back a dead angel."

"Now, work with us, or we'll put you back in that hole," threatened Nate, bringing to light a mean side of him that I had never seen before the Halloween party.

I sighed, thoughts rushing through my head and making my heart race so much that it made breathing difficult. I felt so overwhelmed, unable to process what was happening. All I could think about was that it was either *this* or dying again. I had to accept that this was my new life now – that I had to listen to these witches if I wanted to or not.

Unless, of course, I wanted to spend eternity in a hole, cold and *dead*.

"*Fine*," I huffed, not having any other choice. "Now, who are we bringing back?"

"One of the key ingredients to our master plan," Ivy started, cracking her knuckles as if to prepare for what she was about to say next. "Your beloved *Annabeth*."

The mid-summer breeze blew my blonde curls into my face as I stepped outside and walked along the wooden balcony that Dad had finished renovating recently. Mom was working, and Caleb was off at the park with Jeremiah, his best friend. Dad was home but wanted the house to be quiet since he had a bad headache, which was why I had to go outside.

I was too young to walk to the park by myself. So, I decided to grab my box of chalk and lay down on the hot, empty driveway. There, I started drawing. I was no artist, but I liked to copy the images from my Disney princess coloring books onto the gravel.

I was in the middle of finishing my Belle drawing when a car rolled into the driveway of the old-looking castle across the street. I didn't have many friends, nor did I know many people on the street, but I knew that house. The Peace Disturbers were what I liked to call the twins who found a way to argue about anything and everything. They had recently moved to Ember Falls, and I tried to avoid them at all costs.

I continued to try ignoring them, though it was hard when their loud squeals about what board game they should play after supper kept breaking my concentration.

A little part of me wished that I could join them since my family never played games.

It was when I spotted the princess Barbie doll laying on the sidewalk in front of their house, though, that I decided to advance with caution, wanting to see the toy up close. Once I got to the doll, I picked her up in awe. She had perfect golden-blonde curls and sapphire-blue eyes. However, her purple dress's hem was torn, and her face was painted with a red marker.

"Where did you put her?" I heard a young girl shriek in the distance. I looked up to see a girl my size in a pink t-shirt and a pair of black shorts. Her bright blue eyes immediately grabbed my attention, along with her golden curls that went down to the middle of her back.

"Put what?" asked a boy with just-as-curly hair and brown eyes.

"Princess Rosetta!" the girl cried as the siblings walked down the sidewalk together after getting out of their car.

"I didn't take her," the boy exclaimed, but the girl didn't seem to believe him.

"Oh, yeah? Well, what if I took your..." The girl searched the sidewalk until her eyes fell on a stick of pink chalk. She picked it up and waved it in his face. "Your chalk?

Maybe you'll tell the truth now!"

"I didn't take her!" the boy wailed. I felt really bad for him – I hated it when people thought I was lying when I was telling the truth.

I looked down at my hands, which still held the Barbie doll.

"Is this your doll?" I asked, raising the toy in the air as the kids looked my way.

"Yeah!" the girl cheered with a big smile as she ran down the sidewalk. Once she was in front of me, she pulled the doll out of my hands and hugged her. "Thank you!"

"You're welcome," I replied before the boy came to join us with a warm, welcoming smile on his face.

"Now can I have my chalk?" the boy asked, sticking his hands out in front of the girl.

"No, I want to draw – you know how much I love to draw," the girl remarked after putting down her doll. She moved away from me and the boy so that she could start drawing a huge rose with a bunch of letters next to it, spelling Annabeth.

"That's a pretty name," I told the girl, making her smile wider. "Is that your name?"

"Yeah, but Mom and Dad like to call me Anna 'cause it's shorter," she replied as she dusted her hands off and stood up.

"Now, it's my turn!" cried the boy, who grabbed onto the other end of the chalk stick and pulled.

"No, it's still mine!" Anna hissed, tugging the stick closer to herself and making the boy fall.

"Anna, that's not fair!"

"Yes, it is!"

"No, it's not."

"Yes, it–"

"Enough!" I cried, annoyed by their arguing. I stepped forward and removed the chalk stick from their hands. *"You have to share. That's what my mommy taught me."*

"But how are we going to do that?" Anna asked.

Without a word, I snapped the chalk stick in half and handed each of them a piece. "There. Now, you can both draw."

"Thank you. Do you want to draw next? You can have one of our pieces when we are done," Anna told me, and I nodded with a smile as we all sat down on the sidewalk. Anna continued to draw more petals for her rose, while the boy began to draw a robot. I admired their artwork until Anna asked, *"So, what's your name?"*

"Adley," I responded as I watched the boy draw a face onto his robot.

"That's Ethan, my twin brother. Where are you from?"

"Across the street," I told her as I pointed with a finger toward my house. *"How old are you?"*

"Five!" Anna exclaimed as she held up five fingers to demonstrate.

"Me too!" I remarked as Anna colored in the petals of her flower.

"Do you want to draw something now?" Ethan asked as he looked up at me.

I looked down into his chocolate-brown eyes and

caught myself smiling. "Sure, I'm really good at animals," I bragged as Ethan handed me his piece of chalk.

"Ooh, me too! I love puppies," Anna exclaimed as I started to draw a cat.

Ethan flinched, whimpering, "But dogs are scary."

Ignoring her brother's statement, Anna began to draw a puppy next to my cat. "Would you like to play a board game with us after supper?"

I looked up from the sidewalk drawings. "What game are you playing?"

"We're gonna play The Game of Life," Ethan said, and Anna nodded, shaking her golden curls.

"Sounds fun!" I cheered, though I had never heard of the game before.

After months without my other half, I was finally accepting the fact that Anna would be gone forever, even if I kept replaying the day that we met on a constant loop. When Ivy told me that we would resurrect my dead best friend, though, *everything* changed.

"What? I thought you *hated* her," I reminded Ivy before looking at Nate. "And I thought *you* would want her gone after the truth came out about your little hook-up sessions."

"As if *my* secrets are worse than *yours*–"

"We need angel blood for our plan. Whether we like it or not, she's our best shot," Ivy stated, cutting off Nate.

"Aw, she's your *only hope*?" I chuckled.

"*No*, we can summon someone else if we want to," Ivy said, rolling her emerald-green eyes.

"Like *who*?" Nate whispered, and I muffled a giggle.

"*Anyway*, we don't have long. So, do what we say, or else."

"Or else *what*? You'll kill me again?" When no one laughed, I fidgeted uncomfortably with a loose curl.

Then, sighing, I stepped aside from the grave. I watched as Ivy broke off a nearby tree's branch and drew into the dirt a huge star over Anna's grave, making sure that each point ended where the grave did. She then traced the most accurate circle possible around the star, connecting every point.

"What's that for?"

"It's a *pentagram*," Nate explained to me as Ivy tossed the stick away and pulled out five black dinner candles. "It's the most-used symbol in witchcraft and the best for powerful spells."

Ivy placed a candle on each point of the star, then went around clockwise to light them with a match. Afterward, she walked into the middle of the circle with a sharp knife, while Nate stood at the tip of the star diagonal to me. "Now, step into the circle and let me draw your blood."

"*What?* You want my *blood*? Are you crazy–?"

"As we said before, we need demon blood to perform black magic rituals," Ivy stated. "Now, give me your hand, or else."

Groaning, I walked into the center, and Ivy pulled my hand out before I could give it to her. Then, she twisted my palm up and sliced across the surface, drawing a line of ruby-red blood. Knowing what to do next by instinct, I made a fist and watched as the blood dripped onto the ground beneath us. Once Ivy looked satisfied, she allowed me to shake the excess blood off my hand and wipe the remains on my black funeral dress, which finally registered in my mind.

"Wait, so everyone thinks I'm *dead*?" Panic rose in my chest again.

"Yes," Ivy stated bluntly, "and it's going to stay that way, understand? After this ritual, we're going to need you to follow our orders for the next part of our plan."

"What *plan*–?"

"Just some spell. Nothing for you to worry about." Ivy then brushed her hair out of her face before continuing. "I know it will be tough, but we have no choice. I mean, how can you explain to a human that you died and were then resurrected?" When I didn't know how to respond, Ivy snapped, "Now, hurry your ass out of the circle and stand on the point across from me and diagonal to Nate."

Without thinking, I did as I was told. I had no reason to fight anymore. No matter how long I would live, Ethan couldn't know what had *actually* happened.

Will I ever get to see him again?

"The last step is to join hands and chant the spell. You can just follow my lead," Ivy said as she grabbed my hand.

"Wait, I have to hold *her* hand? Do you know how awkward it is to hold your ex's–"

"Shut *up*!" Ivy and I cried, cutting Nate off. I grabbed his hand roughly, not caring about anything anymore.

Once the triangle was formed with our arms, we closed our eyes and repeated the chant that Ivy began to say in a loud, powerful voice.

Taker of life,
accept my offer.
Bone, breath, flesh,
resurrect her.
Bone, breath, flesh,
return her to me.

Once the ritual was completed, I opened my eyes to see the orange flames of the candles skyrocket into the air, flickering intensely. When they died out, I took a deep breath and watched as Ivy removed the blown-out candles, while Nate walked over to the two shovels laying on the grass a few feet away.

"Are you just going to stand there? Help me out," Nate commanded as he began to dig around the grave.

Quickly, I reached for a metal shovel and began to dig on the opposite side of Nate. When we were able to see the top of the glossy, burgundy casket that was identical to mine, we dropped the shovels and worked together to pull the casket out from the ground. Surprisingly, it didn't take much effort since I had much more strength than before — probably due to my increased amount of diabolism. I dusted off the top of the casket and traced with a finger the rose carvings that decorated its sides–

"Let me *out! Let me out!*" screamed a voice from inside, startling me, and I jumped back.

"Wow, I forgot how feisty she was," Ivy mused as she pulled out a bobby pin from her hair and kneeled to pick open the casket's metal lock. Once I heard it unlock, Ivy removed the lock from the metal clasp that was keeping the casket shut. "Okay, you can come out, now."

The casket lid tumbled off with a push from inside, and the familiar blonde-haired girl sat up with a look of anger directed at Ivy. "You *bitch*!"

Chapter 3
Annabeth
The Final Girls

Y ou want us to continue to act as if we're *dead*?"

"Yes," Ivy answered me blandly as she folded her arms on the table. "You can't just go around revealing to mortals that you're alive again."

I rolled my eyes and slouched in the booth, frustrated by the response.

I hadn't even been alive for *four hours* and this bitch was already controlling my life. I should have been thankful that she and that asshole revived me, but I *wasn't*.

They were the ones who had wanted me dead in the first place, after all.

Adley had *technically* been the one to kill me the night of the slumber party three months ago. But I knew by the way that she looked at me when I had been resurrected that she *did* care about me. Besides, Ivy had reasons to kill me, while Adley *never* did. Ivy and Nate weren't telling us something, and they were letting Adley convince herself that it had all been her.

I wanted to tell Adley not to blame herself, but Ivy and Nate hadn't given me much of a chance. Since I was resurrected, she had been ranting about the supernatural shit that I had no intention to listen to. I knew damn well my role in all of this – I was the chosen angel sent from Heaven to eradicate evil.

What she *should* have been explaining was how I ended up dead since I knew that it hadn't fully been because of Adley. But it felt like they weren't ready to explain that yet.

The flickering 1950s ceiling fan that hung above our heads began to sway. I then caught sight of a broken mirror hanging on one of the café's walls, which sent a shiver down my spine.

A bad omen.

"Why, again, did you bring us *here*?" I asked Ivy, surely cutting off whatever she was ranting about still.

The building looked as if a tornado had once hit it. Its white siding was crumbling off the exterior, and its gray, unpolished floor tiles were scratched to death. Every booth had seats with peeling black leather, and the tables were all marked with what I guessed was coffee from years of spills that had never been cleaned. The walls were beige and looked run down, and the wooden shelves behind the counter were empty. I would have sworn that the café had been abandoned decades ago if not for the little *Open* sign that still hung on the outside of the glass entrance door. Somehow, the café had gotten a middle-aged woman to work here with a proper uniform – a beige dress and a white apron with the words *Crystal Lake Café* printed in light blue cursive at the top.

"So that nobody notices that you two freaks are back to life," Ivy told me. "No one from this deserted town will recognize us."

"If anyone *actually* lives here," Adley mumbled from beside me as she glanced out the large, dusty window next to her, which displayed the café's vacant parking lot.

"This will give us the time we need to plan out your new aliases," Nate finished, acting all smart with his *big* words. I was still trying to wrap around the fact that the douchebag was working with Ivy, who hadn't yet kicked him to the curb due to his stupidity levels.

"New *lives*?" I asked, not wanting to believe what he said. "Is that *really* necessary?"

"You're acting like you haven't reinvented yourself before," Nate muttered, looking at me with judging eyes.

"That was during my *improvement* phase," I reminded him.

"Some improvement you made. You just hid the world from knowing the kind of bitch you *truly* are–"

"*Enough!*" Immediately, Nate and I stopped bickering to look over at Adley. For the first time in a while, Adley then grabbed my hand and looked directly into my eyes. "Anna, I know that you may not trust me anymore, but I think we should just listen to what they have to say–"

"I trust you, A," I whispered so that only she could hear over the low music of the café's radio. "I know that you didn't intentionally kill me. You *wouldn't*."

"Wait, *what*? How? I was the one who–"

I pressed a finger to her lips as the blonde-haired waitress walked over to our table with an overly exaggerated smile on her face. "Hi, I'm Amanda, and I'll be your waitress today." The nice-sounding woman pulled out an old-fashioned notepad and a blue pen from her apron's side pocket. "Do you want to start with drinks, or do you already know what you're ordering?"

"We decided to each have a stack of pancakes, please. And a pot of coffee would be nice. Thank you," Ivy said before any of us could speak up and order for ourselves.

"Great, I'll take your menus." Amanda picked up the laminated menus that none of us even got the chance to look at. "I'll be back with your order soon," she told us, then walked away with a smile.

"You were spelled into doing it," I continued to tell Adley once Amanda was gone. "These witches wanted me to shut up because I knew too much. So, they got *you* to kill me."

"All you had to do was not say a word," Nate stated, glaring at me.

"I never *did* say anything!" I shouted in frustration. "You made sure she killed me before I could tell her the truth."

"And now that I know, I think we should just listen to them—"

"Are you actually falling for this bullshit? This does not sound like you, A," I cried, not believing how weak my best friend had become. "I'm not just going to stop living because they say so—"

"They killed us to shut us up," Adley hissed, her eyes big with fear.

"*Technically*, we killed Adley so that she wouldn't go

to jail. She should be thanking us," Ivy retorted.

"Oh, I'm sorry. Thank you for *killing* me," Adley hissed sarcastically before rolling her eyes. "Anna, you aren't going to stop living. You're just going to live as someone else."

"Like when we'd play our make-believe primary school games?" I looked around the table. "We aren't little kids anymore. You can't just *be* someone else."

"Well, in the *supernatural* world, you technically can be. We can use a spell to alter your appearances completely, and you can come up with new names," Ivy declared as if I was *agreeing* to this plan. "All you have to do is follow our instructions so that we can get our master plan's last ingredient. Then, the plan is set in motion, and we're done with you."

"*Fine*, we'll do it," Adley huffed after a moment of pondering. "It's not like we have a choice."

"No, you really don't—"

"Um, *I* didn't agree to anything," I protested, cutting Ivy off. "Adley, I know the three of you are friends, and you are dating Nate, but they *killed* us."

"*Actually*, we aren't friends anymore, and Nate and I broke up," Adley admitted, and my eyes widened in shock.

"Oh, wow, I missed a lot. Why *do* you trust them, then?"

Adley folded her arms over her chest and closed her mouth. Confused, I glanced away and caught the perky waitress walking toward us. We all sat up straighter as the waitress placed down four plates of fluffy pancakes, then came back a few seconds later with a pot of coffee and a dish of cream cups. "Here you go, darlings. The maple syrup is on the side, you have your utensils, and the sugar packets are next to the condiments. Can I get you anything else?"

"No, everything looks great," Ivy replied in her phony, polite voice. "Thank you."

"Enjoy!" The waitress disappeared behind the counter again, and we dug into our meals.

"I... I'm not saying that I trust them, because I don't. But I think we should go along with the plan because, well, there's nothing else," Adley explained a few moments later in between bites of her pancake. "Plus, if we do what we're told and don't look too obvious, we *could* talk to our friends again. This also saves me from getting caught by the police for your murder if *Jessi* decides to ever say anything–"

Jessi?

Before I could question how Jessi would possibly know the truth, Ivy interrupted.

"Great! We'll buy you each a prepaid phone when we're out. But *first*, we need to give you your new looks, and you need to choose your new names. Your backstory, on the other hand, will be that you two are friends and both lost your family members in a recent car accident. You are now new to town and are living together with Adley's aunt. But in reality, you will be staying at the Ember Falls Motel since Nate knows an employee there – that way, you won't be paying for your stay."

I didn't want to do this – why would I *ever* want to help Ivy Blackthorn? She wouldn't even tell us about this plan of theirs.

But Adley was right. We had no other choice.

"I guess we have nothing to lose. It's this or death," I sighed, then glanced around the deserted café as I thought about who I wanted to become. "*Fine.* My name will be Aurora Dickinson, and I want to be a redhead with peach-toned skin and brown eyes."

"Wow, it's as if you had already planned this out," Nate observed, chuckling.

Adley's eyes grew at the remark, and I caught myself smiling. "She *had.* When we were kids and played pretend, this was always her character."

"Aurora was my favorite princess, and I was a huge fan of Emily Dickinson's poetry," I laughed, thinking back on my childhood, and a warm feeling spread through my body.

"What about your tattoo?" Ivy questioned as I noticed her staring down at my ankle. It still had the tracings of a pair of angel wings and a halo that I had gotten two years ago. It used to originally be the image that I would draw with my gold tattoo pen, but one night, I had snuck out alone to get a real copy.

Something to subtly showcase who I was.

"Whoa, I am *not* removing that. You know how special it is to me," I reminded Ivy, bending down to try to hide the tattoo but realizing that I couldn't. I was still wearing the white heels that my parents had put me in for my funeral, along with the white, pearl strap V-neck dress. "I'll just make sure to buy socks and wear them with boots from now on."

"Fine," Ivy sighed, pulling out a few candles from a black duffel bag that sat next to her on the floor. "Since your alias is approved, we can start with you."

"Right *now*? We're in a café. How are you going to

transform me?"

"The lady is in the back. So, all we need to do is form a circle of candles around this ring" –Ivy stopped talking to show us two matching labradorite stone rings– "then describe how you want to look by using a chant, which I will say. These are rings made specifically for cloaking spells so that when you wear them, they'll keep your appearance. They'll also alter your voice and facial features so that no one can recognize you."

"That's why you *can't* take them off at any costs," Nate warned as if our exposure would destroy him more than us.

"Shall we begin the ritual?" Ivy pushed aside our plates, made a circle with five purple dinner candles, and placed one ring in its center.

Just as Ivy closed her eyes, though, ready to start chanting, the kitchen doors swung open.

"What the *hell* is going on here? We don't allow people to make fires," the waitress cried as she stormed over to our booth.

Ivy looked toward Adley without faltering. "You're a full demon. Now, use your powers! Along with telekinesis, you can read minds when you touch someone and focus on their thoughts, and you can control the minds of non-supernatural beings."

"What about *me*?" I remarked, confused and a little hurt. "I'm an *angel*. Where the hell are *my* powers?"

"They've been blocked by the dark magic we used to resurrect you. You can't just snap your fingers and have them." Ivy's eyes then shifted over to Adley again. "Unlike *her.*"

"What?" Adley exclaimed as she shook with worry.

"Look into the waitress' eyes and demand what you want. That way, you can erase her memory and force her to leave us alone," Ivy murmured.

As if she was born to do so, Adley then stared into the woman's olive-green eyes and said, "You never saw anything. Walk away and go back into the kitchen."

The lady blinked a few times as Adley snapped out of her trance. Without a word, the woman then retraced her steps back into the kitchen.

A smile grew on Ivy's smug face once the woman disappeared. "Not bad, newbie," she told Adley, keeping her eyes on the kitchen door. "You'll need to work on your precision, but you've impressed me."

Adley tried to smile just as smugly. "Maybe this whole demon thing isn't so bad."

After performing the ring rituals and leaving the creepy café, Nate drove us back into Ember Falls in his bright blue pickup truck so that Adley and I could go shopping for a change of clothes.

The strip mall in the center of town looked abandoned as we drove into the parking lot – not to our surprise, though, since it was early in the morning and the town's population was smaller than average. Once the truck stopped, Adley and I pulled on the black fall coats that Ivy had brought for us. We then hopped out of the vehicle and walked to Fiona's Fashion House.

It was odd walking beside the girl who looked

nothing like my best friend. She now had long, wavy black-brown hair and dark brown eyes, and she went by Jenna Adams.

"You know my favorite Final Girl is Jenna from *Friday the 13th,*" Adley had explained when she chose her name. "And Adams… is a *great* last name."

She didn't know, but I had a strong feeling that Adley hadn't picked her father's middle name coincidentally.

After hardly giving us time to search through the racks of clothing in the empty store, Nate and Ivy waltzed into the shop, and I sighed dramatically. "Why are *you* two here?" I asked them as they stared out the display window.

"Yeah, I didn't think this was your scene, Nate," Adley laughed as she came across a rose-pink crop top in the racks and tossed it at me. I held it up to my torso, then threw it back onto the rack since it looked too big for me.

"We need to keep an eye on you," Nate declared, rolling his eyes.

"*Fine*, but while you're here, make yourself useful. What color looks best on me?" Adley held up two identical shirts, though one was dark red, and the other was black.

"Red always brings out the blood that ends up on your hands," Ivy scoffed, and Nate snickered. Adley huffed and chose the black shirt instead, which she paired with a pair of blue jeans and black combat boots.

After a few minutes, I decided on a blue off-the-shoulder long-sleeved shirt, a black pair of jeans, and beige, knee-high lace-up boots. Once we paid for our new clothes, we then got permission to change into our items in the changing rooms.

However, as we walked over to the store's exit, where Nate and Ivy stood, Adley's jaw dropped in horror – along with mine as I fell upon the most disturbing image presented in front of me.

Nate and *Ivy.*

Kissing.

"What the *hell*? You go and kill me, then you stick your tongues down each other's throats?" Adley yelled as she stepped between them. "How long have I been dead?"

"Sorry to hurt your feelings, but while you were making out in closets with Ethan Landers, we were *kinda* already together," Ivy remarked with a grin, throwing aside a pair of black ankle boots. "It's been about, what, a year now?"

"A fucking *year*? Weren't you in Paris?" Adley narrowed her eyes at Ivy.

"Let's just say I had better places to be – big things to plan," Ivy retorted, batting her lashes at Nate with a sickening smile. "You didn't actually think I had an aunt in Paris, did you?"

"Were you ever even in New York?" Adley questioned Nate.

"Yeah, *that* wasn't a lie – Ivy just joined me a year later."

I was so lost in the conversation, taken aback by the truths revealing themselves, that it took a few moments for anger to rise inside my chest. "Wait a second," I began, looking back at Adley, "you *kissed* my *brother*?"

"And they probably did a *lot* more too," Nate added as he scrunched up his facial features in disgust.

"Oops, I thought Adley would have said something to you by now, Anna," Ivy remarked in a tone that sounded sympathetic, but knowing her, it was just an act. "Aren't you two *BFFs*?"

"That was because we were *dead*!" Adley shouted at the two lovebirds, and everyone tensed at the statement, hoping that nobody was around to hear. Luckily, the employees were in the back storage. "You're acting as if you never even *cared* about me, Nate."

"Well, I guess that was where the message had wrongly been delivered," Nate remarked, and I could see the tears welling in Adley's eyes. "I never *loved* you. Since I've been back from New York, it has all been just a *lie* – a way to get you closer to us so that we could *use* you."

My heart broke for Adley as she stumbled on the words that she tried to make into sentences. "W-Well, I never loved you either. It was *always* going to be Ethan!"

Wait, what?

"That's right. I *love* Ethan no matter what anyone thinks," Adley shouted confidently before she pushed open the store's glass door.

We followed behind her, but Adley stopped when I began to speak. "You know, you're being more of an ass than usual, Nate. You think Adley is bad, but *you* aren't any better." I hated that Adley decided to put her hands all over my brother – who had been desperately *in love* with her for years – but I had already hated Nate for centuries. "First me, then Adley, and now, Ivy. Who's going to be next?"

"You know, I don't even care." I could tell by the look in Adley's eyes that she was hurt, but she wasn't letting the pain get to her. "All you were to me was a safety net, and honestly, you were a pathetic choice," Adley snapped, her eyes blazing with anger. "You know, eventually, nobody will want you if you keep acting so immaturely. And, after all, Karma's a real bitch."

After blasting Ivy and Nate, Adley took off toward the restaurant area of the strip mall. She seemed pretty upset by the look on her face as she began to walk away. So, I decided to follow her, even though I could tell that she didn't want me to.

I was still frustrated that she had chosen *my brother* out of anyone in the *entire* universe to date, but that didn't mean I didn't love her. I could put my anger aside for a moment.

Once we were far enough from Ivy and Nate, I put my hands on Adley's shoulders so that I could look her in the eye. "Are you okay?" I asked Adley cautiously, afraid that she may scream at me.

"Yeah," she sighed, glancing back at Ivy and Nate. "I know that I shouldn't be mad, but—"

I pulled Adley closer and hugged her tight. "It's okay. Everything will be *okay*." I then looked back into her brown eyes and smiled. "Let me get you a drink."

"Okay," Adley agreed as she sat down on the wooden bench in front of Danny's Diner, which faced Main Street.

I pulled open the glass door of the diner, sounding the familiar jingle of the bell that dangled above the entrance. I looked around the small, 90s-inspired restaurant and noticed that nobody was seated in the cushioned booths, which was odd since I was used to it being packed around this time of day.

Shrugging off the confusion, I ordered myself an iced peach tea and got Adley a mocha latté before taking a seat on one of the red high stools in front of the counter. I couldn't stop looking around as I waited, wishing that life could be like old times – that at any moment, Jessi would walk into the room with her huge smile.

It was after I received the beverages that I heard a familiar laugh from behind me. I spun around, and my heart leaped in my chest.

Jessi.

For a moment, I didn't recognize the girl who was entering the diner. She was wearing a navy-blue t-shirt with a pair of black jeans, and her hair was now shoulder-length and cocoa-brown.

It was still Jessi, though. I just didn't understand how she had *changed* so much.

When I blinked out of my thoughts, I noticed that she was pointing at my to-go cup. At first, her expression was different than I was used to – sad and closed off – until she looked up at me. "Oh, I-I didn't think that anyone ordered that drink anymore," Jessi laughed shakily, and I tried hard not to look her in the eye.

I couldn't stand staring at the reddish-brown birthmark that circled her right eye. It only reminded me of the truth.

"You see, one of my best friends used to order it. It used to be *so* unpopular here, but since then, it became, like, *her* drink," Jessi informed me.

How could I have forgotten?

It was *my* famous drink.

And, *of course*, people remembered that kind of detail – *especially* Jessi.

"Really? Well, *I* had heard someone whisper the drink's name when I entered. So, I thought I would try it."

"Well, it's very good." Just as I was about to duck by Jessi, wanting to leave before I slipped up and exposed myself, she continued to speak. "*So*, are you new here? I don't remember seeing you around."

God, why was Jessi so attentive? What was *so* special about *me*?

"Oh, yeah. I just moved here," I lied, vaguely using the story that Ivy had told me to follow.

"Well, then, welcome to Ember Falls. It's nothing impressive, but it'll feel like home in no time." Jessi walked over to the counter and ordered what I had predicted she would say. "One coffee with three-quarters cream, lots of sugar, and a sprinkling of cinnamon." Jessi then glanced back at me and added, "Please, don't judge."

"I would never," I whispered, glancing around the room for an escape route. I was terrified that, any minute, I would screw something up–

"What's your name?" Jessi suddenly asked, jolting me back to reality as she started walking toward the corner booth – *our* booth.

"Um, uh… A-Aurora," I replied, on the verge of crying my real name.

"Oh, I *love* that name," Jessi commented, her smile

growing. "I'm Jessi."

"That's a-a lovely name too," I said while cracking my knuckles nervously. "*Anyway,* I need to go. So, I'll, um, see you around."

"All right. Just don't be a stranger, okay?" Jessi called out as the diner door slammed shut behind me.

If only you knew, Jessi Alvarez.

Chapter 4
Ethan
Memories are the Worst Form of Torture

T hank you all for coming," Ms. Mattson, the Ember Falls High principal, said into the microphone. She stood on the small stage that had been set up for that day's assembly in the gymnasium, a sad smile on her face. "Please, take your seat quickly so that we can begin."

We hadn't had an assembly since the first day of school that year. That was why it was so odd to be seated on the bleachers. *Especially* since I knew what was coming – I had already heard this same speech a *thousand* times during the past few weeks from my parents.

I fidgeted uncomfortably, glancing constantly toward the gymnasium doors whenever they'd open. A part of me still hoped that my girlfriend, Adley, and my sister, Annabeth, would walk in, laughing together as they'd sit down beside me.

Instead, everyone filed in silently, looking at me

every so often. *Of course* – because after getting caught making out with Adley during the Halloween party, rumor had spread. Now, I was known as "the dead girl's boyfriend."

I couldn't decide if it was a step up or down from "the dead girl's brother."

Once the audience of teenagers that had been disrupted from their first-period classes quieted down, Ms. Mattson began. "I want to start by saying that Adley Morgenstern will be missed tremendously. She..."

I stopped listening to the principal when I caught sight of the side gymnasium door opening. However, it wasn't who I had dreamed it would be. Instead, Calvin Walsh, Dylan Guerra, and Kyle Meester sneaked in, then climbed the bleachers to sit next to me.

"Are we late?" Calvin asked as he sat beside Dylan, who sat on my left.

"What do you *think*?" Kyle hissed, patting me on the shoulder and trying to smile as he took his spot on my right. He adjusted the undone button of his cherry-red buttoned-up shirt, then said to me, "Sorry, we were held back by a teacher."

"But we're here for you now, man," Dylan told me, fixing the gray beanie that covered the top of his messy, shoulder-length, brown hair. "God, I still can't believe any of this *happened*. Adley seemed totally fine the night of the party. A little *too* fine, if you know what I mean–"

"Shut up!" Calvin scolded, punching Dylan in the shoulder. "That's the thing about being in the position that she was in. You never know what somebody is going through on the inside. One minute, they're smiling. But the next, they're wishing they had never existed."

"All we are trying to say is that Adley didn't deserve this. I wish we would have known how she was feeling," Kyle stated, cracking his knuckles and staring down at the floor.

I couldn't remove my eyes from the stage, though I tuned out the suicide prevention speech that Ms. Mattson was sharing with my year. My friends were right – I had known Adley inside and out, yet I had never expected her to have been thinking such horrible things.

That's why none of this made any sense.

You take two *pills, Adley – not* four, echoed in the back of my mind, though, and I was suddenly brought back to *that night.*

Maybe she *was* wanting to end her life.

Maybe I just *didn't* know her at all.

Maybe this is all *my* fault.

"Pay attention to if you or someone you know is experiencing a loss of appetite, a loss of interest in activities, a withdrawal from others, energy loss, substance abuse, self-harm, or a large change in personality. These are common signs of depression, which can lead to suicidal thoughts," Ms. Mattson explained as everyone nodded their heads in comprehension like robots. "This is why it's important to ask others how their day is going. Simple things like that can change everything."

Memories of Adley and the moments we had shared during the last few months flooded my mind. I felt a tear come to my eye.

God, Adley, what was I missing?

"Remember that you aren't alone. If you or someone

you know needs to talk, there are people out there ready to listen," Ms. Mattson explained as she tried to keep on an Everything-Will-Be-Okay smile, though I caught it falter for a moment. "Also, keep in mind that we have our school's counselors who are always here if you need to talk. They are especially open to extra counseling sessions for those who may need them during these difficult times." Ms. Mattson took a deep breath, and I could tell by her shaking posture how hard of a speech this must have been to deliver. "There is only one of you out there. Don't make a permanent decision based on temporary feelings."

Sleeping had become something foreign to me ever since Halloween – whenever I closed my eyes, all I could see was Adley, lying dead against Anna's headstone. A thousand thoughts would constantly buzz in my head. Even when I'd try to think about the good parts of the past day to distract me, it would never work.

That's why instead of staring up at my ceiling for hours every night, I would sneak down to my makeshift workshop in the garage and spend my time disassembling and reassembling anything I could find. I *did* have a small robot that I had been building, but lately, I didn't have the brainpower to work on it either – I just didn't have the motivation. After all, the robot had been something that I intended to give Adley.

So, it was a worthless project now.

I lifted my head, sleep deprived, from the picnic table, then looked around the schoolyard of Ember Falls High. On the basketball court nearby, I spotted Nate, laughing loudly like nothing was wrong in the world.

What did Adley ever see *in him?* I wondered, narrowing my eyes at him. *Or Anna, for that matter?*

I had known forever that both girls were with Nate. But ever since he had become someone cruel, I couldn't stand the sight of him.

On the opposite side of the schoolyard, I watched my friends play a game of soccer as an unfamiliar burn of jealousy boiled in my veins.

None of them had a sister who'd been murdered.

None of them had a girlfriend who'd killed herself.

But I had *both.*

Tearing my eyes away from the game, I stood up from my seat and gathered my books, which I stuffed haphazardly into my school bag. When I started to walk back toward the school building, though, I caught a glimpse of a short brunette sitting under a tree with a phone in her hands.

Normally, I would have gone over to see her, but now I hesitated — I honestly didn't feel like I knew who Jessi Alvarez *was* anymore. In the last few months, she had turned from the shy, trustworthy girl into someone who threatened and backstabbed people — she had even changed her hair, and her colorful wardrobe had disappeared.

I looked away from her but couldn't seem to make myself walk any further. Jessi was the only person who would be able to help me figure out what had *really* happened to Adley, after all. Even with all the evidence, it just didn't add up. Why message me to meet her at the graveyard when, all along, Adley wanted to end her life?

Jessi was the only other person who had seen Adley's

dead body on Halloween night. And I knew that she —
superstitious, detail-obsessed, Jessi — *must* have noticed that
something was off, even if she wouldn't admit it.

For Adley, I told myself. *Just do it for Adley.*

I slowly walked toward Jessi, but she didn't look up,
intensely focused on her Blackberry. I scuffed my black
Converses in the grass, hoping that she'd hear the sound and
glance up from her phone. But her dark brown eyes stayed
glued to the miniature screen.

"What are you doing?" I asked, hoping that talking
would get Jessi's attention.

My voice seemed to startle Jessi back to reality —
though, maybe a little *too* much. Her head snapped up so
quickly that she knocked it against the tree trunk behind her.
She muttered something that I didn't understand, then
glanced up at me, her eyes narrowing in anger. "None of your
damn business."

It still shocked me how smoothly she could lie
nowadays.

"It seems quite interesting from the way you're
staring at it. What's the harm in sharing?" Before Jessi could
protest, I threw my school bag down and sat beside her on
the grass to look at her phone.

She was on TheTea.com, Ember Falls' gossip site,
which surprised me. But then again, Jessi wasn't *Jessi*
anymore, so she might as well have been scrolling through a
gossip site article.

I quickly skimmed the article that she was reading,
then instantly felt sick.

The article was about *Adley.* Somebody had posted a

picture of Anna's gravestone, which was covered in Adley's dried blood, at the top of the article. I was instantly taken back to Halloween night.

Adley's dead body, the blood, the screaming, the police lights—

I clenched my fists, my nails digging into my palms, and forced myself to focus.

For Adley.

I took a deep breath and continued reading the article. It wasn't very long, and it didn't tell me anything besides the fact that Adley had been found crumpled against Anna's headstone. It also said that there had been an empty pill bottle next to her.

"Seriously? You're looking at this stuff after the assembly this morning?" I asked, dragging a hand down my face. "What's the point? This stupid article only seems to state what we know."

"Says the person who thought something else was up a few days ago," Jessi scoffed before pushing the screen closer to my face, which I began to read. "And it's these *comments*… They're, I don't know… They're kinda making me question things."

<TeA_SpilleR_125> Dying on a gravestone? That's either super ironic or really SUSPICIOUS.

<idK-008> that pill bottle. anyone ever see it full? could have been fake evidence.

<MaYbE_L8r> There IS a killer in Ember Falls. We all know about Annabeth Landers' death. Who's to say that THEY didn't kill Adley, too?

<sk8r4ever> i heard the police got a call on halloween, right b4 adley died. it was a murder accusation for annabeth landers' case. no one knows who called but ik that the police showed up at adley's. i think the killer was at adley's halloween party and someone knew.

<iNEVERLiE> I think Adley called the cops that night. And the killer found out. And then they killed Adley.

I felt shaken — I clearly wasn't the only one who thought something else had happened to Adley. Though Jessi's expression was impossible to read, she was clearly unnerved.

"See?" I protested, but my voice was weak. "Something *else* happened that night."

"I mean, they're just conspiracy theories. I said they're making me *question* things. That doesn't mean I *believe* them. They don't *mean* anything."

"Then why are *you* reading them?"

Jessi opened her mouth, then closed it and glared at the ground.

She knows something else happened too.

I had algebra homework, but there were more important things to do — like solving Adley's murder.

After all, it wasn't a suicide.

It never *had* been.

That hadn't made any sense.

Adley had been texting me from the graveyard. She had said that she did something bad — I still didn't know what she meant, but it wouldn't have mattered — and she needed to get out of Ember Falls. I had told her that I would go with her – it wasn't like there was anything left for me here.

Then, after she had agreed to let me come, I showed up at the graveyard and saw her splayed against Annabeth's headstone.

Dead.

I rubbed my eyes, staring at the opened, ancient math textbook on the cluttered desk in my dimly lit bedroom. The numbers and letters blurred in front of my eyes, so I looked away and out the window.

What Jessi had shown me at lunch opened my eyes because I wasn't alone. Other people had noticed that something was wrong with the situation, and Jessi – as hellishly stubborn as she was – knew it too.

I'm not alone. We all know that something else happened.

I sighed, letting my head fall onto my textbook.

But what happened? *And what am I going to do once I know?*

I pushed my chair back from my desk and grabbed my unzipped school bag. I needed to write down what I knew – I needed somewhere to start, at least. I reached into my school bag and pulled out a bent, spiral notebook, then searched for a pencil. In my search, my fingers knocked against something hard, and I wrapped my hand around the object and pulled it out–

I dropped the object onto the floor instantly as if it was made of hot metal.

It was a small, empty, orange pill bottle – the one that carried Tylenol just in case I needed something to weaken a bad headache – almost identical to the one that had been found next to Adley.

The room started to spin as I saw black spots. I felt like I was going to puke.

Adley didn't kill herself. That pill bottle means nothing, I told myself. *It's nothing.*

But the possibility – the *idea,* that Adley had taken her own life–

It's all your fault.

I pressed my fingers to my temples, trying to focus on breathing.

No, she didn't kill herself.

But the idea loomed over me since, after all, Adley *had* had a problem with pills in the past. The night that she had almost taken four, *well…*

She could have taken more, a voice in the back of my head whispered. *She could have done it so easily.*

I felt tears burn in my eyes. "A-Adley," I whispered, frantically running my tongue over my dry lips. "Y-You didn't. I know you didn't."

But she could have.

I felt like I was drowning – like someone was choking me.

I could have helped her, that night. But instead, I kissed her and never asked if she was okay. Never brought it up. Never tried to help.

I curled into a ball on my desk chair, shaking so hard that my teeth chattered.

It's all my fault.

I hastily rummaged through my school bag,

searching for a pencil, an eraser, a marker – *something* that I could fidget with. I didn't find any of the objects that I wanted, though. Instead, I found a folded piece of lined paper with a faded red stain on the corner. I put my head between my knees, positive that I was going to be sick. I coughed, tears dripping down my face, but nothing came out of my mouth besides a choked sob. I then looked down at the paper, my shaky hands nearly tearing it in two.

That paper… I had found it beside Adley on Halloween.

Maybe it had been wrong, but I took it with me. I hadn't been able to stomach the idea of the police shoving it in a plastic bag and keeping it as evidence as they did with Adley's bags.

I hadn't yet brought myself to read it either, though.

My breath hitched as I gently unfolded the letter and smoothed it out. I only had about half of it – the first half of the paper was torn off, and I wasn't able to find it in the graveyard. The letter was written by Adley – without a doubt – but her handwriting became increasingly sloped and messy as it went on.

Maybe things were supposed to turn out this way, though. Is that what the universe was trying to tell me – that you weren't supposed to be in my life? I have no clue how that could be. After all, ever since you've been gone, my life has been falling apart like that clay sculpture I had made during art class in first grade. Remember that? It was supposed to be Belle, my favorite Disney princess at the time, but her arms kept falling off and crumbling into a million pieces.

I hope you remember. You're the only one that knows these stories – the only one who knows the real me.

Or, at least, I think you do...

Dammit, Anna! I need you. I need you on this complicated-as-hell planet where nobody loves me like you did. And screw writing letters to the dead! You're never going to read this. YOU ARE DEAD, AND YOU'RE NEVER COMING BACK!

I just have to accept that.

I dropped the letter as everything hit me at once.

They are never coming back–

Not Anna–

Not Adley–

Never.

I buried my head in the front of my black hoodie, my chest aching with pent-up sobs.

They are never coming back.

"Fuck!" I cried, roughly wiping tears off my cheeks. I hated how everybody kept telling me that it would eventually get easier – that I would soon move on, and everything would be all right. The fact was, though, life being easier meant that I would be forgetting Adley, and forgetting meant that I would eventually stop loving her.

An awful realization then rolled in, and my heart felt as if it was being squeezed extremely tight. Anna and Adley were only the first people that I knew to go – the longer I lived, the more people I was going to watch slowly leave me.

I smacked my hands – and, accidentally, one of my

arms – on the desk's surface, frustration flowing through me. I then winced, though the pain that crawled across my skin didn't seem to bother me. I glanced down at the soon-to-be bruise on my left arm, then caught sight of a small gash, ruby-red blood slowly bubbling to the skin's surface. It burned slightly, but it somehow didn't hurt like it should have.

Due to the lack of energy that I now had, instead of cursing like normal, I just watched as a drop of blood dripped down my arm like a tear of sadness.

Nothing mattered anymore.

Chapter 5
Adley

A Dream is a Wish Your Heart Makes

A velvet-cased pillow smacked me in the face, and I shot up from the motel's uncomfortable queen-sized bed to see my worst nightmare. I had to fight back a groan.

"Aw, looks like someone was having a nice dream. Too bad dreams aren't real," Ivy teased from the doorway before entering the motel room and closing the door behind herself.

As luxurious as the exterior of the Ember Falls Motel looked, the inside looked beaten to death — stained white walls, rusted metal, squeaky beds, and dusty windows. However, it did the trick since nobody would have ever expected two teenagers to be hiding here.

Still exhausted, I lay back down. When I realized that Anna was up and eating a blueberry muffin on her bed, though, I rolled over and covered my face with the throw blanket that Ivy had given me the night before.

She was always the morning person.

"Oh, get *up* already," Nate groaned, and I peaked around the throw blanket to see him entering the motel room dressed in a pair of blue jeans, a white T-shirt, and his signature brown leather jacket. "You don't want to miss your first day of school, do you?"

"Well, I *would* prefer to sleep all day. But I guess I don't have that option," I retorted, tossing the bundled blanket to the foot of the bed.

Ivy walked over to the bench next to the TV stand, where two black suitcases sat filled with clothes that she had packed for me and Anna. Ivy then tossed through the wrinkled clothes until she found a black t-shirt and a pair of denim shorts.

"Wow, you're not even letting me pick out my outfit. A little bossy, are we?" I snickered tiredly as I sat up.

"Put this on, *okay*? It's the best we can do since you can't go and buy an entirely new closet," she told me, ignoring my comment as I got out from under the covers. "You're *welcome*."

"You know, if you wouldn't have *killed* me, you wouldn't have to lend out your clothes," I reminded her as I stood up. I then grabbed the outfit from Ivy's hands and marched into the small bathroom.

"She seems grumpy," I heard Nate mumble on the other side of the door.

"She's just not a morning person. You would know that if you had been her *real* boyfriend," Anna hissed, and I smiled as I pulled on my shirt.

It was weird how awkward it had been between us the past day — someone would have thought that Anna would have been happy to be alive and by my side again. But I knew that it was all because I had kissed her brother a few times and she was mad about it. At least it wasn't because I killed her since that had all been a lie. I still didn't know the full story, but I *had* been set up by Nate and Ivy. It was a relief – I felt as if a heavy weight had been lifted off my shoulders. But it didn't change the fact that if Jessi had reported me to the police, I could still be guilty of Annabeth's death.

The scary part now was that I was going back to school, and only one terrifying thought raced in my mind.

Is word out that Adley Morgenstern was a killer?

"Now, I know how excited you must be to be back here. But we are trusting you to *not* break cover," Ivy remarked as we walked onto the school grounds.

Everything still looked exactly how it used to – the small school building was still burgundy bricked and covered in windows, the grass was still a burnt green, and the parking lot was still the famous douchebag hang-out spot.

"Keep those rings on, and we're all good," Nate reminded us before kissing Ivy quickly. "Now, I'll see you guys later. I gotta go act normal and say hi to the guys." Without another word, he then jogged off as if it was just another, casual day at Ember Falls High.

"So... *what* are we supposed to do?" Anna asked a moment later, though she sounded distracted as she gazed around the schoolyard.

As I followed her stare, I realized that her eyes were glued to a girl sitting alone at a nearby picnic table, her nose stuck in a hardcover copy of *Divergent*. I did a double take, however, when I noticed that the girl I used to consider a friend was barely recognizable. She was wearing a black hoodie and a dark pair of jeans, and her once-short hair was cocoa-brown and past her shoulders.

What happened to Jessi Alvarez while I was gone?

"Keep your eyes on the brat who looks as if she will stop at nothing to make this more than what it was," Ivy told Anna, bringing my attention back to the two girls. "*Apparently*, Adley's death story isn't as convincing as we thought it was – at least, not to *her*."

"Wait…" I trailed off, alarms blaring in my head as pieces fell into place. "*What* death story?"

"When we hit you with the shovel that night, you fell and smacked your head onto Anna's tombstone. Before we could do anything else, we heard footsteps and calling – which was your little boyfriend–"

"Where was Damion? He was with me in the graveyard that night." I looked up at Ivy after cutting her off – I had a feeling that she knew who I was talking about.

"Oh, you mean your puppet master?" Ivy snickered, and I rolled my eyes. "The minute you died, he was pulled out of your body – without a living soul to attach to, he couldn't stay. Before he could search for another body, though, I trapped his soul in a jar. There, he'll wait to gain power so that he can be a full demon on his own. Only then will he be released so that he can help us with the final step of our plan.

"*Anyway*," Ivy continued, dragging out the word as she examined her razor-sharp nails. "Concluding my story about your death, Ethan had later come upon the empty pill bottle that was in your bag. Everyone from then on assumed that it was a suicide."

My head felt heavy as I took a step back, trying to

find balance. I felt as if I was going to be sick.

Ethan found my dead body. He thinks I-I...

"Ethan thinks I *killed* myself?" I whispered under my breath, trying to hold back the tears that stung my eyes at the thought. I knew that I couldn't lose control at school, but the thought of *him* coming across my blood-splattered body on his *sister's* grave with the *one* thing he told me *not* to take made my body shake in pain.

"Yeah, which *should* make him believe that it wasn't a murder," Ivy huffed bitterly as if she didn't see that I was freaking out. "But from what I've overheard, he knows you a lot better than we thought. Plus, with Miss I-Can-Solve-Anything also questioning things, I'm afraid that our coverup is failing, momentarily."

For a moment, I wished that the rest of town could find out what had truly happened – I hated that everyone believed that I killed myself. But I soon remembered what Ivy had told us about how the human world should not mix with the supernatural world.

"That's where you come in," Ivy proceeded, looking directly at me. "You need to keep an eye on our last ingredient until we need him for our master plan's spell." I followed Ivy's stare toward the table next to Jessi's, where I fell upon a blond boy with curls that made butterflies flutter in my stomach. I couldn't help but smile giddily as I caught his chocolate-brown eyes glimmering, though they seemed to be filled with an unfamiliar sadness.

That was when Ivy's words sunk in.

"You need *Ethan*?" I shrieked, my eyes widening as my heart skipped a beat.

How could she even suggest *that?* I thought, watching as he sat at a picnic table with his three moronic friends, who were talking and laughing under the morning sun.

Ivy shushed me the minute that my boyfriend's name escaped my lips. "No, we need one of his *friends*."

My eyes flicked back over to the table, where I caught Ethan's three friends – Kyle, Calvin, and Dylan. I didn't know the boys much since we had barely talked before – the only times we ever crossed paths were during the Halloween party and the corn maze competition.

"You poor soul. You're stuck with *them*," Anna snickered as she glared at the group of boys. Growing up, they had always been over at her house, so she had known them a lot better than I had. She had always talked about how they made googly eyes at her and how uncomfortable they made her feel.

To me, though, they always just sounded like teenage boys.

I didn't know them as much as Anna did, but as I watched them laugh and fool around together at the table, I couldn't see what was so bad about them – they seemed *fun*. Plus, it wasn't like I could back out of this.

"Who do you need?" I asked, my eyes still glued to Ethan, who was scrolling on his phone and seeming to be out of the conversation.

"This guy who was born into a family of witches that my mom knows. We need to make sure that he stays a *virgin witch* – also known as a witch who hasn't tried to get in touch with their powers," Ivy explained as I nodded in comprehension. "All you need to do is get close to him and his friends to make sure that there's no temptation to perform any magic. No virgin witch, no spell."

"What's his name?" I asked, curiosity edging my thoughts as I focused on the group.

"His name's Kyle Meester. Do you know him?"

It was weird being back at the same school but with a different life.

However, not much had changed, though, since I had already found a way to be late to my first period class.

So much for the squeaky clean record, I thought, remembering the fake transcript that had gotten me into school, which Ivy had made me. *That could have been the best part about starting over.*

It was hard to not get swept up in nostalgia as I traveled the halls, trying to find that day's classes while not catching too much attention. It was especially challenging, though, once I fell upon my old locker since as the last bell rang and students bolted into their classrooms, I was able to see the black locker in all its dented glory – along with the stickers, cards, and pictures that now decorated it.

A tear pricked my eye as I approached the locker and noticed an enlarged photo of my most recent school ID picture, which was taped in the center of the locker. Many cards that said things like "You will be missed" and "You were such a wonderful person" were also glued around it. Some of the cards were even signed by people that I didn't know went to our school. It surprised me that my death had impacted so many lives.

Unless, of course, all these people had done this out of guilt because I was "the girl who committed suicide."

I closed my eyes, listening to the echoes of teachers beginning class in nearby rooms, their lessons spilling into the hallway.

He thinks I'm dead.

He thinks I killed myself.

But why? was what I couldn't stop asking myself. *I had asked him to join me, to run away with me—*

Unless Ivy was right – maybe he wasn't believing the bullshit of a coverup. No matter what theories popped into my imaginative head, though, the conclusion was still the same.

He thinks I'm—

"She was a really nice person," I heard from beside me, and I turned around at the familiar voice to come face-to-face with Ethan, my heart leaping in my chest. As he looked into my eyes, the corners of his mouth turned up a little, and he reached out to flip open a card. "I can't believe so many people put this together – that so many people cared. I honestly thought Lucy Montgomery *hated* her for some stupid reason."

That was because she *did*. We were archrivals in gym class during tenth grade since we were both always trying to be the best.

I suddenly wanted to pull Ethan into my arms – I wanted to kiss him so hard and never let him go—

But I *couldn't*.

Not *there*. Not *then*. Not *ever*.

It was crazy how every part of him drove me wild – I

wanted to never stop looking into his chocolate-brown eyes; I wanted to kiss his lips until he smiled again; I wanted to pull off his black hoodie and have his grease-stained fingers run over my skin—

"Are you new here?" he asked, snapping me out of my thoughts.

I blinked hard and realized that none of it was a dream. He was *actually* standing in front of me, and I was *actually* staring at the locker of who everyone thought was the dead girl.

"Yeah," I sighed, combing a hand through my long dark brown hair that didn't even feel like my own. "I-I never really knew this girl, so..." I trailed off, glancing at the ground before looking back up at Ethan. "Wh-What are you doing here?"

"I forgot my calculator for math," he laughed, rubbing the back of his neck. "And, you're, um, blocking my locker." He nodded toward the locker next to me, and I gasped in realization before taking a step back so that he could get into his locker.

God, how could I have forgotten?

"Sorry about that," I laughed awkwardly, cracking my knuckles. "I need to leave anyway."

After exchanging a smile, I took off down the hall, deciding that it was about time that I got to class—

"Wait!" I turned back at the sound of Ethan's voice and caught him jogging my way. "Why were you standing at this locker when you never knew the girl? Was there some sort of reason?"

My heart palpitated at the thought of screaming out

the truth. Though I hesitated, all I wanted to say was—

"That *is* my locker. Ethan, it's *me!*" I cried, tears coming to my eyes. "It's Adley — it has always been *Adley!* I'm not *dead*. I'm *not!*"

Ethan's facial features were unreadable, but his eyes widened in confusion as his smile grew with hope. He looked me up and down, his eyes sparkling with happiness. "But-but *how*? I found your dead body in the graveyard."

"It's all a long story, and there is so much you don't know," I confessed as I stroked his face with the back of my hand. I suddenly caught the sun peeking out from behind the dark clouds in the sky, its sunshine pouring into the hallway windows. Birds even began to sing. "But what matters is that I'm here. I *swear*, I'm not dead." Before giving him a chance to say anything more, I pulled him into my arms and brought my lips to his—

I blinked hard and realized that Ethan was walking down the hall with his calculator now in hand.

After we had talked, and I left his locker…

Of course, it had all just been a *dream.*

Chapter 6
Jessi
There's a Theory for Everything

 D id *Adley kill herself?* I chewed at the end of my pencil, trying and failing to concentrate on my algebra homework before classes started after lunch. *Of course, she did,* I told myself, scratching out a mistake in my workbook. *You saw her. You saw the news.*

However, thinking back to the TheTea.com post I had read recently, I couldn't help but notice how strange it was that so many people thought otherwise.

Something messed with Adley's death, and I just don't know the full story.

I felt a sudden surge of anger flash through my body.

Then again, I never do seem to know the whole story until it's too late–

I slammed my math workbook shut, interrupting my inner monologue. I then glanced at my watch and decided to wander around the schoolyard, hoping to find a tree to spend the rest of my break in. Once I found a suitable tree, I hauled myself onto a branch, got comfortable, and stared out at the bright blue sky. I leaned my head against a nearby branch, closing my eyes.

Sleeping still didn't come easily, but as strange as it may have sounded, I had been sleeping *better* since Adley died. The night that she was found dead, my nightmares about Anna and Damion had disappeared. It was as if since Adley was gone, Damion's haunting voice was gone from my head too.

Thank God for that — the way he had talked to me and Adley, saying things I wanted to pass off as crazy but that had somehow made sense… It was chilling, especially since the more I thought about what Damion had said, the more I wanted to believe everything about demons and angels, and good and evil—

No, I scolded myself, toying with the ukulele charm on my silver bracelet. *You're* not *allowed to believe the stuff that Damion said. He's nuts—*

"I think the brunette is the hottest, honestly," remarked a loud voice from below, interrupting my thoughts. Sighing, I leaned over my branch to inspect whatever madness was going on and found Ethan's group of soccer friends.

I swung down from my branch, landing beside the picnic table where the boys were sitting. "God, do you *have* to be so loud? I don't think everyone needs to know how hot this brunette is."

"Trust me, it's a very pressing matter," Dylan exclaimed, nudging Kyle in the arm. "Right?"

Kyle's face pinkened, and I stifled a laugh. "Seriously, what is going *on*?"

Calvin pointed over to a faraway bench, where two girls were sitting – one brunette and one redhead, who were both dressed in dark-colored shirts and blue jeans. The two of them didn't seem to be talking to each other – the brunette was scrolling on her phone, and the redhead was scribbling in a notebook. "You see those two girls over there? *They* are what the two morons are so excited about."

I squinted, trying to make out the girls' faces. "Who *are* they?"

"They're–"

"The new girls, and the *smoking hot* new girls at that," Dylan stated with a grin, cutting off Calvin. "You see that brunette? She is gonna be Kyle's *girl*–"

Kyle tackled Dylan, pushing the guy onto the grass and messing up his hair. Calvin watched, shaking his head in disappointment. "Cut it out, you two! I swear, sometimes, I feel like a parent."

Ignoring the fight unraveling in front of me, I looked back at the girls, trying to put a finger on where I had seen them before. They looked so familiar, especially the redhead.

Where have I seen her before? Was it the mall, or the Speedway, or Danny's–

"Oh! I know one of those girls."

Kyle and Dylan stopped fighting and looked back up at me. "Yeah?"

"I met the redhead at Danny's Diner the other day. Her name's Aurora."

"Do you know the *brunette*?" Dylan inquired, a smirk spreading across his face as he stood up and brushed the dirt off his gray sweats.

"No, only the redhead," I responded, turning around to face the boys with a fake sad face. "Sorry to disappoint."

"It's just *too bad*. I guess we'll have to find out Kyle's true love's name on our own—"

"I swear, I will *not* hesitate to suffocate you with my backpack!" Kyle threatened through gritted teeth, cutting Dylan off. When Dylan didn't seem frightened, Kyle began chasing Dylan across the soccer field with his blue-and-green plaid school bag raised above his head. Calvin shook his head, crestfallen once more before smiling at me and walking after them.

I chuckled to myself once Calvin was out of earshot, wondering how desperate Ethan was in the friend department to be hanging out with those idiots. I then remembered how he surprisingly wasn't around like he always was, though, and I wondered if I should reach out – he had seemed to be a lot quieter and unlike himself ever since Adley passed away.

However, the other part of me remembered the words that Ethan had said the night of the Annual October Bonfire, and I immediately thought against it.

Annabeth would have been ashamed of you.

I wandered the school halls, pretending to have a purpose for being there so that the teachers wouldn't force me back outside. Feeling the eyes of Mr. Fisher on me, I leaned forward to inspect the school bulletin board. Randomly, I pretended to be interested in a vague audition flyer for *Raven and Josie*, the school's senior play.

"Are you thinking about auditioning?" a familiar

voice asked.

I whirled around to come face-to-face with Aurora. She had her long, red-orange hair in a loose braid, and her eyelids were dusted with a rose-gold eyeshadow.

"I-I don't know," I responded, fidgeting with my charm bracelet. "I'm no actress."

"I'm sure you aren't that bad," Aurora remarked, a sweet smile on her glossed lips. "You just need a push. I mean, we *could* always audition together if you'd want. Maybe it would take the pressure off you if you did it with a friendly face – that's if you even *consider* me as one." Aurora blushed, and I found myself laughing despite how much I wanted to tell her no.

What the hell? Why not?

There was just something about her that made me want to try.

"All right," I told her, a smile spreading across my face as I imagined us for a quick second together onstage. Maybe this wouldn't be such a bad idea. "No promises that I'll do good, though."

"Oh, don't be like that. You'll need more confidence if you're trying for the leading role."

I took a step back as her words processed in my mind. "Wait, you want us to try out for the *leading role*?"

Aurora shrugged. "Whoever doesn't get the leading role usually gets a side role."

"I-I was ready to settle with the role of the tree," I laughed nervously, my palms becoming sweaty. I casually wiped them on my black jeans so that it wouldn't be noticeable. "If it isn't clear, I've never done this before."

"That doesn't matter," Aurora laughed, toying with the silver, blue-stone ring on her middle finger. "Just take a chance. I mean, what do you have to lose?"

"N-Nothing, I guess."

"So, it's settled. You're doing this with me," Aurora decided, picking up the purple pen that was attached to the sign-up sheet clipboard. She passed the pen to me so that I could write first, and I signed my name and wrote my grade before giving it back to her. I then watched as she scribbled her name in loopy cursive penmanship that looked oddly familiar – but all cursive looked like that, right?

"*Aurora Dickinson*," I read. "It's a pretty name. Sounds like a poet from the medieval times."

"It kinda does," Aurora laughed, blushing ever so slightly. "Anyway, I guess I should start heading to class. I'm still learning my way around here."

Smiling from the extra confidence that signing the sheet gave me, I asked, "Where are you headed? I could, um, help you find your way there."

"Yeah," Aurora said, looking down at the stack of books in her hands. "Yeah, I'd like that a lot, actually."

Chapter 7
Adley
In Loving Memory

So, you're telling me to just bump into him on *purpose*?"

"Yeah, pretty much," Anna remarked as she slammed her locker door shut. "It's been two days, and you've got to start your assignment eventually. Plus, it's not like you two have anything in common. Therefore, just casually bumping into Kyle in the halls and dropping your books would force you guys to talk and meet each other. From then on, you can have a reason to know him, and you don't have to just randomly walk up to his lunch table and ask to eat with him."

"Hey, that was better than my original idea of trying to get a match with him on Bumble," I laughed, remembering Ethan telling me months ago about how Dylan had signed him and Kyle up for shits and giggles, though Kyle had never taken down the account when Ethan had. "Are you *sure* there's no better way to meet somebody?"

"Without any parties or common hangout places, this is my best advice." Anna smiled wider as the bell signaling the end of lunch rang, and Ethan and Kyle entered the hallway, walking in our direction.

My heartbeat speeding up, Anna and I walked toward the boys as if nothing was. We were just two girls laughing and chatting. But, deep down, I hated how nervous I was, even when Ethan disappeared into a nearby classroom, leaving Kyle alone.

I wanted to *murder* the butterflies in my stomach.

Come on, it can't be that hard, I told myself. *Just bump into him.*

I looked up at Kyle, my arms shaking as I tightened my grip on my books. He was barely five feet away from me, and all I could think about was what he would say. I felt my heart thump at the bottom of my stomach, and I was starting to want to abandon this stupid plan—

Anna shoved my shoulder *way* too hard for it to have been an "accident." I then tumbled into Kyle's path, dropping my books – and crushing him against a locker.

For a second, I just stood there, startled by his bright azure eyes. I then remembered that I had to make my way to class, though, and got off him so that I could gather my belongings in the middle of the now-empty hallway.

"I am so sorry," I told Kyle, though he picked up my books before I could, handing them to me before flattening the wrinkles that formed on his blue buttoned-up shirt.

"It's fine. I needed a smack in the head anyway." I looked at him, puzzled until he laughed and combed a shaky hand through his dark hair. "I'm *kidding*."

"I knew that," I laughed, trying to act calm when I was afraid that he could hear my racing heart trying to escape my ribcage. "Thanks for picking up my things."

"No problem." Without another word, he flashed me a smile and disappeared down the next hallway.

Sighing, I turned around, hoping to find Anna. But she had vanished, along with the butterflies in my stomach that had been fluttering for no reason at all.

"I can't believe that *this* is what they wrote on my tombstone," I exclaimed with my hands on my hips. I kneeled in front of the stone, brushing off the dead leaves that had fallen onto it. "*Loving daughter and friend.* It's the same generic bullshit that was on yours."

Anna and I had decided to take a trip to the graveyard after school that day since, as depressing as the place was, we knew we wouldn't run into people we used to know. Plus, we wanted to avoid Ivy and Nate as often as possible, which meant the motel was not an option.

"At least your headstone was never vandalized," Anna reminded me, kneeling beside me before looking toward her headstone at the end of the row.

I followed her gazed and sighed. "So, you knew about that?"

"I knew about everything," she admitted, raking a hand through her curls. "I was there – in *spirit* – when it all happened."

"Who actually did it, then?"

Anna took a deep breath. "It was Nate."

"*Nate?*" I questioned, biting my lip in an attempt to not laugh.

"I saw him walk over to the headstone with a

baseball bat. Then, after it was broken, he covered it with Ivy's spray paint. I knew that it was her paint since she signed her name on the can with a Sharpie." Anna laughed quietly to herself. "She can be so dumb, sometimes."

"Do you know *why* he did it?" I asked as the facts registered in my brain.

"Something about wanting to stop me from sending messages? I'm not quite sure. He was mumbling it to himself."

"He meant *the* messages... Wait, were *you* the one sending me all those warnings?" I questioned, and Anna glanced back at me. "The hand, the tombstone, the fog–"

"Oh, yeah! I can recall faintly doing so," she told me, smiling sadly. "While I was in the In-Between, I wasn't allowed to leave the graveyard. That's why, when I realized that you couldn't have killed me, I knew that I had to try warning you when you'd visit. I knew something odd was going on – I just didn't know *what*. That's why the messages were vague and threatening – I needed you to stay alert." Anna laughed to lighten the mood, then twirled a strand of hair around her finger. "Sorry if I scared you."

"What about the message in the bathroom?" I asked as I remembered the evening of Anna's death. I had come home to see "I KNOW YOU DID IT" written on the bathroom mirror with what looked like blood. At least, that's what I had thought until I blinked and it vanished.

"I never did that." Anna's eyes were wide. For a moment, she gazed at me as if I was crazy. "Unless it was all in your head? When people go through traumatic scenarios, their minds can mess with them – make them see things out of guilt."

"Maybe," I mumbled, staring down at the ground. I then shook my head and stood up. "I hate that this all happened. I hate that I killed you, and I hate that we are both *dead*."

"You mean *'were* dead'," Anna corrected as she stood up too.

"Anna, we have tombstones and different lives — Adley and Anna *are* dead." I sighed, brushing a tear away. "All we've got are the memories to hold on to, and it's all because of Ivy and Nate, and their *fucking vague plan*!"

"Then, why are we listening to them?" Anna looked up at me, a mischievous glint in her brown eyes.

"Because I don't want to die *again*," I exclaimed, remembering how easily Ivy and Nate had murdered us before. "Besides, after bumping into Kyle this morning, I think I gave him a concussion and I don't want that to have all been for nothing."

Anna giggled at my dramatic behavior. "And *why* do you think he got one?'

"Because I caught him checking me out at the end of the day when we were exiting school," I laughed, my face burning in embarrassment.

"Oh, boy," Anna chuckled, but then her face fell serious. "It's just... I don't get why we're doing Ivy and Nate's bidding when we won't get anything in return. Just saying, it sounds like a one-way streak. Get the boy, help them with the spell... What's this spell even *for*?" I opened my mouth to answer but shut it immediately when I realized that I didn't know what to say. "We can't even know *why* we're doing this, Adley."

Anna *did* have a point – why help when we couldn't know the full story? But I was afraid of what could happen to us if we abandoned the plan. Plus, we had already started to put our parts into action.

Unless...

"What if we played our roles to convince Nate and Ivy that we are doing as told, but in reality, we are turning *against* them?" I remarked, a smug smile spreading across my face. "You can keep an eye on Jessi for our sake, and I can get close to Kyle to *teach* him magic."

"Holy shit, that's a *fantastic* idea!" Anna cried, her eyes sparkling with excitement. "Awaken the virgin witch without Ivy and Nate even knowing."

"Therefore, we can destroy their plan once and for all." Anna and I smiled at each other, and it was then that I remembered how much I had missed my partner in crime.

I knew that to move on and become best friends again, I had to be honest with her.

"Anna, I think it's time that I tell you the truth."

"I love Ethan Landers," I finally confessed as I kicked the sand underneath the swing that I now sat on.

Anna and I had decided to leave the graveyard and spend some time alone at the park that we used to live at when we were kids. It felt fitting, especially since we always had our best conversations there – and Nate and Ivy had never known about this spot.

I knew that I needed to talk to Anna about this. I had been putting it off for long enough.

"I know that before everything happened, I always claimed that Nate was *the one*. But when I started getting closer to Ethan after your death, he was there for me more than Nate ever was. I can't believe that I wanted to spend the rest of my life with Nathaniel Tucker."

I scrunched my nose in disgust, and Anna laughed. "I know that you're upset that I kissed your brother, but I

promise you that he is the one I want. I can't even explain how much I care about him."

"I'm sorry that I was mad at you," Anna said after a moment of silence. "It just felt weird since the minute I died, it was as if he sorta replaced me. I was also *horrified* because, like, he's my brother and you're my best friend. But I can tell how much you care about him – I can see it in your eyes whenever you mention his name."

"Really?" I smiled wider, then glanced away so that Anna wouldn't notice my blushing.

"Yeah, I always had a feeling that you liked him. Plus, I trust you with his heart."

Hearing those words come out of Anna's mouth brought tears to my eyes.

If only I could still be with him.

I then began to cry. At first, it was muted, but then, I let go of the fear of falling apart and cried harder. I couldn't hold in the pain anymore, and all I wanted was to be in Ethan's arms.

"Ethan's *gone*. He-he's always there but never with

me, and I can't ever get him back because I'm supposed to be *dead*." I looked up from my shaking knees to see Anna's watering eyes. "I don't know how I'm supposed to keep an eye on Kyle when I don't like *him* – when all I want is *Ethan*! I-I just wish that if *I* couldn't be with him, then I wouldn't have to see him every day of my fucking life. I can't live with him *not* by my side."

Anna stood up and pulled me off the swing so that she could hug me. I buried my face in her chest, sobbing into her gray sweater and inhaling the sweet scent of her coconut shampoo. "God, if only I could find a way for you to be with him. Unless you want to try to date him as Jenna–"

"*No!*" I yelled, anger consuming me rapidly. I stepped away from Anna, sitting back down on the swing. "I'd rather not talk to him at all than date him as someone else. It wouldn't be the same… I'd never get to be myself. We'd never get to be *us*."

"You know, I completely understand how you feel. Right before I died, I also fell for someone *really* hard – and it wasn't just some act. It was real," she confessed, grabbing my attention.

"You mean *Drake*?"

"Oh, God, *no!*" she laughed, bringing a smile to my face. "He was *such* a douche. This person was *much* more special – they were like family."

"Sounds like how I feel about Ethan."

"Yeah, well, maybe we could have had what you two did – if only I didn't die before getting the chance to say anything. That's my biggest regret – not ever getting to say I love you."

A heavy silence hung over us as I tried to decipher who he was. Why hadn't I ever heard of him before today?

I didn't want to pry, though, so I decided to say, "Well, if you ever want to talk about it, I'm here to listen. I'm *dying* to know all about this mystery man. He seems pretty special."

Anna chuckled almost uneasily. "I'm not ready to do so just yet if that's okay with you." Anna pushed a stray lock of hair behind her ear, and I nodded.

Sometimes, we deserved to have our own secrets.

"I'm really happy that we can be like this again," I said, smiling at Anna. "*Best friends,* I mean."

"You thought two murders would separate us? Bitch, *you* are my ride-or-die. Nothing can tear us apart – not even death." Anna grabbed my hand, and I interlocked my fingers with hers. "Now let's give these witches a taste of their own medicine."

Chapter 8
Ethan
The Fine Art of Screwing Up

I *never* expected to see Jessi try out for a play – or get on a stage, for that matter. Yet there she was, standing stiffly centerstage beside Aurora Dickinson, the new girl in our year. They were both trying out for the leading role for this year's senior play, and their audition was in a few minutes.

I had dropped off my backstage application form in the designated bin at the front of the auditorium. But then, instead of walking home as I had originally planned, I sat down in one of the wooden auditorium chairs, intrigued. When I had seen Jessi enter the auditorium afterward, I assumed that she was dropping off a backstage application form too – it was what we would usually do when it came to the yearly plays at our school.

But then, I had seen her get up on the *stage.*

I couldn't imagine *what* had convinced Jessi to take up acting. It was strange even seeing her up on that stage because I knew that she – just like myself – was more of a backstage kind of person. After all, I knew from having been in her classes in the past that she struggled just with oral presentations.

But then again, I don't even know who Jessi is anymore.

I sighed, leaning my head against my seat and closing my eyes. Even though the Ember Falls High auditorium chairs were far from comfortable, I honestly could have fallen asleep – feeling drained and having the capacity to turn off all your thoughts were two very different things, though.

A loud voice boomed from onstage. I opened my eyes to see Aurora twirling around and throwing her arms out as she passionately recited a piece from *Romeo and Juliet*.

But soft! What light through yonder window breaks?
It is the East, and Juliet is the Sun!
Arise, fair sun, and kill the envious moon.
It is my lady; O, it is my love!
O that she knew she were.
She speaks, yet she says nothing. What of that?

For a moment, I looked away from Aurora, who was still absorbed in her performance, and over to Jessi, who was standing off to the side. She was gripping her script very tightly, and even from where I was sitting, I could tell that she was shaking. I was no expert in theatre, but I was pretty sure that the actors onstage *weren't* supposed to look like they were about to pass out.

Maybe Jessi hasn't changed that *much,* I thought, feeling sorry for her as Aurora smiled encouragingly at Jessi.

When Aurora took a step back and Jessi took a shaky one forward, though, Jessi started to worry me. A mixture of uncertainty and fear painted her face as she cleared her throat. "Um— R-Romeo, Romeo, w-where-fore art—" Jessi cut herself off, freezing. She glanced back down at her paper, wanting to continue her audition even though we both knew how badly this would end. "D-Deny... um... thy..."

Aurora, from Jessi's other side, looked both mortified and sympathetic. She was mouthing something, almost as if she was trying to prompt Jessi.

But I knew that it was hopeless.

"I-I'm sorry," Jessi stammered, then she dropped her script and ran off the stage.

"Jessi!" I heard Aurora shout as I watched Jessi sprint out of the auditorium doors.

Despite everything, I then found myself standing up to go after her. I ducked out of the auditorium and looked both ways quickly, searching the empty halls for Jessi but was unable to find her.

"Jessi?" I called, stupidly hoping that she would respond.

When I heard footsteps coming from the hallway to my left, I turned, following the noise. I finally caught sight of Jessi, who was slowly walking out of the front doors of the school.

I chased after her and headed out the doors, shielding my eyes from the sun once I was outside. I then searched the trees, knowing that I would find Jessi somewhere nearby. It only took me a minute to spot her sitting on a high branch, staring out at the street nearby. Part of me worried that she was going to fall and break her neck, but the other part of me knew that Jessi had been climbing trees since she was able to walk.

"Jessi?" I called breathlessly as I stumbled upon the tree. I looked up, trying to make out her brown eyes, which were shadowed by the last few leaves that dangled off the branch above her.

"Go *away*, Ethan!" she snapped, not looking away from the Speedway across the street.

"I just wanna make sure you're okay," I admitted, rubbing the back of my neck and looking down at the ground. When I glanced up again, I noticed that Jessi was now looking my way. "What happened back there?"

"Of course, you witnessed that," Jessi scoffed, rolling her eyes. "You're just always there at the *perfect* moments. Why do you even care?"

I tried to go for something lighthearted. "Well, when you see someone running out of the auditorium like their shoes are on fire—"

"I get it. I made a fool of myself."

"Would you *stop* twisting everything I say?" I snapped, losing my patience. "I'm *trying* to help you out."

Jessi sighed angrily. "I screwed up. End of story."

"But why did you even audition? You're not the type of person who would — no offense."

"Maybe I wanted to try something new."

"Yeah, but *acting*?"

Jessi looked away, biting her bottom lip. She mumbled something that sounded like, "I didn't have much choice."

"Did that new girl make you do it? Because—"

Jessi jumped down from her spot in the tree, landing a few inches away from me. "No one *made* me do anything," she declared, her voice quiet but harsh. "Aurora *wanted* to audition with me. But thanks for the vote of confidence."

"That's *not* what I was trying to say. I just meant—"

"That you don't think I can stand up for myself? That I just let everyone else *drag me along*?" Jessi laughed bitterly. "Maybe I was that person once, but not anymore."

"I don't even *know* who you *are* anymore!"

Both of us fell silent.

I saw a flicker of sadness cross Jessi's face. "Funny," Jessi mumbled, looking down at her sneakers. "I get that a lot." Jessi sighed once more, combing a hand through her dark hair. "I auditioned with Aurora because she actually *wanted* to audition with *me.* It doesn't happen often that someone wants to associate themselves with me."

I didn't say anything, waiting for Jessi to continue.

She tucked her hands in the sleeves of her red-and-black plaid sweater. She then added quickly, "It doesn't matter, though. You saw me up there. I'm not cut out for acting."

"You know, you *could* always do backstage."

Jessi smiled sadly. "I... I'll have to think about it."

"Okay, but the application forms are due next week—"

"I'll see," Jessi stated, cutting me off and starting to walk away. She looked back at me after a moment, though, taking a long breath. "You know, Anna always used to tell me to try new things. She would say, 'Take a chance. What do you have to lose?'" I watched as Jessi fidgeted with the ukulele charm that my sister had once given her. But once Jessi looked into my eyes, her expression was impossible to read. "Honestly, though, I think Anna would have been ashamed of that performance. I think she would have been ashamed of *me*."

I only figured out why Jessi had said what she did the next morning. She had repeated the same words that she brought up at the Halloween party when we last fought – the words I told her back in October when we got into a fight at the Annual October Bonfire over her threatening to reveal that Adley and I were secretly hooking up.

Annabeth would have been ashamed of you.

I hadn't thought much about what went down between me and Jessi in the last few months – besides the fact that Jessi had turned into someone that I wanted to avoid. Now that I had, though, I realized that I played a part in everything too. Jessi *had* said – *and* done – stuff, but maybe there was something to be said about equal blame.

I kicked a rock on the sidewalk, keeping my eyes down as I passed the graveyard. I had always hated that I needed to pass by it on my way to school every day. But now, I despised it even more.

Now, it only reminded me that two of the people I cared about most were dead.

They're never coming back–

I stopped walking as if my feet had sunk into the cement. Something heavy pressed down on my chest, and I found myself unable to breathe.

You're never going to see them again.

I sat down on the edge of the sidewalk, lowering my head and trying to breathe – which was more of a task than it should have been.

Come on, Ethan, I told myself. *You can't keep doing this. Why can't you just* breathe?

I looked up, and black spots momentarily blurred my vision. I closed my eyes and took a deep breath, trying to focus.

You're going to figure out what happened.

Then, I forced myself to stand up and continue to walk to school. I looked down at my hands, which were – as usual – stained black. I sighed and tried to wipe them on my sweater, not caring that my parents were surely going to be mad about the stains on the gray fabric. It wasn't like I talked to my parents much these days, though. They were both always either at work or "too tired" to do anything. I didn't blame them, but sometimes, I wanted to shout at them – tell them that *I* was still there.

I crossed the school's soccer field, heading for the usual table that I would sit at with my friends. Once I got there, I spotted Kyle a few feet away, pacing and mumbling to himself as if someone was in front of him. Oddly confused, I sat down and decided to eavesdrop on what he was saying.

"Hey, how's it going?" Kyle shook his head, his stare fixed on the ground a few inches in front of him. "No... *Hey,* how's it going?" A wide smile appeared on his face. Nodding with satisfaction, he remarked, "Yeah, *that* sounds better."

What is he doing? *Why is he—*

Someone grabbed my shoulders from behind, and I jumped and lost concentration. I was about to yell at the person until Dylan came into view, laughing and taking a seat next to me. "What are we watching?" he whispered, and I rolled my eyes in response.

"If I'm not wrong, he's practicing *pick-up lines*." Calvin sighed, joining us as he watched Kyle.

Dylan snorted, combing a hand through his dark hair. "Preparing for the real thing, isn't he? He must be planning to ask out that brunette."

I just barely stopped myself from sighing.

Kyle had been obsessed with that other new girl – Aurora's friend – since he first saw her. I didn't understand how someone could have such a crush on someone they barely even knew. I felt like I needed to know someone before I could like them – not that relationships had been on my mind lately.

I'd had my chance with that, and it didn't end well.

"So, Kyle," Dylan shouted, standing up. Kyle's head shot up, and his face tinted pink as he flinched. "Are you *finally* gonna ask out the girl of your dreams?"

When Kyle rolled his eyes and didn't move, Dylan smirked and made his way over. Calvin and I followed with apologetic smiles.

"W-What are you *talking* about?" Kyle mumbled, his face now bright red.

"I *mean*, that *drop-dead   gorgeous* brunette that you've been staring at. You *are* gonna ask her out, aren't you? Unless you're losing your mind and talking to yourself—"

Kyle kicked Dylan in the shin, remarking, "Shut *up*, asshat. Don't act like I haven't caught you practicing pick-up lines on Ally."

"Ally?" Calvin and I asked in sync. Dylan's face flushed the same color as Kyle's.

"Ally is Dylan's stuffed alligator. She was his *first* girlfriend–"

"When I was *six*."

"Make that *twelve*." Kyle smirked, then added, "She's how he practiced kissing and–"

"You said you'd *never* bring that up," Dylan hissed, mortified. I honestly felt embarrassed *for* him.

"Maybe if you weren't such a dick–"

"Can we *not* do this now?" I groaned, cutting Kyle off. I was fed up with his and Dylan's bickering. "If you're into that girl so much, Kyle, just ask her out already. Or maybe start by *talking to her* instead of telling us about her."

Kyle's face brightened, and his smile widened. "You know what? I *should.*"

Dylan grinned, slinging an arm over Kyle's shoulders. *"Finally."*

Stepping away from Dylan, Kyle fixed his buttoned-up shirt and combed a hand through his hair. "Wish me luck," he called as he walked toward the school.

Dylan chuckled once Kyle was inside. "Twenty bucks if he doesn't go through with this," Dylan stated, putting out a hand in front of me and raising an eyebrow. "What do you say?"

"I don't know," I said, looking between my two friends. "I have a strange feeling that he'll prove you wrong."

Chapter 9
Adley
Getting What You Want 101

How are the assignments coming along?" Ivy asked as she paced in front of the motel beds, arms crossed in front of her chest like an investigator.

Anna sat up from leaning back against her bed's pillows and raised a hand, acting as if we were *actually* in a meeting. "I think I've got Jessi under my radar," she explained when Ivy called on her.

I raised an eyebrow in confusion.

How had *she* done her part so effortlessly?

"How so?" Ivy questioned as I slouched further into my seat in the corner chair.

All I wanted was to get more sleep. Why Ivy had woken us up by pounding on our motel door for a gathering at seven o'clock on a Friday morning – while Nate got to use *our* shower and *not* attend – was beyond me.

It was so unfair. Especially when I was the one awake all night because I was sick over the fact that the one person I loved most believed that I was *dead*.

"Well, I was able to push her into auditioning for the school play yesterday afternoon. I did an *outstanding* job," Anna bragged, tossing a lock of red-orange hair over her shoulder. "However, Jessi ran off mid-audition and I haven't seen her since." Ivy laughed hysterically, and so did I before Anna held her hand up in protest. "Look, even *if* she doesn't make the cut–"

"Wow, the amount of faith that you have in Short Stack cracks me up," Ivy chuckled.

Anna narrowed her eyes at Ivy. "Even though she *won't* make the cut," Anna began again, a frown now on her face, "I have still found a way to get her closer to me. I think we're already friends."

"Well, 'I think' isn't good enough. I want an affirmative answer." Ivy then turned her gaze toward me, not giving Anna a second to comment. "Now, how's Mission Kyle?"

I swallowed hard, knowing that my answer wasn't going to satisfy Ivy. "I have *nothing*, okay?" I admitted, and Ivy's jaw dropped in shock. "I bumped into him one morning, and he kinda checked me out the other day, but that's *it*. It's a lot harder to get close to some guy that you have *no* relation with, let alone don't know anything about. I just need a *little* longer. I know that I can get him under my control," I explained, trying to make the situation sound better than it was.

After a moment of silence, Ivy sighed. "Fine."

"*Fine?*" Anna and I both questioned, and a smile spread across my face.

"Yeah. If it's done soon, that's what matters," Ivy told

me, and I could see her hiding a small smile from us. "We're not in a rush."

"Huh?" I asked, hoping for clarification.

Ivy waved me off. "Never mind, just get to school. The more time you get, the better."

As the first-period warning bell rang, I headed down the bustling halls. I was so mad at myself – how hard could it be to become friends with some guy? It wasn't even like I cared what he thought. I needed him for the plan, and that was that. I just needed us to talk, for him to hang out with me, and for him to *maybe* introduce me to his friends so that I could *maybe* talk to Ethan.

I shook my head, wanting to empty my head of all the feelings and thoughts I had about Ethan.

It was *never* going to happen.

Not *then*. Not *there*. Not *ever.*

I looked up from the dirty school floor to see my new chemistry classroom. I had no clue how to even *do* chemistry – I always sucked at science, and the only reason I was in this class was because Ivy had stuck me in it.

Damn her and that fake transcript.

I couldn't believe that she actually thought I took chemistry at the start of the year.

I tried to smile. It was my last new class, and I *had* to think positively – *maybe* Kyle would be in there, unlike he had been in every other fucking class I entered.

The classroom was decently large compared to all the other classrooms in this school. There were two sections to the room – the desks, which were in rows at the front of the class, and the lab stations, which were set up at the back. The teacher stood at the front of the class near his desk and the SMART Board, eating a container of blueberries and talking with two of the students upfront.

The teacher seemed quite friendly – he had a wide smile on his face, and he was wearing one of those science pun shirts that I couldn't quite understand. After squinting at it for a while, I remembered who I should have been looking for.

I turned to look at the rows of desks, then noticed that only two were empty.

And *none* were already taken by Kyle Meester.

Discouraged, I grumbled as I walked over to the teacher, who welcomed me into his class. We talked for a few minutes, then he handed me the books that I needed for his class. He said that he'll have office hours soon, so if I needed help catching up, he would be happy to help.

I knew that if I was wanting to pass – or at least not look like an idiot when it came to bonds and atoms – I was going to be taking him up on the offer.

It wasn't like I had Ethan who could tutor me.

The final bell rang, and I sat down at the empty desk in the back of the room. Just as I was taking out a pen from my bag, though, the last student flew into the classroom, grabbing my attention. He stumbled into his seat at the front of the room, and the teacher, Mr. D, smiled, holding back a laugh.

I, however, grinned like a fucking moron, and I couldn't care less.

"Mr. Meester, late *again*?" Mr. D laughed, shaking

his bald head.

"I *technically* entered the classroom before the bell was *done* ringing," Kyle replied, and everyone in the class burst out laughing. I caught Dylan laughing the hardest from his desk, which was behind Kyle's.

"You're lucky I like you," Mr. D chuckled as he turned on the SMART Board. "You get away with too much in my class." When he spotted Dylan, who was still laughing, the teacher added, "And so do *you*!"

"And I appreciate that you let us off the hook," Dylan replied quickly.

I didn't understand at all how *he* made it into chemistry class.

"Anyway, guys, today is going to be a simple class," Mr. D announced, returning his attention to the students. "All we'll be doing is working on the first few pages of the new chapter's booklet. Marissa, can you hand them out?"

Marissa Langford, the head of the volleyball team, grabbed the stack of thick packages from off the teacher's desk, then handed them out. She surely was the teacher's pet.

When she tossed mine, I flipped through the package, trying to understand the material. This chapter was all about energy changes and rates of reaction – it didn't seem too hard until I saw all the labs we were going to have to do.

I knew that I was screwed.

"Great work today," Mr. D said when there were only a few minutes left of class.

I was thrilled that the class was about to end. The topic started to make a bit more sense once we went over the answers for the worksheets, but when you had no clue what many words meant, it was hard to keep up.

"Now that you know more about the material, next class, we'll be doing a lab," Mr. D continued, and the class erupted into excited whispers. I had thought that I heard wrong for a second – who gets this excited about mixing chemicals? "However, since you know how I like to change lab partners every few weeks, I thought we could pick the new pairs today. We also have a new student with us, so she'll need a partner."

"Does that mean no teams of three?" Dylan whined, and Mr. D nodded.

"Now, you all know the drill. I'll be calling on students randomly, who will draw a name from the bowl." The teacher grabbed the see-through container from his desk and held it up for everyone to see. "If you draw your name, you just pick again. Clear?"

When everyone nodded, Mr. D began calling names. Each student then went to the front of the class and moved their hands around inside the bowl of folded papers. They then grabbed the slip that they wanted and read the name aloud.

This is my chance, I couldn't help but think. This is my way to get to know Kyle. If the stars align for just this once–

"Miss Adams?" Mr. D called, slicing through my thoughts.

It took a second for me to realize that he was calling *my* name, but once I noticed, the entire class was staring my way as I stood up and walked to the front of the class. I then shoved my hand into the bowl and fished around carefully. I knew that the paper that I would grab was going to decide my fate. I then pinched a slip of paper once it felt right and pulled it out. My hands trembled as I unfolded the slip.

Please, be Kyle...

"Who did you choose, Miss Adams?" the teacher asked, attempting to read my paper. My eyes widened when I read the name.

You've got *to be kidding me.*

"*Dylan,*" I mumbled, trying hard not to scream in frustration. I looked over at my new partner and caught him sticking his tongue out at Kyle. When he noticed my staring, however, he smiled widely and waved.

"I'm sorry," Mr. D whispered in my ear, and I smiled at him in response as the bell rang. "See you guys tomorrow," he then told the class as I arrived at my desk.

"Howdy, partner," Dylan remarked seconds later as he wandered over to my desk. I rolled my eyes discreetly as I picked up my books. "Okay, here's the thing. While I'm sure you'll be an *amazing* partner and all, my friend, Kyle, *kinda* had dibs on you."

"Excuse me?" I choked, and I felt heat rush to my cheeks.

"And, I mean, there's this exchange student, Alejandro, in our class that Kyle was partnered with, who is pretty hot too," Dylan rambled. "So, I was thinking, why don't we *switch*?"

It was as if he had read my mind.

I blinked hard, making sure that this was real and not

just another dream. When Dylan still stood in front of me, his pleading eyes wide with hope, I smiled. "Deal," I remarked a little too quickly. "I-I mean, yeah, sure. If you *want*."

"Nice. I'll go let the teacher know." Dylan smiled wide before shouting over to Kyle, who was waiting – probably for Dylan – at his desk. "Yo, Kyle! She's all yours."

When Kyle heard his name, he turned in his chair, and his eyes widened in horror. "Dylan, *what* did you do?"

"Nothing," Dylan insisted as Kyle joined us with his books. "I just got her to work with you. You're *welcome*." Before we could say anything more, Dylan noticed that Mr. D was leaving the room and chased after him.

"Well, *that* just happened," I laughed awkwardly as I pushed my chair and walked out of the classroom with Kyle. "What were the odds that I'd see you again?"

"Very slim, but I guess you were lucky," Kyle answered, blushing and rubbing the back of his neck nervously. "I guess I'll be getting to see a lot more of you now."

"Yeah." I suddenly noticed that I couldn't stop smiling, which weirded me out. "So, chem class is fun. Atoms, molecules, and *stuff*."

Kyle chuckled. "You're the new girl, right?"

"Is it that obvious? I laughed nervously, playing with a strand of my dark hair. "I swear, I've visited the town before!"

"Really?" Kyle questioned with a grin before glancing forward. I followed his gaze and spotted his friends, who were gathered around their lockers.

"Yeah, my aunt has lived here all her life. I just moved

in with her recently," I told him, going along with the story that Ivy created.

"Oh, wow. That's pretty cool." Kyle then stopped at his locker, and as he opened his locker and shoved his books inside, I caught sight of Ethan and smiled. When Ethan grinned back, Calvin raised an eyebrow in confusion.

"So, dude, did you *do* it?" Dylan asked teasingly, slipping in front of me to speak to Kyle.

I shot Kyle a puzzled look as he responded quietly, "No." Kyle responded quietly.

"*Coward*," Dylan mumbled, then moved to lean against the locker beside Kyle's, his smile wide. He combed a hand through his long hair slowly before looking at me and saying, "*So*, I know we kinda already met, but do you have a first name, Mystery Girl?"

"Jenna," I responded slowly, confused and a little terrified.

"Oh, Locker Blocker. I knew I had seen you before," Ethan responded, and the original smile I had been wearing came back on my face.

He remembers me.

"Well, I'm Dylan, and that's Calvin and Ethan," Dylan explained, ignoring Ethan's comment. "I guess you already know Kyle."

"Wait, who are you, exactly?" Calvin asked me.

"I'm Kyle's new lab partner in chemistry class," I explained.

"Which is why you should *definitely* join us for Movie Night," Dylan exclaimed, grinning at me. "You know, so you guys can work on your *chemistry*." Dylan burst out laughing, though Kyle's face turned beet red.

"Movie Night?" I questioned, changing the subject so that it wouldn't become awkward. I looked at Ethan as if he was the one who was supposed to answer. But when I noticed what I was doing, I glanced over at Kyle, who looked like he wanted to smack his head against a locker.

"Oh, yeah, it's just this thing that I do with the guys," Kyle responded, and I could pick up on how tongue-tied he was. "I mean, you could join if you *want*, but you don't *have* to–"

"When is it?" I asked, more intrigued than I should have been. But it was my chance to weasel my way into their group.

"Tuesday night at Ethan's house around seven o'clock," Dylan responded before Kyle could.

"Okay, I'll be there. Unless, of course, you want to just be the guys–"

"No!" Dylan and Kyle both cried, one happier than the other. I watched Calvin facepalm in disappointment.

"*I'm* cool with it," Ethan answered, smiling at me welcomingly. "What about you, Cal?"

"I just wanna see what's so special about this girl–"

"So, it's a yes," Dylan responded quickly for Calvin.

"I'll text you the address," Kyle told me as the guys began to walk together, and I followed. "Are you *sure* you want to join?"

"Yeah, of course. Besides, I'd like to get to know my partner before we work together. Labs take a lot of trust."

"Well, the first thing you need to know is that this geek is *one with his playing cards*," Dylan laughed, and Kyle narrowed his blue eyes at him. "He was *practically* Houdini in primary school–"

"You *asshole*!" Kyle yelled, pushing Dylan against a locker before they began to tackle each other wildly.

I then felt someone cup my shoulders with their hands, pulling me away from the boys. When I looked over my shoulder, I noticed that it was Ethan, and I felt myself blush despite how much I tried not to.

God, it was *never* going to happen. Yet I kept acting as if he was *still* my boyfriend.

As if I was *still* myself.

"Now, the second thing you need to know is that there has *always* been a never-ending rivalry between these two," Calvin explained as if I couldn't have already assumed. Our eyes were all still on the bickering boys.

"Yeah, they kind of remind me of these two girls that I used to know. They used to *always* have something to argue about," Ethan commented, laughing sadly to himself.

"You mean Jessi and your *girlfriend*?" Calvin asked, and my heart caught in my throat.

"Yeah." Ethan stopped walking, a look of sadness and heartbreak consuming him. It reminded me of the feeling that always wrapped around me when I thought about him. "God, I miss Adley."

What killed me the most was the fact that those four words tore my heart in two – especially since I was standing right in front of him.

Chapter 10
Annabeth
Sarcasm on Speed Dial

Did I make it?" I asked Adley as we arrived in front of the school's bulletin board. I closed my eyes and crossed my fingers.

After a moment of silence, I heard Adley sigh. "Wow, the leading role once again," she remarked, and I opened my eyes, squealing. Adley covered her ears, wincing in response. "You know, I thought after three years, they'd consider starring someone else."

"Stop being so bitter," I scolded Adley, who smirked in reply. "Besides, they starred Aurora Dickinson, not Annabeth Landers."

"Do you think Jessi made it?" Adley chuckled as if it would have been a joke if Jessi was cast in the play. She leaned toward the list with her pointing finger out as if she was ready to scan the sheet.

Before she had the chance to, though, I pulled her away and directed her down the hallway. "It's useless looking," I said quickly, shrugging my shoulders nonchalantly.

"My name is there, and that's all I need to know. I can then be surprised with the rest of the cast at rehearsal this afternoon."

"Ooh, I can't wait to find out who will play your Romeo," Adley gushed.

"Yeah, I can't wait either," I agreed in a whisper, stopping and opening my locker to get my first-period books.

"He better be hot, for your sake," she laughed.

I smiled at her before her eyes left me to look down the hall. I followed Adley's stare, falling upon Ethan and his group of idiots.

"Seriously? You already got them to hang out with you. I don't think you need to stare in interest anymore," I told her, twirling a strand of hair absentmindedly. "That'll just boost their already-large egos."

"Yeah, I know," she replied, but it didn't look as if she was even listening to me since her eyes were still glued to the gang. "You know, I'm shocked you haven't attempted to speak to your brother yet."

My eyes widened at the mention of Ethan. "I-I guess I've been so distracted with everything that I haven't had the chance to."

"Well, you know how easily our lives can be taken away from us." I closed my locker and realized that Adley was now looking at me. "I'd at least say hi and see from there so that I wouldn't regret not trying. Who knows what'll happen tomorrow, right?"

Adley's words repeated in my head throughout the rest of the day. I forgot about them, though, when I walked into rehearsal and saw that I was officially living my worst nightmare. Because right in front of me was Nathaniel Tucker, pacing on the stage with a thick script in his hands.

No.

He looked up from the booklet as the loud, heavy doors of the auditorium closed behind me. A smirk appeared on his face.

I walked down the aisle and up the stage's stairs, my hands forming into fists at my sides. "What are you *doing* here? I don't recall basketball tryouts taking place on a stage," I remarked bitterly.

"Seriously, don't you remember how I was a huge theater geek in ninth grade?"

"Yeah, but that was *three* years ago! I had high hopes that you would have changed," I grumbled, rolling my eyes. "Plus, you didn't care to ask me if I was *okay* with you partaking in my extracurriculars?"

"Your *what*?" Nate questioned. I rolled my eyes at his lack of vocabulary as he shook his head dismissively. "Point is, I didn't think I had to get your permission to star in this year's play."

I choked on my saliva, my heart racing. "*What?*"

"That's right. You are looking at the actor for *Raven Morningstar*," Nate cried, his voice booming off the walls. "I hope that our past relationship won't affect things," he then whispered to me.

No. I could *not* pretend to be *in love* with Nate Tucker, the murdering son of a bitch that had a brain too small for his own good.

I swallowed hard. "I'm just excited to see what Ivy is

going to think of this—"

Nate and I turned at the sound of slow clapping. When we looked toward the right wing, Jessi revealed herself with a grin that matched Nate's smirk. "Well, well, well. Who would have seen *you* coming up here and playing Mr. Romeo? I didn't know you were such a romantic," she laughed, her brown eyes not meeting mine.

"At least I got a role, unlike *you*," Nate bragged. "Though, maybe you're stuck backstage for a reason. It would be *so* awkward when no one can see Josie on the stage because she's so fucking *short*."

Jessi feigned a yawn. "You act so high and mighty because you think you're so *tall*. But have you seen yourself beside your new girlfriend? Honestly, it's a shocker that you can make out with her without getting squished."

I stood there, gaping at the conversation that I was hearing.

When had Jessi become such a—?

"You can be such a bitch, sometimes," Nate snapped at Jessi, finishing my thought.

"You call it being a bitch, I call it, 'telling it like it is,'" Jessi told Nate, her hands on her hips. "Though I suppose that your oversized ego has trouble handling reality, doesn't it?"

The lines coming from her mouth reminded me so much of—

Oh, shit.

"I don't think you can judge what's oversized and what isn't. How tall are you, three-foot-five? *Everything* is oversized to you, Short Stack," Nate bit back. I could see the anger in Jessi's eyes flare up like a campfire at the use of the nickname that Ivy had given her years ago.

"Using Ivy's lines, are you? You must *really* be getting desperate–"

"Enough!" All three of us looked toward the left wing, where my twin brother emerged. His hands were forming into fists at his sides.

Now, *that* was another shocker.

"Ethan, I don't *need* your help," Jessi hissed through gritted teeth, but she couldn't seem to be able to look him in the eye.

"I'm not *saying* you do. I just know that someone is going to do something stupid," he answered, stepping in between Jessi and Nate before meeting my eyes for a brief second.

"*She* started it! She's probably just pissed because she didn't get the lead role," Nate exclaimed.

Jessi leaped for him, though Ethan held her back. "I do *not* care about some stupid role!" she yelled, looking as if she was a rabid bear that was ready to attack its prey.

"Just, please, *stop* already!" I cried, and the tension broke as everyone's eyes landed on me.

"*Fine.*" As if a switch had flipped inside her, Jessi dropped the act and marched down the stage's steps. She headed out the exit doors as more cast members entered.

I wanted to go after her as Nate walked over to his chair in the corner of the auditorium where his school bag sat–

Ethan blocked my path, holding me back. "I know you don't know me, but I know her *really* well." I stopped trying to go against his will, wanting to listen to what he was going to say next. "Jessi… She's been through a lot these past few months. After losing her close friend – my, um, sister – she became someone different… *cruel*… But I know that she doesn't mean everything she says." Ethan sighed, his brown eyes glancing at the doors that Jessi had just exited. "She's a real piece of work, sometimes. But she was once this nice girl who would *never* hurt a living soul. The Innocent One, her friends would call her."

"I can tell how much you care about her," I remarked, staring at the moving curtains behind Ethan.

"She's all I've got now," he admitted as he sat down on the edge of the stage.

I tried to hold back my tears as I took a seat, joining him since I still had a few minutes until rehearsals began. "What about your family?"

Ethan's eyes widened as if he was confused by the question. "They-they're too busy with work to acknowledge me anymore. But that's beside the point." Ethan looked up from the ground to look into my eyes. "Jessi needs a friend. And from what I've heard, you may be the only chance at getting through to her these days."

"What do you mean?"

"She won't listen to me, but she speaks so fondly of you whenever the topic comes up. My sister used to be the one to keep her under control – which was why Jessi never acted this way before now. But with Anna gone, you're, like, the best replacement… Not that you'd be replacing Anna, but–"

"I get it," I told him, nodding in agreement. "I *promise* to try my best, though I can't make miracles happen."

Ethan stood back up on the stage, and so did I as Ms. Mitchell walked up the steps on the left side. "I don't need miracles. I need my best friend back," was all Ethan said before slipping behind the curtains on the right-wing side of the stage.

"*Finally*, you got to see the bitch in all her glory," Adley laughed after I shared with her what had happened at rehearsal.

We were sitting together on my motel bed, each sipping a mug of hot cocoa. We were now waiting for Ivy and Nate to arrive since they had just texted us that they were coming over for *another* meeting.

"Since *when* have you known Jessi to start fights with sarcastic retorts?" I asked, confused by Adley's not-shocked reaction.

"Since when have I known Jessi *not* to, is the question. She was Miss Perfect for the first bit after your death, but once she started to become annoying and obsessed over finding your 'killer,' she lost it. She began to be bitter twenty-four-seven, hating me the most. Especially after Ethan confided in her about the night that he kissed me, and..." Adley trailed off, her face turning pink.

"And *what*?" I couldn't just let her get off the hook. I had to know what she wasn't telling me.

We were *best friends*, after all.

"And I stayed at his place for the night." Adley blushed, looking down at her hands. "Before you ask, no, we didn't do *it...* I just slept in his bed that night, and it was *really* romantic–"

"Okay, okay, *please,* stop. I've heard too much," I groaned, covering my ears and wincing in disgust.

Adley frowned. "But you always said that I could tell you anything."

"I didn't mean *everything*!" I cried, cringing at the thought of them *being* together.

"Never mind," Adley mumbled. "I don't even know why I told you."

"I'm sorry," I apologized, shaking my head. "That was just... so *sudden*."

"I-I know," she stammered, looking away. "I didn't mean for it to come out like that."

I took a deep breath, trying to calm myself down. "It's okay. I... I'm happy for you."

"Really?" Adley smiled softly, and I nodded.

I *was* happy for her since she'd had someone that made her feel comfortable and safe.

Someone I wished that *I* had.

"So, why did Jessi care about this?" I asked, wanting to get back on track before the facts weirded me out too much.

"I honestly have no clue. But since I was still with Nate, she decided to threaten me and Ethan with our secret. From then on, Ethan was so mad at Jessi that they stopped talking – if sarcastic retorts didn't count. That's just the brief breakdown," Adley explained before taking a sip from her mug. "Point is, she has been like this for *months.* I don't think anyone will ever change her."

"Maybe *I* can."

Adley almost choked on her beverage. "*What?*"

"Ethan said today at rehearsal that he believes that I can change her, and I will. I *promised* him that, and I know she's all that he has now. Without us, he's all alone."

"And miserably stuck with Jessi the Loser," Adley mumbled, laughing to herself.

"I *will* fix her, I promise."

If not for Ethan, then for Jessi herself.

"Don't you have your hands full with Mr. Nate Capulet?" Adley chuckled.

"Romeo's family name is *Montague*—"

"Are you *kidding* me? You left the spellbook at *school*?" Ivy snapped as she barged into the room with Nate, not caring to knock. "You know we needed it for tonight's meeting."

"I always keep it in my locker," Nate remarked as if Ivy should have known this. He then mumbled, "You know it's how I get good marks in chem." His smile turned into a smirk, and Ivy chuckled, interlocking her fingers with his.

I realized then that Adley had also caught the act since her eyes sparkled with mischief. "Well," she exclaimed, looking at Ivy with a smirk. "I guess you're okay with his new role?"

"Huh?" Ivy's brows shot up, and she looked over at Nate. "What is she talking about, Natey Boo?"

Adley bit her bottom lip, stifling a laugh. "So, I'm guessing he *didn't* share the amazing news?" I caught Nate's eyes widening in fear. "Well, let's just say that Anna auditioned for the leading role in the school's senior play, and she got it."

"Congrats?" Ivy remarked, confusion lacing her voice.

"*But*," Adley continued, "not only did she get cast in the play – your *Natey Boo* did too." Adley looked back at Nate, a wide grin on her face. "Tell her, Natey Boo, what role did you get?" Nate opened his mouth, about to remark something, but Adley didn't let him speak. "He is going to be Anna's *prince charming*!"

Ivy dropped Nate's hand. Her usual smirk flipped into the scariest frown I had ever seen. "*What?*" she questioned in disbelief. "You're in a *play*, and you never *told* me?"

"Um, uh, I didn't think you'd care," he stammered, and Adley snickered.

"Well, it *kinda* matters when you're going to have to *kiss* your *ex*!"

"Ivy, it's *just* acting–"

"*Bullshit*, it is." Ivy stomped toward the door, a scowl on her face. "God, I thought we were open and honest with each other. And to think that I looked past your stupidity for *this*." Ivy pulled open the motel door and mumbled "Forget about the fucking meeting" before slamming the door shut behind her.

"I think *someone* is a little jealous–"

"Stop *ruining* things, Adley. For once, stay out of it before you make everything worse," Nate yelled, cutting Adley off before running to the door and chasing after Ivy.

Adley spun around to grin at me, no remorse in her eyes. "Well, I guess our evening is free after all. Wanna watch a horror movie?"

Chapter 11
Jessi
Everyone's Got a Weak Spot

We're on the same page, then? You agree that something else happened to Adley?"

"I'm not *agreeing* or *disagreeing*," I told Ethan, twirling a pencil between my fingers. "It's just a possibility – a *theory*."

He sighed, looking annoyed by my refusal to pick a side.

However, if I was being honest, I wasn't ready to admit that something else had happened to Adley. After all, that meant that there was another piece in this messed-up puzzle that I didn't know about.

Ethan twisted one of his white shoelaces around his finger. I followed his gaze to his friends, who were currently passing a soccer ball around on the field by using their heads instead of their feet.

"Why aren't you over there?" I asked. Instead of hanging out with his group of weirdos, Ethan had sat down in front of me under the tree, interrogating me about Adley.

"They may be my friends, but sometimes, I can't stand them. They're completely incapable of talking about anything *except* that new girl, Jenna. It gets annoying," Ethan admitted, rolling his eyes. He paused, licking his lips nervously. "Plus, I can't talk to them about Adley – not like I can with you."

My face fell. I felt sorry for Ethan – sorry that he had fallen for a killer and didn't even know it.

What would he think if he knew the truth?

The situation was so messed up that, sometimes, *I* didn't believe that Ethan was in love with his sister's killer. The killer who was now *dead* – maybe had even been murdered.

Ethan looked away from me, twisting his grease-stained fingers in his lap. Ever since Adley died, I had noticed that his hands were always stained. "Have... Have you talked to Aurora since the auditions? Like, one-on-one."

"What?" I sputtered, caught off guard.

"Aurora. Have you talked to her?"

"I understood you the first time," I snapped, rolling my eyes and sighing. "No, I haven't."

"I think you should."

"Why?" I questioned, crossing my arms and looking away from him. "She probably thinks I'm a loser."

"I don't think she does. She seems to care about you."

I looked up after he spoke, and a mixture of anger and confusion consumed me. "And how would *you* know? Did *you* talk to her?" I was asking him jokingly, but when Ethan looked away from me sheepishly for a second, my eyebrows raised.

"*Maybe* a little."

"Oh, *great*. Did you guys have a nice, long, heartfelt discussion about how *pathetic* I am?" I laughed bitterly. "How I can't even audition for a *school play* without–"

"It wasn't like that," Ethan interrupted.

"No? Then, tell me, what *was* it like?"

"We were just worried about you, Jessi. After you blew up on Nate the other day–"

"You didn't think he *deserved* it?"

Ethan smirked, laughing softly. "No, he definitely did. You looked ready to tackle him, though, and I *know* that that's not the real you."

I raised an eyebrow. "What exactly are you trying to tell me?"

Ethan sighed, combing a hand through his golden curls. "I just talked to Aurora because I didn't want her to have that first impression of you."

I felt my cheeks get hot, and I bit my lip. "You didn't have to do that."

He smiled sadly, and I realized then how strange — but *nice* – it was to be talking to Ethan as if we were friends again. "I know, but I *wanted* to. I think you should get to know Aurora."

I fidgeted with my charm bracelet, twirling my volleyball charm with a finger. "Ethan, you don't have to help me make friends."

"I know, but I think she'd like to get to know you too."

"Maybe." I honestly wasn't sure if I had enough

courage to go up and talk to Aurora, though. Especially after the way I had surely embarrassed her during the auditions.

Ethan stood up as the warning bell sounded, announcing the end of lunch. "Well, I hope you do get to talk to her. I think it would make her happy."

Would *it make Aurora happy to talk to me?* I stood in front of my locker, hastily shoving my homework into my school bag. *Would Aurora want to talk to me, even after the audition?*

I glanced down the hall and spotted her at her locker. She was shoving a few papers into a bright blue folder, and I sighed softly to myself.

Just go talk to her. What's the worst that could happen?

Taking a deep breath, I walked over to Aurora's locker. She was now gathering her books and tucking them neatly into her school bag. "Hey, Aurora," I said tentatively.

She turned and closed her locker at the sound of my voice, a smile growing on her face. "Hey," she remarked as she slung her bag over her shoulder.

"I wanted to talk to you—" I froze when I realized that Aurora and I had said the same thing in sync. We stared at each other for a beat, then laughed.

"I guess that's a sign that we *should* talk," Aurora said, tossing a lock of red-orange hair over her shoulder.

"I guess so," I agreed, walking down the hall beside her. "Isn't that other girl waiting for you, though? I always see you guys walking together."

Aurora shook her head. "Jenna can wait," she stated as we stepped outside.

I scanned the yard for a good place to sit. My eyes found an empty spot at the base of the tree that I usually sat under, and I pointed it out to Aurora. "We can sit there if you want. It's a pretty nice spot. Unless you aren't a fan of trees – we could then just find a table–"

"Under the tree sounds great," Aurora interrupted.

Once we settled ourselves in the grass, I took a deep breath to steady myself.

"Listen, I'm really sorry–" I stopped talking, realizing that Aurora had *also* said the same thing.

Aurora laughed, but this time, she sounded a little uneasy. "You go first."

I swallowed hard. "I... I'm really sorry for what happened at the audition. I'm sure that I embarrassed you up there."

Her brown eyes looked sad. "Jessi–"

"Let me finish," I said, fearing that if she cut me off, I would lose my nerve and wouldn't be able to complete my statement. "When you asked me to audition with you, I got over excited since no one's ever asked *me* to do something with them. I shouldn't have led you on, though." I looked away, biting my lip. "I'm no actress, Aurora. If you must know, I suck at doing *anything* in front of a crowd."

Aurora burst out laughing, and my eyes widened, taken aback by her reaction. "God, *I'm* sorry for making you audition. I never asked if you were comfortable with it, and I should have."

I shrugged, wanting to act nonchalant. "It's fine – I could've said something. Besides, it's hardly the first time that I put on a show here."

Aurora's smile shifted into a serious line, and I caught her cracking her knuckles. My stomach dropped. "I was wanting to ask you about that, actually."

I cocked my head to the side, intrigued. "Yeah?"

"What was all that, the other day, with that guy… *Nate*, was it?"

I flinched. I despised Nate in general, but when I had seen him with Aurora at rehearsal, I snapped. What I had experienced was the same feeling that I used to get when Anna was in some sort of trouble – the feeling that I needed to *fight*.

But that doesn't make sense, I told myself. *I knew Anna for years – I've only known Aurora for a few* days.

Either way, that hadn't stopped me from wanting to knock Nate upside the jaw. If Ethan hadn't stopped me, I was sure that I would have. But, instead, I had walked out of the auditorium, not wanting to have to deal with seeing Nate's smug, stuck-up face. I had later forced myself to go back, though – for the sake of the play – and I had spent the rest of that afternoon glaring at Nate so much that it gave me a headache.

"So, what happened?" Aurora repeated, snapping me out of my thoughts.

I shrugged, trying to go for an I-Couldn't-Care-Less look. "You're new here, so you don't know. *But*, to put it simply, Nate Tucker is an asshole." Aurora's eyes widened, probably at my choice of words. "Good luck having *him* as your co-star in the play. If he's too annoying, feel free to punch him in the face – or ask me to do it."

Aurora laughed but it sounded a little shaky. "Okay.

Good advice, I guess." She then checked her phone and stood up. "Sorry, but I have to go. If not, Jenna is gonna kill me," she remarked, then flinched as if she was offended by her own joke.

"Oh, um, okay," I stammered, standing up as well.

Aurora unzipped her bag and tucked her phone back in it, then frowned. "Shit. I just realized that I forgot my history homework in my locker." She sighed, shaking her head and sending strands of her hair flying. "God, I'm so behind in that class."

"Do you, um, need help?" I asked hesitantly. "I'm pretty good at history. Not-not that I'm bragging or anything."

I felt my face flush as Aurora giggled softly. "That would be amazing, actually. When are you free?"

"Uh, I think Monday or Tuesday next week would be best. But I-I could make do with any day, I'm sure–"

"Tuesday sounds great," Aurora chirped, interrupting my nervous rambling. "Jenna has plans that day." Aurora then pulled out a piece of paper from her notebook, then scribbled something in a blue pen before handing it to me. "It's a date."

What exactly did she mean by, "It's a date?" I wondered as I wandered through the school parking lot in a daze. My heart was beating quicker than normal, especially whenever I looked down at the piece of paper Aurora had given me with her phone number.

Did she mean something by it? Or am I just overthinking–

"*Still* don't know your way home, Short Stack?"

My smile dropped, and I lost the bounce in my step as I looked to my left. There, I found Ivy leaning against an ugly, blue pickup truck next to…

Jenna? What's she *doing with Ivy?*

I peered at the girl with long, black-brown hair, who looked a little nervous. She lifted her brown eyes from the ground and looked right at me—

It was as if someone had punched me in the ribs – if that person's hand was on *fire*. I stumbled backward, pressing a hand to my chest. I remembered having felt this exact way before around Adley.

That doesn't make sense—

"Are you having a heart attack, Short Stack?" Ivy snickered. "Do I need to call the ambulance?"

I gritted my teeth, forcing myself to breathe against the pressure in my chest. "*Shut up*, Ivy."

Ivy leaned forward so that her face was uncomfortably close to mine. "Just for the record, I'd let you die."

I took a step back from Ivy, trying to regain my composure. "Likewise."

"You're not gonna tell me that you'd save me no matter what? Be the *good one* in this situation?" Ivy laughed bitterly. "Oh, wait. I forgot you're a total bitch now."

I made a fake sad face. "Aw, are you mad that I made fun of your boyfriend at rehearsal?"

Ivy didn't respond, settling on sending me daggers with her eyes.

I turned to Jenna, trying to ignore the tightness in my

chest. "I don't know what you're doing here, New Girl, but *trust* me. The last person you want to be hanging around with is Ivy Blackthorn. As her name implies, she's *toxic*."

Jenna looked at me, and the force of her glare shocked me. "I was just asking her a homework question."

I stifled a laugh. "Hate to break it to you, Jenna, but Ivy Blackthorn *never* does her homework. She probably doesn't even know the definition of it. How else could she have failed *second* grade–?"

"Jenna was hanging out with me because she clearly has taste," Ivy interrupted, pretending as if I hadn't just called her out on her academic failure. "*She* can tell the cool kids from the losers."

"'Cool kids'?" I mocked. "How old are you, *ten*?"

Ivy snorted. "I don't think *anyone* would mistake me for a ten-year-old – but *you*? You could still order off the kid's menu, and no one would think anything of it."

I pretended to be deep in thought, my hand resting on my chin. "What about this, Ivy? What if we agree that neither of us are ten-year-olds, but that your new boyfriend has the *brain* of one?"

Ivy's face flushed an angry shade of red, and for a second, I thought she was surely going to kill me. However, all she did was mumble "whatever" before she stalked off with Jenna.

Chapter 12
Adley
N is for Nostalgia

What do you wear to a movie night with a group of guys?"

Anna laughed as she joined me in front of the motel's cracked mirror. "You look perfect the way you are," she stated, pointing at the cropped, white T-shirt and the black pair of jeans that I was wearing.

"*Fine*," I sighed. I walked away from the mirror and over to the bedside table, where I picked up my ring. I then slipped it on my finger, transforming into character. "You don't look bad yourself. Where, again, are *you* going?"

"Jessi offered to help me catch up in history class," she said in a tone that I could have mistaken for *bragging* – as if studying with *Jessi* was so special.

"Wow, people *do* like you no matter the body," I teased, fixing my long hair in the mirror. "So, what will you be doing on this *study date*?"

"St-Studying, of *course*," Anna stated almost nervously as I noticed her face redden slightly.

Before I could think much of it, I glanced at Anna's

appearance in the mirror. I noticed that she was wearing a red long-sleeved shirt and a black skirt with her black heels.

A little fancy for studying, huh?

"You think it's weird for *me* to want to look good for the guys, yet *you* are dressing as if you're attending a party," I remarked, pointing toward her outfit. "You know there's no one to impress."

"Same goes for you. You've already got the *entire* gang staring at you non-stop. You might as well marry one of them now."

I rolled my eyes and walked away from the mirror to grab my phone and purse from the nightstand. "So, you'll be home by eleven?" I confirmed as Anna picked up her white canvas bag and slung it over her shoulder.

"I can't make any promises," she laughed as she walked out the door.

For a second, I wondered if she was lying and was going to meet up with some guy. After all, she was never this happy about anything else.

I knew we now told each other everything, though, so she couldn't have been lying.

Right?

I didn't even have to read the text that Kyle had sent me to know where I was going. I could have walked to Ethan's familiar, blue-painted Victorian house with my eyes closed. I couldn't help but feel a wave of comfort wash over me as I walked up the porch steps.

"Hey, you made it." I looked up from my stare at the gallery swing, as Ethan opened the front door.

"Yeah, it wasn't that hard to find," I laughed quietly. I walked up the steps and entered the house that smelled of buttered popcorn, rather than its usual Lysol odor. "Thanks for letting me come," I told him as I took off my black boots in the entrance.

"It's my pleasure," Ethan replied with a smile.

I gazed around the room as memories came flooding back to me. I could practically see six-year-old me, Ethan, and Anna running down the stairs as we raced to the back porch to go swimming. "It's a nice house you have," I commented casually, trying to find something to say.

"Thanks," he laughed, combing a hand through his blond curls before glancing into the living room. "Um, I have to go get the bowl of popcorn in the kitchen, but feel free to make yourself at home. The guys are in the next room playing a game."

I nodded, then walked into the living room to find Calvin, Dylan, and Kyle sitting in a circle on the floor. There was a pile of cards in the middle of them, and they were each holding a small number of colorful playing cards in their hands.

"Uno!" cried Kyle, waving his card in the air.

"You're supposed to say that when you only have *one* card left," Calvin sighed, shaking his head.

"But I *do* only have one card left," Kyle protested, though his face said otherwise.

"I'm not blind. I can see that green three tucked in your sleeve," Calvin commented, rolling his eyes.

"Yeah, we all know you aren't *that* good at magic," Dylan teased, leaning over and pulling the card out of the sleeve of Kyle's navy-blue hoodie.

"So, you think I'm good at magic?" Kyle smirked, and Dylan narrowed his eyes before Kyle reached over and pulled a card from under Dylan's leg. "Cheater! *You* were hiding a card too."

"*No*," Dylan remarked, stretching out the single syllable.

Kyle flicked the red plus-two card at Dylan's face before Calvin stood up and broke the boys apart. "How about we set up the movie?"

As Calvin said that, all three boys looked up and saw me standing in the doorway of the living room.

"H-How long have you-you been there?" Kyle stuttered, standing up and walking over to me.

"Long enough to see how immature you guys are," Ethan chuckled as he entered behind me with a bowl of popcorn. He then walked over to the couch and sat on the far-right side with the metal bowl.

Calvin walked over to the flatscreen TV and kneeled in front of it, pulling out a DVD case from the movie shelf that belonged to the television stand. I then decided to sit beside Ethan, knowing that it would be the closest way of feeling as if it was like old times. Once I was sitting, Dylan and Kyle dove for the spot next to me, pushing me against Ethan's chest awkwardly in the process. Kyle won, and I sat back up, trying to get comfortable.

But it felt like an impossible task, even with a knitted blanket.

"What are we watching?" I asked, making conversation so that, hopefully, Dylan and Kyle would stop glaring daggers at each other.

"*Back to the Future.* Ethan recommended it. *Again.*" Calvin rolled his eyes at the mention of Ethan's favorite film. A flash of Ethan dressed as the movie's main character on Halloween night appeared in my mind, and I tried hard not to smile at him.

"Oh, come *on*! It's the best movie of all time," Ethan exclaimed from beside me.

"Sure, it *was*. Before the *eighth* time," Dylan whined, leaning back against a pillow. I then caught him staring at me over Kyle's shoulders from the corner of my eye.

"We're watching it, okay? It's not like we have any *better* options," Calvin decided. He popped the disk out of its case and stuck it in the DVD player.

"Well, there's always *American Pie*–"

"No!" Calvin and Ethan cried in disgust, and I fought back a chuckle at the thought of sitting through that film with them.

However, as I spotted a familiar DVD case on the shelf, a better idea came to mind. "Why don't we watch a scary movie?"

I didn't choose *Scream* because it was my favorite horror movie and a cult classic. I chose it because it was the least scary movie that I could think of – it was supposed to be funny, after all.

The boys all wanted to watch something scary, but since they hadn't watched much horror before, I knew that they couldn't handle the scary stuff that Ethan, Anna, and I used to watch together. But while watching *this* film, Dylan,

Calvin, and Kyle were terrified by the most *basic* jumpscares. Every five minutes, someone was screaming – it almost ruined the experience.

What made it even worse, though, was the fact that I wasn't able to focus at all on the movie – every time Kyle yawned, he'd wrap his arm around my shoulders, and my body would tense from the uncomfortable feeling.

What the hell is going on?

As afraid as he was of the film, every so often, I still spotted him blushing in the dark, making my heart skip a beat. Sure, it could have meant so many other things, but as everything then clicked as I replayed in my head every moment that Kyle and I had spent together, it had all finally made sense.

The way he would look at me.

The way he wanted to be partners without knowing me.

The way he called "dibs" on me.

Shit, Kyle has a crush on me *– of all people.*

I didn't know how to feel. Part of me was scared to hurt him since I couldn't stop thinking about Ethan – I was still in love with him, after all. But the other part of me knew that Kyle's liking of me could be useful when putting the plan into action. It would be easier to keep an eye on him.

I closed my eyes since the thoughts rushing through my head were making me feel sick. I hated how I was put in this position – *chose the boy you want to love or the one who will get you what you need.*

Not that I would ever be able to have the boy I wanted, though...

I looked between Ethan and Kyle, knots forming in the pit of my stomach.

"I need water," I stated as another scream came from the TV – as well as the three, terrified boys. "I-I'll be back." I stood up abruptly, then grabbed my phone and exited the room.

It was odd standing outside on Ethan's front balcony, gazing out at the quiet street that was glowing in the light of the scattered street lamps. The crescent moon was blocked by the large clouds, and the stars weren't twinkling, but the cool breeze felt as if it was washing my worries away. During all my seventeen years of living on this street, I had never paid so much attention to the little things like the street signs that awaited at every corner.

I had been outside on the porch for about ten minutes and was drinking from the water bottle that I had found in the kitchen when I heard the front door creak open. I turned around in my spot on the steps to see Kyle.

"Hey," he whispered as he closed the door. "Are you okay?"

"Yeah, I'm sorry. All the screaming was giving me a headache," I lied, tucking a dark strand of hair behind my ear.

"Maybe you *shouldn't* watch horror movies with us anymore. I have a feeling that Dylan may be paranoid for the next week because of this," Kyle chuckled.

I stood up to be at his height, taking a deep breath. "Anyway, I think I might get ready to leave if that's okay."

"Yeah, definitely." Kyle looked more nervous than usual, pacing with his hands in his pockets, while his body shook.

Oh, he so likes me.

"I'll, um, go get your purse." Kyle then entered the house again, and after sitting down on the porch swing, I continued looking at the streetlights, the houses, the cars–

"Mind if I join you?" Before I could look back around, Ethan took a seat next to me. I nodded, smiling as my heartbeat quickened. "Are you okay? If gore isn't your thing, maybe you shouldn't have recommended a *slasher*."

"No, I just got a bad headache," I said, looking away from Ethan. "I actually *love* horror movies. They are super cliché, and the gore is stupid and unrealistic. But they also keep you on your toes – you have no time to think about anything else besides when the next jumpscare will be."

Ethan chuckled, and I looked back to see that he had an odd look on his face. "You sound just like Adley. She loved horror movies, especially the classics like *Scream* and *Carrie*."

I smiled and blushed when he mentioned my name. "Adley?" I questioned since I then remembered that I wasn't supposed to know much about this girl.

"Yeah, the girl on the locker that you visited the day we met… She was my girlfriend. We weren't official, but we had just gotten closer before her passing." Ethan looked down at his black Converse as a tear came to his eye. "She was all I had left. Sure, the way we got close was messed-up – we were hooking up secretly, while she was still dating Nate Tucker. But our relationship… You wouldn't get it."

"No, I do," I confessed as a tear rolled down my cheek. When Ethan looked at me encouragingly, I said, "I-I was dating someone back where I used to live before I moved here. It was pretty messy too, but I won't ever forget him."

"I told Adley that I loved her over text, right before I found her *dead*," Ethan laughed sadly. "It's been hard, especially since she wasn't the only person that I lost this past year."

"I'm really sorry… My friend, Aurora, told me about Anna." I placed a comforting hand on his shoulder. "I actually just lost my parents. They died in a car crash about a month ago. So, now, I'm living with my aunt."

Ethan's jaw dropped, and I could tell that he understood what I must have been feeling – if only the story *wasn't* a lie. "I-I'm… Shit, here I am, crying about Adley, and–"

"*Stop.* It's okay. We understand each other," I reminded him, and he nodded sadly. "2015 has been quite a bitch," I chuckled, trying to smile when all I wanted to do was fall in Ethan's arms and cry.

"*Nostalgia* has been a bitch – without the memories, we'd be fine," Ethan mumbled, and I nodded in agreement. "Sometimes, I just wish that our memories would die with the people we lose." After a moment of silence, where we sat and stared at the sky full of stars, Ethan added, "You-you know, I like you. You're caring, understanding, and honest. You and Kyle would make a good pair."

My face burned, but I felt the sensation vanish as Ethan's eyes met mine again. "You-you think so?"

"Let's be honest – he's *terrible* at keeping his crush a secret," he remarked, and I burst out laughing with what felt like relief. "You would be good for him. He doesn't have many people to rely on besides the three of us idiots. You make him smile, which makes me happy."

It makes him happy…

Just as I was about to comment, I heard the door creak behind me. Ethan and I both turned and stood up to see Kyle in the doorway with Ivy's black crossbody purse.

"Good night, Jenna," Ethan told me, then passed Kyle and disappeared into the house.

"Sorry, that took a while. I got held back by the boys," Kyle stated as he handed me the purse. "And I'm sorry that it was a shitty night for you. It was probably a *horrible* date–" He cut himself off and blushed.

"Oh, so this was a *date*?" I asked, raising an eyebrow as Kyle froze. I contemplated for a moment how to reply, then decided that I didn't have anything to lose now – this would help the plan. This would help me get Ethan back. Besides, this would make Ethan *happy*. "Well, luckily, it was a *great* one. I hope we can have another soon."

The smile on Kyle's face grew, making his blue eyes sparkle.

"Anyway, I better head out–"

"W-Want me to-to walk you home?" Kyle stuttered, and I giggled at his nervousness.

I fell upon the small, two-floored Cape-Cod style house across the street. It looked abandoned if not for the small light in the living room, where my mother was most likely watching her evening TV dramas. I was suddenly already home, and I most certainly didn't want to leave.

"No, I think I'll be okay on my own."

Chapter 13
Jessi
Games are a Girl's Best Friend

I'm sure she'll be here soon," I mumbled to myself, pacing from my bedroom to the main room of the basement. I then turned around and did it back again, biting a nail. I had told Aurora to arrive at my place at 7:00 PM. But now, it was already 7:10 PM.

Maybe she just got lost. She's new and probably doesn't know the neighborhood. I looked in the direction of my front door, hoping to hear the doorbell or a knock. *Or maybe she won't show up at all.*

The thought of that made me sadder than I had expected it to.

Why do I even care so much? I wondered, picking up a black-framed picture from the tall bookshelf in front of me.

I looked down at the photo in my hands, then felt myself wince a little. The picture was a candid shot of ninth-grade me, Ethan, Adley, and Anna, sitting on the Landers' wooden back porch. We were each holding an oversized, vibrant-colored popsicle.

We were so happy back then—

The doorbell rang, and my heart leaped – so much so that I almost dropped the photo frame. I placed it on the coffee table in front of the couch, nerves bubbling inside of me. With a wide smile on my face that I couldn't quite control, I darted toward the stairs.

I yanked open the front door to find Aurora in a red top and a black skirt, and a white fabric tote bag was slung over one shoulder. I took in her sweet, vanilla perfume, then felt underdressed. I had just thrown on my favorite black jeans with a gray lace-trimmed T-shirt.

"Hey!" Aurora exclaimed, smiling wide. "Sorry if I'm a little late."

I stepped aside to let her enter. "It's fine. I was just chilling."

"Well, I know I *am* kind of late. But let's just call it 'fashionably late,'" Aurora offered playfully, kicking off her black boots.

I felt myself blush and looked away so that she wouldn't be able to tell. "Yeah, we'll call it that," I responded, trying to channel her easy confidence. "Um, you can come downstairs. I have my books there."

Aurora nodded but didn't say anything. Her gaze drifted around my house almost wistfully before she followed me downstairs slowly as if she was nervous. I headed over to the coffee table, where I had haphazardly placed my books. But before I could ask Aurora what she needed help with, she picked up the photo that I had left on the table.

"Who are these people?" she asked softly, her brown

eyes sad.

I felt a sharp stab in my stomach. "Oh, um, my friends. Two of them, however… Well, they're the girls who recently passed away in this town."

Aurora's eyes met mine, and her lips pulled into a straight line as if she was unsure how to react. "I-I'm so sorry. From this photo, you guys seemed close."

I sat down on the couch to stop my legs from shaking, and Aurora took a seat beside me. "Yeah, we *were,* but Adley – the one with the straight, blonde hair – died in October. And Annabeth – the girl with the curly hair – was murdered back in August."

By Adley–

I couldn't breathe. It was as if the walls were collapsing in on me. I was vaguely aware that I was trembling, and I knew that I must have been freaking Aurora out big time. But I couldn't get control of myself.

"Hey," Aurora whispered gently, laying a hand on my shoulder. "Are you okay?"

"Fine," I choked, squeezing my eyes shut. I dug my teeth into my bottom lip.

"Why don't we go outside?" Aurora offered. I opened my eyes to see her standing above me and holding out her hand. "It's a little cramped in here, no?"

Aurora took my shaking hand, pulling me up and off the couch. I felt my pulse speed up even more, and all I could focus on was the feeling of Aurora's soft, warm hand against mine.

"Do you want to grab your books?" Aurora asked, keeping my hand in hers. I nodded dazedly, and Aurora gave me a soft smile. She dropped my hand so that I could pick the textbooks up, though my hand then felt cold without the warmth of hers.

Shaking my head, I snatched up my books and stuffed them into my backpack. I then followed Aurora up the stairs, out the front door, and onto the porch. I sat down on the top step, letting out a breath.

Aurora sat beside me, her brown eyes wide with concern. "Feeling a bit better?" she questioned, setting down her bag beside herself.

"Yeah," I admitted, though I still wanted to hide after everything – I felt like a *freak*. "Thanks."

"I'm sorry. I shouldn't have asked about that photo," Aurora apologized quietly.

"It's fine," I assured her, biting at the corner of a nail. "I overreacted."

Aurora shook her head. "You didn't. All this... it must be hard." I noticed a catch in her voice as if she was getting choked up. Neither I nor Aurora then said anything, not meeting each other's gaze. After a minute of silence, though, she stood up. The dim evening sunlight reflected off her red-orange curls, making them shine effortlessly. "Why don't we find somewhere else to study?"

Aurora and I walked down the sidewalk of the strip mall on our way to Danny's Diner, chatting about annoying teachers, good books, and what songs we liked on the radio. It was funny how easy it was to talk with her – it was as if I had known her forever.

Once we entered the diner, Aurora made a beeline

for the corner booth by the windows – the *exact* booth that had been my, Anna, and Adley's spot. I walked over to where Aurora sat, then slid onto the bench across from her. A waiter came to take our order, and I asked for my usual drink, while Aurora chose the peach iced tea.

"So," I said slowly, setting my history books on the table. "What do you need help with?"

Aurora sighed, raking a hand through her loose curls. "What *don't* I need help with?"

I laughed nervously. "I guess I'll start with the first chapter, then."

"Sure, that'd be great," Aurora replied with a smile. She then rummaged through her bag, pulling out a marble-covered notebook before frowning. "Shit, I forgot a pen."

I quickly dug through my pencil case and found one of my pencils. "Here, you can use this one."

As Aurora grabbed the pencil out of my fingers, I flinched slightly. I noticed that the pencil I had pulled out was one of Anna's old purple ones, which she once lent me. I had been supposed to give it back a while ago, but whenever I used it, it was like a part of her was still with me, and I had never *wanted* to give it back.

I hadn't touched it in months, but now, sadness flowed through me.

A part of her was still with me, yet it wasn't the *same*.

I looked up from the pencil, then realized that Aurora was also staring oddly at the purple stationary. I never got to ask what had come over her, though, since I was interrupted by the waiter, who came to our booth and handed us our drinks.

After studying for a while, Aurora set down the purple pencil and stretched, leaning forward as she reached with her arms across the table. She then took another sip of her iced tea, which was almost empty. "All right," she remarked, sounding tired but confident. "I think I get it, now."

"Yeah?" I asked, my voice sounding more hopeful than I intended it to.

"Yeah," Aurora responded with a smile. "I think I'll ace the next test. Thank you so much – you are a *lifesaver*."

I felt myself blush as I tucked my books back into my bag. "Anytime."

When I looked back up, Aurora had a pensive look on her face. "Hey," she started, chewing on the end of her straw. "What if we played a game?"

"Oh, sure. What kind of game?"

"Something like… Would You Rather," Aurora replied, her lips curving into a smile.

The title of the game pulled at my heartstrings since it had been Anna's favorite game growing up. The last time I played had been with her.

"Sure, we could play that."

"Okay, I'll start," Aurora exclaimed, her exhaustion vanishing. "You love books, right? Would you rather be able to only reread the same book for the rest of your life, or never be able to read the same book twice?"

"Ooh, tough question," I laughed, thinking through the pros and cons of each scenario. "I really love rereading books... I guess I'd rather reread only one book for the rest of my life. I can never get bored of *The Hunger Games*." I tucked a loose curl behind my ear as I then said, "Aurora, would you rather... only watch horror movies or only watch comedies for the rest of your life?"

"Horror movies, as weird as it sounds," Aurora chuckled. "I know, horror movies are lame after a while, but so are terribly-written comedies. Horror at least keeps you on your toes." She then glanced around the room as if pondering her next question. "Now, Jessi, would you rather go skydiving or—"

"Kiss the girl across from you?" a familiar, bitter voice snickered, and my stomach dropped.

I turned around in the booth to find Ivy strolling toward us, the green streaks in her hair popping out in contrast to her black outfit. She then stopped at the front of the table with a latté in her hand.

"Come on, Short Stack," Ivy snickered. "Answer the question."

I felt my face burn, both with anger and embarrassment. As I opened my mouth to reply, though, Aurora cut me off.

"I need water," she stated before standing up and sliding out of the booth.

Ivy and I followed Aurora with our eyes as she walked over to the diner counter. Then, once Aurora was out of earshot, Ivy looked back at me with a smirk on her plum-colored lips. "Wow, you moved on *already*?"

I choked on my saliva, then coughed. "What?"

Ivy slid into the booth, sitting across from me. She folded her hands on the table, her green eyes sparkling with mischief. "Don't act like I don't see the way you look at that new girl. It's cute, really."

I felt as if I had traveled back in time to the day of the corn maze in October. Ivy and I had been paired to work together, but instead of solving the riddles that would help us find the maze's exit, Ivy was always discussing the topic of my crush on Anna.

"Shut up," I seethed, glaring daggers at Ivy.

"Relax, I don't give a shit about your love life." Ivy leaned closer, looking from me to Aurora. "I'm just happy you've found yourself a distraction."

I stifled a laugh. "You're never happy about anything."

Ivy rolled her eyes, though the smirk on her lips showcased her amusement. "That's actually very true," she admitted, shaking her head as she laughed. "Anyway, I have to go. I think I've interrupted your date for long enough." Ivy stood up as Aurora approached the table with a bottle of water in her hand. "Now, don't stay out too late, crazy kids." Before I or Aurora could find something to respond with, Ivy flounced out of the diner.

I rolled my eyes as Aurora sat down, her eyes still fixed on the diner door. "God, Ivy is the literal *worst*. Sorry about that."

I heard a phone notification chime, and Aurora glanced down at her phone. "Don't be sorry," she answered, though it was more to her phone than me. She then stood up abruptly with her bottle.

"Where are you going?" I questioned, confusion lacing my voice.

Aurora sighed, glancing at her phone again before

tossing it into her bag. "Jenna just texted, reminding me that it's ten-thirty. Our curfew is eleven o'clock *exactly*."

"Oh, okay," I responded, trying not to sound disappointed.

Aurora gathered her things, packing the purple pencil in her haste. Before I could point it out, she told me, "Thanks again for everything. I owe you big time." She then darted out of the café, leaving me alone and confused as I stared at where she was sitting just moments before.

Chapter 14
Adley
The Truth Doesn't Change the Way You Lie

Just like it had been for the last few weeks, sleep was foreign and unreachable. No matter how dark and quiet the motel room was as I lay in bed, alone since Anna was still out with Jessi, I couldn't stop tossing and turning. I continuously tried to focus on small details, such as the low hum of the air vent or the ticking of the clock, but rushing thoughts were always overpowering.

Kyle likes me.

Ethan wants me to be with Kyle.

If only he knew that—

A blinding light flashed into my eyes, and I winced, closing my eyes, regretting not shutting the blackout curtains. Once the light went out, I realized that Nate's blue pickup truck had just parked in front of the window, and my heart skipped a beat as the motel door creaked open. After years of pretending to be asleep when my parents would come home late from parties, I closed my eyes, my first instinct being to act as if I wasn't awake – especially when hushed voices followed the sound of shoes scuffing the old floorboards.

"I'm impressed. You *did* follow through with your task," Ivy mused, and I could practically hear her smirk. "Can't believe you took her out on a *date*."

I stopped breathing for a second, confused by Ivy's words.

What date*?*

"God, it *wasn't* a date. She was just helping me out with history class stuff," Anna mumbled as the door shut.

"*Sure*, she was." Ivy chuckled, and I opened my eyes just enough to see Anna's now red face in the darkness. "Come on, it's obvious that she likes you – as *more* than just a friend. Open your eyes."

A knot formed in my stomach. *Nothing* was making sense.

Were they talking about *Jessi*?

"Shut up. You don't know anything."

"Come *on*, I've been seeing how she makes those hopeless puppy eyes at you. The real question is if *you* feel the *same*."

Ew, why would Anna ever feel the same? Firstly, we're talking about Jessi Alvarez, and secondly, wasn't Anna just with Drake? I know that she said there was someone else, but the girl is as straight as they get–

"I'm not talking about this with you."

"You aren't *denying* anything," Ivy sang, her tone playful yet bitter.

"Shut up!" Anna yelled, jolting me awake, though I tried hard not to stir. I closed my eyes shut, afraid that someone would catch me. "Don't you have somewhere else to be? Thanks for the ride, but it's getting late."

Ivy laughed, and I heard the door open again. "Sweet dreams, Annabeth. You know I'm right."

A chill traveled down my spine as the door closed. Ivy's words had been so similar to the ones that Damion said to me about my crush on Ethan...

Ivy had to be wrong, though. The Anna I knew would have never fallen for some fucked-up monster – my *nemesis*, of all people.

She wouldn't do that to me–

My thoughts were cut off by the sound of crying. I opened my eyes slightly to see Anna sitting on the floor, her back against the motel door and her hands cupping her face.

Shit.

Was there more to this than I was thinking? Why would Anna be crying if Ivy was only joking, and if Anna didn't–

No.

Anger coursed through my body, and my mind swirled in a panic.

No, there has to be some other reason...

Anna couldn't have fallen for her guardian angel, could she have?

I hadn't spoken to Anna for a few days after I overheard the bizarre conversation between her and Ivy since school had taken over our lives. However, as I watched TV from my bed one afternoon, the creak of the motel door shook me awake.

"I got you a little something."

I glanced away from the TV screen and spotted Anna, who had just closed the door behind her with a small box in her hands. Her smile was wide, and I raised an eyebrow, confused. "You got me something? Christmas isn't for a few days."

Anna laughed as she walked over to the bed, taking a seat beside me. I turned the TV volume down, uninterested in the news anyway. "I know, but I couldn't help myself. While I was window shopping and trying to distract myself from everything, I saw this… And, well, I *had* to get it."

I mirrored her grin, snatching from her hands the tiny, white box adorned with a pink bow. "Anna," I whispered in a joking tone, "you know I'm committed to Ethan."

"God, it's not a *wedding* ring box," Anna chuckled, her eyes watering with joy. "Just open it!"

At her demand, I flipped open the box, and my jaw dropped with surprise. I brought a hand to my heart as I gazed at two thin, heart rings, one silver and one gold. "You didn't have to get me *two* rings!"

Anna rolled her eyes, then shoved my arm playfully. "They're friendship rings. That means we *each* get one."

"Anna, you didn't have to!" I exclaimed, my chest warm and fuzzy. The gesture was so nice, especially since the past forty-eight hours had been odd between us. I hadn't know what to do after overhearing the conversation Anna had with Ivy about Jessi the other night. We were so close, and to think that Anna was hiding something that big from me… I had decided that the best thing to do was pretend that

I heard nothing.

Besides, Jessi *couldn't* have been the reason why Anna was crying that night – I *knew* it.

"I have dibs on the silver–" A burning shock zipped through me, prickling across my skin as I touched the silver ring. I dropped it back into the box, moaning in pain.

What the fuck?

I looked over at Anna, then watched as her face turned red with shock. "You-you never knew about the metal rule, did you?"

"What *rule*?" I huffed, rubbing my fingers as if the motion would remove the pain.

Anna laughed softly. "Supernatural creatures all have weaknesses – besides witches, since they have to work with each other to be powerful. Angels can't touch gold, Guardians can't touch bronze, and demons can't touch silver." As I looked down at the silver ring on my finger that I had found in Ivy's things, Anna added, "Fake jewelry is okay, though. That's how I always wore gold rings."

I nodded in comprehension, sighing. "So, we're like each other's weakness when wearing these rings?"

"Exactly!" Anna cheered, slipping the silver ring on her finger. "Isn't it cute?"

"Sure," I answered, though I was still wrapping my mind around another rule I had never been told about. "*Interesting.*" Once the gold ring was on my finger, Anna sighed. I looked up to see her staring at her phone. "What's up?"

"It's Jessi." A tightness formed in my chest at the mention of her name, and I bit my bottom lip. "Ever since I ran out on her the other night – during our study session – she's been wanting to hang out again, and…"

"And?" I prompted, curious to know where she was going with this. I needed more answers since I still couldn't grasp the idea of Anna having a *crush* on Jessi.

There had to have been something that I was missing.

"God, I don't know." Anna laughed again, though this time, it was filled with nerves. "Jessi… she's been making me question everything." Anna took a breath, then asked, "Adley, can I be honest with you?"

I gulped, unsure how to answer. The more she talked about Jessi, the more terrified I got – and the less certain I was about my theory. "Y-Yeah, of course."

Anna laughed nervously again, twirling a lock of red-orange hair. "I don't know how long I've been thinking this – maybe I don't know anything at all. But I've been feeling nervous. Like, I want to see her, but I'm always wanting to say the *right thing* – like, I'm afraid of her judging me even though I shouldn't be. My hands get all clammy, and my stomach, it does these somersaults–" She stopped herself, cupping her face with her hands. "God, I can't believe what I'm admitting."

"You like Jessi." The three words tasted bitter in my mouth as they came out slowly in disbelief. When Anna glanced up from her palms, nodding her head, I couldn't breathe. "You like Jessi," I cried, anger lacing my voice.

Anna's eyes widened in alertness, taken aback by my change in mood. "What, you *aren't* happy?"

"It's Jessi fucking Alvarez! Of course, I'm *not*."

"What did she ever *do* to you?"

I laughed in bewilderment. "Have you lost your memory? I told you *everything*. She-she went after my and Ethan's relationship – fuck, she can't stop going after the people *I* love–" I stopped talking, my last words sinking in.

She takes everyone away from me.

"You started this war. *You* could have been nice to her on the first day of ninth grade, but you were a bitch and made fun of her instead."

"And so did *you!*" I pointed out, and Anna's face turned bright red with shame. "Besides, what's so special about Jessi?"

"She's not afraid to be herself. You, on the other hand... You always have been."

I looked back at Anna, glancing from her ring to mine. I felt as if she had just slapped me across the face. "I can say the same thing about you. I don't even know *who* you are anymore – but since when *have* I?" I abruptly stood up, walking away from the bed and toward the motel door. "Maybe you guys *deserve* each other – you're both fucked in the head."

"Adley–"

"I can't deal with this right now," I yelled, cupping my hands over my ears like a child. "I-I need air." Before Anna could do anything to stop me, I walked out the motel door.

Then, tears stinging my eyes, I sprinted down the sidewalk, away from the situation, away from the truth, away from Jessi and the memories that followed.

Away from Annabeth's confession.

Though I wasn't sure if I would ever be able to escape

that.

Chapter 15
Ethan
It's Beginning to Look a Lot like Murder

With Christmas only a few hours away, my home was bustling with activity since my parents were having the entire family over to celebrate the holidays. Socializing with family members that I barely knew while forcing a smile onto my face wasn't close to being on my wish list, yet here I'd been, putting up wreaths on every door, decorating the large Christmas tree in the living room, and helping my mom bake cookies.

Now, I had just been sent to the corner store to pick up a new cartoon of milk so that my mom could bake the chocolate cake.

My brain power on battery saver, I dragged myself down the icy sidewalk as the chilly air nipped at my skin. My feet felt as if they were sinking into wet cement whenever I would take another step. My eyes kept drifting shut, and I had already almost crashed into *three* different street signs.

"Stay awake, Ethan," I told myself, ignoring the weird looks that nearby people shot at me as I grumbled to myself.

God, how could people be so happy about the holidays? I wondered as I glanced around at bypassing people. Their smiles were so wide that they felt forced. *How could their lives be so perfect?*

I stuffed my hands into the pockets of my black sweater, fighting back tears.

2015 has been quite a bitch.

I laughed a little to myself, remembering what Jenna had told me the night she came to my house with the guys. I wasn't the only one who'd had a shitty year. She had said that she lost her parents in a car crash, and honestly, I had no idea how she was holding up so well—

A dog barked from nearby, making me jump and trip over my untied bootlaces. I tumbled onto the pavement, scraping my right palm and knee on the icy ground. For a second, I didn't move since I didn't have the willpower to do so. After getting a couple of stares from people driving by, though, I slowly stood up. I then raised my right hand to see a thin stream of blood dripping down my wrist and soaking into the sleeve of my sweater. When I pulled up my sweats, I noticed that my knee was also torn, smeared with blood, and burning. The sweatpants were only torn a little, though blood was seeping through at some spots.

Shaking my head, I forced myself to get up and start walking even though the pain buzzed through my body. I hardly paid attention to my surroundings as I stepped into the street—

A car honked at me as it zipped by. I hurried my pace,

nearly tripping as I darted onto the sidewalk on the other side of the road. I took a deep breath to steady my pounding heart, then pulled open the door of Monet's Drugmart, my thoughts racing so fast that it made me dizzy.

"Give me one reason why you think you're the favorite."

"Well, I did better than you — the A+ student — on that last science test," I boasted to Anna as I slid down the slide at the park. Once I stood back up, I looked at the top of the slide to see Anna roll her eyes. She didn't seem to have liked the answer.

"Come on! You were better by one percent. One percent, Ethan!" Anna cried in frustration, sliding down next and landing in front of me.

"I am the oldest too," I added, feeling confident in this answer. "Everyone loves the oldest."

Anna rolled her eyes again. "You're only older by twenty minutes."

"So? It still counts."

"Fine, then," Anna said, her voice taking on a challenging edge as she placed her hands on her hips. "If you're everyone's favorite, make me a list of ten people that prefer you over me."

I opened my mouth to give her one, but my mind was blank. From on the swings a few feet away, I could see Adley wincing as if she felt bad for me.

Anna smirked, tossing her curly hair over her shoulder. "That's what I thought."

I looked at the ground, kicking a rock in the dried grass. "Whatever."

"So, you're not everyone's favorite," she continued as if she wanted to rub it in. "But you could totally be Adley's favorite."

My head snapped up involuntarily, and I caught Adley stop swinging at the comment. "Huh?"

Anna nodded toward Monet's Drugmart across the street from the park. She then whispered into my ear, "Go grab her a bag of Sour Patch Kids. You know she loves them."

"But-but I don't have any money," I stuttered, glancing from Adley to Anna.

"I didn't say buy, did I?" she asked, cocking an eyebrow.

I felt all the blood drain from my face. "You-you mean… steal?"

Anna looked at me like I was the dumbest person alive. "Duh."

"Anna," Adley called, hopping off her swing and running over to us. "What's going on?"

"I'm just encouraging Ethan to have a little fun," Anna giggled, leaning against Adley with an elbow resting on her shoulder. "He has to enjoy being a teenager while he can."

"'Teenager' and 'felon' are two very different terms," I reminded Anna, but she waved me off.

Ever since we had started ninth grade a few weeks ago, Anna seemed determined to have Adley to herself as much as she could. I had a feeling that she didn't want me around anymore since we were now in high school. Why she had to be mean about it, I didn't understand.

"Well, go on," Anna remarked, pushing me toward

the park's gate. "Stop being a coward and live a little."

I looked at the glass door of Monet's Drugmart, then back at the two girls. Anna was standing with a hand on her hip, while she examined the other one as if she was already bored. From her side, Adley looked at me doubtfully as if she also didn't expect me to go through with Anna's suggestion.

You can do this, Ethan. Show Adley that you're not a coward.

"Fine. I'll do it," I said, taking deep breaths to calm my nerves.

"Great!" Anna cheered, clapping her hands. "We'll wait out here. You better be quick."

I swallowed hard, then jogged across the street and into the corner store, not looking back. As I stepped inside, I felt a gust of cold wind from the air conditioning smack me in the face. Feeling like everyone's eyes were on me, I then made my way to the small shelf in the back of the store that held multiple neon bags of candy. The green bag of Sour Patch Kids immediately caught my eye, but I didn't reach for it, frozen in place.

Come on, Ethan, *I thought, licking my lips nervously.* Just do it, already!

Slowly, I reached for the bag of candy. My heart was racing so fast that I was sure it was going to suddenly stop functioning. I took the bag off its shelf, the package's crinkling sound startling me.

God, I can't do this.

I shoved the bag back onto the shelf. I then turned around and darted toward the store's exit, my head down as if everyone was laughing at me. Once I walked out the door,

I leaned back against the small display window, trying to catch my breath. When I spotted Anna and Adley crossing the street and heading my way, I straightened my posture.

However, the laugh that escaped Anna's lips when she saw my empty hands made me slouch again. "So, you wimped out, huh?"

Maybe it was that flashback, or maybe it was just muscle memory, but either way, I found myself standing in front of the candy shelf at Monet's Drugmart, rather than the milk fridge. The bright green packaging of the Sour Patch Kids stood out like a beacon, and I felt a familiar nervousness return to me, my palms sweaty.

Take it, a voice in the back of my head whispered.

I reached for the bag of candy—

Shit, I shouldn't do this.

I let go of the bag, then turned away, a tight feeling rising in my chest.

But they were Adley's favorite…

A wave of anger crashed over me, and I turned back around and grabbed the candy bag off the shelf, then shoved it into the front pocket of my sweater. My pulse racing in my ears, I walked away from the candy shelf and headed for the door of the corner store—

"Hey, kid!"

Shit.

I turned back to look at the cashier, forcing a neutral look onto my face. "Yeah?"

"Your knee's bleeding," the blonde pointed out, her eyes wide with concern. "Are you okay? I could get you a band-aid—"

"I'm fine. Thanks, though," I answered, trying not to reply too quickly as a strange, giddy relief filled my body. "Merry Christmas." Once the blonde looked distracted by her phone, I ducked out of the store. I half-expected the cashier to yell at me again, though she never did.

I did it.

In a daze, I wandered into the alleyway behind the corner store, then sank onto the snow-covered pavement, my body shaking. I pulled out the bag of candy from the front pocket of my winter jacket, placed it on my lap, and stared at it.

Then, out of nowhere, I pitched forward, laughing so hard that it hurt. "I did it," I gasped between laughs. "Am I everyone's favorite *now*?" I continued chuckling, not even caring that people were probably hearing me and thinking I was crazy. "Maybe I *am* crazy," I wheezed, tears leaking from the corners of my eyes. "'Cause everyone I love just *dies*!" I buried my head in my hands, my laughs dissolving into sobs.

I knew that this time, Adley and Anna wouldn't be coming to look for me.

This time, I was all alone.

By the time I had dragged myself back home, the sun started to set. I slipped my key into the front door's keyhole, then stepped inside the warm house. I took a breath, trying to focus on the simple task of untying my bootlaces at the entrance—

"I already told you, Officer Hale. I can't remember Anna ever having an enemy. I don't know *why* she was murdered," I heard my mother say in the kitchen. She sniffled, then added, "I always knew about her friends. She constantly talked about Adley Morgenstern and Jessi Alvarez. She mentioned many girls on the volleyball team too, like Kristen Decker and Marissa Langford. It always seemed *positive*."

Intrigued, I stepped silently toward the kitchen. Soon, I was able to spot my mother and Officer Hale, who were talking while my mother cooked on the stove. She stood in her white apron as she stirred a pot, and Officer Hale sat at the table, a notepad in hand. I remembered the man vaguely from the investigation of my sister's murder – early thirties, dark hair, scary eyes.

Were they picking back up the case?

"What about Ivy Blackthorn? Have you ever heard about her?" Officer Hale asked, his voice deep and emotionless.

"*No*, actually..." My mother trailed off, looking away and stirring the pot. "However, if I come to think of it, once, she showed up at our doorstep."

"Really?" Office Hale exclaimed as I wondered the same thing. "Why have you never mentioned this before?"

"Because it was *nothing*. Ivy was already off the suspect list by the time I remembered." I could tell that my mom still suspected the girl since her face then twisted in suspicion.

"Can you at least recall what she said? Maybe this can help."

"It was late one night when the kids were fifteen. Ivy had come to our door, saying that she *feared* Anna and was worried that Anna might hurt her. She went on about these crazy things that Anna was stating. I can't remember for the life of me what they were – *witches*, maybe?" My mother chuckled uneasily. "I knew this girl must have been pranking me – my Anna would never say such odd things."

"Did you ever ask Anna about this?"

"Oh, no. Like I said, it was nothing," my mother exclaimed. She turned to face the officer again, sighing. "Do you think you'll ever find out who the killer was?"

"Right now, we still have no leads, which is why the case has still been put on the backburner," Officer Hale admitted, looking down at his black boots. "I came here to see if there was anything else that you could tell us. If we find out anything more, though, we'll make sure to give you a call." After giving my mother a reassuring smile, the officer then snuck out through the back door.

What? Ivy was scared of Anna? I wondered as a thick fog of drowsiness settled over me. I didn't know Ivy well, but she didn't seem to get terrified. *Why my sister?*

Shaking my head and trying to forget what I had just heard – I felt too tired to think straight – I wandered into the kitchen. When my mom spotted me, she wiped her hands on her apron and grinned as if nothing had just happened.

"Hey, honey," she greeted, turning toward the stove. I collapsed onto a high stool at the kitchen island, folding my arms onto the marble countertop and burying my head in them. "Where's the milk?"

"Forgot," I muttered, cursing myself for forgetting.

"Ethan!" my mom scolded, though it wasn't in a harsh tone – she sounded more concerned than anything. I glanced up at my name, wincing as she approached me, her apron dusted with flour. There was also a white streak across her forehead, though she wiped it away as she sat down next to me. "Are you coming down with something?" She felt my forehead, her wedding ring cool against my hot skin. "It doesn't feel like you have a fever."

"I'm not *sick*," I grumbled, leaning back in my chair – I didn't feel like I was anyway.

"Then what's up? You've been so out of things lately."

"You wouldn't get it," I snapped. "*Nobody* would get it!"

"I'm sure I would," she remarked, which only annoyed me more.

"*No*, you wouldn't. You know *why*?" I yelled, my throat dry as I choked back tears. "Because you didn't lose your sister *and* your girlfriend!" My face flushed at the last word, especially when I watched my mother's jaw drop in shock. I felt so numb that I couldn't care less, though. "Just forget it. I need air."

I pushed back my chair, then stood up and walked toward the entrance. My mother just watched as I slipped on my coat and boots. She didn't even follow me as I walked out the door and into the cold.

I hated this perfect family Christmas card – the way the lights hung brightly around the house, the way the tree sparkled in its elegant glory, and the way the blue Victorian house smelled of freshly-baked cookies.

It wasn't *real*. It was just a cover-up to remind everyone that the picture-perfect family wasn't broken.

But the truth was that it had *never* been whole.

By the time my adrenaline had faded, I made it to the park, which was – *thankfully* – empty at this hour. I leaned against a tree, trying to catch my breath.

Keep it together, I told myself, feeling my sanity slipping through the cracks.

I then opened my eyes after taking a deep breath, watching as the world tilted for a second, then stilled. I left my leaning position against the tree and slowly walked around the park, watching as the swings on the rusty swing set swayed back and forth in the cold wind. I came upon a patch of trees, and after selecting one, I scanned its branches. A tiny part of me hoped that Jessi would be sitting up there, even though the branches were covered in fresh snow.

As much as I wanted to be alone, I didn't really want that.

After a thorough search, though, I concluded that Jessi was nowhere to be found. I sighed, surprising myself with how disappointed I felt. It shocked me more, however, when I found myself reaching for a low branch and deciding to pull myself up with it, its rough bark rubbing against my scraped palm. The irritating motion burned as I climbed my way to the top of the tree, but I didn't care – I wasn't *able* to.

Once I settled myself onto a stable branch, I looked out at the last traces of the orange-and-blue sunset. I only snapped out of my trance when something in my hoodie's front pocket made a crinkling noise. I reached into the pocket and pulled out the bag of shoplifted Sour Patch Kids, which I had almost forgotten about. I stared at the neon green bag, my hands shaking.

Just the thought of its bittersweet sugar coating made me want to throw up, not that it shocked me. My appetite had been smaller than normal lately. I was down to eating one meal a day, and even supper felt forced.

Anger consuming me once again, my grip tightened on the plastic bag. I threw it out into the distance as hard as I could, then watched as it dropped to the ground.

"Well, *damn*, what did that bag of candy ever do to you?"

For a split second, I thought it was Jessi who had spoken. My heart skipped a beat in surprise before I quickly realized that the harsh voice hadn't matched hers.

I scowled down at Ivy as she came into view at the bottom of the tree, her plum-purple lips twisted into a smirk. Just as she was about to pace away, I found myself hopping down from my branch and landing in front of her in the snow.

It was odd how my body and mind didn't seem attached anymore. I was almost a stranger to my body, unable to control myself.

"Had you ever felt threatened by Anna?" I blurted, suspicion edging in my voice.

Ivy froze in her spot. She spun around to look at me, her eyes wide with alarm, but her lips revealed a playful grin. "Of course, *not*. That girl was about as dangerous as a kitten. Hissed and spat a good deal but posed no real threat..." She trailed off, and even in the fading daylight, I could see her expression shift as if a puzzle piece had been put into place. "But-but there *was* this one time, I think. No offense, but your sister could be cruel when she wanted to be."

I rolled my eyes, frustrated by Ivy's back-and-forth behavior. "So, *were* you or were you *not* ever scared of her?"

Ivy huffed, folding her arms over her chest. "You Landers *never* know when to shut up. Just leave me the fuck alone – that's my one Christmas wish." She then bent forward to pick up the plastic bag, laughing softly to herself before walking toward the park's exit. "Thanks for the free candy."

"You're welcome?" I found myself remarking before sighing in defeat.

However, as everything lined up in my head, I realized that I *was* getting somewhere. Somebody had been lying, and I had a pretty good feeling that it was Ivy Blackthorn.

Ivy couldn't have feared Anna, I thought as I sat down on a wooden park bench. *But then, why would she go and tell my parents that?*

Chapter 16
Jessi
Speaking of the Devil

W e need to talk."

I pressed a hand to my heart, startled as I watched Ethan climb up the snowy tree that I had been spending my lunch hour in. Without giving me a chance to question him, he motioned with a hand for me to slide over, giving him space to sit next to me.

We didn't talk for a moment – I was still trying to catch my breath, and Ethan was staring down at his hands, grease-stained as always. A minute later, after looking around the yard below us as if afraid someone might overhear, he stated, "I want to talk about Ivy."

I blinked, stunned by Ethan's words. Since when did Ethan care about Ivy Blackthorn? I had learned a while back that his sister and Ivy had been *friends* – if you could even call it that – but why the sudden interest?

Ethan took a deep breath as if what he was going to say next required a large amount of energy. "Over the Christmas break, Officer Hale came over, and I overheard him talking to my mother about Anna and the people she knew."

My eyes widened as hope filled my chest. "Wait, are they opening back up the case?"

"That was their intention if my mom could give them new leads," Ethan explained, and I sighed. "She gave none, in the end, but I overheard something really odd."

"Like what?" I questioned before my body froze at the thought of what he could say next.

"That Ivy came to our house one night. She told my parents that Anna was *crazy* – that she was *scared* of Anna."

"Crazy?" I laughed, though it sounded unnerved. "Like, what, mentally insane?" Ethan nodded slowly, and I couldn't believe what he was saying. "You're joking."

"That's exactly what my parents thought. That's why it never came up until now." Ethan sighed, raking a hand through his messy curls. "I just don't get it."

"Yeah. It makes no sense," I replied, trying to think back to the way Ivy had talked about Anna in the past. "Anna had her moments, but she couldn't *ever* scare Ivy Blackthorn."

"*Exactly* – I thought the same thing." Ethan licked his lips, and I could tell that he was holding something back. When I raised an eyebrow in question, he added, "Plus, when I ran into Ivy on Christmas Eve and decided to ask her if she *had* been afraid of Anna in the past... Jessi, Ivy seems suspicious. I think she *did* lie to my parents about Anna."

"Obviously!" I shouted, and Ethan hushed me. "But *why*?" I questioned in a lower tone, trying to understand what was going on.

"I know Ivy was claimed innocent, but what if

Ivy *did* do something?" Ethan exclaimed, his eyes wide and glossy. "I-I'm not saying that she killed Anna, but–"

"Hey! Jenna!" Ethan was suddenly cut off by the burst of excitement at the picnic table close to the tree, and I rolled my eyes as Kyle shouted. Jenna had just exited the school's side doors and was now approaching the table that Kyle was sharing with Dylan and Calvin. "What are you doing here?"

I stiffened as Jenna got closer to the table. That familiar, uncomfortable tightness bloomed in my chest as I looked at her.

Jenna ruffled Kyle's hair affectionately before sitting down beside him. "I came to see if you had my chem textbook. I think I forgot it at your place the other night," she chuckled as Kyle searched through his bag.

Moments later, he handed her the large textbook with a smile, though I caught him sighing in annoyance as Dylan raised his eyebrows suggestively. "We were *working* on our chem lab report. How's *yours* coming along, by the way?"

"Alejandro and I are working *great* together," Dylan recalled, though his face had suddenly flushed.

"*Anyway*," Kyle laughed, bringing his attention back to Jenna. "Is there anything else?"

"Seriously, you're trying to shoo me *away*? I just thought I would come by and say hi."

"Thanks, but you *really* didn't have to," Kyle laughed nervously, eyeing his friends – especially Dylan.

"Oh, is it because you're afraid that we'll end up saying something to *embarrass* you?" Dylan teased.

"Yeah, I don't think there's anything that we could use against you that she *doesn't* already know," Calvin remarked, his tone laced with annoyance.

"So, have you asked her out yet?" Dylan questioned, leaning across the table. "And I mean, *for real.* Not a lame movie night. Something" –he paused dramatically– *"intimate."*

"With the way that he talks about her, he *surely* must have by now," Ethan muttered from beside me, rolling his eyes.

I couldn't help but stifle a laugh.

Kyle, from what I could tell, looked utterly mortified. He was staring at Dylan as if he wanted to attack him – which was probably the case – and he kept anxiously combing a hand through his hair.

"Aw, come on," Dylan continued. "You're always telling us how beautiful she looks in the sunlight, and the way her laugh makes you smile–"

"Dylan, cut it *out,*" Calvin interrupted, and Dylan frowned in disappointment.

"Um, you know what? I would *love* to stay longer, but I just remembered that I had planned to meet up with Aurora," Jenna said suddenly. "But, I'll, um, see you later, Kyle." Jenna stood up from the table and made her way over to the tree that Ethan and I were sitting in, not seeming to notice us. When she made a move like she was going to sit down on the grass, though, suddenly, Kyle – who had come after her – grabbed her wrist–

Well, this is just great.

Right under *my* tree, I watched from above as Kyle

pulled Jenna closer and pressed his lips to hers. Jenna stepped away afterward, her look dazed and filled with shock before she wrapped her arms around his neck and kissed him again, this time more deeply – much to my horror.

I quickly glanced at Ethan, and his expression looked mostly shocked – but I caught a glint of sadness in his gaze as well. I then covered Ethan's eyes with a hand, trying to distract him. "Don't look. As the older one, it's my job to protect your innocence."

"You're only five days older," Ethan mumbled, but he didn't make any attempts to move my hand away.

My God, how are they not done *yet?* I thought, watching Jenna and Kyle continue kissing, practically eating each other's faces while Dylan mocked them in the background like an eight-year-old.

It was very tempting to drop something on Jenna and Kyle's heads – it would have been hilarious, and it would have also broken them apart – but I held myself back until the lovers ended their make-out session, staring at each other with wide eyes. I let my hand drop from in front of Ethan's face before I swung down from my branch, landing right beside the pair.

"Great show, *really*," I said sarcastically. "Now, excuse me, but I've got to go and bleach my eyeballs."

"You were just *watching*?" Jenna hissed, her face flushing red. She glanced down at the snowy ground as she wiped her lips with the back of her hand almost sheepishly.

"Unfortunately," I replied. "Trust me, I'm not any happier than you are."

"*Seriously?* Why were you–" Jenna stopped talking

as she looked over my shoulder, and as I followed her gaze, I noticed that she had spotted Ethan, who was slowly climbing down from the tree. "Oh, hey, Ethan."

"Um, hi," Ethan responded awkwardly. "I, uh, wasn't watching you guys or anything. Jessi had her hand in front of my eyes for most of it."

Before Jenna could say anything in response, the warning bell rang, reminding us that lunch was almost over. The group then broke apart, and Jenna and Kyle went their separate ways, leaving me and Ethan alone.

With a smirk on my lips, I elbowed Ethan playfully as we made our way to the school's building. "Well, *that* was certainly an interesting lunch hour."

Ethan shook his head, running his grease-stained fingers through his hair. "Interesting is one way to put it."

Chapter 17
Annabeth
To Kill or Not to Kill

Marry me, then! We could run away and escape our families, once and for all."

"But where would we go? It's either Heaven or Hell," I reminded him.

"We would go to Limbo and make a new life for ourselves. What do you say? Will you take my hand in marriage?" He went down on one knee and flipped open a velvet-covered box, in which a cherry-red Ring Pop sat.

"Of course—!" I cut myself off mid-cry and stopped the fake tears that were coming to my eyes. I glanced down at the script in my hands once I was out of character and re-read the line. I then looked up at our drama teacher, my brow furrowed. "Wait, you want Josie to instantly marry Raven, this guy who she *barely* knows, all because of their parents' history?"

Ms. Mitchell looked up from her computer and smiled at me forcefully. "Yes, just like in the *original* story."

I rolled my eyes, thinking back to the plot of the play.

Raven and Josie: two star-crossed lovers who fall in love and must sneak around together without their parents finding out.

I was all for classic Shakespearean plays – *Romeo and Juliet* was one of my favorites. But this play was supposed to be a *retelling*.

One where Romeo was a demon, and Juliet was an angel.

Somehow, the cast was perfect – besides how Nate and I played *lovers* – since we all knew who the saint and devil were.

"But we're in the twenty-first century!" I pushed, wanting my case to win even when I knew that we weren't in court. "Don't teenagers know better?" I searched the eyes of the cast that stood around me, hoping to find at least one other student who agreed.

"Yeah, they *do*, which is why maybe Josie *knows* what she's doing," Nate remarked after standing up from his kneeling position across from me. He closed the box in his hands, and it snapped shut loudly. "Not everyone has trust issues, *Aurora*."

I rolled my eyes again, annoyed by Nate's voice. "And not everyone has a good head on their shoulders, *Nate*." I then whispered to him, "*You* of all people should know."

Fists formed at Nate's sides. "Let's just take it from the top, okay–?"

"And pretend as if Josie isn't wise beyond her years like this script made her out to be? Maybe we should change this ending. *Maybe* Raven dies alone, while Josie runs away and makes a better life for herself."

"Miss Dickinson," hissed Ms. Mitchell from her seat in the house. "This is *my* script, and *I* decide what happens."

"And I'm just trying to help," I explained, putting on my nice girl act. "Why do the girls always have to depend on the guys–?"

"I think you're going a *little* off-script," Nate said beside me, his white knuckles making it seem as if he was fighting the urge to yell.

God, he just always wants to be the teacher's pet, I thought, mentally rolling my eyes.

"All I'm trying to say is that maybe Raven isn't the best guy for Josie. After all, didn't Raven just stop loving Roxie?" I asked, remembering how Romeo had loved Rosaline at the beginning of the original play.

"Maybe Raven never *did* love Roxie," Nate told me through gritted teeth. "And, *maybe*, Josie just needs to *shut up*."

"Or *what*?" It was getting personal, and it only made me feel more powerful.

I was Josie. Nate was Raven. Adley was Roxie.

It all reminded me of that spring break, and I knew it sure as hell reminded Nate of the same.

"Or *I* will be the one who kills you next," Nate whispered to me with a smirk on his face, sudden darkness consuming him.

"I would *love* to get back at you for that statement because it's just so *fun* to insult you," I purred into his ear, my hand sliding down his arm until my fingers wrapped around his wrist aggressively. "But I think that nature already does a good job at constantly reminding you of that – I mean, have you *seen* your face–?”

“That’s *enough*, you two,” Ms. Mitchell roared.

Nate acted as if he hadn’t heard the teacher’s warning. “And you’re going against nature since you’re supposed to be *dead*,” Nate reminded me, taking me aback. “Which one is better?”

“I think dying as a legend is better than living as a loser,” I bit back, feeling a surge of confidence–

I couldn’t breathe, and it took me a moment to realize that Nate’s big hands were now wrapped around my neck. He started to squeeze my throat, and I squirmed in his grasp.

“Nate, *stop*!” I whisper-cried as I gasped for air. Tears pricked my eyes as his thumb pushed against my voice box, triggering a burning pain in my throat. His hands kept pinching tighter, and my heartbeat sped up. Black spots began to blur my vision as I heard cries around me. I clawed at his hands desperately. “Nate, you fucking *psychopath*! Let *go* of me!”

Nate’s grasp then softened. As I stumbled back, gasping for air, I swore that I saw a tear slip down his cheek, though. I was confused since, instead of walking off in triumph, Nate was bending over, his face flushed. A hand was covering his right eye, and I glanced around to see what the hell *happened*–

That’s when I spotted Jessi, who now stood in front of me. Her right fist was coming down to her side.

Did she just...?

“Leave her *alone*, Nate,” Jessi snarled, hands on her hips. “You’ve got to learn that you can’t put your hands all over *every* girl you meet."

No fucking way.

I looked away from the scene in front of me, then spotted Ethan. He was now slipping out from behind the right-wing curtain, his eyes wide and eyebrows raised in fear.

I then watched as Ms. Mitchell stood up from her seat. Her face was red-hot like a volcano that was about to explode. "Miss Alvarez, *what* has gotten into you?"

Jessi stepped away from Nate, and an expression of sheer panic appeared on her face as she realized what she had just done. "He was *hurting* Aurora. I couldn't just stand there and *watch*."

The teacher was silent for a moment as if considering the statement. "Jessi and Nate, in my office. *Now.* The rest of you, practice your lines amongst yourselves until I get back."

"You little *bitch*," I heard Nate hiss into Jessi's ear before walking over to Ms. Mitchell. He was still covering his eye with a shaking hand. "Lori, you know me. Aurora was doing it on purpose. She knew that I was going to flip–"

"That's no excuse to hurt a student," the teacher sighed, silencing Nate. "Now, come along."

Nate didn't look back at me as he left the room with Jessi, while I stood on the stage, frozen in fear. But when nobody was looking, Nate held up his middle finger – which I knew was directed at me.

Once the main auditorium door swung shut, all stares shifted over to me as I tried to comprehend what had just happened–

I felt a warm hand on my shoulder and turned around to come face-to-face with Ethan. I guessed he had come to my side without my noticing. "Are you okay?"

"Yeah," I mumbled, trying to find my words. "It just all happened so fast."

"Why did Nate come at you like that? Was it something you said–?"

"I don't know, E," I lied when I knew *exactly* why Nate had gotten so mad. I realized what I had just said to Ethan, though, and corrected myself with "E-*than*." I smiled wide, hoping that I had covered my slip-up. "I'm safe all because of Jessi, though. I didn't know that she could do that."

"Neither did I, but when Nate threatened me at a party once and was about to throw a punch at me, Jessi protected me too." Ethan's gaze became distant. "It's what she does best, I guess. She can be a moron, but she means well. *Usually*, anyway," he laughed to himself. "Lately, though... She's been worrying me. Maybe it's because of Anna's death, but..."

"I'm sure she's just going through a phase. It's always hard to deal with tragedy," I reminded Ethan.

He nodded in agreement before the auditorium door opened, revealing Ms. Mitchell. Nate and Jessi trailed in behind her, and as they passed me and Ethan, Nate grinned wickedly at me. Jessi just stormed past before ducking behind the back curtains.

"I'll talk to her," I told Ethan as everyone fell back into their positions onstage as if nothing had ever occurred. "I made a promise, and I'll stick to it."

"You don't have to–"

"But I *want* to," I explained with a smile. "You aren't the only one who cares about her."

After giving in to the terrible storyline of the play, I escaped rehearsals and made my way out of the building so that I could walk back to the motel. Just thinking about how the afternoon had gone gave me a headache – especially the part where Jessi had knocked the living daylight out of Nate.

If he ever *had* something living in him, that was.

"What a rehearsal *that* was!" Jessi exclaimed with barely any worry in her voice.

I looked beside me to notice that she was standing next to her usual tree, which was near the side exit of the school. I turned around and walked in her direction, smiling. "No kidding! You were a *badass*! I mean, smacking Nate like that? Not that he didn't deserve it, but that was brutal." I paused, my smile dropping. "Wait, what did Ms. Mitchell tell you and Nate when she pulled you out? Are you going to be in trouble?"

Jessi shrugged as we started walking together toward the front of the school. "Well, I'm going to be suspended until Founder's Day next week, but Nate, on the other hand, is suspended for the next *two* weeks. So, I didn't *really* lose anything. I just have more time to study for that geometry test."

I laughed, relieved for Jessi. "You are *so* lucky, you know. You could have been kicked out of the show."

"Maybe that would have been a blessing," Jessi remarked, fixing her bag's strap over her shoulder. "I'm getting exhausted by seeing Nate's obnoxious face when I don't have to."

That widened my grin. "At least you don't have to

kiss him!"

"Yuck! I'd rather kiss a poisonous snake–" Jessi cut herself off and stopped in her tracks. I soon noticed that she was staring at Nate and Ivy, who were a few feet away and sitting on a wooden bench near the front of the school. "Speaking of poisonous, what is *she* doing here?"

I pulled Jessi behind a tree so that we wouldn't be spotted. When she was about to say something, I pressed a finger to my lips to remind her that they could possibly hear us.

"Oh, come *on*, Ivy!" I heard Nate plea as he looked into Ivy's emerald-green eyes. "*Please*, just give me another chance. I didn't *do* anything. It wasn't even my choice to be opposite her in the play."

It looked as if Ivy was wanting to say something, her lips parting to speak but no words coming out.

Oh, my God. Nate's begging for Ivy's forgiveness.

Just when I was beginning to think that Nate was full of surprises, he had to go and display his vulnerable side.

He was *desperate.*

For *Ivy Blackthorn.*

I tried hard to hold back a giggle alongside Jessi. Ivy, on the other hand, looked a mix between embarrassed and frustrated, her face reddening as Nate spoke. "*Nate–*"

"Please!" he cried, not letting Ivy speak. "I promise, nothing will happen between us. I care about *you–*"

"I can't *believe* it. Ivy Blackthorn dates the desperate," Jessi laughed, cutting Ivy off as she advanced toward the couple. I wanted to go after her but knew that it was better to stay hidden. "I gotta say, I didn't take you as the type. Is it because no one else could ever like a poisonous plant like you?"

"*Jessi,*" Ivy hissed, standing up and dropping Nate's hands. "You little bitch! Why are you eavesdropping on our *private* conversation?"

"If it was *actually* supposed to be private, you should have done it behind closed doors – *not* on school grounds," Jessi remarked, putting her hands on her hips. "Now, seriously. You're dumping this puppy just because he has to kiss another girl in a *play*? It's not like he even cares about Aurora. Unless, of course, he shows his affection by grabbing girls' throats and almost choking them to death in the middle of rehearsal."

"You did *what*?" Ivy's eyes widened and flickered over to Nate.

Nate scowled at Jessi. "It was a fucking *set-up*. Besides, look what this bitch did to *me*." Nate pointed at his eye with a frown on his face. He then winced in pain as if it would get him sympathy from Ivy.

"Remember, you still have another eye that I can smack my fist into," Jessi snapped, rolling her eyes. "At least then they'd look *even*."

"You bitch!" Nate hissed again at Jessi, only making Jessi laugh harder.

"Oh, stop exercising your vocabulary for me," Jessi remarked, pretending to seem flattered by Nate's repetitive word choice.

"Why do you care about *Aurora*, anyway? Need a replacement in the friendship department after your loss? Or *many* losses, might I say, since everyone is practically walking away from you now," Ivy stated, examining her long, sharp nails as if preparing to attack Jessi. "Somehow, Ethan is *still* hanging on by a thread–"

"*Stop!*" Jessi screamed as if hearing my brother's name burned her eardrums. "You know, you two screwed-up weirdos *deserve* each other."

"And I know that there's a weirdo just waiting around the corner for you," Ivy purred at the same time that I stepped out from behind the tree to pull Jessi away. Ivy's smirk widened as I stood next to Jessi. "*Aurora*, how nice of you to join us."

"Why do you guys keep saying her name like that?" Jessi questioned before looking at me with concern.

I didn't give Ivy time to reply. "I'm not staying. *We* were just leaving," I declared and grabbed Jessi's wrist tightly. Our eyes met for a quick second, and the touch of her skin sent electric waves up my arm, but I ignored the feeling.

Before Jessi could argue, I tugged her away forcefully. Her shoes scraped the ground as she pulled the opposite way. "Why are you *doing* this?" Jessi asked me once we were far enough from the Terrible Two.

"Because I was once just like you, and I had no one to pull me back when I was about to do something I knew I would regret," I admitted.

I then remembered every time that I had lashed out and made mistakes big enough to scar myself. I shivered at the memories.

Jessi sighed, looking at the couple, then back at me with a smile. Once she looked down at our hands, though, I dropped her wrist as much as I wanted to hold it longer. "I'm sorry–"

"You don't have to apologize for anything. You got *suspended* for me. I think that means that I owe *you*," I laughed, which somehow lit Jessi's face up even more.

"Then how about we hang out once my suspension is over? I know that once my dad finds out, I'll be grounded the entire time," Jessi said, and a small giggle escaped my lips.

"Okay, sure. When?"

"Founder's Day. I'm volunteering in the morning with Ethan, but afterward, if you *want*, we can hang out together," Jessi exclaimed, reminding me of the town's holiday.

"Just us two?" I asked, hoping that, for once, we could be alone.

"I mean, Ethan might tag along for a bit. After, however, *sure*. It can be just us."

Us.

I liked the sound of that.

Chapter 18
Adley
Murderers in the End

W*hy* do we have to be here?" I moaned as I stared in confusion at Ivy. "Don't you already have your boyfriend to drag to stupid events?"

"Yeah, now that you're back together, I don't see why you would need *us* to entertain you," Anna grumbled from beside me.

It was odd standing next to Anna – it had been weeks since our argument, and we hadn't spoken alone since. She was still mad at me about how I had reacted when she told me that she had feelings for Jessi, and I wasn't willing to apologize. However, now we were in the town roundabout, freezing our asses off as the town set up for Ember Falls' most famous event.

Founder's Day.

We were gathered around a stack of unopened folding tables and chairs, which Ivy was trying to set up as she had been instructed to do. Other volunteers were scattered around, setting up carnival game stations and bake sale tables. I didn't see how the Founder's Day committee could need any more help, yet Anna and I were still forced to help Ivy.

"I'm part of a Founding Family," Ivy reminded us. "Since my mom couldn't be here, she wanted me to step in and represent. I hate it, but I know it will make her happy. As for you two, you're here because I need to talk to you, and this will probably be the only moment for a while that we can chat privately." Ivy then motioned with a hand for me and Anna to start helping.

"I swear, you've *got* to learn the definition of 'private.' Anyone *here* could hear if they tried," Anna exclaimed as she picked up a folding table and moved it to its designated place.

"No one is close enough to hear us whisper," Ivy stated, though her tone clearly indicated that she hadn't thought this through.

"So, what's there to say *now*?" I questioned, pulling out the legs of the folding table. "Are we finally going to discover what this stupid plan is? Why have we been taking so long to put it into motion?"

"Because we're waiting on a *celestial event*," Ivy informed as she moved another table. "And it won't be happening for a while. I already told you that you don't *need* to know anything." She sighed, looking down tiredly at the five other tables that we had to set up. "We need to talk about *today*."

"Today?" Anna questioned, stepping away from the folding tables. "You mean Founder's Day? What else is there to know? We grew up learning *every* year in primary school how back in 1824–"

"*1872*," Ivy corrected, rolling her eyes.

"Some colonist named Winston–"

"*William*," I cried, amazed by how even *I* remembered more than Anna, though we were both horrible at history.

"Founded this town along with a dozen other people, naming this place – as well as that popular bridge – after his beloved wife, Ember," Anna finished confidently as if she *hadn't* screwed up the story. "The end."

"You see," Ivy started, leaving the folding tables and leaning against a nearby tree pensively, "that's where you're *wrong*."

"Wrong? How could our teachers all be wrong? How could *you* know more when you weren't even alive back then?" Anna exclaimed.

"Unless she's immortal – like a *vampire*," I joked, though a part of me was afraid Ivy would say that my guess was correct.

"They're wrong because they don't know the *real* story," Ivy stated, clearing her throat. "In school, you learn the simple, *non*-supernatural story. There's much more to this town than you know, though, and you must be aware of this.

"Before the town was infested with humans, angels and demons roamed free, though it was very chaotic. After all, the demons, competitive in nature, wanted to rule Earth since they thought they had the most power. The angels were completely against this, of course, since they thought they were better and wanted a world of *peace* and *happiness*," Ivy exclaimed, looking disgusted by her last words. "To sum it up, both races thought that *they* were the rightful rulers of this world.

"Ember Smith knew about everything going on in the supernatural world and hated the sight of the chaos being created. That's why she decided that change needed to be placed. One day, she went to each leader of the supernaturals on Earth – Lucifer for the demons, and the Archangel Gabriel for the angels – and *begged* for a part of their power. She promised to banish the other party with that given power, and both sides agreed. But Ember – being the little bitch that she was – didn't *technically* stay true to her promise.

"The night of the full lunar eclipse, on the bridge that was named after her, Ember created two new worlds. She then banished both sides of the supernatural creatures to the world best suited for them – demons to Hell to torture other souls, and angels to Heaven to have peace. Ever since then, the demons have been trying to get back on Earth. They would do so by finding ways to send their kind, like having the demon attach itself to a human to use as their puppet. The angels, on the other hand, hated the confinement at the beginning but oddly realized that the banishment was for the best. That *was* until they discovered that demons were escaping Hell slowly, then began sending down angels – like Anna – who infused their light and power into a five-year-old human they thought was worthy. Occasionally, these angels would be accompanied by a Guardian, which is a descendant of a failed angel."

"What about the witches, though?" I asked,

confused. It sounded as if angels and demons were the only supernaturals back then.

"After Ember banished the angels and demons in 1872, there was a fallout caused by the radioactive explosion made from the power that Ember used. This fallout then touched Ember Falls while it was being built, and the people there inherited a small portion of the supernatural power," Ivy told us, a smile spreading across her face. "This power has since then spread through bloodlines, creating more witches like me and Nate."

At the mention of his name, Nate spotted us from the center of the roundabout. He then strolled over and kissed Ivy once he joined us.

My eyes widened in shock, though, at the sight of the reddish-brown bruise that circled his right eye. "What *happened* to you?"

"Nate tried to strangle me to death at rehearsal last week," Anna snapped angrily, though I could see fear blaze in her eyes.

"*She* started it by going off-script and trying to persuade Ms. Mitchell into rewriting the story," Nate explained calmly. "But, of course, my anger got the best of me, and I got a little reckless."

"A *little*? You tried to *kill* me," Anna shrieked in a whisper. "There are no excuses for that. Which is why Jessi punched him in the face."

"So, what you're saying is that because of a little improvisation, that tree stump gave you a black eye?" I clarified, laughing at Nate.

"I can't believe I can still stand next to you," Anna

cried. "You know, you're *all* murderers. *I* am the only sane one here!"

"Well, that's what you think," Ivy told Anna with a smirk. "But I know that you'll go just as crazy when your little girlfriend, Jessi, gets pulled into this."

Anna's face turned red as a tomato, and my heart stopped. "Don't call her that," Anna mumbled, and Ivy snickered.

"What, your *girlfriend*?"

"You've been known as Jessi's girlfriend for years," Nate remarked nonchalantly as if this wasn't news, and both my and Anna's heads snapped up.

Anna's face flushed a deeper shade of red. "What?"

"Anna?" Ivy asked in a playful tone. "Are you that *blind*?"

"What do you mean?" Anna asked quietly, though she looked as if she was aware of the conclusion.

No, this can't be right. It just can't *be.*

"Jessi has a pathetic crush on you. I mean, it's been like this for *years*. So, I thought by now you would have–"

"How do you know this?" Anna pointed a finger at Ivy. "Are you *messing* with me?"

"Why would I be *messing* with you? You know your Guardian's secret, but it's not like it's going to change anything, *right*?"

I think we all know what the real answer to that question is.

Anna bit her bottom lip, her gaze falling to the ground. "How did you find out?"

"After *lots* of observing the last few years, I realized

how protective she was of you. Not in the guardian angel way, but in the *more* than friends' way. She would speak so highly and defensively of you. She talked about you *all* the time, and the way she used to look at you... It was obvious how hopelessly *in love* she was with you and still is. So, when I was alone with Jessi once, I got her to spill the truth, confirming my conspiracy theories."

Anna was quiet for a good minute, speechless.

I was about to be a good friend and ask her if she was okay when she finally spoke.

"Well, it's too bad Jessi will be sad and alone forever. I'm *dead* now. Plus, I'm sure the list of guys who want to date *Aurora* is way too long. She'd *never* have a chance." Anna smirked at her comment, but I knew that she was lying about all of it.

"We need to talk," Ivy exclaimed, blocking my view of the bumper car station that I had been watching.

I slouched on my bench, rolling my eyes. "Why does every conversation these days have to start with those four words?" I looked away from Ivy, who had taken a seat next to me. "I don't think there's anything else to talk about."

"Woah, someone is in a mood. Did the truth about Short Stack piss you off?" Ivy laughed teasingly until she noticed my scowl and stopped. "Are you crushing on Anna too? Because that would be pretty fucked up, considering your old status with her brother–"

"What did you want to talk about?" I snapped, annoyed by Ivy's theories.

Could a girl just be upset that she may lose her best

friend to a weirdo like Jessi Alvarez?

"Fine," Ivy sighed, twirling a lock of green hair. "I thought that since I was finally telling you about the town's history, I thought it was time that you learned about your own story."

"Huh?" I questioned, raising an eyebrow. "Ivy, *what* are you saying? I know that my father's bloodline is a part of the Founding Families, which is why my mom's speaking today on his behalf. And every family has skeletons in their closets, but some *story*?"

"About a hundred years ago, one of your ancestors, who was a witch at the time, was killed," Ivy began in her matter-of-fact tone. "The complex spell that he was performing had gone wrong, setting flames to his body and burning him to ashes. He was then sent to Hell, where he got so upset about his fate that he did the unthinkable. He went to Lucifer and asked to make a deal – one that would bring him back to life.

"Lucifer, seeing an opportunity to get the upper hand, accepted this deal. However, he asked your ancestor to sacrifice his bloodline to the demons. That way, they could possess the bodies of his descendants and use them as their Charges. Your ancestor was selfish and took the deal, then returned to Earth. He was no longer a witch – which is the reason why you don't have those powers – but now a half-demon, and his descendants were bound to the same fate as he was.

"That was why your family's last name was originally known as *Morningstar.* It was given to your family by Lucifer but was changed over time," Ivy finished with a smirk.

"So, what you're saying is that it's my stupid ancestor's fault that I'm here as a *demon*?" I cried, and Ivy shrugged.

"Sort of, but it was mainly because of your father." When I gaped at the mention of my dad, Ivy continued. "Jack was Damion's anchor to Earth for years before his tie to Jack's body weakened. You see, demons can't possess bodies for very long since the human mind grows, which makes the tie much harder to keep. But for a demon to become whole on Earth, they have to inhabit Charges for a certain amount of time. That's why Damion then chose you."

I swallowed hard, my heart beating extremely fast.

"You were five years old when Damion had to switch bodies. He was lucky that he spotted you – a fresh, innocent, and easy body to take over. You were the youngest in your bloodline too, which made it simpler for Damion to slip into your mind," Ivy concluded.

"But if Damion needs a human body to help him become a full demon, why didn't he inhabit another possible Charge when I died?" I questioned, confused that someone like my brother hadn't been an option.

"He was almost a full demon by the time you died," Ivy remarked, leaning in closer so that the people who passed by wouldn't hear. "So, in the jar that I've been keeping him locked inside, he can still finish charging. It will take him a little longer than in a human body, but we now have him so that he can help us when he's ready and needed."

I nodded in comprehension as everything registered in my brain. "Wow, I can't believe what I'm hearing. All this time, my father was involved in the supernatural world."

Suddenly, I could remember the day that I met Anna and Ethan as if it was yesterday. I remembered sitting in the living room on the couch beside my dad, who had been watching a baseball game on the TV. I had been distracted with my Barbie dolls – which I was trying to sit in my brother's toy trucks – not noticing how much pain my father was in until he pressed his fingers to his temples, moaning.

I had dropped my toys and looked over at him, asking what was wrong. He had explained that he was just having another episode of his terrible migraines. I stared at him as he walked to the kitchen island and swallowed two pills without water. Then, he turned back to me with his hands balled into fists, telling me to go play outside since he wanted silence. Scared yet worried, I had done as I was told.

If I thought back to that day hard enough, I swore that as I had opened the front door, I had heard my father mumbling – *talking* as if someone was in the empty house.

He had probably been talking to Damion.

That had been why I left. The only reason I met the Landers had been because of my father.

Because of *Damion*.

"Why do you know all of this?" I asked Ivy, blinking away the memory.

"Because my mom knew a lot about demons. Our parents also knew each other quite well – especially before Jack passed away," Ivy confessed, looking away from my eyes.

That's when I knew that I had to ask. "Was... was *Damion* part of the reason my dad died?"

Ivy gulped, seeming taken aback by the question. As

she sighed deeply, though, I could tell that she had known that this question was coming. "You want the truth?" I forced myself to nod, even though I was tired of hearing things that I didn't want to know. "Damion drove him mad."

"*Mad?*" I asked through gritted teeth. I had not been expecting *that* answer. "*Damion* is the reason that my father is *dead*?"

Ivy shushed me as a few people glanced our way. "You know how, even though Damion was connected to you, any supernatural being was able to see and hear him? Well, that was how I met Damion — that first time you and I had a sleepover in ninth grade. Damion and I bonded while you were sleeping that night, and we became friends. I don't know much about Jack's death, but Damion told me that once a demon leaves its Charge, it drives the human mind crazy. The action probably drove Jack so insane that he drove himself off the road."

"So, he just killed himself?" I whisper-cried, trying to act calm so that I didn't draw attention.

"He crashed into a lamppost on a cloudless evening. Why *else*?" I was silent for a moment, and so was Ivy. She then placed a cold hand on my shoulder, though I brushed it off. "I know this must be hard—"

"You *think*? My entire *life* is a *lie*." A tear slipped down my cheek, and I quickly wiped it away.

"If it helps, my dad died by supernatural means too—"

"No, it *doesn't* help, Ivy," I seethed, standing up in frustration. "You *killed* me! You, Nate, and Damion destroyed my *entire* life. Just... just leave me *alone*." Before Ivy could say anything else, I then stormed off, wishing that everything could have just been a terrible nightmare.

My head spun as I searched the dark streets with a broken flashlight for the fifth evening that week. Voices boomed around me, but they said nothing important. I remembered my mother wanting me to stay home and not get involved, but I always found a way to join the search parties.

"Are you okay?" I glanced to my side to look at Ethan, who was smiling at me reassuringly.

"I'll be fine," I sighed, looking up from the ground and into Ethan's warm, chocolate-brown eyes.

He placed a hand on my bare shoulder, and I shuddered, the sudden warmth in the freezing rain shocking me. Ethan then pulled off his plaid blue-and-black sweater and draped it over my shoulders awkwardly.

"I just don't get it." I looked around at the town citizens who had volunteered to help look for my father. I watched as they called his name and waved their lights around in the trees. "He was perfectly fine that morning. Since he left for work, though, no one has been able to reach him... Why?"

Ethan shrugged, just as clueless as I was.

Anna then sprinted over to us from her spot next to her parents, who were also helping. My mom had stayed home in case my father showed up, but Mr. and Mrs. Landers insisted on coming and watching me.

"Any new leads, Nancy Drew?" Anna joked, though none of us laughed. I could barely smile.

"It just makes no sense," I mumbled, burying myself

in Ethan's sweater and hoping for his familiar scent to bring me comfort.

As the three of us huddled under a nearby tree to hide from the rain, I heard a booming voice from across the street. "Hey, I think we found something."

Maybe they've found him.

Curious, I sprinted away from the twins and dodged the adults, making my way to where a group was now forming. It was brighter there, and I soon realized that it was because of a blazing fire.

A car crash.

In front of me was my father's olive-green Jeep smashed by a lamppost. The windshield was shattered, and the hood was drenched in flames. The lamppost's light flickered somberly, and tears ran down the sides of my face as five men searched the truck. They found my father's wallet and car keys, but there was no body.

How can this be?

Frustrated by the outcome, I pushed past the adults and investigated the car myself. I opened the door of the passenger seat and crawled inside cautiously. I ignored the cries coming from behind, instructing me to get out. I looked around, tracing every object with my fingers.

I just had to find something...

I came across three scratch marks, one beside the other as if nails had dug into the side of the driver seat cushion. The marks seemed rough, almost animal-like. Before I could get a better glance, though, two hands pulled me out of the car by my shoulders. I turned around to see Anna and Ethan.

"Look! Look at those marks! They have to mean something," I tried, but it was useless when I could tell by their tired faces that they didn't believe a word that I was saying.

"I know you want to believe that something more happened to your father, but there's nothing. You're just looking into something unimportant," Anna told me as Ethan pulled me away from the crime scene.

"No! There has to be something we're not seeing," I insisted, but Anna tugged me toward her parents harder.

Ethan took a deep breath and stopped walking to look into my eyes. "You need rest, Adley. It's been a long week for you."

Chapter 19
Ethan
Crazy Runs in the Family

Here's *another* one," Jessi sighed, wiping a hand across her forehead as she dropped a cardboard box next to my feet. "Damn, this is a *lot* more work than I thought it'd be."

"Agreed," I replied, combing a hand through my sweaty curls.

Jessi and I had been running around all morning. We were setting up the stage for the parade since the Founder's Day committee had decided that preparing a stage only required two people — which was *not* true. That was why, by mid-morning, both of us had known that we would never finish setting up in time for the noon parade, and Jessi had taken matters into her own hands, dragging Kyle, Dylan, and Calvin over. She had then gotten them to help to varying degrees of success.

"Hey!" Jessi shouted at Dylan, who was staring off into the distance. "Hurry up! We've only got half an hour left until the parade." Jessi marched over to where I was standing with Dylan, then dropped the box that she was carrying at our feet. "We still have to hang these with the names in *alphabetical order*."

I picked up from inside the box a velvet banner reading "Kennedy" in big, golden letters. "What are these for?"

"They're banners with the Founding Families' last names," Jessi answered, rolling her eyes. "Honestly, I think it's a *little* excessive."

"Did they go *this* all-out last Founder's Day?" I questioned.

Jessi shrugged, grabbing a couple more banners from the box. "Probably, though all I can remember from last time is my twelve-year-old self being terrified of the crowds. Maybe that's why they only celebrate it every five years." After laughing to herself, Jessi shoved a few banners into Dylan's arms. "Go hang those at the back of the stage."

"A 'please' would have been nice," Dylan grumbled as he walked off, though Jessi didn't seem to notice his remark, too busy fixing other banners in their designated places.

"Gross," she snorted, holding a dark green banner away from her as if it was poisonous. "*Ivy's* family is a *Founding Family*?"

I looked at the banner in her hand, which read "Blackthorn." "So is Nate's family, it seems," I added just as unenthusiastically, holding up a navy-blue banner with "Tucker" printed on it in gold.

"Nice, my banner's orange," Kyle exclaimed as he walked over with a roll of tape.

As it turned out, he was *also* a Founding Family.

I handed him the banner that was in my hands so that he could check it out. Then, as Kyle left to hang up his banner, I continued to search through the box. I soon pulled another one out that removed the air from my lungs, though. I read the name in loopy, silver letters, which were printed on a ruby-red fabric.

Morgenstern.

Now that I was seeing the banner, I *did* remember hearing once that Adley's dad had been a descendant of a Founding Family. Seeing the name printed there, though, still made me feel like I had been punched in the stomach.

You can't keep doing this, I told myself. *You can't keep losing it every time you think about her.*

Taking a deep breath, I hung the banner up on a peg, then looked away from it.

Of course, I still wanted to figure out what had *really* happened to Adley, but life still had to continue, whether she was there or not.

I need to move on...

I glanced back at the banner, feeling a tightness in the back of my throat.

Right, Adley?

By the time noon rolled around, I was ready to fall asleep standing up. The five of us had managed to finish setting up the stage – with less than ten minutes to spare. Now, we were standing at the front of the crowd that had gathered, waiting for the parade to begin. First, I knew that there were going to be speeches from some of the Founding Families – the ones that bothered to show up, anyway. Despite being important in Ember Falls' history, as I've heard, some of the Founding Families were notorious for being absent on their day.

I don't blame them for not showing up if it's this much of a drag every time, I thought, impatiently checking the time on my watch.

Finally, Mayor Shay made her way onto the stage, waving as everyone applauded. "Welcome to Ember Falls' twentieth Founder's Day!" she announced into the microphone. "Today, we are honored to kick off this special day with speeches from two of our prestigious Founding Families: the Kennedys and the Morgensterns."

Everyone applauded at the names as I watched two women step onto the stage and stand beside the mayor.

"Presenting Ms. Kate Morgenstern and Ms. Cecilia Kennedy!" Mayor Shay exclaimed before stepping aside and leaving the microphone to the two women.

Cecilia... Why do I know that name? I wondered, unable to place where I had heard it in the past.

I looked at Ms. Kennedy, who was standing at the microphone and smiling warmly. She had shoulder-length brown hair and tanned skin, and I noticed a large white scar circling over her right eye. I squinted at her, confused. I knew that I had never seen her before, but something about her features was almost *familiar–*

"Hey, E," Dylan called, breaking my focus. "Your plus-one looks like she's gonna pass out."

Alarmed, I glanced over at Jessi and realized that she was standing painfully stiff beside me. Her lips were pressed into a thin line, and all the color was drained from her face.

"Hey, Jess, are… are you okay?" I asked carefully, placing a hand on her shoulder.

Jessi didn't respond, her eyes fixed on the mystery woman onstage.

"Uh, hello?" Kyle said, waving a hand in front of Jessi's eyes, though she still didn't flinch.

"What's so interesting over there?" Dylan questioned, but Jessi didn't answer.

Instead, she started backing away quickly, though she ended up running straight into Calvin, nearly knocking him over. He gave her a confused, wary look, then opened his mouth to say something. But Jessi shoved past him, disappearing into the crowd.

"Jessi!" I called, even though I knew that she wouldn't respond.

"What's up with *her*?" Calvin asked, adjusting his Badgers baseball cap.

"I have no idea," I admitted, shaking my head, " but I'm going to go find out." Forcing myself to keep calm, I turned away from my friends and waded through the crowd. I then searched for Jessi, though it was hard since she was able to hide easily due to her height. "Jessi?" I shouted, trying to get my voice to carry over the roar of the crowd. "Jessi, where are you?"

As expected, once again, I didn't get a response.

Standing on my toes to get a better view, I scanned the crowd, looking for any sign of Jessi. I then spotted a tree-filled clearing nearby, though, and knew instantly that must have been where she ran off to. Once I made it into the clearing, I scanned the naked, snow-covered trees for Jessi, but oddly, she wasn't up there.

Instead, I found her leaning against a tree trunk as she shook furiously.

"Jessi?" I asked cautiously, slowly approaching her. I rubbed my gloved hands together, trying to stay warm in the shaded area.

"Seventeen years," Jessi murmured, lifting her head to look up at me. "Seventeen *years*... And *now* she shows up?" I didn't respond, anxiously waiting for Jessi to go on. "Just when I thought things couldn't *possibly* get any more screwed up, *she* comes back."

"Are you going to tell me who 'she' is?" I asked, my voice coming out louder than I had intended it to.

Shit. That sounded harsh, I realized as Jessi's lip curled into a snarl.

"*She* is no one to me," Jessi said coldly.

"What are you *talking* about, then?" I demanded, feeling both panicky and annoyed at Jessi's vagueness. "Jessi, I don't understand—"

"She's my *mother*!"

I took a step back, shocked by the exclamation.

"She's my mother," Jessi repeated softer, closing her eyes and gritting her teeth as if what she was saying was causing her physical pain. "The woman onstage — the brunette — she's my *mother*."

"But... that... that doesn't make any sense," I stuttered once I regained the ability to talk. Jessi's mom had left after Jessi was born — and now, she was *back*? I didn't know what to say. "It's... gonna be okay," I told her, trying to sound comforting.

"Don't be stupid," Jessi snapped, but her voice lacked force. "I *know* it's not okay, and it's never going to *be* okay." A tear slipped out the corner of her eye, though she quickly wiped it away.

I gently pulled Jessi into a hug. At first, Jessi seemed a little startled, but after a few seconds, she leaned into my touch, burying her face into my shoulder. I heard her sniffle softly and knew that she was crying.

I had to admit that it scared me a little.

"Maybe everything's not okay. But I'm here, all right?"

"I don't know what to do," Jessi whispered, lifting her head from my shoulder. I tightened my arms around her, feeling like *I* was protecting *her*, for once. "This wasn't supposed to happen, Ethan. She wasn't *supposed* to come back."

"I know, Jess," I said softly, looking into the distance. "I know."

"I'm sure you know my messed-up family story, Ethan," Jessi said flatly, fidgeting with the charm bracelet on her wrist. We now sat on a nearby bench since we were too exhausted to climb a tree. "I came into existence, then my mother decided to leave – probably *because* of me."

I shook my head. "Jessi, no. You can't blame yourself for that."

"I can do whatever I want. It's a free country." I opened my mouth to say something more, but I was interrupted by the chime of a text notification from inside Jessi's pocket. "Oh, crap, It's Aurora. I had promised to meet up with her this afternoon, but…" Jessi's eyes drifted away from her phone's screen and back to the parade that was happening in the distance.

"But you don't want to go back there."

"Not really," Jessi sighed. "I promised Aurora, though."

"So, invite her over here. We can walk to the diner together or something."

Over the last few weeks, I had come to like Aurora. She seemed caring and kind – *and* she was the only other person that I could share my concerns about Jessi with.

"Hey! There you are!" Moments later, I looked to my left to see Aurora jogging up to us. She smiled wide in her ruby-red t-shirt and black-and-white plaid skirt, which she wore with a pair of black tights and a winter coat. "I see Ethan has joined."

"I hope it's all right. I was thinking we could go grab a burger or something," I suggested as Jessi and I stood up.

Aurora beamed, especially once she made eye contact with Jessi. "Yeah, that sounds good."

The diner wasn't far from the town square, but even in the short amount of time that it took us to walk there, Aurora had seemed to pick up on the fact that something was wrong with Jessi. She kept looking over at her, then at me, tilting her head to the side in a concerned manner.

The three of us soon stepped into the diner, then sighed as the heating melted our winter chills.

"Hey, Jessi," Aurora said as we pulled off our coats. "Ethan and I will go find a booth. Would you mind grabbing some water?"

"Sure," Jessi — who normally would have given a sassy retort at that request – mumbled, then headed toward the counter.

"What *happened* to her?" Aurora questioned in a low voice as she sat down across from me in a nearby booth. "She's so *quiet* – so un-Jessi-like."

I quickly glanced over at Jessi to make sure she couldn't hear us. "Jessi... she's had a rough day."

"What do you mean?" Aurora asked as she twisted a lock of red-orange hair nervously.

"Jessi's mom – who's been gone for seventeen years – just showed up today for Founder's Day, and it's been hard on Jessi," I explained as simply as I could.

I expected Aurora to ask more questions, but she surprisingly just nodded, understanding exactly what I was talking about. She then glanced over at Jessi, who was still standing at the counter. "Do you think she's going to be okay?"

"Jessi's tough," I replied, though it felt like too short an answer.

"Of course, she is. Just think about the way she took on Nate last week," Aurora laughed, then sighed. "I know she's *tough*, but I still worry about her."

"Me and you both–" I was cut off mid sentence as the bell above the diner's door jingled, and a loud crash sounded behind me. I turned in my spot at the sound, following Aurora's stare.

My eyes found Jessi, who was frozen, her stare locked on the door. There was a cup at her feet, and water was all over the floor, but she didn't seem to notice it at all. I followed Jessi's gaze to the door, then realized why she looked like she was going to puke.

Her mother had just entered.

Aurora jumped up from the booth and made her way over to Jessi, a huge grin plastered on her face. I followed behind, unsure about what Aurora was up to. "So sorry," Aurora remarked loudly. "My friend is a bit of a klutz. She's *always* dropping things, *right*?"

Aurora shot me a meaningful glance, and I tried my best to play along. "Oh, um, yeah. Human hurricane, that one."

"Come on," Aurora continued in her overly peppy voice, grabbing Jessi's arm and directing her toward our booth. "I think it's about time we sit down."

I picked up the cup that Jessi had dropped, then set it back on the counter, mumbling an apology to the nearby waitress. Back at the booth, Aurora was seated beside Jessi, who was aggressively biting her nails. I sat down in front of them, starting to feel panicky just watching Jessi.

"I-I can't be here," Jessi choked, attempting to shove past Aurora. "I have to leave."

"Jessi, wait," Aurora pleaded, grabbing Jessi's wrist and forcing her to sit back down. She held Jessi's hands in hers, stopping Jessi from chewing her nails.

"Maybe you should talk to her," I suggested, watching as Jessi's mother sat down at a table on the other side of the diner.

"Are you *insane*?" Jessi hissed. *"No!"*

"I think Ethan might be right," Aurora added, smiling at me hopefully. "Maybe the best way to face this is head-on."

Jessi pulled her hands out of Aurora's grip and pressed them against the sides of her head as if she had a bad headache. "I-I *can't*. I can't just go and *talk* to her. I *can't*."

Aurora gently patted Jessi's back before her phone chimed, and she quickly checked the notification, a scowl forming on her face. "Shit, it's Jenna. She's pissed because I disappeared on her. I… I have to go back to the parade. Will you guys be okay?"

I tried to give Aurora a reassuring smile. "Yeah, we'll be fine. And, um, tell Jenna that I say hi." I felt myself blush a little at my last sentence but pushed any thoughts of it away.

Aurora, thankfully not seeming to notice my awkwardness, stood up and gave Jessi's shoulder a quick squeeze. Jessi didn't look up, and Aurora gave her a sad, concerned glance before slipping out of the booth and exiting the diner.

Sighing, I turned around and stole a glance at Jessi's mother. She was sitting by herself at a two-person table, staring out the window.

"I'm such a coward," Jessi whispered, and I looked back at her to find her staring at her mother. "Anna would be ashamed of me."

"*No*," I said forcefully. "Jessi, Anna *wouldn't* be ashamed of you." Jessi shifted her gaze to the table, biting her lip and not saying anything in response. "Anna would *never* be ashamed of you. I know that she would have wanted you to face this head-on, though."

Jessi looked into my eyes, and I saw a single tear

stream down her cheek. "Okay, I'll do it," she said softly, a look of subtle determination crossing her face.

I smiled, a little caught off-guard. "All right. I can wait here if you want–"

"No. You don't have to be involved in my screwed-up family life. Besides, I don't know how long this is going to take."

"Okay," I answered, not wanting to start an argument. "Let me know if you need anything, though."

Jessi nodded, standing up from the booth and walking with me to the door. "Thanks."

"And, hey, if everything ends in a disaster, and this turned out to be a horrible idea, you can punch me and say, 'I told you so.'"

Jessi cast me a small, nervous smile. "I have a feeling you're gonna regret saying that, Ethan."

Chapter 20
Jessi
Mother Knows Best

I *can't do this.*

I glanced at the exit door behind me, wanting nothing more than to escape.

No, I told myself, tearing my gaze away from the diner door. *You're going to go over there and talk to her.* My eyes found the table where my mother was sitting and staring blankly out the window. *For Anna.*

I slowly walked over to the table, each step feeling like it took more effort than the last. Once I reached it, I forced myself to sit down and tried hard to resist the temptation to chew my nails. "Hi, Mom."

My mother looked away from the window and over at me. Her eyes widened, and her face paled as if she had just seen a ghost. "Jessi?"

"You mean the daughter you left years ago without explanation?" Just looking into her eyes – wide and dark brown, like my own – made a sudden wave of nausea crash over me. For a terrifying second, I was sure that I was going to puke all over the table. "I'm surprised you recognize me."

My mother chuckled, which took me aback. "You are so much like your father – it's *crazy*. I still follow him on Facebook, you know. I've been watching you grow up through posts. Might I say, you look so *beau*–" My mom cut herself off as I smacked her hand away from my face, which she was about to caress. She frowned but didn't look surprised by my reaction. "You must have a lot of questions for me."

"Oh, no. No questions at *all*," I snapped, though my voice was shaking. "Why would *I* have *questions*?"

My mom chuckled, tucking a lock of hair almost identical to mine behind her ear. "I suppose I should just start at the beginning, shouldn't I?" she asked, giving me a tentative smile.

I glared at her in return. "Yeah, why don't you start by telling me why you've come to screw up my life even *more*?" My mother flinched, but I kept going. "Ooh, better yet, why don't you explain why you *left*? I honestly can't imagine what I did to make you hate me so much."

"This world is a lot more dangerous than you think it is, Jessi."

"*Cryptic* much?"

"I know you may not want to listen to me – with good reason. But, *please*, hear me out. There's a lot that I need to tell you."

I leaned back against my chair, keeping a glare pasted on my face. "You're right. I *don't* want to listen to you. Since you came *all the way* from California to tell me whatever it is you have to say, though, I *suppose* I can try."

My mother took a deep breath as if she had to prepare herself. "Okay, well... I think we should start with the history of Ember Falls."

I rolled my eyes. "I already know that, thanks. For your information, I'm quite good in history class."

My mother shook her head. "No. That history is a lie – a *coverup* story." Before I could make another retort, my mother continued. "Before humans arrived in this town, angels and demons roamed free. But they were in a constant battle about which race should be the rightful rulers of the Earth–"

"Whoa, whoa, whoa," I interrupted, unable to keep myself from laughing. "*Angels* and *demons*? They must have skipped over *that* bit at school."

"Of course," my mother murmured. "You don't *know*... I don't know why I figured that you did–"

"Know *what*?" I hissed, fed up with her rambling.

"Jessi," she said, and I realized how much I hated the way my name sounded coming out of her mouth. "Angels and demons – *supernaturals* – are real."

"*Right,*" I responded, drawing out the word. "And so are unicorns and flying pigs."

"Have you ever seen, heard, or felt something that you couldn't explain?" my mother asked, ignoring my remark. "Or maybe something that someone else couldn't see, hear, or feel?"

Yes, I thought before I could stop myself from agreeing with her.

"That would most likely have been something supernatural, or supernaturally influenced. I'll get into that more later, but let me start by telling you the *real* story of this town."

My mother then launched into a tale of angels and demons who were fighting each other for possession of Earth, and how a single woman – Ember Smith – had changed all of that. Apparently, Ember had begged the leaders of the supernatural parties – Lucifer and the Archangel Gabriel – for a portion of their power. But then, she had banished both supernatural races to either Heaven or Hell on her bridge – *Ember's Bridge*. This bridge had been built strategically so that, during the witching hour, the moon would be perfectly aligned with the rapids below.

"If you've ever visited that bridge, it's likely that you would have felt a rush of some sort. That would be the remnants of the fallout," my mom explained. Flashbacks of crossing that bridge, as well as the pain of doing so, then crossed my mind, and I shivered. "When Ember banished the supernaturals – which led to her death – she used an immense amount of power, which resulted in a fallout of sorts. This touched the Founding Families and created witches."

"So, wait," I interjected, my head in a million places at once. "You're telling me that the Founding Families are *witches*?"

My mother nodded. "Yes, but some families refuse to acknowledge their power, or so I've heard."

"So, then, *you* are a witch?"

My mother gave me an almost sad smile. "No."

"But you're part of a Founding Family, aren't you?" I asked, wishing that she would get her damn story straight.

"Yes, I am, and I *was* a witch. When I was seven years old, though, I was hit by a car—"

"*What?*" I cried involuntarily.

"Let me explain," she said calmly, taking a deep breath and combing a hand through her hair. "When I was seven, I nearly died. But while I was hanging between life and death, I was approached by an angel, who offered me a second chance. I, of course, accepted, and that angel took me as their own."

I blinked twice in confusion. "As their own? What is *that* supposed to mean?"

"It's hard to explain, but angels use a sort of body-possessing tactic when coming to Earth." My mom began speaking with hand gestures almost nervously, and I found myself leaning forward with curiosity. "I'm an angel, but I'm still myself... You could say that I'm a human with angelic powers. Either way, when I was saved from dying, I became an angel, and I was no longer a witch."

"You said that angels came to Earth." I sighed, my patience starting to evaporate. "What exactly does that mean?"

"After the supernaturals were banished, the demons began to rebel. They didn't want to be stuck in Hell – they wanted to rule Earth. Of course, they had no way of doing this until Lucifer was able to make a deal. Lucky for them, the blood deal with the Morgenstern family – which allowed demons to return to Earth using anyone from that bloodline as a tether – helped the demons get to Earth.

"Once the angels realized what the demons were doing, they had to retaliate. So, they started to send down some of their own to fight against the demons. The way that they did this, of course, was very different from the demons. Angels, who have no real form – they are mostly creatures made of light – can simply 'become' someone–"

"So, angels choose *dying kids* to possess?"

My mother shook her head, glancing to the side for a quick moment. "No, I was a special case. Usually, an angel will choose a human that they observe until they are the age of five. Then, the angel will decide if that person is worthy. If they are, that person will become an angel. That's how the angels get to Earth.

"As for the demons – who are remarkably human-like in appearance – they continue to tether themselves to a human, who is known as a Charge. They then turn the Charge into a half-demon and accompany them on Earth. This way, they can have a bit of control over the human mind. Demons *can* interact with the living world, but only to a certain extent. So, they use their Charge to do their... *dirty work*."

"How do you even *know* all this?" I questioned accusingly. I was baffled by the facts, which were still registering in my brain.

My mother smiled sadly. "I'm part of a Founding Family, and stories are passed down through generations. It's our job to remember them because we are the only ones who *really* know the danger of Ember Falls."

"Why don't you just *tell* people, then? Why keep everyone in the dark?" I began picking at the skin around my nails, shifting in my seat as my mom pressed her lips into a thin line.

"Telling everyone would only hurt them. Knowledge

can be dangerous, Jessi."

"Knowledge can be *dangerous*? Isn't it more dangerous *not* to know?"

"In my experience, knowing always puts you in *more* danger," my mother replied, her gaze drifting over to the window. "When I was in high school, I dated Jack Morgenstern–"

My eyes widened, and a gasp escaped my lips. "Wait, you mean, Jack *Morgenstern*, as in..."

Adley's father?

"I'm assuming that means you know of the Morgenstern family," my mother said as I trailed off. "So, yes, I'm sure we're thinking of the same person. He and I dated from ninth to twelfth grade, when I found out that he was a *half-demon*.

"I had caught him talking to his demonic tie and confronted him about it. He explained everything and begged me not to leave, but I *couldn't* stay with him. It was too dangerous, especially for an angel. It was too late, though, since the demon – Damion – was already out for me since I had revealed my angel identity."

Damion? I was too speechless to say anything aloud. *Damion was* there*? He's a* demon*?*

"Damion hunted me down, forcing Jack into it, as well. For a couple months, I was able to escape him. But then, Damion – along with Daniel Blackthorn, who was a bad witch – finally caught up to me. Jack – controlled by Damion – and I fought, and, well... I lost."

I licked my dry lips, trying to find my words. "You *lost*? What is *that* supposed to mean?"

"I was *defeated*. I lost my angelic powers and became one of the Fallen. Do you see this?" She pointed at the large, white scar that circled her right eye. It looked uncannily like *my* birthmark. "This is proof of my failure."

I narrowed my eyes. "You're a *useless* angel, then?"

My mother flashed me a strange, happy-but-sad look. "Pretty much. After that fight, I ran away and went into hiding for a while – not that I needed to. Damion was off my tail since I wasn't a threat anymore.

"More than ten years passed, and I eventually let my guard down. I shouldn't have, though – in a small town, people hold grudges. Daniel Blackthorn – who was strongly allied with the demons – came after me again, wanting to finish what was started. He cornered me on Ember's Bridge, wanting a fight since, I assume, he knew that I was weaker and posed less of a threat. I tried to talk him out of it – his daughter was just born – but it was useless. He attacked me, and I had no choice but to fight back.

"In the end, Daniel was killed. I managed to shove him into the rapids below the bridge, and those rapids are nearly – if not *completely* – impossible to survive."

"You *killed* someone?" I was frozen in fear and shock.

I noticed a single tear slip down my mother's cheek. "It was self-defense. But, *yes*." When I didn't comment, she added, "Then, about a year passed, and you were born."

"And you decided 'Nope, this is a mistake,' and *left*," I snapped, feeling a strange mixture of anger and sadness bubble in my chest.

"It *wasn't* like that," my mother argued, her eyes glossy with tears.

"Then, what *was* it like? I just *can't* seem to find a good reason for abandoning your child."

My mother closed her eyes and blew out a long breath. "I left because I thought it would keep you safe, Jessi."

I laughed bitterly. "*Right*, because running away *totally* helped protect me."

"I thought you wouldn't have to face your true nature if I was gone," my mother said, glancing down at the table.

"My *true nature*?" I questioned harshly, raising an eyebrow.

She looked into my eyes, her expression serious. "You're a half-angel, Jessi."

I didn't say anything, raising my eyebrows in disbelief until the facts registered, and I realized the familiarity in the statement.

Damion had told me the same thing.

"You're a half-angel," my mother continued, giving me a weak smile. "Or a Guardian, one might say. Your job is to protect an angel that has come to Earth. You have a set of abilities tailored for that, like enhanced fighting skills and demon sensing. I'm sure you've noticed that, when you're in a stressful situation with an endangered loved one, your first instinct is to fight – and you're *really* good at it.

"As for demon sensing, it's just this feeling that a Guardian gets around a demon. This will act as an alarm, alerting the Guardian of danger." My mother then stopped talking, looking at me as if she was expecting some sort of reaction, but I was too busy processing everything.

I hated how all this made sense.

"Guardians do, of course, have weaknesses. Your main one is bronze," my mother added. "Any contact with a bronze object will harm you in some way, and a large wound caused by a bronze weapon can be fatal."

"Wait," I started, thoughts racing through my head at a million miles per second. "How… *Why* am I even a-a *Guardian* in the first place? Was I *chosen*?"

My mother shook her head. "No, that part is *my* fault. I told you that Damion had defeated me. I had taken a final punch to the eye from Jack's hand, which had been adorned with rings made of gold – an angel's weakness. That last blow had sapped my power – which wasn't that impressive since all angels have is extra strength and a healing ability, which only works to an extent. But the blow also gave me this scar – which, I'm sure you've noticed, looks exactly like the birthmark on *your* eye.

"That birthmark is the mark of a Guardian. It mirrors whatever scar the failed angel parent has. Since I was defeated – and therefore failed my assigned mission – you are the one who has to make up for my failure."

"So, you're telling me that because *you* were defeated, *I* am stuck being a Guardian to make up for *your* screw-up?"

"It's not fair, I know—"

"*None* of this is fair!" I cried, throwing my arms out in frustration. When the waiter glanced up in alarm from behind the counter, I covered my mouth with a hand. I had forgotten we weren't alone. "This world is so screwed up."

My mother laughed softly. "I'm sorry, but this was

one of the reasons why I came back. I couldn't keep you in the dark anymore, no matter how much I wanted to."

"Why *now*?" I whispered, tired of the lies and secrets.

She sighed, twisting a strand of her brown hair around her finger. "I've kept track of Ember Falls all these years. In the last few months, though, I noticed strange things on the news... *deaths*. Within a short period, two girls died, and I recognized the name 'Adley Morgenstern.' She was *Jack's* daughter. So, I had a feeling that — given the Morgenstern history — something supernatural was involved. I was afraid that you were in danger."

"Well, *now,* I feel safe," I scoffed. "Thanks *so much*."

"Listen, Jessi. I know that I've made a lot of mistakes in the past, but I *am* trying to help."

"You want to *help*? Why don't you try and *fix* things?"

"Fix things?" my mother asked softly.

"Yes!" I cried, my voice turning desperate. "Fix your *family!*"

My mother flinched. "Jessi, I can't do that."

"Why *not*?" I questioned, feeling tears burn my eyes.

"Because I don't belong here," my mother answered, not meeting my eyes. "I'm leaving on Friday."

"What? You show up, tell me the craziest things that are *life-changing*, then pack up and *leave again*?"

My mother looked toward the floor. "I'm sorry, Jessi, but I can't stay. I have a purpose in California. I'm part of the team that discovered the Test — the blood exam that determines how guilty a person is by the shade of their blood that shows up on a Tester paper.

"No one knows this, but supernatural blood reacts differently to a Test compared to how human blood does. Human blood will show somewhat accurate levels of guilt – it can vary from person to person since some people can hide their guilt well. But demon blood will always show up guiltless – pure red – since evil is a demon's soul purpose. Angel blood, on the other hand, will always show up dark since they are meant to be good and therefore can't hide their sins."

I blinked, disoriented by her sudden rant. Despite how insane it sounded, though, it made sense. My blood had come back dark when I had taken the Test since I had some angel blood in me. Even though I had never been a rebellious child, I was certainly not perfect – and my blood just couldn't hide any sins.

I shook my head, refocusing on the present. "Well, good for you. I'm so *glad* that you were able to build yourself a nice, new life without me."

"It isn't like that–"

"*Why* are you leaving, then?" I snapped, though my voice came out shaky. "You *just* came back. You might even have a chance to fix *our* family."

"Jessi, I can't *fix things*. It's too late, and staying here would only make things worse. I don't want to live a *lie*, Jessi."

My heart sank to my stomach, and that was when I glanced at her right hand and caught a silver, bedazzled ring on her ring finger. "What?"

My mother sighed. "Jessi, your father was just an

escape – someone safe for me to be with after Jack. I... I'm remarried now."

I felt like I had been punched in the stomach. I knew that my father still loved my mother – I had seen the way he would look at their old photos longingly.

But *she* moved on as if my dad and I had never existed.

"Wh-What?" I stammered, tears slipping down my cheeks. "You don't *care*?" I looked directly into her brown eyes, not caring that I was crying freely now. "Do you... do you even love *me*? Or do you have this new life with other children who aren't fucking *screw-ups*?"

"Of course, I love you," she responded, but the split-second of hesitation she'd had was enough for me to know the truth.

She doesn't love me.

She had avoided my second question for a reason.

I angrily wiped the tears pouring down the sides of my face.

She doesn't love me.

"Jessi," my mother said urgently as if she didn't see my crying. "You... you can't tell your father that I was here."

"Why *would* I?" I snarled, but my voice kept breaking. "You don't love *him*. You don't love *me*. You don't *care*. You just wanted to come and dump all this information on me so that you wouldn't have any more secrets to keep." My mother opened her mouth to say something, but I didn't let her talk. "We don't *need* you," I spat, repeatedly wiping tears from my face. "And you don't *deserve* my father. You don't deserve *me*. You don't deserve *anything*."

My mother looked down at the table, her expression unreadable. Then, she pushed her chair back, stood up, and slowly made her way over to me. "You're right," she said quietly, cautiously reaching out and cupping the side of my face in her hand. "Of course, you're right."

I wanted to pull away, but I found myself leaning into her touch and hating myself for it.

My mother leaned down, quickly pressed a kiss to my forehead, then dropped her hand from my face and turned away, heading for the diner's exit door.

She's leaving, I realized, a cold feeling settling into the pit of my stomach. *Again.*

She stopped walking and looked over her shoulder, her eyes shiny with tears but her face stern. "I'm sorry that things have to be this way, Jessi."

Chapter 21
Adley
Misery Loves Company

My stomach twisted with nerves as I walked down the quiet, dark streets on my way to Danny's Diner. I knew that it was about time that this happened.

It *needed* to happen, and tonight was the perfect night.

After Founder's Day, Kyle and I started spending more time together. Almost every night for two weeks, we had been at his house, studying and completing chemistry labs. We actually got along really well, I had learned, and I caught myself looking forward to our work sessions more every time.

I had only learned a week before now that Kyle's friends were getting a little jealous since I was keeping them away from Kyle for so long. That was why I had planned for us to all hang out at the diner. Dylan, Calvin, and Ethan would get Kyle, and since things seemed to have blown over between me and Anna, we'd get to hang out and clear the air – with *Jessi*, of course, since Anna had also invited her.

Plus, I would get the chance to talk to Kyle seriously. I had to start my side of the plan, and that meant that Kyle had to know the truth about who he was so that he could start practicing magic. That was why I had invited him to meet me earlier at the diner. We needed a few extra minutes alone to chat.

As I pulled the door open and entered the diner, I noticed that only one booth was occupied. Forcing a smile – as nervous as I was – I waltzed over to the corner booth and slid onto the bench across from Kyle.

"Hey," I greeted as I pulled off my winter coat and tucked it in between me and the large window. It was the moment when I glanced into Kyle's piercing blue eyes that I questioned if what I was doing was the right thing.

He was so *innocent* in all of this...

"Hey, how are you?"

I bit my lip to stop myself from smiling. I could tell by his sweaty hands how nervous he was. "I'm okay," I sighed as I tucked a lock of hair behind my ear. I had to rip the Band-Aid off, especially since I knew that I didn't have all night. "Look, Kyle, we need to talk. I've needed to be honest and tell you everything. Before you get worried" –I had already noticed his eyes widened in fear at the word "talk"– "this isn't about us. It's about who we are."

"What?" Kyle's eyes widened in confusion.

I licked my lips, trying to think of a way to explain everything without him freaking out *and* making a scene. "There's, um, a lot you don't know about me – and a lot that you don't know about *yourself*," I began, looking from Kyle to the table as my heartbeat quickened. "We're *special*.

I was pulled into this devious plan that I have no choice but to help with – or at least *pretend* to – and I met you for a reason because you're also needed for this plan. But I *promise* that everything will be fine if you *listen* to me."

"Okay, seriously, what the *hell* are you talking about, Jenna?" Kyle questioned, his eyes watering in fear. He glanced over at the door behind him as if he was debating if he should run or not. "You're scaring me. Aren't we supposed to be here to *chill*–?"

"You *need* to be afraid, Kyle. There's a world out there that you don't know about, and you need to be careful from now on," I continued, knowing that if I stopped for a moment, I would never finish. "You won't get hurt if you stick by me, I promise."

"So, let me get this straight. Your meeting me was a *set-up*? All because you're being pulled into some plan?"

"Yes," I told him, trying to be as honest as possible without giving huge amounts of information away. I didn't trust him to keep a secret that big, especially when my life was at stake.

"But… You still like me, right? Everything you feel–"

"Is completely *true*," I insisted, though I hated myself for still lying about that part. I just knew that if I *was* to have told him the complete truth, he wouldn't have listened to the rest of the explanation, and I *needed* him to make this work.

"And you're in danger… You know, we could go to the police together and not solve this on our own," Kyle reminded me, grabbing my hands and cupping them in his. "We don't have to be victims–"

"But we *can't* go to the police, and you *can't* tell this

to anybody. Only Aurora knows. There's a whole other world out there," I repeated, squeezing Kyle's hands. "A world that's out to get rid of humankind. A world of *magic.*"

"Okay, Jenna, what drug are you on–?"

"Kyle," I hissed, losing my patience as my eyes flicked to the wall clock across the diner. I knew that the gang would arrive at any minute, and I had to finish my explanation. "I need you to trust me. I need you to understand that this is all *real.*"

Kyle stopped shaking as if he was ready for whatever came next, though I knew that he wasn't.

I wasn't.

"Kyle, I'm a demon, and you're a witch–"

"Who's ready to get this party started?" Dylan cried from the diner's entrance as he, along with the rest of the gang, walked into the diner with wide smiles.

Fuck.

I glanced over at the gang with a weary smile before looking back at Kyle, whose eyes were wide with fear. He had definitely paled, and his hands were shaking as he pulled his hands out from under mine.

Scared that I had fucked everything up, I smiled at him and mumbled, "We'll talk later. Just... don't stress too much. We're gonna figure it all out."

Kyle smiled faintly, which at least showed that he hadn't lost it yet.

At least the hard part was done.

Now, all I had to do was explain *everything...*

"Ooh, are we interrupting something?" Dylan laughed as he slid in next to Kyle, who combed a hand through his dark hair as if to shake off our previous conversation. "If you need a second—"

"We're *fine*," I exclaimed as I found Ethan in the crowd and smiled at him.

I then locked eyes with Jessi for a moment, who coughed in response, almost as if in pain. She seemed a little uncomfortable, actually. Her arms were crossed over her chest, yet her everyday smirk — which she wore like an accessory — was glued to her face. Honestly, she was beginning to look *just* like Ivy, especially in her all-black t-shirt and shorts. The only difference was how Jessi was wearing a purple-and-black plaid sweater, which Ivy would never wear.

Dylan pulled Ethan down next to him, and Anna sat down beside me, along with Jessi. Calvin pulled over a stool, sitting at the head of the booth.

"So," he started, glancing around the table. "What's everyone having?"

After ordering two large, cheese pizzas and a round of Cokes, the girls and the boys had split. The boys had decided to show each other games on their smartphones, while the girls had moved to the booth next door to gossip.

However, it had been more like Jessi and Anna were the ones gossiping. I, on the other hand, had eavesdropped on the guys' conversations since their topics were way more interesting than history class, which Jessi and Anna were discussing. After a few minutes, though, the boys' conversations became more personal.

"So, do you think things are going to get more *intense* between you and Jenna?" Dylan asked Kyle with a smirk on his face.

Kyle glanced my way, and I quickly looked at the girls until his eyes went back to Dylan, Ethan, and Calvin. "Eventually, probably," Kyle said casually, making my heartbeat speed up – just the way he acted as if nothing had happened before gave me hope. "When we're ready. I... I just feel like, sometimes, the girl has her mind in two worlds. One minute, she seems so into things, but the next, it's as if I don't matter."

"That's girls for you," Dylan sighed, and I wasn't sure if it was a happy or sad remark. "It's the mood swings."

"Or *maybe* you're just overthinking this," Calvin implied, but Dylan waved him off.

"All you need to do is show her how much you care. You could buy her flowers, chocolates–"

"*Or* you could just show her how much she matters with an action," Ethan suggested, cutting Dylan off.

"Oh, I see where you're going with this," Dylan chuckled, and I felt myself blush at the idea.

"No!" Ethan cried, shaking his head as if wanting to get the thought out of his mind. "I meant, make *memories* – talk or help her with something. Once you can prove how you'll always be there for her, she'll commit herself to you."

"Ah, yes. Ethan the love expert," Dylan remarked, rolling his eyes. "Look, all you've got to say are three magic words."

"But only say them when you *truly* mean it," Ethan added with a smile.

"How do you know you mean it, though?" Kyle questioned, his tone serious.

Everyone glanced at Ethan expectantly. "Well, I mean, I told Adley because I just couldn't stop thinking about her – every song I heard was about her, and every story seemed to be written about us. I knew she checked all the boxes – there was no one better out there for me. She just got me, and I wanted to spend my life with her.

"I never got to say it to her in person, but I wish I would have. Because, yeah, I meant every letter."

My heart skipped a beat at his last line, and I caught myself grinning like a fucking weirdo. The warmth that spread through my chest when I heard his words was indescribable – he had felt the same way I had, which only tore at my heart more. I suddenly had an urge to tell him that I loved him, and I wanted to say it over and over again–

But, of course, I couldn't.

After a while of everyone having their separate conversations in the diner, Jessi oddly pulled Ethan aside. Curious to know what was up, I watched as they walked outside of the diner to have a few moments alone. I couldn't stop wondering about what they could have possibly been talking about.

Why pull him aside like that in the first place?

That was why, once Ethan and Jessi had been gone for a few minutes, I told the group that I was getting a phone call from my aunt and needed to step outside to answer.

Luckily, when I exited the diner, nobody was around to spot me. Ethan and Jessi were sitting on a bench a few feet away, staring out at the main road and not seeming to notice my presence. Not wanting to get caught for spying, I lurked in the shadows, watching closely but not too close so that they wouldn't see me.

"Okay, *seriously*," Jessi began, though she looked stiff and uncomfortable. "What the hell is up with you? Are you already moving on from Adley?"

My eyes widened at the remark. For a second, I thought I had heard wrong.

"What?" Ethan asked, looking just as bewildered as I was. "What are you talking about?"

"It's just…" Jessi looked down at the ground, then took a deep breath. "I have a feeling that you're being stupid."

"About what?" Ethan crossed his arms over his chest in disbelief.

"God, do I have to *say it*?" When Ethan didn't comment, Jessi remarked, "I've been *watching* you all evening, Ethan. And I've been seeing how you're acting whenever… whenever *Jenna's* name comes up."

My heartbeat sped up at the mention of my alias. My eyes flickered over to Ethan, who I caught gaping in the dim light of the streetlamp.

"I don't understand what you're *getting* at–"

"I see you look away every time. I see you *blushing*, E!" Jessi cried in what looked like disgust. "Do… do you have feelings for *Jenna*?"

My heart caught in my throat.

What?

Ethan's face flushed red, and I bit my bottom lip. "Yeah," he whispered.

I covered my mouth to stop myself from gasping,

then fell to the cement sidewalk from my leaning position against the diner's brick wall. My heart started to beat rapidly in my chest, my insides squirmed around, and I felt my face go hot. It felt like *that night* all over again – when he had first admitted to me that he liked me.

No matter whose body I was in, he still loved *me*.

I couldn't decide if that was romantic or screwed up.

"Are you *serious*?" Jessi looked so mad that, for a second, I thought she was jealous. "I thought you *loved* Adley–"

"I'll always love Adley!" Ethan shouted, tears coming to his eyes. "But she's *dead*, and she's *never* coming back." Ethan licked his bottom lip, and I could feel my eyes watering too. His words stung like nothing ever had. "And Jenna–"

"Do you remember who you're talking about? That's *Kyle's* girlfriend."

"I know, I know. It's bad," Ethan cried, shaking his head. "But it's just something about her. It's not only that she's pretty... She just reminds me so much of Adley. From the way she acts, to how close we've gotten so quickly–"

"Stop!" Jessi shouted, covering her ears with her hands as if hearing the words pained her. "Just *stop*. Adley is *dead*, and no one can be Adley besides *her*. This is all in your head, Ethan." Jessi put her head in her hands. "You need to move on, but this is not the way to do it. Sure, you took someone's girlfriend *once*" –a smirk appeared on her face, but it then quickly vanished– "but your close friend's? You can't do this to Kyle."

At her words, I heard the diner entrance's bell ring. Not wanting to be spotted, I dodged into the dark alleyway next to the diner, then watched as a figure approached Ethan and Jessi, who were still seated on the bench. I couldn't hear what they were saying to each other, but once I heard a shriek, I knew that I had to get closer to hear.

I sprinted over to the nearby garbage can and hid behind it, praying that I was small enough to not be seen. I noticed at that moment that it was Kyle who had come out of the diner, and he was now standing next to Ethan, whose face was back to being red as a tomato.

Oh, shit.

"Kyle, I just thought I should tell you because I want to be honest," Ethan admitted, his hands up as if they would protect him from Kyle's reaction.

"Oh, that is *certainly* one way to put it," Jessi snickered nervously, trying to break the tension, but the guys continued to glare at each other like I had never seen them do before.

"People and their *honesty*! You like *Jenna*?" Kyle asked, his tone laced with anger.

Ethan Landers, you idiot!

"Yeah," Ethan mumbled, and Jessi slumped on the bench awkwardly as she watched the boys. "But-but I *promise* that I won't interfere with your relationship. I'm happy for you. Like I've told Jenna, you two are good for each–"

"I can't *believe* this. I thought you were just *friends,* but no wonder you guys are so close. And you're always quiet when we talk about her… Everything just makes *sense*," Kyle stated, pacing under the moonlight and ignoring Ethan's statement. "She doesn't know, does she?"

"Of course, not. I wouldn't do that to her."

A little late for that, I think.

Ethan swallowed hard. "Look, just hear me out–"

"I'm going back inside and waiting for *my* girlfriend to return," Kyle declared, cutting Ethan off before he could apologize. Kyle then marched back toward the diner's entrance. "If you ever make a move on her, though, I *swear*, our friendship is over."

The rest of the evening was strange, to put it mildly. After Kyle and Ethan had fought, Kyle had come storming into the diner. Once I had come back in to see him, he sat next to me in the booth and didn't leave my side.

When Ethan – trailed by a hilariously, uncomfortable-looking Jessi – had come back into the diner, Kyle glared at him with enough force to start a fire. Ethan hadn't stuck around for long after that, though, saying he needed to get air alone.

I hated how the evening had unraveled.

I felt as if it was all *my* fault.

That was why I snuck out a while later, saying that I had to use the washroom but escaped through the diner's back door instead. I soon found Ethan on a bench in the alleyway, staring up at the starry sky.

I snuck up behind him, watching him with a smile on my face. It suddenly felt like it was just me and him – like old times. "It's a nice night, isn't it?"

Ethan jumped in his seat but smiled when he spotted me emerging from the inky darkness, his face tinting pink. "Oh, yeah."

"Mind if I sit?" As Ethan nodded, I sat down next to him on the bench, then looked back up at the sky. "What are you looking at?"

"Every night, I search for the Leo constellation," Ethan told me, glancing back up at the stars. "It's the horoscope that my sister and I share — *not* that it relates to me, by what my sister used to tell me." He chuckled softly, combing a hand through his messy curls. "But it *did* relate to my sister, and this is like my way of remembering her, you know?"

"You like astronomy?" I prompted, trying to find something to talk about as Ethan looked away from the sky and focused on me.

"Yeah. I like how we feel so alone, sometimes, but aren't actually. When you look up at the sky, you're always reminded how small we are compared to the Universe — how there's an entire world of people out there."

"Yet somehow, we managed to be in each others' worlds," I added, feeling myself blush and hoping Ethan hadn't noticed. "Tell me about yourself," I then blurted, and when I caught his face scrunch in confusion, I laughed and elaborated. "I mean, since we're friends, I'd like to know the real you. So, tell me... What's your favorite ice cream flavor?"

Ethan's eyebrows raised, but he shook his head, laughing at my subject change. "Bubblegum. I know, childish—"

"It's not childish," I remarked, bringing a smile to his face. "I've always been a chocolate and peanut butter fan, though."

"You do look like the type," he pointed out, and I

shoved him playfully. "What's your favorite past-time activity?"

I pulled at a lock of my hair, debating if I should admit the truth – what I would have said if I was Adley. I then sighed, knowing that it *was* the truth – I shouldn't have had to change because I realized that my life was more complicated than I had thought it was. "It's going to sound silly, but I write scripts."

"Yeah?"

"Nothing interesting. It's kind of like my diary – I re-write scenarios that happen to me. It's like my way of coping with things. I know, I know; it's stupid–"

"No, it's not." Ethan looked into my eyes, and I felt a sense of comfort – because, of course, he wouldn't judge; he's my Ethan. "I like to build. Some nights, I'll stay up and take apart appliances just to rebuild them. I guess it's *my* stupid way of coping with things."

I looked down at his hands and finally realized why they were always covered in machine grease. I then felt so idiotic for not knowing beforehand.

"What's one thing you regret?"

His question surprised me, but I answered without a second thought. "Not telling the guy that I loved my true feelings for him sooner," I confessed as my heartbeat sped up. I knew that I shouldn't have said it, but in Ethan's presence, I felt compelled to be honest. "What about you?"

"Not kissing the girl that I loved sooner than I did."

"What did you love most about Adley?" I couldn't even control the questions slipping out of my mouth.

He licked his lips before they pulled up into a sad

smile. "I loved how she was always honest – how she would say things like they were and never lied about what mattered. Sure, she could lie about the little things – like that time when she claimed to have not stolen my laptop in class." He laughed tearfully at the memory, and so did I. "But when it came down to the big things, she would tell me the truth."

That statement slapped me in the face, and I felt drugged by the emotions resurfacing. Ethan thought I was *honest* when I was one of the biggest liars.

He *trusted* me, and I had left him without ever telling him the truth.

"What's up between you and Kyle? Why are you close one minute, then so distant with him?"

I realized then that we were so close that our shoulders were rubbing against each other. I was so consumed by the moment that I could barely think straight. "Because I'm not so sure I even like him like that when there's this other guy I would rather be with–"

I closed my eyes at the impact of his soft, familiar lips on mine, then I leaned into him, wrapping my arms around his neck to close the gap between us. I kissed him back, wanting every inch of him as I felt his hand slide up my thigh. I combed a hand through his hair as he held my face, his touch the most exhilarating feeling–

I pulled back, realizing what we were doing.

"We can't," I breathed as our foreheads touched and we looked into each other's eyes for a moment. I grabbed his hand, interlocking my fingers with his before letting go and backing away. "If Kyle sees..."

Ethan combed a hand through his curls as I stood up,

fixing the strands of hair that had gotten tangled between his fingers. He then cupped his hands over his face, out of breath. "*God*, what were we *thinking*?"

My heart ached as I watched him fill with regret, though the worst part was that *I* didn't regret anything.

I had kissed Ethan Landers.

He just hadn't known that he had been kissing *me*.

An idea then popped into my head, and before I could stop myself, I sat back down beside him, meeting his eyes. Then, after taking a deep breath and brushing a tear from my cheek, I whispered, "Forget everything that just happened. You came outside to look at the stars and never saw me." I then pulled away from Ethan, then quickly ducked into the diner the way I had exited at first.

Thank God, I had mind-control powers.

As much as I hated the fact that he wouldn't remember the moment, I knew that it had to be done. I loved him, but I couldn't love him as anyone but Adley.

It was too bad that she was gone forever.

Chapter 22
Annabeth

A Match Made in Hell

He still likes me."

I choked on the water that I was drinking, taken aback by the statement. After swallowing the liquid in my mouth, I stopped walking to look her in the eye. "What? Adley, it's been *three months*–"

"I mean he likes *Jenna*," Adley cried, throwing her hands up in the air in defeat. Her eyes looked pleading as if she was tired of this never-ending game of plot twists.

Oh, Ethan. I shook my head, frustration swirling inside me.

"Okay, seriously, what have I missed?" I asked, confused since, though we had hardly been talking during the last few weeks, I didn't understand how she couldn't have told me this sooner. I looked down at the sidewalk, thinking back to the fight we'd had a month ago. "I *know* things have been off between us, but we've been best friends *forever*. You kinda have to tell me these things, *especially* if they involve my brother."

"Honestly, I've barely had time to process this." Adley sat down on our usual park bench, and I took a seat next to her. We were, once again, on our way back to the motel after school, but neither of us actually wanted to go "home."

Not when Ivy or Nate could show up at any moment.

"I-I overheard Ethan talking to Jessi and admitting his feelings for me – *Jenna* – during our hang out at Danny's the other night. And… when Kyle came outside, looking for me, Ethan told him the truth." Adley's face pinkened as she shook her head in disappointment, and I couldn't help but copy her. "It was so stupid of him, but he had good intentions. He wanted to be honest, but all it did was get Kyle riled up."

"I mean, that's predictable," I responded, playing with the ends of my hair. "I think many people would have reacted like Kyle did."

"Yeah, but Kyle said that if Ethan ever made a move on me, their friendship was over – right *before* Ethan and I kissed."

My eyes widened, and my jaw dropped. "You guys did *what* now? *Adley–*"

"We-we were just sitting outside and talking together. But then, we were sitting closer, and our faces were inches apart, and suddenly, our lips were *touching*!" Adley's face was red as she blurted her recollection of the memory. She then covered her face with her hands, sighing. "I didn't *mean* to. You know I'd never play games with these guys. I knew it was wrong, but I couldn't help it. I *love* Ethan, yet I had convinced Kyle that I liked him to keep a closer eye on him. I finally told him a bit of the truth that night – about how he's a witch and all — then finally clarified everything with him during lunch today. But I can't admit to his face that my feelings are *fake*."

I nodded slowly, understanding where she was coming from. "So, now, you can finally teach him some magic. That's good. Does he know that you're Adley?"

"Fuck, *no!*" Adley stared at me for a moment as if I had two heads. "He knows I'm a demon and that he's needed for this plan, but that's it."

"You think Ethan will keep his mouth shut about your kiss?"

Adley looked away from my eyes. "*Well,* I *may* have erased his memory of the moment he had spent with me," she admitted, slowly cracking her knuckles. "At least I'm using my demon abilities for the better."

Silence hung over us as we stared into the distance. I was proud of Adley's maturity — not that I *wanted* to admit it. After the way she had behaved when I came out to her, I wasn't so sure she was able to take things seriously.

The way she had looked at me as if my feelings *weren't* real...

"I guess we'll both end up alone," Adley laughed sadly. "We'll always have each other, though. We can be those ladies who live together in a beach house and have fifty cats."

"Why, because you don't think Jessi and I can be together?" I snapped, taking immediate offense. Adley jumped, shocked out of her daze. "God, you act like my feelings for Jessi aren't real."

"Anna, not this again," Adley sighed, raking a hand

through her dark hair. "Sure, I don't get how your feelings can be real. I mean, have you *met* Jessi? She's a bitch, and she's not a–"

"A *guy*?" My voice cracked on the last word, and my body shook in anger. "A guy? *Really?* Adley, how could you possibly *say* that?" I bit my lip, trying to hold back tears as I collected my thoughts. "When I came out to you, you made me feel as if I didn't know who I was. But I *do*, and though sometimes I wish that my feelings were simpler, they aren't. I don't control how I *feel* about people.

"When I met Jessi, I tried to deny what I thought I was feeling. I told myself that I was just longing to feel loved, and I pushed myself toward other guys. No matter how hard I tried convincing myself out of what I was thinking, though, I *couldn't*. I *still* can't. Though I may be attracted to guys, I can't help but wish that *her* arms could be wrapped around me. That-that *her* lips could be on mine." A tear slowly slid down my cheek before it splashed onto the collar of my shirt. I was breathing deeply, my heart racing.

Saying the truth aloud made me feel better. But it also made everything so much more real.

I *loved* Jessi.

I looked over at Adley, her lips moving but no words coming out. "I didn't mean that," she responded a few moments later. "I was just going to say that she's not a good person. Anna, I will *always* love you for who you are. You know that, right?"

I wanted to nod, but I couldn't.

"If that means you like guys, you like girls, or you like *both*. I just hate that it's *Jessi* you've fallen for." Adley laughed softly as she toyed with the hem of her gray t-shirt. "I guess that's the difference between us. You like to see the good in people, but I like to see the truth."

"I don't try to see the good in *everyone*," I snapped, though I was laughing with relief.

"Like who?" Adley crossed her arms over her chest, ready to prove me wrong.

"Nate Tucker."

"I don't think *anyone* can see the good in that douchebag," she laughed, lifting the sudden awkwardness. "I can't *believe* I ever dated him."

"He was different back in ninth grade. At least, he *pretended* to be. He seemed like a good guy."

"And that's why *you* hooked up with him?"

The question struck me by surprise, and I felt my face go hot. I hadn't thought about that week in ages. "It's a long story–"

"Which you *haven't* yet explained. So, why don't you start talking?" Adley leaned back, a smirk now on her lips.

"Well," I began, jogging my memory of the long-ago moment. "It all happened during the ninth-grade spring break. You were gone to Chicago with your family and had just broken up with Nate. For *what*, again? Not lending you lunch money on the last day of school before the break."

"I was only asking for *three* dollars. It wasn't that hard to do," Adley protested with a smile.

"Anyway, we had crossed paths at Monet's Drugmart the Monday after, and he told me how upset he was about the breakup. We then started talking, and we ended up buying hot chocolate together and taking a walk.

Nate was sad about you, and I was still sad about the recent breakup I had with... what's his name? Oh, Scott, *yeah*." I forced a smile, though I knew it was terrible that I couldn't remember the names of my exes. "I didn't feel bad because I knew you had broken up with Nate, and you were out of town..."

"But when things got serious?" Adley prompted, and I sighed.

"When things began to get serious, however, I told Nate that we should tell you. He silenced me, though, and told me that he wanted to stay a secret. I didn't get why, but I went along with it. It was the night that we were going to *do it* that things changed. I'll never forget that night," I added, looking at the ground in shame. "It was supposed to be a memorable night, and though it was, it only destroyed the rest of my life."

"This movie's getting lame," Nate whispered into my ear, his warm breath sending shivers down my spine. "Are you tired?"

I lay curled in a ball on the sofa as we watched Scary Movie *– Nate's pick. My head was resting on a throw pillow, while my feet were propped up on Nate's legs. He continued to trace the side of my bare legs with a finger, making me tremble so much that I pressed my knees together to try to stop.*

He seemed to notice but continued since I wasn't saying anything.

The front door had just slammed shut, so it was now quiet in my house. My parents had decided to go out for dinner together, and somehow, they didn't seem worried about leaving a fifteen-year-old girl and boy home alone.

Well, Ethan was hiding somewhere, but he practically wasn't there.

My family thought that Nate and I were just friends. No one knew that it was anything more because Nate wasn't ready to share with the world his new girlfriend. He and Adley had just broken up four days ago, after all. It came with some perks, like easily getting the house to ourselves, but I hated lying to my best friend, even if she was out of town.

I nodded slowly, trying to decide what I was wanting to reply with. I was insanely bored, no matter how hard I tried to focus on the terrible movie that we were watching. "What do you suppose we do, then?" I finally asked, smiling mischievously before he kissed me.

Kissing him back, I blindly fumbled for the remote with the hand that wasn't holding onto the back of Nate's neck. I then paused the movie as he pushed me back against the couch's arm. We continued to kiss intensely, the soft pressure of his lips on mine making me dizzy.

His fingers combed through the roots of my hair, his body pressed against mine...

I wanted the feeling to never end.

"I'm ready," I said shakily against his lips, only noticing afterward what I had said. I didn't regret it, however, when Nate sat back up with a wide grin.

"Are you sure?" It didn't seem as if he wasn't ready. It was as if he had already done it before, which wouldn't have shocked me.

"Yeah," I exhaled, smiling as I slid my hand down his arm slowly. "Yeah, I want you, Nate Tucker."

Without another thought, I turned the TV off. Then, we made our way upstairs, Nate leading me as if I didn't know the way to my own bedroom.

Once we entered the room and I closed the door, Nate raised an eyebrow. "Wait, isn't Ethan—"

"He won't leave his pathetic idea of a workshop. Don't worry," I insisted as I walked over to my bed, which Nate sat on the corner of. "Now, kiss me already."

The doubt vanishing like a flick of a switch, Nate pulled me on top of him, and we continued to kiss, Nate slipping his tongue to meet mine. His hand slowly slid down my leg, and a moan slipped out of me before I could control myself. Just his touch drove me wild, and this weird and indescribable feeling squirmed around inside my body while his kisses traveled down my neck.

After a while, I sat up and pulled my tank top over my head. My ring got stuck on the shirt's lace trimming, so Nate had to assist me. Just during the moment of taking off my shirt, I knew that I couldn't stand leaving his lips for air.

I wanted them more than oxygen.

I leaned down and kissed his neck, my fingers toying with the hair on the nape of his neck. He then pushed me over and kissed my chest, tugging off his white t-shirt afterward. I pressed a hand to his tanned chest, overwhelmed by his beauty. We continued to kiss until my lips felt numb and sore, and I pulled away, sighing and taking a breath of air. Once he'd gotten the message to get off me, Nate sat up and stared into my eyes.

I then turned around and moved my hair to the side, displaying the hooks of my bra. Nate began to un-do the hooks, and the two white straps slid down my shoulders and off my arms. Nate's finger then traced down the curve of my spine, making me whimper–

I felt Nate's finger leave my back, and I looked around to see him standing up on the other side of my bed, his eyes bigger than I had ever seen them before. "Fuck!" he gasped, a hand covering his mouth as he stared at my back.

"Wh-What is it?" My eyes widened in fear as my heart thumped faster in my chest, afraid but unsure about what he was looking at.

I stared into the full-length mirror on my closet door, my curls frizzy and my upper body bare. I crossed my arms over my chest, insecurity leaking through my fear for a quick moment. I then turned to the side, trying to look at my back through the mirror.

"It's... it's your back. There are these lines..." Nate kept trailing off as if he couldn't believe what he was seeing.

I stood up and walked over to him. "What lines?" I asked, grabbing my phone and handing it to Nate.

He then turned on the phone's camera and moved my hair for a second to take a picture. When he handed the phone back to me, I saw the image on the screen and cried in horror, almost dropping the device as I realized what he was talking about.

On each side of where my spinal cord was, there were two, long scars.

I tapped around frantically on my back, trying to find the marks but failing. "What the fuck? I haven't done anything to get these," I cried, hyperventilating. "I-I don't understand." I sat down and took a few deep breaths, trying to stop the tears in my eyes from escaping.

"Actually, you did do something," Nate mumbled as grabbed my white bathrobe from the back of my bedroom door and handed it to me.

I tugged it on, covering myself while Nate sat down next to me. "What?" I laughed, confused by the sudden accusation.

"It's…" Nate sighed, looking at the ground and shaking his head. "God, I can't believe this."

"Believe what?" My palms were so sweaty that I began to continuously rub them against the sides of my bathrobe.

"It's a long story."

I waited for him to elaborate. When he didn't, I screamed, "Tell me the fucking story, Nathaniel."

That's when he stated as bluntly as ever, "Annabeth, you're an angel."

He then dove into an insane story that I couldn't quite understand about a world with demons and angels that were battling to rule Earth. Apparently, I was an angel who was supposedly sent to kill the evil beings on Earth. He admitted how he was a witch – his entire family was – and so was Ivy. That's why he knew so much. He told me how the faint lines were scars from where my wings should have been, but since I had infused my light and power into a human baby, my wings had disappeared, leaving scars behind many years later.

At first, I thought he was screwing with me. But after a while, everything began to make sense. It terrified me so much that I stood up, storming over to the bedroom door.

"Get out," I whispered at first, but then, I repeated it louder. "Get the hell out of my house!"

"But Anna—"

"Stop!" I cried, a tear rolling down my cheek. "None of this can be real. Supernaturals don't exist. I don't know what you're on. Get out of my house, or else."

Nate stood up cautiously, his hands up in innocence. "I'm not trying to scare you, Anna. It's about time you found out the truth—"

"Oh, stop with that lie! I can't take it anymore." I knew that he was right about everything, but I couldn't let it be true. I wouldn't accept it. "Leave or else."

"Or else what?" he pushed, crossing his arms over his chest and staring into my eyes.

"Or else I'll tell Adley about us."

"You wouldn't sacrifice your friendship with her for—"

"You don't know what I would sacrifice! Just leave and make this easier on all of us."

He hovered in the doorway of the bedroom as he watched my body tremble. I knew that what I was doing was wrong — that he just wanted me to know about what was out there.

But I couldn't deal with it now.

Plus, a part of me was pissed that he hadn't told me sooner. By the way that he was talking, he'd had a good feeling about my angelic powers for some time.

"Fine, have it your way," Nate said before walking down the staircase.

I didn't even give him time to leave before slamming

the bedroom door shut angrily. I then pulled myself over to my wrinkle-sheeted bed and flopped onto the pillows.

For a second, I wanted to punch the pillows since the thought of Nate burned me like fire. But I burst into tears, curling into a ball and crying until I had nothing left inside me.

"I broke up with him that Friday," I told Adley as I stared down at my leather boots in shame. "I called him over and lied straight to his face, deciding to act as if I didn't believe him. I said he was delusional. He tried to argue, but I left before he could say anything convincing.

"At least, that was how things had been left between us before I accepted that everything he had said was true. I then got back in contact with him secretly, and that was when he and Ivy roped me into their lives and told me about what you are." I smiled sadly and Adley, who sighed in comprehension.

"And you began to threaten them about telling me the truth..." Adley trailed off, biting her bottom lip pensively. "We still don't get how the marks suddenly appeared, though. Maybe they became darker with age?" It was my turn to sigh, frustrated by the crazy life I had been tossed into. "All of this to say, I guess you can't trust anyone anymore."

"No kidding. As we've learned, people are always hiding something," Adley laughed bitterly. "And people always wondered why I had trust issues. That's all thanks to Jessi – no offence." Adley caught me wince, and she sighed into her hands. "She just… she knows that I killed you because right before I died, she had overheard a conversation between me and Damion."

"That's why you said you could go to jail…" I trailed off, everything finally making sense. "Why didn't you say something sooner?"

"Because… why make a thing out of it? You know the truth, Anna." Adley glanced into the distance, blowing a curl out of her face. "We're dead. And even if this plan works out… things won't go back to normal. Adley and Anna will still be gone forever."

Chapter 23
Adley
A Show to Remember

Are you ready, or what?" Ivy hissed, her tone laced with annoyance.

I turned around in my short, navy-blue dress that I hoped might get Ethan to glance my way – as much as I should have been wanting Kyle to be looking at me. After glancing in the mirror, I spotted Ivy barging into the motel room and slamming the door shut behind her.

She definitely didn't seem to be in a good mood, and I couldn't blame her. It was the evening of the school play, and Ivy was going to be forced to watch her boyfriend kiss his ex in front of the entire school.

I hated any kind of play or musical, but I was actually *excited* to see this one unfold.

Plus, Ethan was supposed to be going. How could I *not* go?

"Yeah, I'm ready," I replied to Ivy as I slipped on my black flats and grabbed my purse. We then exited the motel, closing the lights behind us and entering the dark evening.

Since Ivy didn't own a car, we were forced to walk over to the school. Though I was used to commuting that way, it felt different in just the glow of the street lamps. We didn't talk for half the walk, but eventually, I was tired of the awkwardness.

"So." I paused, then glanced over at Ivy to see if I had grabbed her attention. However, her eyes were still glued to her phone. "That plan of yours... *Why* haven't you cared to share it?"

The abrupt question was what made Ivy's head snap up, and her eyes glared my way. "Because it's none of your damn business."

"You keep saying that, but I feel like since I'm part of the plan, I have the right—"

"Look, we need a virgin witch. That's all you need to know."

"*Okay.*" I tried to think of a better way to get the truth out of her. "What's the *point* of this spell? There's *always* a reason."

"A *reason?*" Ivy laughed as if this was a stupid thing to say. "I have no fucking clue, okay? Let's just say that I was asked to do this."

"But *why*—?"

Before she could snap at me again, I was cut off by Ivy's annoyingly loud ringtone. She then answered the call in a peppy voice, and I knew exactly who was on the receiving end.

"Hey, Natty Boo. Sorry, we're almost there." Ivy narrowed her poison-green eyes at me before quickly walking ahead of me on the sidewalk as if to have some privacy.

I rolled my eyes, frustrated. I *had* to know what this plan was about! If only there was a way that I could see into that twisted brain of hers...

That's it.

Along with telekinesis, you can read minds when you touch someone and focus on their thoughts, and you can control the minds of non-supernatural beings.

Ivy had told me this in Crystal Lake a while ago, and I couldn't believe that I had forgotten about my *powers*.

Reading minds.

Ivy and I arrived at Ember Falls High and entered through the front doors to see a line-up forming near the bottom auditorium doors. There, I spotted Calvin, Dylan, and Kyle, who were standing at the back of the line.

"Jenna, hey!" Kyle exclaimed as Ivy and I joined them.

I forced a smile, especially when Ivy nudged my shoulder a little too hard. I knew I was slipping out of character, but after seeing the way Kyle boiled with rage when Ethan admitted his feelings for me – Jenna – I couldn't see Kyle the same way.

I shrugged the feeling off, knowing that it wasn't helping. "Hey, are you guys ready for the show?"

"Uh, *yeah*," Dylan remarked in an overly dramatic tone. "It's going to be *too good* getting to see Mr. Tucker play a *romantic*. It's just too bad Aurora has to be the one to get kissed by him." Dylan sighed before looking in Ivy's direction almost cautiously, which made Ivy laugh.

"*God*, you look at me like I'm plotting your murder," she stated, and we all laughed, though my reaction felt forced. "You can speak about my boyfriend however you like. I love him for who he is."

"Which is a douchebag who can barely count to *ten*?" Dylan snickered.

This time, Ivy's face flushed red with fury. "I didn't say it was a *free-for-all*—"

"So, I'm guessing Ethan is already backstage?" I remarked, remembering how he and Jessi had applied to work behind the scenes like they always did. I also hoped that cutting Ivy off would prevent the conversation from continuing – she had already killed enough people in one school year.

"You haven't heard?" Dylan looked my way with concerned eyes. "Ethan hasn't been at school all week."

"What?" I questioned, blinking hard in disbelief. I didn't want to act as if I cared too much, though, so I toned back my reaction. "I-I hope he's okay."

"Yeah, we do too," Calvin added as Kyle glared at the ground. "He hasn't responded to any of our texts or calls. He was fine last weekend, but ever since the night that we hung out... I don't know."

"Anyway, we should get inside," Kyle suggested, wrapping an arm around my shoulders as the line moved forward.

I tried to mirror his smile, though I had a pretty good idea why Ethan hadn't been at school.

The first part of the play had been hilariously good. There

were many issues with the script involving gender roles, but I couldn't lie and say that I *wasn't* enjoying myself. The best part was watching Ivy cringe every moment that Nate and Anna had to be "romantic" with each other. The moments distracted her so much, though, that I knew it would be then that would work best to simply slip into her mind and find out the truth about this plan.

I just had to choose my moment.

It was during the classic balcony scene that seemed the most appropriate. A balcony of clouds had been built on the stage, and Anna looked gorgeous in her long, red velvet dress. Once Nate joined the scene, however, I was taken aback by his *rapping.*

They made him rap. *I can't believe this.*

Her name is Josie,
if only she could know me.
She is the East and the West,
better than the rest.
Too good-looking for me,
as I'm barely royalty.
If only we hadn't met,
I wouldn't be so upset.
I love her to the moon and back,
and if only she knew the slightest of that.

The audience and I were laughing so hard, and though I couldn't tell how Ivy was reacting to her boyfriend's awful performance, I knew her thoughts were nothing positive. That was why I knew I wouldn't find a better moment than this one to slip into her mind.

I closed my eyes and lightly touched Ivy's arm, hoping that she wouldn't realize anything. I then took deep breaths and cleared my mind, focusing on reading her thoughts. Once I was able to tap into that mindset, though, I was overwhelmed by a thousand exclamations in her mind.

"Oh, what are you doing? *You just fucked up that line!* Why *are we dating?"*

It took some effort, but finally, I was able to grab hold of the small thought that was still lingering in her mind.

The meaning behind the plan.

My head began to ache since reading Ivy's mind was taking so much of my energy, but even as the pain grew, I knew that I couldn't back out now–

"How can she not leave it alone? It doesn't even involve her… It's just between me and my mother – our family…"

What? I tried to stay focused on hearing her thoughts, but my own questions were bubbling to the surface. *Ivy's mom is a witch too? What does* she *have to do with any of this?*

"It's not my fault she asked me to do this. My mother just wants to get revenge for the death of my father–"

I let go of Ivy since my head ached too much to concentrate any longer. My thoughts then raced through my mind, making me feel dizzy.

The poisonous apple never falls far from the twisted tree, I guess.

The scene from the play was over, I realized, as I snapped back to reality. The audience clapped as the curtains closed, and the room went dark again.

I could feel Ivy's eyes on me as she asked, "Are you okay? I was expecting some commentary from that scene."

"Yeah," Kyle remarked from my other side, and I could hear him fidget in his chair. "What's up?"

Clearly, no one had noticed a thing, and I was able to breathe again. I knew there was more to find out, but I had enough intel for now.

"I'm okay. I just have a bad headache," I lied, rubbing my temples before searching through my purse for something.

The lights for the next scene went on just as I pulled out an orange, see-through pill bottle. I always dragged one around with a few pills in it just in case, especially since I had more headaches than normal after coming back to life. Every time I fell upon the bottle, though–

What in the world are you doing? *You take* two *pills, Adley – not* four.

It felt like a sin even taking *one* as Ethan's words echoed in the back of my head.

I shoved the pill bottle into my purse. I knew that I wouldn't be at risk of overdosing, but I realized then that I preferred putting up with the pain.

Headaches didn't last forever, but one false move and a mistake could be permanent.

Chapter 24
Ethan
You Can't Love Her Back to Life

I wasn't sure what exactly had brought me to Ember's Bridge, but there I was, leaning against the rickety railing as the harsh sounds of the current rushed into my ears. The wind picked up, blowing dead leaves and gravel across the forest floor and making me shiver. The sky was dark and the park was empty except for the few birds that would fly by occasionally. The only light came from the flickering lamp post above the bridge, along with the bright full moon.

My head burned with memories that I wanted to forget, making me feel dizzy and overwhelmed. I kept glancing down at my phone every few minutes, feeling stupid because though I had received a few texts from the guys who were questioning my whereabouts – not that I even believed they cared – all I had hoped for was one special person to message me and ask how I was.

But that wasn't her job. She was Kyle's girlfriend, not mine.

And that was why I hadn't been to school all week,

and that was why I had abandoned the play. I didn't want to face my friends – *especially* Kyle. I was too embarrassed after the other night when I had admitted that I had feelings for Jenna – Kyle's fucking *girlfriend*, of all people.

I had always known that I was fucked up, but that was a low blow, even for me.

I closed my eyes as if that would erase the fact that my life had been a complete mess since the day my sister died.

Since Adley died–

I kicked the railing of the bridge with my shin, then winced in pain. However, the burn only made me feel more alive when my emotions had felt so numb recently. The more I thought about everyone and everything that I'd lost, the less I was able to feel – to *care* – about.

There wasn't *anyone* or *anything* left for me.

I was alone.

I had Jessi who wasn't mad at me anymore, but how long was *that* going to last? I just keep doing things to fuck up everyone else's life.

Maybe it would have been better if I just *didn't* exist...

I let out a cry as the wind picked up, trying to release my pent up anger and frustration. My body shook, and tears slipped from my eyes as my vision blurred for a moment. I leaned over the railing of the bridge, staring down at the rushing water.

I wondered what it might have been like to fall into those inescapable rapids.

I wondered who would even miss me if I just so

happened to lean a *little* too far over the railing—

"Ethan!" a panicked voice cried from behind.

The disappointment that took over me scared me more than ever.

It could have been over.

All of it.

Why did someone have to show up now? *Do they even care–?*

"Ethan, *please*, get down."

I recognized the sweet tone—

The realization shook me, and I looked down and noticed that, in my haze, I had climbed the railing of the bridge. I was wobbling inches away from tumbling into the angry rapids.

And Jenna was now nearby, scared out of her mind.

Black spotted my vision, and I swayed, unable to control my balance – not caring to try and stand up, not *wanting* to—

Just as I felt air below one of my feet, about to fall off the bridge, two arms pulled me backward. I tumbled onto the wooden bridge, smacking my spine and head against the hard surface. My eyes drifted shut as tears continued to pour down my face. My body shook uncontrollably.

I was this *close to—*

It could have been over.

"Ethan," Jenna breathed, her voice wavering as I felt her stroke the side of my cheek, wiping my tears away. "Are you okay?"

Yes, of course. I'm perfectly fine, I wanted to tell her.

But I couldn't. I *wasn't* fine, or okay, or even *happy.*

I hadn't been in a long time.

"No," I whispered, my words barely audible. I couldn't look her in the eye since I felt too embarrassed. I felt like a coward for not wanting to face my issues.

I'm not okay.

Jenna pulled me into her arms, then squeezed me so tightly as if she was afraid that if she let go, I would try to end my life again.

Maybe I would. But momentarily, I had no energy left to try.

It could have been over.

I'm not okay.

"It's okay. It's all going to *be* okay," she reminded me, and I tried to focus on her voice and the softness of her winter jacket against my ice-cold face.

"Help me," I pleaded into her jacket. "*Please*, help me. I can't feel like this anymore. I'm *tired*."

I was about to give in to the blackness when Jenna grabbed my hands. "Look at me," she demanded forcefully. "Ethan, *look at me*." I met her stare, still shaking uncontrollably and breathing in short gasps. "Breathe, Ethan," she told me, keeping her eyes locked with mine.

"I-I *can't*."

"Yes, you *can*. Just copy me, okay?" She took a long, deep breath. I tried my hardest to copy her but failed and continued to hyperventilate. "Come *on*! You've gotta *breathe*!" I took a shallow, shaky breath, trying to find a normal rhythm. "That's it," Jenna encouraged. "Again."

I forced myself to take a deep breath.

Then another.

And another.

Finally, I managed to regain a normal breathing pattern. The black spots started to subside, leaving me with a clearer image of the distressed Jenna sitting with me.

I licked my lips nervously. "I-I'm sorry—"

"Does anyone know?"

"Kn-Know what?" I stuttered, unable to think clearly.

"Know about how you've been feeling." Jenna licked her lips, looking from me to the bridge. She inhaled deeply. "Ethan, I almost lost you – *we* almost lost you. If you need help—"

"Don't say *we*!" I shouted, my hands balling into fists. "I don't have anyone left."

"But you-your parents, and Jessi, and the guys—"

"I don't have the guys, okay? None of them care about me, *especially* Kyle... I don't deserve them, anyway."

"*Ethan*—"

"I *betrayed* him, okay?" I choked on my saliva, my mouth dry from crying and my head pounding in pain. "I-I have feelings for his *girlfriend*, and he knows," I blurted, too overwhelmed to think straight.

Fuck.

"And, well, now, so do *you*." I didn't give Jenna time to comment. "And Jessi's only talking to me because she doesn't have anyone else. I've always been the second-best Landers. No one has ever loved me besides..." I trailed off, unable to say her name.

Adley.

"I miss her, I miss her so fucking much. I just wish that someone still cared about me. Why-why live if no one *wants* me? I just keep ruining things for everyone, and I'm only wanted when I'm useful, and—"

"Stop." Jenna took a breath, and so did I. "What about *me*?"

"You love Kyle, remember?"

"That-that doesn't mean you don't matter to me." Jenna lifted my face, and I looked into her sparkling eyes. "Ethan Landers, you matter so much to me. And if you leave me… I'll never forgive myself."

The way we connected in the moment – the way our eyes locked… I felt as if I had known her *forever*.

How could a girl that I barely know care about me so much–?

"How long have you been feeling this way?" she questioned.

I couldn't even remember the last time I had felt happy. "Since-since November, maybe. I-I don't remember."

"And nobody knows?" When I shook my head, Jenna sighed deeply, hugging me harder. "I-I'm going to help you through this, okay? We are going to find someone who knows what to do so that you can talk to them. And I'll always be here if you need—"

"I-I don't think I should be talking to you. I don't want to make Kyle hate me more than he already does."

"Oh, okay, then." Disappointment and hurt filled her voice, only tugging at my heart more. "We'll find you someone who knows more – who can help more than I can."

I nodded slowly as she spoke. "I-I'm sorry—"

"Don't apologize, okay? This isn't your fault."

"But it *is*—"

"No, it's *not*." Jenna tucked a long strand of dark hair behind her ear. "Just, please, if you ever… try to *jump*—"

"I won't," I interrupted, feeling my cheeks burn. "You-you aren't going to tell anyone about this, right?"

"I won't if you promise to talk to the school's counselor on Monday."

I sighed, despising the idea but knowing that she was probably right.

I *needed* help.

"Okay." A few moments later, I whispered, "Will I ever be okay again?"

Jenna sniffled. "Were we *ever* okay?"

Chapter 25
Adley

It Will Painfully Be Clear Soon Enough

It had taken me a while, but finally, I came upon Nate's locker. It hadn't been hard to find the blue, rusted locker in the senior hallway, especially since *NT & IB 4Eva* was scratched into the chipping paint.

I rolled my eyes as I knelt on the floor, then turned the lock until the locker door popped open. I had visited Nate's locker a thousand times while dating him, so it helped since I remembered the lock combination by heart.

I glanced down the hallway to make sure that no one was coming – especially *Nate*, who was in math class while I had a free period, and who was unaware that I was about to steal the spellbook.

Then, I took a deep breath.

Nate always talked about how he brought the book to school so that it could help him with his chemistry homework – though we all knew that it wasn't *that* powerful.

That was why it had to be there, and I *needed* that spellbook – I had kinda accidentally told Kyle in class that I already had it, after all. He had been talking about how we would have his house to ourselves that night, and I knew that there wouldn't have been a better opportunity to teach him a few spells.

Once the coast was clear, I opened the locker to see inside–

I gaped, taken aback by the monstrosity that the locker was. There was a pile of folded papers stacking up from the bottom, Nate's jacket and school bag were hung up sloppily on the two hooks provided, and both shelves were bombarded with ripped notebooks. I was able to spot Rice Crispy Square rappers shoved between binders, a few empty smashed plastic water bottles decorated the floor, and the odor did *not* smell natural, especially near the black drawstring gym bag and Nike running shoes.

However, I smiled in relief when I spotted the leather-bound book wedged between a couple of notebooks on the top shelf. I slipped it out of its spot like a sensitive bomb, then cradled the book in my arms as I closed the locker.

It was *done*.

"Hey, Jenna," I heard a voice call, and I jumped in my skin, almost dropping the book. When the voice registered, though, I realized that it wasn't Nate or Ivy, and I spun around to come face-to-face with Ethan.

Startled, I pressed a hand to my chest as if that would calm my racing heart. "God, Ethan! You scared the shit out of me," I exclaimed as he walked up to me. I forced a smile as I tried shoving the spellbook inside my leather jacket discreetly. "I'm happy you're back at school."

"Yeah, me too…" Ethan trailed off, then glanced up at the locker number. "Um, what are you doing here? I thought your locker was in the E-Wing of the school–"

"I was getting something from a friend," I blurted, cursing Ethan for being so observant.

"Isn't this *Nate's* locker, though?" Ethan leaned closer toward the locker, then laughed when he spotted the engraved initials.

"What's with all the questions?" I snapped, and Ethan's eyes widened in shock. I felt myself blush, then bit my bottom lip. "I mean–"

"Look, I know it's none of my business, but–"

Ethan was then cut off by the bell, signaling that class was over. And, right on cue, Nate exited the classroom across the hall and began walking in my direction.

"Shit," I cried, glancing under my arm, where the spellbook was still hidden under my coat. "He's coming."

"Who–?" Ethan began, but I didn't give him time to finish.

Instead, when I caught sight of the janitor's closet, I grabbed Ethan's hand and pulled him down the hallway with me. Luckily, the closet door was unlocked, and the halls were so crowded that no one caught us jumping inside the room and slamming the door.

It was so dark inside the janitor's closet. I was only able to see Ethan's silhouette with the help of the light that was coming in through the slit under the door. I dragged my hand up and down the wall closest to the door until I found a switch and flipped it up, turning the small ceiling light on and immediately spotting Ethan's body close to mine. In the silence of the room cluttered with cleaning products, I could hear his heart racing.

The sense of déjà vu was too strong, and all I could think about was Halloween night.

All I wanted to do was push Ethan up against the wall, kiss him deeply, and forget *everything*–

"Okay, *please,* explain why we're hiding in a *closet,*" Ethan cried, looking at me with wide eyes. "You're lucky I'm not claustrophobic."

"Ethan!" I yelled, slipping the spellbook out from under my arms and holding it to my chest. "Please, I just need to get this book back in my locker without Nate knowing, okay?"

"What is that, anyway?"

"It's nothing."

"Uh, if it was *nothing,* you wouldn't mind being caught with it."

I sighed in frustration. "Fine, it's, um… It's his *diary.*"

To my surprise, Ethan believed it more than I thought he would. "You're *kidding,*" he laughed, bending over to catch his breath. "Wow, what a–"

"This is *not* the time for insults," I snapped, then pressed my ear against the door. I closed my eyes, trying to see if I could hear any ruckus in the halls.

I was just about to open the door to the silent hallway when I heard squeaky wheels rolling on the tiles. The sound was growing louder every second.

It's the janitor with his mop bucket.

The jingling sound of keys came next, and I started to panic. I paced back and forth in front of Ethan, breathing heavily as I tried to think of another plan.

"Wh-What is it?" Ethan whispered, tensing up at the sight of my breakdown. "Are you okay–?"

I shushed him, pressing a finger to his lips. My heart skipped a beat at the action, and a sudden idea then came to mind. I knew it was far-fetched, but it was also probably so crazy that it might have just gotten us out of the janitor's closet with a free pass.

"Ethan," I mumbled, wrapping my arms around his waist and pulling him closer. My heart was beating so fast that I wouldn't have been surprised if Ethan could hear it wanting to jump out of my ribcage. "Do you trust me?"

"Sure–"

As the closet door flew open, almost smacking us in the head, I held Ethan's face and kissed him hard. Ethan seemed taken aback at first, and he was about to lean away from me until he realized that *this* was my plan.

To make the janitor feel so uncomfortable that he would let us off easily.

Maybe the kiss only lasted for a second, but the familiar feeling of his lips on mine as he kissed me back softly drove me insane.

It only fueled me and reminded me why I was doing all of this.

For *him*.

"What the *hell*!" roared the janitor in his navy blue jumpsuit, just like I had hoped he would. Ethan jumped away from me, licking his lips and gazing down at the ground cowardly. I copied him, though I had to try harder not to laugh.

"We're so sorry," I said sheepishly.

"Yeah, whatever," the janitor remarked, combing a hand through his thin, salt-and-pepper colored hair. "You kids do this all the time. Just leave before I decide to send you to the principal's office."

Trying to hide my smile, I darted for the exit, grabbing Ethan's hand and bringing him with me. The halls were empty, so we were lucky to not be seen by anyone else. With five minutes until classes would start, I walked toward my locker, the spellbook snug in my jacket again.

"So, are you going to try explaining what that just was?" Ethan called out, and I glanced back to see his mouth twisted in confusion.

I suddenly remembered the night at the bridge, and my smile then dropped – his body so close to the edge of the bridge, his uncontrollable shaking–

We weren't supposed to be *talking*, let alone…

God, I'm supposed to be helping *him, not giving him more issues! It's enough that I was the reason he–*

No. You can't think that way.

"It was acting," I stated, trying to brush off the moment. "Thanks for playing along. Just pretend that it never happened."

"You think that's possible?"

No, I wanted to say. *But what other choice do we have?*

"Jeeze, this is *huge*," Kyle exclaimed, flipping through the pages of the spellbook as he took a seat next to me on his basement floor.

We had just set up a circle of white candles on the floor, which were now lit and flickering, casting an almost romantic glow in the dark basement. With the fireplace next to the leather couches, it was nice and cozy – and the perfect ambiance for casting spells.

I grabbed the spellbook from Kyle, eager to look inside. On the way to his house, I had searched for spells to try, but it had been hard when walking in the dark streets. There were also too many spells to count, and some were more common than others.

"I know, I don't even know where to start..." I trailed off, glancing at the book's old pages.

It was hard when I knew that Kyle didn't have the full story about what was actually going on. If he knew what was happening, or if I was a witch myself, I would have leaned him toward a spell that was more useful than fun. But since I didn't have powers and had only picked up on a few techniques after watching Nate and Ivy perform rituals countless times over the last few months, I had no idea what spell to teach him.

"Well," Kyle started, taking the book out of my hands and placing it down in front of us, "there are protection charms, cleansing rituals–"

"Which are labeled under *'advanced,'*" I pointed out, underlining the word with my finger. "Why don't we start at the section for beginners?"

"*Right,*" Kyle mumbled, blushing as he flipped to the start of the book. "Okay, there are spells for speed, lock picking, healing... Or how about a memory spell? This one clears your mind to help you remember what you forgot."

My eyes widened at the idea, and a smile tugged at my lips.

That's perfect.

I knew instantly that it would help with what I needed most – recalling the night that I had killed Annabeth.

"Give me the book," I demanded, pulling it closer to me before Kyle could get the chance to pass it over. I skimmed the old, torn pages, looking to see what we'd need for the spell. "Sounds pretty simple," I stated, ransacking through the basket of ingredients I had bought off a very sketchy website with Nate's credit card. "It says here that we need salt, rosemary, and crushed amethyst, which I have all in here." I stuck my hands in the basket and pulled out three cork-stopper glass vials, which I placed on the other side of the book.

"Okay, let's do this." Kyle cracked his knuckles, preparing himself. "Whose memory are we trying to restore?"

"We're restoring mine."

"*Yours?* What, did you forget again where you put your chemistry textbook?" Kyle teased, elbowing my arm playfully.

"I want to… *confirm* something, okay?"

"Okay, fine. But I'm next." Kyle then slid over the mortar and pestle that he had taken from the kitchen. "What do we have to do?"

"What *you* have to do is mix those three ingredients, form a circle with the products, and" –I glanced over at the spell, then winced– "add three drops of blood from the person you're doing the spell on."

Kyle's face paled at the mention of blood. Shakily, he asked, "Um, are-are you okay with that?"

I nodded, almost laughing about how concerned he was about a few drops of blood.

Without another word, Kyle ground together the ingredients with shaking hands before pouring the products into the center of the circle of the five lit candles. He then used his fingers to shape the product into an outline of a circle.

Afterward, looking up at me as if giving me the signal to do so, I took out the sharp kitchen knife from the basket. Facing my left palm toward the ceiling, I slowly pressed the blade into my skin, wincing, and dragged the blade across my palm. A line of dark red appeared, and blood bubbled to the surface as I handed Kyle the bloody knife to wipe with a cloth. I then made a fist above the center of the salt circle, and three drops dripped from the cut before I shook my hand in hopes that the cut's burning would go away.

"Hey, let me help," Kyle offered, and I gave him my hand, which he cleaned with a wet cloth and bandaged.

"Thanks," I whispered, then backed away before any butterflies could flutter in the pit of my stomach.

"Okay, it's done," Kyle exclaimed, dusting off his hands. "This is when I close my eyes and chant some voodoo shit, right?"

"You've observed well," I giggled, looking closely at the spellbook. "Okay, just repeat after me. You can channel me." I stood up, moved to sit opposite him, and gave him my hands over the circle, which he grabbed before closing his eyes.

Then, together we chanted loudly.

Water and air,
Sweat and blood.
Bring to light
The memory that was once none.

The more the chant was repeated, the more my head ached with an indescribable pressure. It was as if a fog was being lifted from my brain, and I could finally see clearly again.

But soon, my body started getting tired and numb. I swayed back and forth, the power too strong to handle as it coursed through my veins.

I must stay awake. I must stay strong.

Once the candle flames went out, though, I couldn't hold on. I dropped Kyle's hands and closed my eyes.

All I felt before my vision went black was my back hitting the floor.

The bedroom was dark besides the bright light radiating from the full moon, which shined in through the open bedroom window. The pink curtains blew in the breeze as I lay on the floor, snug in my sleeping bag next to Anna. I watched as she kept tossing and turning restlessly, while Jessi snored at the opposite end of the room.

I couldn't sleep since the excitement and adrenaline from the past evening was keeping me awake. So, when Anna sat up and nudged my sleeping bag with her elbow, I turned to lay on my stomach, smiling at her. "You can't sleep either?"

I whispered as she copied my position in her sleeping bag.

"No, I never can at sleepovers," she confessed, fixing her hair so that it fell over her shoulders in perfect, golden curls. "So... I guess all we can do is talk." She licked her lips pensively. "You know, that small moment you shared with Ethan during Truth or Dare—"

"Stop," I sighed, tempted to smack her with my pillow. "It wasn't a moment. And we are not talking about Ethan like he's some guy that I've got a crush on."

"But with the way you two look at each other... It's like you're the only people in the room." I couldn't tell if Anna was shipping us or making fun of whatever she thought was going on since the giggle that followed was playful. "Pay closer attention, next time. It's obvious he likes you."

"I need water," I said abruptly, fed up with Anna's theories. We had been playing this game for years, and it was always the same conversation that went nowhere.

I was about to stand up when Anna motioned with her hand for me to stay seated. "It's okay, I've got this. I'm thirsty too – and I'm the hostess, after all."

"All right. Make it snappy," I joked, and Anna laughed softly as she disappeared into the dark hallway.

I then waited patiently for a good ten minutes, wondering how long it took to get two glasses of water. After a while, though, I got worried. So, I stood up and made my way down the stairs slowly, trying hard not to let the flooring creak and wake someone up.

"Anna?" I whispered, gripping the metal railing as I made my way downstairs. It was even darker down there, and I already hated the upstairs. It reminded me far too much

of a scene in Halloween. *"Annabeth?"*

As I approached the kitchen, the house felt strangely chilly as if a door or window had just been opened. I shivered, then rubbed my bare arms to keep warm as I entered the dining room.

"Ann—"

"Adley!" Anna remarked, glancing up from the stainless steel dishwasher. We both jumped, startled by the sight of the other. My heart raced as she then asked, "What are you doing down here?"

"I came down to check on you. I thought you were dead or something."

"Nope, all good. I just couldn't find any clean glasses and needed to search the dishwasher," Anna chuckled softly, her face flushed as she grabbed two tall glasses from the top dishwasher rack. When she shut the dishwasher, though, I could tell that something was off. Her body was shaking, and she seemed to be breathing heavily out of fear.

"Are you sure you're okay?" I looked my best friend up and down, positive that something was wrong. "You're shaking uncontrollably."

"I'm fine," *Anna announced in a whisper—*

The two glasses in her hands broke from her grip, tumbling to the floor and shattering at our feet. Anna jumped back from the mess, then looked around with wide eyes. I held my breath, trying to hear if anyone had stirred or woken up by the loud sound.

When nobody came downstairs to see what had happened, Anna and I rushed to the pile of glass. I found a pair of black leather gloves and slipped them on to protect my hands, and Anna opened the garbage can so that I could quickly drop the glass shards inside.

"Shit," Anna whispered, staring at the mess. "My parents won't notice, right?"

"You'll be fine," I told her, hoping that it would calm her down a bit. When it didn't, though, I took a deep breath. "Anna, what is going on?" I questioned as we both stood back up. But before Anna could say anything, my eyes fell on her lilac nightgown. "What happened to your clothes?" I pointed to the left side of the nightgown, which had grimy stains all over its white-lace hem.

The stains were so similar to fingerprints–

I couldn't tell anymore if Anna was talking or not, nor did I care if she was. All I could then see was red, and all I could feel was anger. It was as if a switch had flipped in my brain, and now, I was out of control. One part of me wanted to stop what I was doing – just leave, go upstairs, and get some rest.

But the other, more dominant side wanted to see bloodshed.

"Hey, Adley, are you okay?" Anna asked, her voice sounding far out. She walked over to the counter and picked up her iPhone in its peach-pink case. "You're worried about me, but you don't even look like yourself."

I stepped closer to Anna as my hands reached out uncontrollably toward her. Just as I thought I was about to hug her, though, my hands wrapped around her neck and started to squeeze.

Taken aback, Anna grabbed my shoulders and pushed me away, breathing heavily in panic as my hands let go of her. She then started frantically tapping her phone, and I realized she was about to call 911. Terrified, I smacked the phone out of her hands, sending it flying onto the counter before she could hit CALL.

"What's going on?" Anna shrieked, staring at me with wide eyes after looking over at her phone.

Anger taking over, I smiled viciously as I charged toward my victim, rattling the spoons that hung above the kitchen sink. In response, Anna backed up quickly into the corner of the counter. Her right hand fumbled behind her as if she was looking for something to defend herself with.

I was stuck in such a dark mindset that I couldn't find the exit.

And I was so far gone that I covered Anna's mouth roughly with my hand, stopping her from screaming. Anna kept fighting, squealing, and shaking, but my grip on her was so strong that she couldn't move.

"I finally have her," a cruel, familiar yet unfamiliar voice laughed in my head. "All I have to do is end her."

Smiling wickedly, I reached and pulled out a sharp knife from the knife block on the counter behind Anna. When the weapon glimmered eerily in the moonlight that poured in through the window, a rush flowed through my body.

Anna tried to pull away from me, and that was when I noticed that she seemed stuck. I looked down to realize that the hem of her nightgown was now trapped by the dish towel hook under the sink.

I have her. I really have her.

Out of control, I finally plunged the sharp kitchen knife into the side of Anna's neck the same way that I had *seen every serial killer do so on-screen. I then watched as Anna's sapphire-blue eyes widened from the impact, and an exclamation of pain escaped her lips before her legs gave out.*

I stepped back and stared as Anna's lifeless body fell to the floor. Blood poured from the injury before pooling around her neck on the ceramic floor tiles.

I was certain that she was dead. After all, victims in horror movies never survived a deep stab like that.

Relief filling my chest, I smiled as much as I wanted to bend down, check on her, and scream for help.

I couldn't do any of that, though.

I had no power over what was happening.

All I could do was watch.

I gasped, opening my eyes and sitting up fast. I looked around hastily, realizing that I was still in Kyle's basement and that the ceiling lights were now on but dimmed.

Kyle was next to me, rubbing my back to calm me down. "Hey, are you okay? That spell really knocked you out."

How can I be okay when I finally know the truth?

That night, it had been as if a switch turned on inside me – the demon coming out to play and taking over my mind. It hadn't even been *me* anymore. I still wasn't sure about the spell that had been cast on me, but it had allowed that familiar voice to take over my mind and complete the dirty deed that I couldn't do.

I had a strong feeling that I knew exactly what happened. One night, when I was asleep, Nate and Ivy cast a spell on me that gave Damion easier access to my mind so that *he* could kill the angel.

It was the only theory that made sense.

It was the only theory that could explain why I would have killed my best friend.

Chapter 26
Jessi
The Lies You Tell Yourself

This is odd. Ethan Landers *called* me, wanting to *talk*." I chuckled as I walked down the stairs of my house's wooden front porch, then sat down on one of the bottom steps. Ethan had just walked up the driveway with his sapphire-blue bike at his side, his eyes fixed on the ground as he unclasped his black helmet strap under his neck.

I didn't know he still owned a bike.

"I knew that if I didn't call before, I probably would have backed out at the last minute," he confessed as he walked over to where I stood, his shoulders slumped.

I knew something was up. "Are you okay?"

"It's funny how, all of a sudden, *everyone* is asking me that question," he laughed nervously, raking a hand through his sweaty curls. He bit his bottom lip, and his legs shook. "I need to be honest with you, Jess. Without my sister, and... *Adley*, I-I only have *you*. It took me a while to realize that-that I can't do this alone."

I raised an eyebrow, trying to wrap my mind around

and understand what Ethan was talking about. *"This?"*

"This-this *life*." Ethan took a deep breath, blowing air out between his lips. "I don't really know how to explain this—"

"So, just *say it*." I placed a hand on Ethan's knee, trying to comfort him, though it didn't seem to help as he continued shaking. "There's clearly something on your mind, and I'm here to listen."

It was silent for a long moment before Ethan whispered, "I-I think I'm depressed." Before I could even try to process what he had just admitted, he continued. "I don't really understand how I'm feeling, but there are these days when I wake up, and getting out of bed feels impossible. I question constantly why I'm here, *living*, and what's the point of it all – it isn't like it's *fun*. I'd rather stay home – where I can't get hurt – than see people. But then, when I'm alone, I overthink and start to blame all of this on myself... Like, it's *my* fault that everyone is dead, and-and maybe everything would be better if *I* wasn't here—"

"Ethan," I cried abruptly, tears stinging my eyes. I swallowed hard as his head snapped my way, and I noticed that his eyes were red. "Stop thinking these things. You *aren't* the problem, you hear me?"

Adley is. She is the reason that this all happened.

Not that I could ever admit that to Ethan...

"I *can't* stop feeling this way. I-I want to, but it isn't that easy."

I didn't know what to say.

I barely knew anything about depression. They had that mental health assembly at school after Adley's passing, but it had been hard to listen when all I was thinking about was how Adley hadn't deserved a recognition assembly after what she had done. I felt stupid for not knowing how to help Ethan now.

"I'm talking to a counselor at school. So, *please*, don't worry about me too much. I'm working toward getting better."

"Ethan, it's my job to worry about you," I laughed softly, trying to lighten the mood. I wiped the tears away from under my eyes. "I'm happy you reached out on your own, though. And if you ever need to talk, don't hesitate to call me. You know I'm always available."

Ethan's lips curved into a small smile. "Thanks, I really appreciate that. My counselor wanted me to have at least one emergency contact – someone I can rely on in case they aren't there..." Ethan started chuckling, though his face was red, and he was cupping his head in his hands. "Fuck, I'm so messed up."

I pulled Ethan closer to me, wrapping my arms around him tightly. "And, what, I'm *not*?" I mumbled into his shoulder teasingly.

"I've been depressed for three months. You can't beat me."

"At least you've accepted it." My joking tone flattened as I reflected on what Ethan had been saying before. He was in pain, I knew that much, and he was probably afraid that nobody would understand him – that he would be seen as the "depressed kid" stereotype that everyone turned this mental illness into. I, however, wasn't in pain. I was just afraid of what others would think, and it was about time that I accepted it too. "I'm more messed up than you could ever imagine, Ethan. I have been for *years* because I just can't accept the truth. I can't accept *myself*." I laughed quietly, shaking my head. "I'm sorry, this is *your* therapy session–"

"No. Please, continue. This is honestly making me feel better about myself," Ethan joked, and I laughed shakily.

My hands began to feel clammy as I searched for my words. "Well, I mean, for years, I've been hiding from myself because I knew that there were people out there who would judge me, and I was *so* afraid of that." I swallowed hard, my mouth dry. "If you can accept your flaws, though, I know that I have to. Plus, if you decide to hate me, I'll just have to live with that. I mean, you probably hate me to some degree already – who *doesn't*?"

I looked down at my lap, my heart racing.

Am I really ready to say it?

Tears pricked my eyes. "Ethan, I... I loved Annabeth." When Ethan's eyes widened, and his jaw dropped slightly, I felt my face go hot. "Oh, *God*. I shouldn't have told you that."

Just as I was about to stand up and leave, wanting to hide from the situation, Ethan grabbed my wrist. "Jessi, hey," he said gently, meeting my eyes. "I don't hate you, okay? I couldn't *ever* hate you."

Hot tears poured down my cheeks. "You *don't*?"

"Of course, not. I'm glad you finally told me." Ethan wiped the tears from my face, which only made me cry harder, and I crashed into his arms. "Nothing is *wrong* with you. I, on the other hand, don't understand why you still bother with *me*."

"Because you're my best friend, Ethan Landers," I mumbled into his shoulder, "and we both need each other more than ever now. I'm really happy that I can lean on you."

"Yeah, me too," Ethan answered, smiling shakily at me.

After a moment of silence, as the sun began to dip below the horizon and paint the blue sky with warm colors, I then questioned, "Ethan? Will... will we ever be okay?"

Ethan was quiet for another second as a cool breeze nipped at our skin. But then, he answered, "No, probably not, but I'm okay with that."

And I found myself agreeing with him.

Chapter 27
Annabeth
The Words I Wish I'd Said

Adley officially knew exactly what had happened the night she killed me, and it terrified me to know that she *had* to have been cursed. Because that meant that Ivy and Nate, as well as Damion, were keeping something else from us, and as determined as Adley and I were to figure out what happened, it was impossible to ask the witches. After all, if one of us were to question them, they'd know that Adley unlocked her memories with magic, and we knew no other witch who was willing to help us besides Kyle.

I sighed, my shoulders slumping as I arrived in front of Danny's Diner. Taking a deep breath and trying to forget about the thoughts racing through my mind, I pulled open the glass door and entered, triggering the small bell that chimed above the door.

"Hey," I heard someone call from the back booths, as the smell of bacon wafted in the air. I looked up from the ground with a small grin on my face.

Spotting Jessi at our usual booth next to the large

window, I walked over and sat across from her, pulling off my jacket. Wanting to escape the cramped motel room and the drama attached to it, I had called her to see what she was up to this morning, and Jessi, being herself, then told me that she had the whole day available.

And there was no one I wanted to see more.

"Hey, have you been waiting here long?" I glanced over at the wall clock above the counter and realized that it was already fifteen minutes past eleven o'clock. "Sorry about the delay."

"Don't worry about it," Jessi remarked, and I immediately smiled when I noticed that she was wearing her familiar faded-blue overalls with a white t-shirt. "You've just given me time to decide my order."

"Oh, really?" I was taken aback since I was used to Jessi always ordering the same drink every time — she had always been very indecisive.

Since when was she wanting a *change*?

"Yeah," she laughed, toying with the blue ukulele charm on her bracelet. "I think I'll try a small strawberry lemonade. What do you want? My treat."

"Wow, thanks." I tucked my ten-dollar bill back into the leather wallet in my handbag. "I'll have a small chai latté."

Jessi was gone for a few minutes, but the service was quick since we were the only customers there. When I glanced away from the window and spotted her coming back with our drinks in hand, though, the wide eyes that she wore made my heart leap in fear.

"What's with the look?" I questioned nervously,

insanely confused as she continued to stare at my feet as she approached. I then took the paper cups out of her hands before she could drop them.

"Aurora, is-is that a *tattoo*?"

I choked on saliva when I followed her gaze, then noticed that I was wearing crew socks along with a pair of black sneakers, unlike normal, exposing the gold, angel wing tattoo.

Shit.

"Oh, yeah. I, um, saw this picture on Pinterest the other night and copied it with a Sharpie on my ankle," I stammered, tugging at the white sock and attempting to pull it up to cover the mark.

"*Oh...*" Jessi mumbled, her face flushing red as she took a seat across from me in the booth. She then took a sip of her drink before adding with a small grin, "It looks cute."

"So, what's new with *you*?" I prompted, not giving Jessi the chance to comment any further on the tattoo as I changed the subject abruptly. I sipped my drink, trying to rid myself of the panic caused by the slip-up.

"Oh, nothing really," Jessi stated, looking taken aback before glancing down at her hands. "What-what about you?"

"Same old, same old," I laughed, knowing that I couldn't exactly tell the truth. "I just needed a distraction today."

"From what?" Jessi glanced up from the table, her eyes sparkling with worry, and I swallowed hard.

"You know, history homework," I chuckled, though this weekend's work was already completed and tucked into the folder in my school bag.

I hated keeping my new life a secret – always acting like Aurora Dickinson instead of Annabeth Landers – but I knew that it was my only choice. It was just hard lying to Jessi – anyone else would have been so much simpler...

"Let's play a game!" I shouted before Jessi could question me on the topics of the upcoming test.

"Okay, sure," she answered, taken aback again but sounding excited. "Which one?"

"How about... Two Truths and a Lie?"

"Ooh, sounds *scandalous*!" Jessi giggled, and I was surprised she didn't rant about how the game would be so hard to play since her life was boring and uneventful. "You go first, though. I'm always horrible with these types of games."

"Okay!" I exclaimed since I always loved going first. When my eyes wandered around the diner as I pondered what to say, though, a realization hit me.

I had chosen the *worst* game – because how was I supposed to play without accidentally exposing myself?

"Aurora?" Jessi questioned, reminding me that it wasn't just me and her – it was her and Aurora playing this game.

"Um, sorry, I got distracted," I laughed, hoping it didn't sound as uneasy as it felt. "Um, okay, I've got something. I'm a Scorpio, I love video games, and my favorite ice cream flavor is black forest."

"The second one? I don't know your birthday, but I can't see you as a gamer," Jessi exclaimed, making me laugh.

"Wow, you know me so well," I remarked, leaning

back in my seat with a grin. "You'll never catch me with a controller in hand."

"One point for Jessi!" she cried, and I hadn't seen her this determined and happy in a while. Her extra enthusiasm was a nice change. "*Okay*, I've read *The Hunger Games* eight times, my blood turned dark during a Test, and when I was a kid, I wanted to be a stand-up comedian."

"*Definitely* the second one. That was too easy."

"*Wrong.* I wasn't *that* funny back then." Jessi faked a frown as her confession registered in my brain. "I guess you don't know me that well after all," she teased with a playful smile.

"Wait, what? *Please*, you could never even hurt a *fly*." I knew that Jessi had changed over the last few months, but she would have never done something so bad that it would make her blood turn dark.

Unless I *didn't* know her at all.

"I guess everything changed once my best friend got murdered." Jessi looked down at her hands, and a sudden, uneasy feeling fell over the table. "I was forced to take a Test, and my blood was dark."

I laughed in surprise, unsure about how I was supposed to react to news like this. "Wow, I would never have expected that. Do you have any idea what you might have done?"

For a moment, the question hung in the air as Jessi slumped in her seat. She blew air out between her lips, then inhaled deeply. "Um, maybe? It's a huge guess, but it was probably the cruelest thing I ever did. It had all been out of spontaneity and hotheadedness, but though I regret it completely, I guess that doesn't change things much." I raised an eyebrow, encouraging her to go on. "When I was sixteen, I found out that Anna was seeing this boy named Drake."

I tried hard not to laugh at the faint memory of the boy I thought I loved, though he had been a walking red flag. The number of times that I had been convinced that an asshole like him was worth my time was honestly hilarious.

"Anyway, when I found out, I-I... I was *jealous*. She deserved so much better, you know? He was a total asshole," Jessi continued, her eyes pleading as if she was hoping that I – Aurora – would forgive her. "So, I did the worst thing *ever* and broke them up by creating fake evidence to convince Anna that he was cheating on her."

My jaw dropped. Not because I was mad at Jessi, but because I was *impressed*.

"In the end, they had gotten back together, so all I had done was hurt my best friend. And since then, I've felt guilty about it. All I wanted was her forgiveness, but I was never able to admit it to her. And, well, now she's gone." Tears pricked Jessi's eyes, and when she realized, she wiped them away harshly with the back of her hand.

"Oh, no. Don't cry, Little J–" I snapped my mouth shut as my heart jumped, but it was too late. Jessi stiffened, recoiling from me ever so slightly, and it felt like the world was about to end.

If I had thought the tattoo incident before had been bad, it had just gotten a whole lot worse.

At first, I stopped breathing. But then, I started to cough, hoping to distract Jessi from the nickname that had just escaped my lips.

I just kept screwing everything up.

First the tattoo, and now, *this.*

I can't stay here any longer.

"Sorry about that," I mumbled after my coughing fit, glancing at my phone and pretending to check it. "Shit, my-my aunt's been trying to reach me. I totally forgot my phone is on Do Not Disturb." I slid out of the booth and grabbed my handbag and jacket, forgetting about my drink in my haze. "I'm so sorry to leave like this, but her calls seemed urgent. I'll see you around, though, okay?"

I knew that I was acting suspiciously, but if I had stayed any longer, Jessi would have questioned me.

And as good of a liar as I was, when it came to Jessi, I knew I would break eventually.

"You can't sleep either?" Adley whispered in the inky darkness as I shifted positions to lie on my stomach in my rose-pink sleeping bag, propping myself up with my elbows.

"No, I never can at sleepovers," I confessed, toying with a lock of hair as the breeze picked up outside, blowing the bedroom curtains and sending a shiver down my back. "So... I guess all we can do is talk." I licked my lips as I thought about what juicy story to bring up – until I thought back to the best part of the night. "You know, that small moment you shared with Ethan during Truth or Dare–"

"Stop," Adley sighed, rolling her eyes as she shut the idea down. "It wasn't a moment. And we are not talking about Ethan like he's some guy that I've got a crush on."

Sometimes, Adley couldn't see what was right in

front of her — and besides, every sleepover deserved a little bit of drama to keep it entertaining.

"But with the way you two look at each other... It's like you're the only people in the room." I giggled, hoping to come off playful so that Adley wouldn't smack me with her pillow. "Pay closer attention, next time. It's obvious he likes you."

"I need water," Adley then said abruptly, and I could tell that she was annoyed by my bringing up Ethan. She was just about to stand up when I sighed and motioned with my hand for her to stay seated.

"It's okay, I've got this. I'm thirsty too — and I'm the hostess, after all."

"All right. Make it snappy," Adley joked, and I laughed in response before exiting the room and walking down the creaky stairs. I slowly turned into the dining room, then the kitchen, and I fumbled around in the dark, looking for two clean glasses. I always hated my house at night — the shadows that would cast on the walls, along with the squeaky floorboards, always creeped me out.

So, it terrified me even more when I heard a loud knock on the back door.

I wasn't expecting anyone — nobody ever showed up at 11:55 PM. But when it sounded again, cautiously, I walked over toward the kitchen counter and peeked through the sheer curtains that covered the door's small window.

That was when I spotted Ivy Blackthorn in her all-black ensemble, standing two feet away from the door.

"What the hell are you doing here?" I hissed as I opened the door and took in the cool evening breeze. "It's

almost midnight."

"And?" Ivy raised an eyebrow. "What, are visiting hours over?"

I rolled my eyes and stepped outside, closing the door. "I'm actually in the middle of a sleepover, and not everyone is asleep."

"Well, it's not like I can talk to you in broad daylight," Ivy snapped, looking around as if making sure that nobody could hear.

"Oh, right. I forgot how you burn in the sunlight," I joked, though Ivy didn't laugh, only glaring daggers at me. "Make whatever you're going to say quick. Adley's waiting upstairs—"

"You haven't told her anything, have you?"

"About how you and Nate are witches? It's not like the topic randomly popped up—"

"Stop fucking around, Landers," Ivy seethed, grabbing my arm and pulling me closer. "I'm serious. Do you know how much you'll ruin everything if you don't keep your mouth shut?"

"So, I'm just supposed to keep lying to my best friend and pretending that I don't know that she's a half-demon?"

"Well, I don't see any other way." Ivy folded her arms over her chest and straightened her posture as if to intimidate me.

"What if I do tell her, though?" I challenged, a smirk on my lips. "What would you do to me anyway? I'm an angel. Don't I have God at my side or something?"

Ivy burst out laughing, doubling over as I watched in confusion. "You really don't know how this works." She *stepped closer to me, and her cherry blossom perfume suddenly smelled like poison. "You're useless on Earth. You're just Little Red Riding Hood going up against the Big Bad Wolf. So, you better not go off the trail."*

"You don't control me. I'm going to do whatever the fuck I want," I declared. Then, not wanting to hear any more of Ivy's bullshit, I spun around and twisted the doorknob, attempting to enter the house.

However, before I could walk inside, Ivy grabbed the hem of my lilac nightgown and yanked me backward, smearing her dirty fingerprints all over the silky fabric. "You aren't telling Adley. Do you hear me?" Ivy threatened, breathing down my neck. "And if I discover that you told her, I guarantee you that pretty mouth of yours will never speak again."

I stopped walking, snapping out of the flashback from the night of my death.

The reason everything turned out so badly.

I looked behind and was still able to make out Danny's Diner in the distance.

Maybe I was there because I didn't want to keep a secret any longer. My life had already been over for a long time, after all.

I hadn't truly been living since I learned who I *actually* was.

That was why I couldn't keep hiding the truth from the one person I loved most in this world. It was as if the mishaps were only encouraging me to follow through with the only thing that I had wanted to do since I was resurrected.

Tell Jessi the truth.

Not giving it a second thought, I spun around and sprinted down Main Street. I retraced my steps quickly, hoping I would arrive at the diner before Jessi would have the chance to leave.

Maybe it wasn't too late.

Maybe she'd still be there.

Maybe this entire nightmare could soon be over.

Maybe, just *maybe*.

Once I arrived in front of the diner's door, I peeked in, crossing my fingers in hopes that I'd still see the girl with dark brown, shoulder-length hair. I searched high and low, glancing every way I could.

But the restaurant was *empty*.

She must have already left.

Sadness filled my chest, and tears began to brim my eyes–

I caught motion at the back of the diner and realized that Jessi had just exited the girls' washroom, looking shaken. My heartbeat sped up ten times faster, and I took a deep breath before pulling open the entrance door. The bell above made Jessi flinch as she sat back down in the booth, but she never looked behind to see that it was me.

I'm going to do it.

I'm going to do it.

I'm not going to think about the million ways this could end badly.

"Jessi, hey," I said softly, sliding into the booth with a smile. "Sorry about that, but I couldn't do it any longer."

"Do-do *what* any longer?" I had never seen Jessi's eyes so wide with fear – I caught her bottom lip tremble as she talked, and I knew that my stress was being projected onto her, especially when I grabbed her hands in mine, which were shaking uncontrollably.

"*Lie* to you." I bit my lip, unsure about how I was going to say this.

"Aurora, *what* are you talking about?" Jessi demanded, squeezing my hands harder. "What's going *on*?"

Suddenly, I was overwhelmed by moments of the past when Jessi and I used to be close – when she, Adley, and I were friends. All I could hope was for it to soon be a reality again.

But what if hoping was *useless*?

When I met Jessi's big brown eyes, though, I knew that I was done pretending to be someone that I was not.

I was *Annabeth fucking Landers* – I had always taught others to get what they wanted and to never let anyone stop them.

So, why had I been letting Ivy Blackthorn and Nate Tucker trap me?

I was done with letting these chains of lies hold me back – I was ready to escape this prison cell.

"Jessi, there's something I need to tell you." I inhaled deeply before finally whispering the words, "It's me. *Annabeth*."

Chapter 28
Jessi
Where Do We Go Now?

 A nnabeth?*

"Wh-What?" I squeaked, sitting so stiffly in the back booth of Danny's Diner that it hurt.

"It's me," the sudden stranger of a girl sitting in front of me repeated. "It's Anna." I abruptly pulled my hands out of her grip and stood up, slipping out of the booth. The girl's brown eyes widened as if she was shocked by my reaction to what she had just told me – like it *wasn't* some fucking crazy proclamation. "Jessi–" she started, but I cut her off.

"*No*. You're a *liar*."

"Jessi, I know it seems impossible–"

"It *is* impossible," I snarled, backing away as tears pricked my eyes. "Anna's *dead*, remember?"

As the girl's face fell, I felt a slight stab of remorse. "I-I'm *not* dead, Jessi," she said softly. "It's a long story–"

"Shut up! I knew there was always something strange about you. I can't believe you're crazy enough to try and impersonate a *dead girl*. At least dye your hair next time and try a little *harder*. I'm not saying go the full length as Katie Ryan did on *One Tree Hill*, but–"

"Jessi! Please, sit down. Let me explain."

"What is there to *explain*?" I shouted, glad that the diner was deserted as my voice echoed throughout the room. "You're just one of those obsessive stalkers, aren't you?"

"I'm *not*! What will make you believe me?"

"I'd believe you if you *were* Anna! But-but you *aren't* – you *can't* be..." I trailed off, recent moments that I had spent with this girl flashing through my mind.

Had it all been some twisted *joke*?

"I know it seems that way, but I'm not lying to you. Sit down, and let me prove it," the girl insisted.

Sighing, I obeyed, sitting back down in the booth and reluctantly crossing my arms over my chest. I didn't say anything, settling on giving her a cautious glare.

The girl fidgeted nervously with a lock of red-orange hair before saying, "Okay, I guess I should start at the beginning. You know that I died on August second and that it was Adley who killed me."

I uncrossed my arms, staring at the girl intently. I was insanely confused by the fact that she knew who had killed Anna.

Just as I was about to point it out, the girl remarked, "It's not exactly what you are surely thinking, though. It wasn't *Adley's* fault."

I laughed bitterly. "Yeah, *okay*. Adley killed someone, and it *wasn't* her fault."

"It *wasn't*. To put it simply, I'm an angel and Adley's

a demon, who had been forced to kill me. Adley would never do something like that on purpose."

You're kidding me. Again with the angels and demons bullshit?

I had decided to believe my mother, but now, this *stranger* was telling the same story?

"I love how you're acting as if Adley just broke a plate," I snorted, rolling my eyes.

"I swear, I'm telling you the truth." The girl leaned forward before whispering, "This story is just a *little* more complicated than you'd expect."

"Enlighten me," I replied bitterly in a just-as-low tone, narrowing my eyes.

"Adley killed me, as I was saying, but I didn't go to Heaven like every other angel should have. I stayed on Earth, looming as a ghost. That's how I got to still see you, even if you couldn't see me. Though there *was* that night when you tried to contact me with the Ouija board. I'm not sure if you remember."

"Of course, I remember," I found myself saying as a flashback from that night played in my mind.

The candles, the intricate-painted board, the poem, the planchette—

How could this girl know, though, if—

"Well, as you probably guessed now, it worked. It *was* me who responded to you." The girl smiled softly as if she was remembering a fond memory. "You didn't even doubt me for a second," she exclaimed before her grin faded. "Nowadays, you seem to doubt everything, though, huh?"

I looked down at my hands, which were folded in my

lap. "I don't know."

"But it *was* me. I promise you that. Adley *had* seen me that night, which was why she freaked out. She was so fearful, back then – with good reason. But then, everything changed. Adley died, and soon, I was brought back to life."

As she finished her sentence, I almost choked on the beverage that I had attempted to continue drinking. My heartbeat sped up for a moment, though doubt then laced my thoughts. "And this is possible *how*?"

"Witches. Specifically, Ivy Blackthorn and Nate Tucker. They were the ones who brought me and Adley back to life–"

"Adley's *alive*?" I blurted before I could stop myself. My body started trembling, and my heartbeat increased rapidly. My palms became sweaty, and I took a few deep breaths to calm myself as terrified as I was.

Anna's killer can't *be alive.*

"Yeah," the girl replied nonchalantly as if she wasn't bothered by the fact that a killer was living amongst us. "Just like me, she's been disguised."

"Disguised? What's *that* supposed to mean?" My vision blurred for a second as I tried to focus.

"This isn't my real hair," the girl told me, tugging at a lock of red-orange hair. "It's just an illusion created by magic."

"*Is* it, now?" I chuckled uneasily, looking her dead in the eye. This freak couldn't be serious. Adley *couldn't* be alive, and neither could Anna. "Prove it."

The girl's eyes widened. But then, she closed them, letting out a sigh. "Okay."

I blinked, caught off-guard by her answer. "Wait, you're *serious*?"

She nodded and stood up, slipping on her jacket. "Follow me. We need to find a place where no one will see us."

Flabbergasted, I stood up as well and buttoned up my coat, then curiously followed her to the front door of the diner, then took a sharp left turn, heading down the alleyway behind the building of Danny's Diner.

Oh, she better not be like Katie Ryan, pulling me into an alleyway so that she could shoot me with a gun—-

"Jessi, are you coming?" the girl called from the alleyway, snowflakes beginning to fall and decorate the girl's red hair. I sighed, exiting the diner and following her into the snow, snowflakes gluing to my lashes.

They better write more than "loving daughter and friend" on my tombstone.

Once we were hidden in the shadows, I caught the girl fidget with her silver, blue gemstone ring. Then, in one swift motion, she pulled it off her finger—

"Anna?" I gasped, blinking hard in disbelief.

I felt as if I was about to pass out.

"Hey, Little J," my best friend whispered in that sweet, slightly sharp tone like rock candy.

I quickly pinched my arm to make sure I wasn't dreaming, and when I felt the stinging sensation, I double-checked my suspicions, glancing down at my hands.

Yep, all ten fingers.

This is fucking real.

I reached out with a shaky hand and touched a strand

of her curly, golden-blonde hair, which was soft and damp between my fingers.

"You're… *alive*?" I questioned. When she nodded, her sapphire-blue eyes brimmed with tears, and I felt my eyes fill too. "How…?"

"What kills you makes you stronger, I guess," Anna replied, sniffling with a small smile on her face.

Before I could say anything else, Anna wrapped me in a tight hug, sobbing quietly. I hugged her back, burying my face into her shoulder and feeling tears slip down my cheeks.

I never wanted to let go of her again.

"Anna," I murmured, my voice muffled against her black coat. "I… I missed you so much."

Anna backed up slightly, though she still kept her arms looped around my neck. When she looked me in the eye, a knot of nerves bundled in the pit of my stomach, but I didn't hate the feeling at all.

"I missed you so much too," she confessed, smiling wider. "Every single day, I wanted to tell you who I really was."

"I can't believe it's *you*," I laughed tearfully. "Now, you better not be some doppelganger who is *really* trying to mess with me."

"I cross my heart," Anna replied, pulling me close again.

Suddenly, I had a flash of an old memory – of a poem written in loopy, purple writing – and I began reciting quietly without thinking. "She's the girl who sings in the pouring rain, not making one single moment–"

"Ever feel the same," Anna finished. "You read that

poem?" By the odd smile on her face, I wasn't sure if she was flattered or embarrassed.

"God, I don't even know why it's coming to me now of all times – it's raining, not snowing." I laughed nervously, taking a breath. "But, um, yeah," I admitted, feeling myself blush. "Adley had it, and I saw it…" I paused, contemplating whether I wanted to ask my next question. But then, I decided that I didn't have anything to lose. "Who was it about?"

Anna's face flushed pink. "*You.*"

I was speechless, staring up into the eyes of the girl I loved – the girl I thought I had lost, but had found again, against all odds.

I hated how badly I wanted to kiss her.

A chime from the pocket of Anna's black trench coat snapped me from my thoughts. She rolled her eyes but took out her phone to check it. As her eyes scanned the screen, they narrowed in annoyance as if she had received a message from her least favorite person in the world.

"What's wrong?" I asked, stepping closer to see if I could manage to get a look at the contact name.

"It's *Ivy*," Anna spat, and I almost chuckled. "You see, she and Nate have this plan, and though I have no fucking clue *what* it is, I know she needs me and Adley for it. *That* was the reason why she brought us back to life." Anna laughed bitterly, glancing down at the screen again. "Adley and I have no idea what's happening. All we know is that it can't be anything good. And that's why we have a plan of our own to take them down."

"I want to help," I blurted, my hands balling into fists

just at the thought of Ivy or Nate hurting Anna.

Anna shook her head vigorously. "Jessi, *no.*"

"Come on, Anna. *I'm* supernatural as well, you know."

"I *know*, but I can't let you do that. I don't want to involve you in my and Adley's disastrous lives."

A thick silence spread over us, and I fought the urge to bite my nails. "So, Adley *is* alive?"

"She's been with me, disguised as Jenna," Anna admitted, looking down at the ground. "I know you two don't exactly get along anymore, but it's been nice to have someone who's going through the same thing that I am."

"Yeah, *nice*. It must be lovely to have your *murderer* right beside you every day."

"You've changed a lot, haven't you?" Anna looked back at me, her eyes filled with sadness.

"That's what everyone's been saying," I mumbled, staring down at my black sneakers.

"Hey." Anna brushed a lock of dark hair out of my eyes. "Nothing can ever change the way I feel about you – not how you acted about Drake, which I forgive you for, and definitely not this."

I felt myself blush at the action as my heart jumped nervously. "Wh-What do you mean?"

"I *mean*," Anna began, pausing and exhaling shakily, "that I love you, Jessi. Always have."

"Oh, yeah," I said, feeling my heart sink. "I–"

"I meant as *more* than a friend." Anna cupped my face in her cold hands before I could comprehend what was going on. "Jessi Alvarez, I *love* you. I have for a long time, but

I was never able to face the fact. But now, after everything I – *and* you – have been through, I've realized that my fear is stupid. *I love you.*"

What? But what could I have ever done for her to love me?

"A-Anna," I stammered, shaking with nervousness. I still didn't understand what was going on, though butterflies filled my stomach, and I started to feel myself smile despite everything. "I–"

I didn't get to finish telling her that I loved her too, though, because she was suddenly kissing me, her cold lips wet with melting snowflakes pressing against mine, making me blush at the feeling of the warmth of her body. The sensation was odd, and there was a part of me that wanted to stop – but another part of me wanted the feeling to *never* end. I felt enveloped by the softness of her touch as I kissed her back, letting the moment wash my worries away. She looped her arms around my neck, and I pulled her closer by the waist. I closed my eyes even though I wanted to keep staring at her, reminding myself that this was *actually* real.

Annabeth Landers was mine.

And she *loved* me.

"You... You're a good kisser," I said breathlessly, smiling stupidly when she pulled away for a moment to look at me, though all I wanted was to kiss her again.

Anna laughed, though I could tell that it sounded different compared to normal – it sounded happier and higher-pitched. "*That's* all you have to say?"

"Sorry. You're an *amazing* kisser," I giggled, feeling my cheeks heat up as my heart pumped widely in my chest.

"And I love you too, Annabeth Landers."

302

Chapter 29
Adley
Truth is Our Worst Enemy

I can't believe how crazy this year has been," I exclaimed as I walked down the snow-covered gravel path next to Kyle at GV, the famous nature park in Ember Falls.

It had been quite a surprise when I woke up to a text from my somewhat-boyfriend, asking if we could talk, and it had driven me crazy the entire time that I got ready since I had no clue what he could have wanted to discuss. Though our last date, about a week before, had ended abruptly after the spell since I bolted without explanation – my headache had been horrible and the new memory of killing my best friend had made me want to puke – I couldn't see a reason to *talk*.

Now, we had been walking at a distance in silence for over half an hour, and I was going insane. All I could ask myself was why hadn't he looked me in the eye yet? What was going on between us? Were we breaking up?

My heart ached a little at the thought, but it scared me even more since I needed to keep the charade up for the plan. And if I *didn't…* who knew what would happen.

"I know. Your coming to town has changed everything, hasn't it?" Kyle laughed, finally speaking as he combed a hand nervously through his brown hair. "I mean, I learned that I'm a *witch*. And I even performed my first spell," he continued, staring into my eyes. "You've changed my life."

How can he think that? I ruined it, and when he learns the truth, I'll probably only tear it apart more.

"I don't think you mean that in a *good* way, though," I added in what I attempted to be a playful tone, though it didn't come out as jokingly, as I looked down at the ground.

"Why would you say that?"

My head snapped up, surprised by his remark. "Um, did you just hear what you said? You're a witch, Kyle," I reminded him as he stopped walking, nearing the river that looped around the park. "It's dangerous, and I've probably flipped your world upside down."

"Maybe it's risky, but things happen for a reason. At least I haven't been a sacrifice in a ritual yet," he chuckled.

I laughed uneasily, knowing that I needed to speak up. I couldn't risk concealing the truth any longer and possibly hurting him. Just as I was about to say something, though, Kyle spoke again, blushing.

"Look, it's been an honor to have my world flipped upside down by you. That's actually why I asked you here." Kyle grabbed my hand and walked toward Ember's Bridge – the half-light and half-dark wooden bridge that the park was known for–

I stopped walking, freezing as the memories flooded my mind from the last time I stood near that bridge. My heart started beating rapidly in my chest as the thought crossed my mind of Ethan, so close to *jumping*–

"Jenna?" I heard a voice say, and for a second, I thought it was Ethan's desperate call for help. When a warm hand tapped my shoulder, though, I jumped back to reality to see Kyle staring at me, eyes wide with concern. "Did you hear me?"

"Um, yeah," I replied slowly, inhaling deeply and reminding myself about what Ethan had told me when we last talked.

He's getting help.

"Wh-What do you mean by 'that's why I brought you here?'" I stuttered, trying to focus again on the present.

"I wanted to ask you something," Kyle explained, stepping closer to me and squeezing both my hands.

My heart started to beat fast again – not because I was nervous, but because this was *too much*. Between hiding secrets and dating the wrong boy, I was tired of being someone that I wasn't. And in the moment of silence that hung between us, I knew that I couldn't let him do this. I had no clue what his question could be, but it felt too *big*–

Wait.

"Kyle, are you *proposing*?" I cried, my eyes widening in panic. I started to pace next to the bridge, glancing down at the bridge as the idea raced through my mind. "God, I don't know how to put this, but we barely know each other. We're just *kids*! *I* can't have kids *now*–"

"*Jenna!*" Kyle yelled, and I snapped out of my thoughts when he placed a hand on my shoulder. I turned around to look at him, though my body kept shaking. "Why would you think that I'd be *proposing* to you? I-I mean, you're *amazing*, but you're my first girlfriend. I'm not any more ready than you are – hell, how could we be? This is all still so new."

My face fell, and my heartbeat slowed as everything sunk in.

I felt like a fucking idiot.

"Oh, shit, I-I'm sorry… God, I don't know what's wrong with me." I felt my face go hot with embarrassment, and I covered it with my hands. I felt like I couldn't even think straight anymore.

"Nothing is wrong with you," I heard Kyle say, I removed my hands from my face to look into his blue eyes.

"What-what did you want to talk about, then? If you aren't breaking up with me, and if you aren't proposing…"

"I just wanted to ask if you wanted to go to that school dance together."

"You mean the masquerade dance next week?" I remarked, my tone lacking enthusiasm due to the shock. A poster that announced the school dance on the night of the rare lunar eclipse suddenly appeared in my mind, and I smiled at the idea. Just as I was about to open my mouth and tell him yes, though, another thought popped into my head.

I couldn't be his *date*. Not if Ethan would be there.

And I had to stop lying to Kyle about my feelings for him. It had gone too far.

"Kyle, I can't," I confessed after taking a deep breath.

"Did you just hear what I said? I'm *not* proposing–"

"Kyle, I can't do *this* anymore. It isn't right," I mumbled, tears brimming my eyes. "I can't let you take me to a dance as your date when there is so much that isn't real. You don't love the real me – you don't *know* her. Of course, that's my fault because, all this time, I've been hiding my true self–"

"Jenna, what are you talking about?" Kyle put a hand to his forehead, closing his eyes as if he was in pain. "One minute, you seem to be into me, but the next, you're acting like *this*–"

"Because I care about you, but I've taken this too far. I was never supposed to fall for you."

"Jenna–"

"I'm not *Jenna*!" I finally cried, gasping for air as if the secret was choking me. The minute I realized that I had admitted the truth, though, I felt as if a heavy weight had been lifted from off my shoulders. Kyle's face shifted into an unreadable expression, and I couldn't tell if he was mad or hurt. Before he could comment, though, I continued. "Remember the brief story that I told you about how I'm a demon and you're a witch? How there's this plan, which led me to meet you? *Well...*"

Fuck, just say it.

"There's more that I never told you," I admitted, taking a deep breath when Kyle stepped closer as if on the edge of his seat. "My name *isn't* Jenna." I grabbed Kyle's hands and squeezed them harder. "It's Adley."

"Adley Morgenstern," Kyle whispered to himself, registering the facts that I had just spilled to him.

After walking around the park as I had explained the truth, Kyle and I had sat down on one of the wooden benches that looked out at the river. The world felt more peaceful and alive now that I had revealed the truth – now that I was able to be myself. I was able to breathe steadily again, and I didn't feel the guilt pressing down on my chest.

I felt *free*.

"I can't believe this… I've been dating my close friend's dead girlfriend, who isn't *actually* dead?" When I nodded, Kyle chuckled, his face red. "Shit, you can't make this stuff up, can you?"

I laughed tearfully in response, finally relieved that I didn't have to pretend to be someone else. "Yeah, you can't." I sighed, licking my lips. "These past few months have been crazy– All because of Nate and Ivy, who need me and Anna – *and* you – for that mysterious plan."

"Because Nate and Ivy are actually *witches*? And Anna…" Kyle's voice cracked as if he was trying to hold back tears. "She's *alive*?"

I nodded slowly, taking in a deep breath. "She was dead for a couple of months because of me – *well*, because of Nate and Ivy, to be more precise. But now, she's been Aurora."

"Shit… I'm sorry, I just can't wrap my head around all of this… There's so much to take in – supernaturals are real, there's this plan that I'm involved with, and now, I find out that you and Anna have been alive all this time."

"I know, and I don't expect you to take this like a champ, but you had to know. This plan of Ivy and Nate's is going to go down eventually, and I needed you to know that there was also a reason you did that spell. Not only did it help me gain the memory of the night I killed Anna, along with why I did it, but it solidified the fact that you aren't a virgin witch anymore."

"And you wanted to make sure of that since the plan involves a virgin witch, and you don't want the plan to work." When I nodded, Kyle raised an eyebrow and added, "But my being experienced is a *good* thing, right?"

"Yeah, for sure – you're aware of your powers, which is much better than never knowing. And now, we're finally a step ahead. We're going to teach these bitches a lesson once and for all. As long as you'll help us, of course."

Kyle grabbed my hands and smiled. "Definitely."

After a moment of silence, I glanced up at him, realizing an odd expression of contemplation on his face. "What?"

Kyle sighed, running a hand down his face. "Sorry, I'm just thinking about all those times when Anna – and *you*, especially – hung out with me and the guys. That must have been–"

"Challenging and awkward?" I chuckled, lightening the mood. "Yeah, it was *interesting*, to say the least. I loved hanging out with you guys, but it would have been much better to have been allowed to be myself."

Kyle tugged at a strand of my long, light blonde hair, and I smiled at the memory of myself finally taking off that silver ring and revealing my true self moments before.

"I have to say, you are, um, much hotter without that stupid disguise," Kyle stated, his face flushing red. I nudged his shoulder playfully, laughing before he added, "I don't get why we never hung out before this."

"You guys were *Ethan's* friends, and Ethan was–"

"The annoying brother," we said in unison, chuckling.

"Wait, Ethan…" Kyle trailed off as his eyes widened, and the moment suddenly felt more serious. "He doesn't know?"

I inhaled sharply, holding back tears. "No, I couldn't risk it. And I still haven't thought of a good way to explain how I was his sister's *murderer*."

"You *need* to tell him."

"I know. I've watched enough of his grieving process to know that he hasn't been taking this well." I wiped under my eyes again, shivering at the thought of Ethan that night on the bridge. "God, I *hate* this."

"I know, but it's going to be okay. We'll make sure it all works out," Kyle told me as he leaned forward with his arms stretched out to hug me. Just as he was about to pull me closer, though, he hesitated and leaned back. "Um, I just need to ask one thing. You love *Ethan*, don't you?"

I bit my bottom lip, feeling as if I should contemplate my response even when I knew for sure what the answer was. "Kyle, I'm so thankful to have gotten closer to you. I had never gotten to have a *real* romantic relationship with someone, but you gave me that experience and made me happy every minute. Everything I felt *was* true, but…" I trailed off, unable to formulate the words that I wanted to say.

"It'll always be Ethan," Kyle said for me, and I nodded, a small smile pulling at my lips despite everything. "Well, I guess it explains why I heard him tell Jessi the night that the group hung out at Danny's Diner that he was crushing on Jenna."

"He-he said *that*?" I questioned, pretending that I

had no idea what he was talking about when I had sadly witnessed the entire conversation.

"Yeah, and I got *really* pissed at him." Kyle took in a deep breath, gritting his teeth as if in pain before chuckling softly as if he found it hilarious that he wanted to be upset about something like this after everything.

"Please, don't beat yourself up over anything," I told him, holding his hands in mine comfortingly. "You would have never known."

"Yeah, and what matters now is that everything is over. And you need to get Ethan back."

I blinked in surprise. "Really? You *aren't* mad at me?"

"Sure, I'm a little pissed because, well, *hello*. It wasn't your fault, though, and I don't blame you for anything." Kyle smiled again, though his grin wasn't the same as it had been an hour before. "I promise not to tell anyone about who you are, as long as you admit the truth soon."

"I will. I just need a good moment."

"Why not at the dance?" Kyle suggested, and my heart skipped a beat at the idea that it was only a few days away. "I can apologize and invite him to join me and the guys. Then, you can have the opportunity to pull him aside and talk."

"You'd do that for me?" Tears brimmed my eyes, but this time, they were filled with joy.

"Adley, I signed myself up to help you fight witches and risk my life. I *think* I can help my two friends get back together."

Chapter 30
Jessi
Behind Every Mask is a Secret

No! You're doing that all wrong!"

Startled, I dropped the black-handled makeup brush that I was holding, then sneezed as the bristles released a cloud of peach-pink powder when the brush hit the vanity.

"That is way too much blush," Adley continued, glancing up from the J-14 magazine she was reading on Anna's bed. She was already ready to leave for the ninth-grade dance, dressed in a short, off-the-shoulders, baby-blue dress and wearing matching-colored heels. "You look like a clown."

Embarrassed, I hastily tried to rub the dark pink powder off my cheeks but just ended up spreading it more. I could hear Adley snickering in the background, and my shoulders slumped.

"A, be nice," Anna scolded from her bathroom, where she was braiding half of her hair into an elaborate crown that would circle her head. "You're supposed to be teaching her."

"Fine, fine," Adley sighed, rolling off Anna's bed and

abandoning the magazine. She then walked over and handed me a drenched cotton pad. "Makeup remover. It'll work better than your hands."

"Thanks," I mumbled, wiping the blush carefully off my cheeks. When I was done, I tossed the cotton pad into the trashcan next to the vanity.

"Now," Adley started, looking down at the blush palette, "use less blush, please."

"Right." I looked into the large, oval mirror of Anna's vanity, feeling ridiculous. This was the third time that I was attempting to apply blush, of all products.

"You've never done this, have you?" Adley asked, stating the obvious as she applied a thick layer of clear, pink gloss to her lips, leaning closer to the mirror to see better.

"Not really," I answered quietly, then glanced down at my short fingernails, which Anna had insisted on painting a deep purple to match my dress.

"My mom taught me to do mascara when I was ten," Adley commented in an almost bragging tone, admiring her perfectly French-manicured nails. "I guess you didn't get to do that, though, did you?"

"Adley," Anna snapped as I flinched at Adley's remark. Anna stepped out of her bathroom to scowl at Adley as she slipped the last bobby pin into her hair. "I told you to be nice."

"Sorry," Adley apologized, but I could tell that she didn't feel guilty.

"Come on, Little J." Anna walked over and picked up the discarded blush brush, smiling down at me. I tried to keep my mouth shut, though I was in awe of how mature she *looked with her blonde hair pinned up, while she wore her short, cotton-candy-pink, sleeveless dress. It looked just like my dress with straps, but she seemed to wear it so much better, especially with the pearl necklace that looped around her neck. "Let me help you out a bit."*

I closed my eyes as Anna brushed a thin layer of pink powder onto my cheeks. After she finished applying the blush, she helped me put on mascara, then picked out what she called "the perfect shade" of lipstick for me, which was a coral pink. Afterward, she pulled half of my short hair – which she'd straightened earlier – into a twist, pinning it up with a black claw clip.

"There!" she exclaimed, smiling at her masterpiece. "Much better."

I glanced at my reflection, surprised by how a little bit of makeup changed my face. That, combined with the neat hairstyle and the gorgeous purple dress that Anna let me borrow for the evening, made me feel pretty.

All except for–

"You're not going to try and do something about this?" I asked meekly, gesturing to my birthmark, which was still in plain view.

Anna shook her head. "I think you look pretty just the way you are."

My cheeks heated as I glanced down at my lap. "Oh, uh, thanks. You, um, look really pretty too."

Anna laughed, and I looked up to catch her blue eyes sparkle. "Why, thank you, Little J."

"Okay, break it up, you two," Adley groaned, stepping in between me and Anna. "Move, please. I need to

touch up my eyeliner."

"Are you jealous?" Anna teased as she fixed her loose, blonde curls. "You look very pretty, as well."

"I know," Adley quipped, leaning closer to the mirror to examine her already flawless makeup.

Anna laughed, then grabbed my hand and pulled me away from the vanity. "All right, Jess. Next step: heels."

"What?" I choked as we approached Anna's walk-in closet. My heart skipped a beat, the idea of wearing heels making me shudder. "No!"

"Come on, Little J!" Anna insisted, bending down and glancing through her rack of shoes. "Live a little!"

"Yeah, Little J!" I heard Adley squeal in a mocking tone from behind, clapping her hands together.

I rolled my eyes, then told Anna, "Nope! I'll die."

Anna stopped searching for a moment to glance up at me with a look of disappointment. "Come on! Take a chance! What do you have to lose?"

"My ability to walk!"

"Please?" Anna begged, making puppy-dog eyes at me.

"Ugh, fine," I moaned, trying to ignore how cute she currently looked. "But if I die, it's on you."

"I'll take full responsibility," Anna stated as she continued to rummage through her closet until she began smiling. "Ah! Perfect!" From a cubby in the corner, Anna pulled out a pair of black shoes with what looked like a two-inch heel. My eyes widened in fear as she waved them in front of my face. "These were my first pair of heels, which means they should fit you just right and shouldn't be too *challenging."*

Shouldn't be too challenging?

Sighing, I sat down on the edge of Anna's bed and reluctantly slipped my bare feet into the shoes. Once Anna strapped them on for me, she helped me stand up as I gripped her hands so hard that I was afraid she would lose circulation. When I was standing straight, Anna then let go of my hands and backed away. I wobbled for a moment, waving my hands around at my sides and attempting to gain balance. The minute I did, though, I instantly wanted to take the stupid shoes off — my feet were hurting like hell.

And just as I thought the hard part was over, Anna remarked, "Now, come on! Walk in them!"

"This, I have to see," Adley murmured, sitting back down on Anna's bed with a grin on her face.

Suddenly determined, I took a shaky step forward, shocking myself when I managed to stay upright—

The minute I stepped foot onto Anna's white wool carpet, I flew forward due to the shoes' little grip. I closed my eyes, bracing for impact—

When I opened my eyes, I realized that Anna had somehow managed to catch me.

I felt my face go hot. "I'm so sorry," I apologized quickly, shaking the cursed shoes off my feet and backing away from Anna.

"It's okay," Anna insisted before shooting a glare at Adley, who was doubled over, laughing on the bed. "Maybe heels aren't your thing."

"You think?" Adley snickered after recovering from her laughing fit.

"Oh, shut up, A," Anna hissed, rolling her eyes as a soft knock sounded against the door of Anna's bedroom. Anna then walked over and cracked the door open before letting out an exaggerated sigh. *"What now, Ethan?"* she questioned, opening the door all the way and leaning against the doorframe.

"It's almost time to leave," Ethan stated quietly, tugging on the sleeves of his wrinkled white dress shirt. *"And, um, I was wondering if maybe you knew how to tie a tie? YouTube isn't helping me much."*

Anna laughed. *"Wow. Real impressive, E."*

"Can you help me or not?" Ethan snapped as his face tinted pink.

"Well, of course, I can," Anna answered, stepping aside to let him in. *"I am the fashionable twin, you know."*

Ethan walked into the room slowly and cautiously, almost as if he was afraid. I cast him a smile, hoping that my action might make him seem a little less nervous, but it didn't seem to change his hesitant behavior as he handed Anna his tie. Anna then looped the tie around her brother's neck and started to tie some sort of knot, though it didn't look quite right.

"There!" Anna exclaimed a few seconds later, placing her hands on her hips triumphantly. *"Perfect!"*

When Anna moved aside, though, I got a full glimpse of Ethan and had to cover my mouth to muffle a laugh. Instead of a neat knot, she had turned his tie into a sneaker's bow.

"What?" Anna giggled as Ethan looked down at himself before shooting her a glare. *"Don't you like it? This is

the latest *fashion trend."*

"I asked for help.*"*

"And I gave it to you," Anna told him, then turned toward Adley. "What do you think, A? Doesn't he look charming?"

Adley's face flushed a light crimson, but before she could reply, Mr. Landers called us from downstairs, telling us that it was time to leave.

"We're coming!" Anna answered, grabbing my and Adley's arms. She then pulled us out of the room as Ethan trailed behind.

When we got downstairs, Anna slipped on a pair of pink heels, while I chose to tie on my white Converse since I was hopeless in heels.

Afterward, we headed out onto the Landers' front porch, where Mrs. Landers was waiting with a camera. "Oh, you all look so nice," she exclaimed, smiling as we exited the front door. "But Ethan, sweetheart, I don't think your tie is quite right!"

"I know, Mom," Ethan mumbled, giving his sister a side-eye as he tugged at his tie in an attempt to fix it, though he only made it worse.

"Well, come on, everyone," Mrs. Landers exclaimed, positioning the four of us in a line and holding the camera up to her face. "Smile!"

I blinked, trying to regain my vision after the bright light from the camera blinded me. I wanted to rub my eyes, but I knew that if I did that, I would have ruined the mascara and eyeshadow that I had so carefully applied.

"Are we done with the photoshoot yet?" I complained, shivering in the end-of-February wind as I stood on the front porch. I couldn't believe I hadn't gotten frostbite yet on my bare legs, though thankfully, I was wearing a black trench coat to warm my arms. "I'm going blind – *and* numb, now that I think about it."

"Sorry! It just isn't every night that you get to see your daughter all dressed up," my dad replied from the pathway that led to the car. "Let me have my fun."

I rolled my eyes, my teeth chattering a little. "You're going to be terrible when I go to prom, aren't you?"

"That's my job," my dad told me, coming over and gently ruffling my curled hair. "Now, come on. We should get going."

We walked over to the car, and I hopped into the passenger seat, being careful not to dirty the hem of my A-line scoop, asymmetrical chiffon, forest-green party dress. My feet were already killing me after standing in my black one-inch heels, but I knew Anna was going to be proud of me. I then toyed with the ribbon of the black, sparkly mask that I had brought to wear for the school's masquerade dance.

I never liked parties, but I found myself actually excited about this one.

"So, is there anyone you're meeting at the dance?" my dad asked me as he pulled the car out of the driveway and onto the street.

I smiled at the ground, and my heart started beating quickly at the thought of Anna, who had convinced me to go as her date. "Oh, um… I'm meeting my friend, Aurora," I answered, feeling my face go hot.

I hated how I was lying to my dad, and while I knew I would never be able to tell him who Aurora *really* was, I wanted to at least tell him what she meant to me.

After the dance, I promised myself. *I'll tell him after the dance.*

We traveled in silence until my dad pulled up in front of the school. It was odd seeing the grounds at night, consumed in darkness except for the odd lamppost that towered over the parking lot.

"Now, I want you to have fun," my dad instructed as he parked the car in front of the school's front doors. "That means no reading in the corner, while everyone else has a good time." He flashed me a teasing smile, and I blushed, annoyed. "You know, the things I would do to be back in high school and living a carefree life–"

"Okay, Dad. I get it. Being old sucks," I joked as I hurriedly opened the car door and stepped out.

"Just make sure to check in every few hours. Oh, and don't do anything *too* crazy. I want you home in one piece," my dad added, and I laughed, smiling wide.

"It's just a school dance. I think I'll survive," I exclaimed, tucking a strand of hair behind my ear. "But okay, I promise. I'll see you later."

Music was blaring from the gymnasium, and I could hear it even from where I was standing outside on the sidewalk. Anna and Adley were already heading toward the school doors, chatting excitedly, but I was hanging back, suddenly feeling nervous.

"Hey," Ethan said quietly from beside me. "Are you

going in?"

"Oh, yeah," I replied, forcing a smile. "Just... I don't know. Dances aren't really my thing, I guess. Too many people – and the music's always too loud."

"Yeah, I get that. They aren't really my thing either. At least we have each other," he added with a smile, and I mirrored his grin.

"Come on, slowpokes!" Anna called, waiting at the doors. "We don't have all night!"

"Coming!" I answered as Ethan and I sped up our paces, arriving at the doors when Adley and Anna pushed them open.

As we entered, I was taken aback by how the party-planning committee had managed to turn the disgusting gymnasium into a dazzling party room. There were streamers and balloons up on the walls, the dark gymnasium was lit by strings of colorful lights, and tables were set up around the room with snacks. In the center of the gym, students were dancing to "Love Story" by Taylor Swift, not seeming to mind they were all clumped together.

"Well, this looks exactly how I'd expect a high school dance to look," Anna sighed, playing with a lock of hair in a bored manner. "Underwhelming."

"I mean, come on. We're in ninth grade – this looks like a grade six graduation," Adley remarked, placing her hands on her hips.

Before I could comment, Anna rolled her shoulders. "Oh, whatever. I guess that's what happens when you don't plan things yourself." Anna then grabbed my and Adley's hands. "Now, come on! Let's dance!"

"Wait," Adley shouted, pulling her hand out of Anna's grip. "I've got to find Nate first."

Anna's smile faltered for a second, but she quickly regained it. "Oh, you can find your boyfriend during the slow songs."

"I promised I'd find him when I arrived," Adley insisted, scanning the crowd until she began waving above her head. "Oh, there he is!"

A few moments later, Nate showed up in front of us, wearing a navy blue dress shirt and a pair of black pants. After kissing Adley, the two of them, along with Anna, began talking. I then looked behind, searching for Ethan, but he was nowhere to be seen. Before I could wonder where he had gone, though, Anna grabbed my hands and pulled me into the center of the crowd on the dancefloor.

Immediately, I felt anxious. There were too many people near me, and it was all too loud. Just as I was about to tell Anna that I needed some air, though, I looked up into her sapphire-blue eyes and caught her staring at me. Her smile was so beautiful that I forgot what I had to say and chose to smile back, despite everything. Anna was still holding my hands, and the feeling of her fingers intertwined with mine made me feel as if electricity was dancing across our palms.

For about five songs, I was surprisingly able to stay within that big, noisy crowd, dancing and laughing beside Anna. After we got tired, though, we made our way to the buffet-style tables, grabbed drinks, and headed over to the benches at the back of the room. There, we found Ethan, sitting awkwardly by himself and tugging on his badly knotted tie.

"E!" Anna cried, racing toward him. "What are you doing over here?"

"Sitting," Ethan responded bluntly, glancing around the room.

"Where are the Three Stooges?" Anna asked with a smirk. When Ethan raised an eyebrow in confusion, she clarified, "Your little gang of soccer idiots."

"Cal stayed home, and Kyle and Dylan are somewhere probably trying to talk to girls."

Anna cracked up, and I caught myself giggling at the thought of those two morons trying out different pick-up lines on poor, innocent girls in my year. "And you're just sitting here?" Anna questioned in disbelief. "Surely, there's someone out there you want to dance with."

Ethan didn't say anything, but even in the dim light, I could see him blush.

Before Anna could tease him more, Adley walked over, still looking as flawless as ever, though her hair was a little mussed.

"Where's Nate?" Anna asked Adley, seeming surprised that Adley's boyfriend wasn't attached to her by the hip.

"In the bathroom," Adley replied, glancing over her shoulder toward the doors. "He should be back soon. He promised he would be for the slow dancing."

"Ooh, slow dancing with Nate?" Anna nudged Adley playfully with an elbow. "Very romantic."

Adley shoved her back, then looked over at Ethan. "Okay, E, your tie is annoying the hell out of me."

"I'm trying to fix it," Ethan mumbled, untying the

knot he had just done.

"Let me help," Adley suggested, batting away his hands. "Caleb taught me how to do this last year." In a few seconds, Adley properly knotted Ethan's tie and stepped away, smiling in triumph. "Much better," she remarked, pretending to dust off her hands. "Now, where the hell is Nate? It's been five minutes..."

"Hey, um, Adley?" Ethan then asked, licking his lips nervously, and I somehow knew what he was about to ask — which made me nervous as hell for him. "I was wondering, do you, um, wanna dance together?"

I heard Anna snort-laugh from beside me, then watched as Adley's eyes widened. For half a second, I thought she might actually say yes—

That idea faded, though, as her mouth turned downward into a frown. "Sorry, but I have a boyfriend."

"I-I know that," Ethan stammered, his face going red. "I just meant as-as friends."

Adley shook her head, and I could tell that she was feeling uncomfortable and embarrassed. "Yeah, still no. Sorry."

"Okay," Ethan squeaked, rubbing the back of his neck and looking down at the ground. "M-My bad."

I then stood there awkwardly, not knowing what to do or say. And just as the silence had become uncomfortable, Nate came striding over, then wrapped an arm around Adley's waist and kissed her. "What are you doing over here in the Loser Corner?" he asked her, raising an eyebrow in confusion.

Adley looked between me and Ethan, then over at

Anna and up at Nate. "I'm not too sure myself. But I'm ready to dance, now that you're here."

"Perfect," Nate chuckled before sweeping her onto the dance floor.

"Well," Anna said after a moment of silence. "That was interesting."

"Stop it, Anna," Ethan mumbled, staring at his shoes.

"Oh, come on, E. We all saw this coming. Hate to break it to you, but Adley's way out of your league."

"Thanks for the vote of confidence," Ethan muttered before standing up and stalking off toward the gymnasium doors.

"Welcome to high school," Anna laughed, glancing over at me with her arms crossed over her chest. "It's all crushes and drama and whatnot. It's about time Ethan learns the hard truth, don't you think?"

As I stood by the snack table near the gymnasium doors, I re-tied the ribbons of my mask for what felt like the one-hundredth time. I was still waiting for Anna, even though she had promised me she would meet me here and that we'd have the night just for us.

Us, I thought, twirling my charm bracelet absentmindedly. *If you had told fourteen-year-old you that there would ever be an us, she would have died on the spot.*

I plucked a pretzel from a nearby bowl, eating it without tasting it. I was half-nervous and half-excited to see Anna again, both because I was still in shock that she was *actually* alive and because we were definitely *more* than friends now.

"Jessi! Hey!"

I turned at the sound of my name to see Anna coming toward me – in her "Aurora" disguise. A dark blue, silver jewel-adorned mask covered the top half of her face, matching her floor-length, lace-topped, cobalt-blue gown perfectly. She was wearing silver, open-toed high heels, and – in ways completely unknown to me – was striding confidently over to me, a wide smile on her nude-pink lips.

"Hey," I greeted as she stopped in front of me. Just as I leaned against the snack table in an attempt to be cool, though, my hand slipped on the white, plastic tablecloth and stumbled forward, nearly ending up on the floor.

I was sure that I had made a fool of myself, but Anna just laughed in that beautiful way of hers, taking my hand in hers. "Hello to you too. Falling for me already, are we?"

"You're so cruel," I pouted, crossing my arms over my chest in defeat.

"But I know you love it," she purred, smirking teasingly.

"You look beautiful, by the way."

"As do you. You know, it's almost ridiculous how happy I am to be here, with *you*. I never thought I would feel this happy again."

"Neither did I. Honestly, I never even thought you would like me back."

"I wish I would have told you sooner–"

I waved her off, shushing her. "None of that, please. We're not here to mope about the past. We're here to have *fun*!"

Giggling like two middle school girls, Anna then led

me onto the dancefloor, where a large crowd of students danced. Anna twirled me in a circle as we entered the clump, and we continued to laugh as we showed off our horrible dancing skills.

But I couldn't care less, especially whenever I looked at Anna, who was dancing wildly in the spotlights and smiling wide. Even though her face was flushed, in the bright lights, she looked like an angel.

It was then that I knew that I was the luckiest girl in the world.

Chapter 31
Adley

You're Un*dead to Me*

God, can people be any *louder*?"

"It's a *dance*, Ivy. You can't expect miracles," I mumbled, rolling my eyes as I stepped through the gymnasium doors and entered the school's masquerade dance. "I thought you'd like this kind of thing."

"Ugh, you know I *never* attended school events," Ivy groaned, walking at my side with Nate trailing behind. She shoved past a crowd of freshmen as she made her way to the drink table. "I enjoy *parties*, where people know how to have a good time." She skimmed the selection of drinks, which was either Sprite, Coke, Pepsi, or a cup filled with punch. "This reminds me of your lame attempt at a party on Halloween."

"Wow, thanks," I remarked sarcastically, then grabbed a can of Coke before searching the crowded room filled with dancing teenagers.

I had to admit that since the last dance I had attended in ninth grade, the party committee had upped their game. Tables were stocked with food, monochrome balloons and streamers decorated the walls, tinsel covered the entranceway, and the stringed white lights gave the disgusting gymnasium an eerie glow similar to the lunar eclipse unfolding outside.

The only downfall was having Ivy and Nate hovering around me like annoying fruit flies.

It was odd seeing everyone dressed up. Nate was in a black tux and a black mask that strangely covered only the left half of his face, and Ivy was wearing a silver mask with an elegant, black dress – which was definitely a first for her.

"Still trying to find your *fake* boyfriend?" Ivy remarked from beside me, her plum-colored lips pulled into a smirk.

"Yep, just like I know you want me to," I confessed before catching sight of Kyle, who was entering the gymnasium. He wasn't hard to find since his mask wasn't on his face yet. It was when we locked eye contact and smiled at each other that I began to waltz in his direction. "I'll see you around," I called to Ivy, who I could tell was already yelling at Nate.

I chuckled softly as I found Kyle, who also had his eyes on Ivy and Nate. "Seriously, they are such a toxic couple," he proclaimed as he tied on his black mask.

"But I can't see anyone better for them to date," I exclaimed, staring at the bickering couple. Momentarily, Nate was attempting to teach Ivy how to waltz on the dancefloor. "It's a shame I thought Nate would be *my* prince charming."

"We all make mistakes," Kyle reminded me, but his teasing laughter wasn't helping me feel any better. "At least you've finally found your match."

At his remark, I heard the gymnasium doors open behind us, and I spun around to see Ethan. My breath caught in my throat. He had never looked more beautiful, wearing that black tux and a *properly* tied tie.

I can't believe I rejected him all those years ago.

"So, you got him to come," I said to Kyle, though I didn't remove my eyes from Ethan. "Does that mean everything is good between you two?"

"Well, I told him that we broke up and preferred being friends. I also added that I was an idiot for choosing a girl over our friendship. So, he's supposed to be coming to hang out with me since Dylan had plans, and, as usual, Cal chose to stay home." Kyle chuckled as he placed his hands on my shoulders and looked into my eyes. "Now, go get him."

"I guess it's now or never." I took a deep breath, though it didn't help calm my nerves. "Shit, what if I mess this all up? What if he hates me? What if I lose him *forever*–?"

I was roughly shoved in the arm, making me stumble right into Ethan, whose eyes widened as he caught me in his arms. My face burned with embarrassment as I stood up properly, brushing the front of his tux to flatten out the wrinkles before glancing over my shoulder to see Kyle laughing.

I guess I deserved that.

"Hey," Ethan remarked, blinking quickly — I had surely startled him out of his daze.

"Hey, sorry about that," I laughed, tucking a curl behind my ear. "I, um, didn't know you were one for dances."

"Yeah, I'm *not*, but I figured, what the heck? Plus, as

much as I wanted to stay home and check out the lunar eclipse, Kyle invited me to be his plus-one, so…" Ethan trailed off, his face flushing red. "Shit, I'm so insensitive. I'm really sorry about how things ended between you two. Kyle told me you guys broke up the other day."

I took a deep breath, tears already pricking my eyes. "It's okay, you don't need to apologize. It was a mutual breakup – we both knew we were better as friends, and none of us were hurt." I nudged Ethan's shoulder playfully and added, "I'm honestly happy that I can be here with you and *not* feel weird about it. You look really nice." I looked him up and down with a grin.

"Thanks," Ethan answered, blushing and stepping a little closer to me. "You… You look very pretty."

It was my turn to blush, and I smiled as I glanced down at my knee-length, burgundy-lace dress, which I had paired with my black stilettos. "Thanks." After a small pause, I then decided to bite the bullet. "Would… would you wanna dance *together*?"

It was funny how ironic the moment was, but I had been regretting *many* moments from three years ago.

Especially the time I had rejected Ethan at the dance.

"Are-are you sure?" Ethan glanced over at the dancefloor, then back at me.

"Kyle is fine with it if that's your concern."

When a smile appeared on Ethan's face again, my heartbeat sped up, and I finally had hope that maybe, *just maybe*, things could feel normal again.

"Yeah, that sounds nice." Ethan held out his hand, and I grabbed it, letting him lead me to the center of the dancefloor as "You Belong With Me" by Taylor Swift began to play over the speakers.

At first, it was awkward since once we found a place to stand, Ethan had no clue what to do – clearly, this was his first time. So, laughing, I grabbed his hands and wrapped them around my waist, pulling him closer to me before I put my arms around his neck. He then copied my swaying motion, and we moved in a small circle, staring into each other's eyes. I wasn't nervous anymore, and it didn't feel like he was either.

It was as if the past four months had never occurred.

"You catch on quickly," I whispered, so close to him that I could smell his sweet cologne.

"What, is it obvious that I've never done this before?" When I laughed in response, he added, "Well, I have a good teacher."

"You know, we've always worked well together. We just met, but we've always understood each other, you know? We have many things in common too. Hell, it feels like we've known each other *forever*…"

"Yeah, it's strange, honestly," Ethan told me, not looking away from my eyes. "I feel like I can tell you anything."

"Which…" I trailed off, unsure if it was the right moment, but I knew that it would have to be. "Which is why I want to be able to be myself when I'm with you. I want to be honest about everything."

"I feel like you're trying to say something." Ethan slowed his steps, and I felt his body stiffen. "Jenna, is everything okay?"

"Do-do you wanna go check out that lunar eclipse?"
I offered, unwrapping my arms from around his neck as his
arms fell to his sides. "I need some air anyway."

Smiling and holding hands, Ethan and I then grabbed
our coats and exited the gymnasium through the back doors,
which led us to the school's empty parking lot. It was quiet
besides the distant sound of passing cars on the streets
nearby, making it perfect for stargazing on a cloudless night.

Once I adjusted to the cool, winter wind, I glanced
up, along with Ethan, to catch only a sliver of the bright
moon. It was beautiful and almost breathtaking – I was never
into astrology, and though these eclipses happen almost
twice a year, it felt special to witness, especially with Ethan
by my side.

"This is amazing," Ethan gasped, smiling up at the
sky. "Now, I can officially check this off my stargazing bucket
list."

"Seriously, you have a stargazing bucket list?" I
asked, laughing teasingly.

"Hey, we all have our weird hobbies," he replied
shamelessly, which only made me love him harder.

That's what made everything feel so much more
challenging.

I stepped away from the open area and sat down on
a bench near the back doors. I rubbed my arms, shivering in
the cold as Ethan looked back at me.

"What's up?" he questioned, joining me on the
bench with a smile.

"God, I feel *pathetic*," I mumbled under my breath,
staring down at my bare feet.

"Why?" My eyes darted up to look at him, shocked by his question. It was then that I realized he'd heard me.

Where am I supposed to go from here?

I glanced around myself before looking at Ethan again, though I decided to focus on the burgundy bricks behind him. "*Because* this shouldn't be hard to tell you, but I just don't want to fuck things up." I took a deep breath, then said, "You know how we agreed that it has felt like we've known each other all of our lives?"

"Y-Yeah," Ethan sputtered, his eyebrows raising in curiosity.

"Well, that's because… we *have*." When Ethan opened his mouth to speak, I continued speaking so that I wouldn't lose my thoughts. "Shit, Ethan, I've known you ever since you moved into the house across my street. You and your sister terrified me until I broke that stupid piece of pink chalk in half and changed your lives." I smiled, remembering the warm, pleasant memory.

Ethan, on the other hand, was staring at me with fear in his sparkling brown eyes as he slowly leaned away from me. "Jenna–"

"I've always known that you're afraid of dogs and that you like to tinker in your garage late at night. Your favorite movie is *Back to the Future*, and you have always loved astronomy," I continued, recounting every possible thing about the boy I loved. "You are a terrible cook and a lousy soccer player, but you're such a smart guy who always believed in me, like that time you tutored me in history and helped me get good grades.

"You taught me that pain only vanishes with love,

and you reminded me that at least one person in this fucked-up world loves me." I was now in tears, and I hadn't yet looked into Ethan's eyes, though he was still silent. "Well, *loved* me. I can't say for sure how you feel now."

"Jenna–?"

"Stop saying that fucking name when you must know by now what I'm trying to tell you," I cried, wiping angrily at the tears on my face. I then looked up, though, and smiled when I met his chocolate-brown eyes, brimming with tears too. "I know that we never got to run away together, but I'm happy to know that you loved me too."

It was silent for another moment until Ethan stood up and yelled, "What is *wrong* with you? Get *away* from me. What kind of sick prank is this?"

"What?" I chased after Ethan, who was walking toward the gymnasium doors. "Ethan, how have you not understood this by now? It's *me*–"

"It *can't* be," Ethan whispered, spinning around to look at me with bloodshot eyes. "I'm hallucinating. You're *Jenna*."

"No, I'm *not*." I grabbed his hands in mine, stroking his palms with my thumbs. "Ethan, I know you must be confused, and I promise I'll explain everything. I just need you to know that it's *me*."

"A-Adley?" Ethan squinted at me as if he couldn't see clearly.

"Who else would know everything about you?" I laughed tearfully as a small smile appeared on his face. "It's not like you open up to *everyone*."

"*Adley*," he sighed after a long pause, stepping away

with fear before hesitantly stepping toward me again with curiosity, his body shaking. His breath hitched as he slipped a lock of my black-brown hair around a trembling finger, and he bit his bottom lip. I could practically hear his heart pound with fear in his rigid body. "B-But how? I saw your dead body in the cemetery, and you don't even look like yourself."

I sighed, combing a hand through my hair. "I think you'll need to sit down for this."

"So, you *don't* hate me?" I fidgeted in my spot on the front cement steps of the school, which we had relocated to. I then glanced over at Ethan, who had been staring up at the dark sky for the last few minutes.

Before, as I had told him the real story bit by bit, Ethan couldn't stop asking questions – then completely freaking out. But during the last few pieces of information, he hadn't been able to look me in the eye.

I felt so bad about *everything*.

"How could I possibly *hate* you?" he questioned, but I saw him flinch when I placed a hand on his knee. "I mean, yeah, all of this is *crazy.* My friend's a witch, who is needed for this plan that, surprisingly, Nate Tucker and Ivy Blackthorn are behind. Along with that, all this time these fucking *monsters* killed you and my sister." He spat their names with disgust.

I winced at Ethan's use of words, not used to his harsh language – not that I disagreed with him. A knot formed in my stomach, though, as I allowed Ethan to fill in the blanks himself and believe that *they* had killed Anna, not *me.* I hadn't yet had the chance to get into those complications–

"My girlfriend is a *demon*, and though I'm not scared of you, I'm scared *for* you," Ethan continued to rant. "And-and my sister... she's *alive*– Where *is* she?"

"We came here together with Ivy and Nate, but she took off the minute we arrived. I'm sure she'll show up soon." Ethan wiped away a tear from under my eye, and I felt myself blush. "Thank you for listening and understanding."

"After telling me how well Kyle took all this, I couldn't act worse, could I?" Ethan joked, nudging my knee with his playfully, though I could tell how uneasy he still felt. "I know that none of this is your fault, and now, I get why you were going through so much before you, um, died." Ethan's head fell into his hands. "I'm sorry if I was ever harsh–"

"*Shut up*, do you hear me? You were the only one there for me," I reminded him, toying with the silver ring in my hand that I had taken off to prove to him who I was.

"You were the only one there for *me*. And I missed you while you were gone – more than you know."

"Trust me, *I know*," I giggled, and as if he realized, his face flushed red.

"I just can't believe you're *here*." He slid his hands down my arms, and a shiver ran up my spine. "Don't ever leave me again, okay?"

I sat up straight and put up three fingers. "Ethan Landers, I solemnly swear not to get hit in the back of the head with a shovel today or at any point in the future," I stated, which made Ethan laugh. "But I think there's a pretty good chance that things won't go back to normal."

"What do you mean?"

"Well..." I swallowed hard, thinking of a way to phrase it. "There's still that whole plan that Anna and I need to stop, and I may not even survive that–"

"Don't say that," Ethan pleaded, holding me in his arms. "I won't lose you a second time. Hell, I'll come to fight with you."

"Are you crazy?" I looked up into his eyes.

"Yeah, but didn't you already know that?" Ethan laughed, attempting to lighten the mood.

"Seriously, Ethan. You could get hurt, or worse, *killed*."

"I can't just sit around while my friends fight for their lives," Ethan remarked, and I understood where he was coming from.

Then, finally, through tears, I told him, "I love you, Ethan Landers."

Even with my heart beating so loud, I was able to hear him say the words, "I love you too, Adley Morgenstern."

I pulled him closer to me by the waist as the relief of saying the words aloud and hearing him say it back filled me with a happiness that I could never describe. He then kissed me hard, his lips soft on mine, and I kissed him back, wanting him more than oxygen. A shock of energy shot through me as his hands cupped my face, and I wrapped my arms around his neck, not wanting to ever let him go.

"Ew, *gross*! Get a room! I'm so happy I was dead during your honeymoon phase," I heard a familiar voice squeal from behind, followed by a snicker, which startled Ethan away from me.

Seriously, Anna?

I laughed uncontrollably as Ethan sat up, frozen in fear that his sister had caught us making out.

"Just think, now that they're back together, Honeymoon Phase 2.0 is about to begin." Jessi made a gagging sound, and I rolled my eyes.

"At least you'll have *me* to distract you," Anna chimed, interlocking her fingers with Jessi's, and it was my turn to want to throw up.

I *was* happy for my best friend, who was finally able to be open about who she was. But still – she had chosen *Jessi Cecilia Alvarez.*

I inhaled sharply. "So, she knows?" I asked Anna, wanting to clarify who knew what. At the same time, though, Anna asked me, "So, he knows?"

We both replied with a nod before Ethan stated, "Congrats. I'm happy you two finally found each other."

"Thanks. I never got to say it to you before, but same for you," Anna said, smiling at me and Ethan. "As much as I mocked you back in the day about your little crush, saying that Adley was 'too good for you,' I was... *wrong.*"

"You were *what*?" Ethan asked teasingly, leaning forward as if he hadn't heard what his sister confessed.

Anna rolled her eyes. "I was *wrong*, okay?"

"And speaking of *wrong*," Jessi then exclaimed, a huge smile appearing on her face, and fear zipped through me. "Adley, guess what *I* saw the night of your Halloween party?" I raised an eyebrow, taken aback by the abrupt subject change – especially to the night of my death. "Nate and Ivy *making out* in your storage room. I even have proof."

I started laughing, only realizing then how behind

Jessi was in the latest gossip. "Jess, Ivy and Nate have been dating for a while."

Her jaw dropped and her face flushed red, though I couldn't tell if it was in embarrassment or anger. "*What? How do you know?*"

"We've kinda been four-wheeling them the past few months," Anna chuckled, and Jessi huffed in response.

"Are you kidding me? Why am *I* always the last to know things–?"

"At least you know now," I heard someone laugh, and surprised, we all spun around to catch Kyle exiting the school's front doors with a smile. When Jessi and Anna gave him a questioning look, he replied, "Don't worry. I know about everything – Adley told me."

"So, clarify one thing for me: Why did you and Kyle date?" Ethan asked me, his eyes wide in confusion.

I laughed uneasily, a knot forming in the pit of my stomach. "That's a *very* long story."

"Don't worry, I have time–"

"*No*, you don't." Glancing away from Ethan, my heart skipped a beat as I spotted Ivy and Nate walking toward us. They had just exited the building too and were staring at us as if they had just won the lottery. "It's *time*," Ivy sang.

"For what?" Jessi snapped, stepping toward Ivy. "For us to kick your witchy asses after everything you've done?"

Ivy cackled, throwing her head back. "I see someone couldn't keep their mouth shut," she remarked, glaring between me and Anna. "Look, we don't have much time. It's now or never."

"To perform the ritual," I added slowly, realizing

what was going on. My heartbeat slowed, and I began to shake in fear as I glanced up at the moon in almost full eclipse. "Tonight is the night of the rare celestial event that you've been hinting at."

"For *once*, someone has been taking notes," Nate chuckled, folding his arms over his chest.

"Why didn't you just tell us it would be tonight?" Anna asked, and Nate laughed in response.

"Because then you would have had time to prepare – and we didn't want that."

Ivy then quickly grabbed Kyle so tightly that he couldn't escape her grasp. "Nate, grab these two, and let's get the fuck out of here."

At the command, Nate clutched me and Anna, locking us in place with his arms. We tried to fight him off, stomping on his feet and hitting his arms, but it was no use.

"Let us *go*," I whined, fighting Nate's grasp, but I knew it was worthless.

"Why would we do that?" Ivy walked over to me and dragged a long, sharp nail down my neck, sending shivers down my spine.

"You're better than this," I told her, fighting back tears of fear. "Ivy, you used to be one of my closest friends."

"Even though I was your friend, it didn't mean I *wasn't* a psychotic bitch."

"At least you admit it," Anna mumbled, and Ivy kicked her in the shin.

"I've always been the Big Bad Wolf. Some of us are just better at disguises – like our little, perfect angel *used* to be." Ivy turned away from us to look at Ethan and Jessi.

"Enjoy this last moment before you never see your lovers again. They *may* not survive this ritual."

"What?" we all shrieked, and panic seized me — we had never been told about *that*.

Our plan backfiring better work now so that all of this can be over once and for all.

"Oh! And don't even *try* to stop us or call the police," Ivy warned, advancing toward Ethan and Jessi. "That'll just get you killed."

"You won't get away with this," Jessi spat as Ethan held her back from attacking Ivy.

Ivy spun around to face me and Anna, ignoring Jessi and clapping her hands together in delight. "Let's get this party started, shall we? To Ember's Bridge!"

Signaling for Nate to follow along, Ivy walked past us with Kyle before pulling out a small, black marble from her crossbody clutch. She then threw it hard onto the floor, breaking it and creating a black whirlpool-like portal in front of her. I could feel it sucking in the air around us like a vacuum, creating a wind that made me shiver.

"Ethan," I sobbed quietly, tears falling from my eyes as sadness filled my body.

Even though I had confidence in our plan, I couldn't think about losing him — not after finally making things right.

But that was what fueled me — I was going to make sure Ethan and I would not get separated again.

Effortlessly, Ivy shoved Kyle into the portal, and Ethan and Jessi cried in fear as I felt Anna flinch beside me.

I hated how torturous the past four months had been. This wasn't the way my life was supposed to go. When

I met Anna for the first time, handing her that piece of pink chalk...

Who would have thought that we were going to have to fight for our lives together?

Ivy and Nate weren't going to win, though. I wasn't going to let it happen.

I wasn't going to lose Ethan.

If I could die once and come back to life, I sure as hell could fight to the death again.

For *Kyle*.

For *Jessi*.

For *Anna*.

And especially for *Ethan*.

Chapter 32
Jessi
The End's Not Near, It's Here

I can't believe we're doing what we were warned *not* to do," I roared at Ethan as we snuck around to the back of the school. "And taking a *bike* there? Can you be any more foolish?"

Ethan spun around and frowned at me. "Do you want to save the love of your life or not?" When I didn't say anything, he added, "That's what I thought." Once we stopped in front of the bike rack, Ethan bent down next to his sapphire-blue mountain bike and pulled out a key from his pants pocket.

"But really, you think a bike is the smartest option?" I continued, folding my arms over my chest. "Doesn't this kind of plan involve a get-away car?"

"Do *you* know how to drive?" Ethan snapped after unlocking his bike from the rack, pulling it out from between the other few bikes that other morons had oddly used to get to a school dance. When I didn't comment again, he sighed. "See, this is all we have."

I stared at Ethan as he hopped onto the bike and fixed his black helmet on his head. I then chuckled teasingly, "Aw, you're actually kind of cute with that helmet on. You look ready for war."

Ethan's face flushed a deep red as he adjusted the helmet's straps. "It can be dangerous riding a bike — especially in the dark. I'm just keeping my brain from splattering on the sidewalk if I ever get hit by a car."

My eyes widened at his dark example. "*Okay*, wear your damn helmet." I glanced around the bike as if expecting an extra seat to pop up out of nowhere. "So, um… where am *I* sitting?"

"Up here." Ethan tapped the space in between the handlebars and grinned.

"Are you *mad*, Ethan? You want me to ride with you to stop our friends from being used in a deadly ritual at Ember's Bridge while riding there on the *handlebars*? Are you trying to get *me* killed?"

"Relax. I used to do this with Anna all the time when we were little."

"Yeah, the keyword being *little*."

"Just give it a try," Ethan insisted, unbuckling the helmet straps under his chin. "I'll give you my helmet."

"What a gentleman," I snapped before looking from Ethan's helmet to the dark street ahead. I then shivered as I grabbed the helmet from his hands. "If I die tonight, it's on you."

"I can't believe we just did that." I exhaled slowly, still shaken from the ride as Ethan stopped the bike after entering the deserted, dark GV parking lot. The lampposts were broken, flickering on and off constantly, so we only had the moon's light to help us see – which wasn't much since it was very close to a full eclipse.

Ethan kicked the bike stand down, then hopped off the bike as I sat, shaken. "You can get off now."

I was gripping the handlebars so hard that my knuckles were white and burning. "I'm never doing that again."

"Oh, come on. It wasn't *that* bad – it was only a ten-minute bike."

"Thank God it wasn't *longer*. You almost ran into *five* stop signs!"

"That was because I was in a rush to get here." Ethan walked over to me and pulled me off the bike, then looked me over to make sure that I wasn't actually harmed. Grabbing my hand, he declared, "Now, let's get our friends back."

Ethan was right. This was not the time to act weak and mentally note to never let him bike alone again.

I had to find Anna, *no matter what.*

The way the shadows of the trees loomed over us as we entered the dark woods made me feel slightly trapped. I tried to quickly forget about the feeling, though, as I heard voices shouting in the distance. I sped up my running pace, hoping that we weren't too late.

As the bridge came into view, I could see a faint light radiating from it. I realized that it was coming from the black candles that had been set down in a circle on the wood, then swiftly pulled Ethan behind a nearby tree. I peeked around it, trying to see – and *understand* – what was going on. In the middle of the bridge, right where the light and dark planks of wood met, there was a shape – something like a star inside of a circle – created with a white powder that looked like salt.

What the hell is that shape? A pentagram?

Inside the shape, Kyle – bound by rope – looked unconscious, and Ivy and Nate were standing around him, talking to each other in hushed voices. Adley and Anna were standing on separate sides of the bridge – Anna on the light wood and Adley on the dark wood.

"How the hell are we going to help them?" I whispered to Ethan, shaking in the cold winter wind.

"I don't know… Punch Nate or something," Ethan suggested, and I rolled my eyes at his attempt at lightening the mood. "Fine, I'll grab Adley and run. You get Anna and Kyle."

"Why do I have to–?" I cut myself off, realizing that it was not the time to argue about who had the largest task. "Fine, let's do this."

We darted out from behind the tree, then sprinted onto the bridge, making everyone's heads turn toward us. Both Anna and Adley's eyes widened in fear, but Ivy and Nate just narrowed their eyes in annoyance.

"Oh, *lovely*," Ivy complained, glaring at us. "I had a feeling you two would show up eventually. I have to say, you're faster than I thought you'd be."

"Well, surprise!" I shouted sarcastically, running over to Anna, though I felt that jittery energy fill my body the way it always did when I was on that bridge. Ignoring it, I grabbed Anna's hand and tried to tug her away, but she wouldn't move. I saw Ethan do the same to Adley with identical results.

"Jessi, what are you *doing*?" Anna hissed, but she looked more afraid than angry.

"*Saving* you!" I cried, pulling her hand harder, and it was enough to make her stumble. "Come *on*!"

"No," Anna replied loudly, snatching her hand back. "I'm *not* going with you."

I stared at her, confused and hurt, and I caught Ivy sharing the same reaction as me. "Anna?"

"Just trust me," she murmured, barely loud enough for me to hear. "*Please*."

Across from me, I could see Ethan desperately tugging on Adley's hand. He was speaking so quickly and unsteadily that I couldn't understand what he was telling her, but though she was looking at him with a blank and emotionless expression, I could see her falter as Ethan begged her to run.

Apparently, Nate had also seen Ethan's large attempt to save Adley as he watched from behind with a smirk. Though he didn't seem shocked that she wanted to stay, he was clearly amused. "You really want to save your sister's *killer*, don't you, *E*?"

I then watched as Ethan's entire world came crashing down.

His face dropped, and so did Adley's hand from out of his grip. "What?"

"Oh, did you not have the talk yet? I just assumed since you *apparently* know the entire story—"

"Adley." Ethan's eyes couldn't meet hers as he stared

down at the ground, his face paling. Adley looked just as ill and frozen in fear as her eyes locked on Ethan's trembling body. "Is it... is it *true*?" When Adley didn't respond, Ethan laughed hurtfully, "He's joking, *right*? As fucked up as this all is, you couldn't have..."

"Adley. You-you said Ivy and Nate were behind this..." Ethan's eyes couldn't meet hers as he stared down at the ground, his face paling. Adley looked just as ill and frozen in fear as her eyes locked on Ethan's trembling body. "Is it... is this *true*?" When Adley didn't respond, Ethan laughed hurtfully, "He's joking, *right*? As fucked up as this all is, you couldn't have..."

Adley shook her head, tears dripping down her face. "Ethan, I wasn't lying — it's just so much more complicated than that. You know I wouldn't have done it of my own free will. She-she's my best friend." Ethan backed away from Adley, terror displayed in his expression. "*Ethan*, let me *explain*—"

"I think you should leave the explaining to the professionals," Ivy interrupted, seeming to talk about *herself* as a malicious smile appeared on her face. "I think it's time that you all finally learn the true story.

"Nate and I have *actually* been planning for this exact moment for years, you know. Two years ago, Nate left for New York City since his parents had to move for work. *But*, a few months later, my mother wanted my help with this plan, and, of course, I couldn't do it alone. That's why I called Nate and got my witch friend to help me out. That's why I left for a year — to meet up with him and brainstorm.

"Nate and I then cast a spell on Adley the night

before the sleepover while she was asleep. That way, the minute she would spot greasy fingerprints, her brain would shut off, and then, Damion would be able to have full control of her for just enough time to get the dirty deed done.

"So yes, Adley killed Annabeth. However, it was more like her body had at the stroke of midnight, while Damion controlled her brain," Ivy concluded.

Adley's jaw dropped. "And my memory was pushed to the back of my head and concealed because it wasn't mine."

"Exactly," Ivy remarked with a wide grin as if she had just won an award for Best Explainer. "Just note that Damion had nothing to do with Adley's death. That was all me and Nate."

"So, those fingerprints… They were there for a reason," I sighed as every detail registered in my brain.

"*Everything* happened for a reason – even the blog post on TheTea.com. I can be a fabulous writer when I want to be," Ivy bragged, tossing a lock of hair over her shoulder. "We had to keep attention away from Adley. It was a small price to pay for the success of it all."

"You must be happy that you weren't permanently stuck in jail," I snapped, rolling my eyes.

"Yep, all thanks to *your* daddy, by the way." Ivy smiled smugly, and my hands clenched into fists at the mention of my father. "Though worst case, we could have gotten my mom to help with a spell to get me out. There was always a back-up plan."

"Why did you even *want* Anna dead?" Ethan asked shakily.

"Yeah, though I know you and Nate are psychos, I just *can't* seem to wrap my head around it," I laughed bitterly.

"Well, *you* of all people should know how much of a gossiper your beloved Anna is," Ivy bit back, glaring daggers at me. "*She* wanted to go and spill all the secrets of our world, which, of course, we couldn't have. But also, killing an angel helped us prove our loyalty to the greatest demon of all – *Lucifer.*"

"Who?" Ethan questioned, though I couldn't take any of this stupidity anymore.

"You *psychopath*!" I screamed, jumping at Ivy–

Ivy shot out a hand and shoved me back with much more force than I expected, sending me tumbling back onto the bridge and smacking my spine against the wood. I quickly pushed myself back up onto my elbows, trying to breathe through the pain that was shooting across my back.

"This bridge may give *you* a boost," Ivy declared with a smirk, "but it does the same for *me*. Remember, *everything* is planned out."

I glared at Ivy as I stood back up slowly, wanting to attack her again but thinking better of it. On the other side of the bridge, Ethan was still staring blankly between Ivy and Adley.

"But-but I just don't get it. Why did you kill Adley?" Ethan asked, still fearful but curious.

"For this ritual, of course. We needed an angel, a *full* demon – not just a half one like Adley was before she died – and a virgin witch." Ivy laughed, tossing a lock of black hair out of her face. "I'd be careful if I was you, Ethan. You're surrounded by people who could *easily* kill you."

If Ethan hadn't looked petrified before, he certainly did now.

"Why?" I cried, tears burning my eyes. "Why are you doing this?"

"Why don't we let the demon who started this explain it himself?" Ivy asked, snickering as she reached into her crossbody clutch and pulled out a tiny cork vial filled with what seemed to be black gas. Stepping back, Ivy then uncorked the vial, letting the gas leak out and shape into...

No.

"*Finally*, you release me. It was getting pretty tight in there, you know. Thankfully, I'm all charged up now," a familiar, chilling voice exclaimed, and my heart stopped beating.

There, next to Ivy, was *Damion*, stretching his arms and wiggling his fingers as if he hadn't moved in years. He hadn't changed since the last time I saw him – dark brown hair, scary eyes, beaten leather jacket, and black t-shirt and jeans.

"My dear friend," Ivy called, grinning evilly at the demon that sent an immediate, sharp, burning pain through my body. "I'm happy you're here for the moment we've all been waiting for. But first, why don't you do the honor of explaining to our audience how this all began?"

Damion grinned, placing a hand on his heart. "It'd be my pleasure," he remarked, skimming the forest with his eyes and smiling creepily at all of us. "You want to know why the plan came to be? Well, it was all because of the immortal bloodlines.

"Because Adley's ancestor signed a blood deal with Lucifer, forcing the Morgenstern bloodline to forever be human ties for demons so that they could come to Earth. Because I was Jack Morgenstern's charge and got to know Cecilia Alvarez, who killed Daniel Blackthorn – a fellow witch. Because I became Adley's Charge, who knew Ivy. Because I heard one day that Rose Blackthorn, Ivy's mother, wanted revenge on the angels, and so did the demons. That's why we chose to work together. The only way to get revenge was to break the line between Heaven and Hell so that both angels and demons could roam free on Earth. Ivy and Nate used me to kill the angel not only because she couldn't be trusted, but so that they could prove their loyalty to my father, Lucifer.

"But now? I just want to rule the world, which, of course, involves a very dangerous ritual that you are now a part of. You're creating history."

"I still don't get it," Anna hissed in between deep breaths. "Why *us*?"

"Because you just happened to be the Chosen Ones," Damion laughed as he glanced around at all of us. "Thank your parents."

"Why isn't your mom performing the ritual?" I asked Ivy, folding my arms over my chest. "Isn't she the reason this idea was created?"

"Yes, but after the years of spells she's performed, she doesn't have the strength that Nate and I have to get it done right," Ivy responded, cracking her knuckles. "Now, speaking of, why don't we get this started?"

Without a moment of hesitation, everyone began to work. Ivy pulled a copper-colored knife from her clutch, while

Nate picked up the wooden bowl that was resting by his feet. As they approached Anna, I stepped toward Ivy, anger flaring in my chest.

"*No*. I'm not letting you hurt her," I hissed.

"Move it, Short Stack," Ivy huffed, then looked over at Nate and batted her eyelashes. "Natty Boo, restrain her, will you?"

Nate gave her a wary look but approached me anyway.

No way in hell am I getting beaten by him.

I lunged at Nate, tackling him onto the hardwood bridge. He yelped, covering his face with his hands and whimpering pleas for me not to hurt him. I laughed at how pathetic he was, but as I was gloating, I realized that I had left Anna unguarded.

"No!" I cried, whirling around just in time to see Ivy grab Anna's wrist. Ivy then dragged the knife across Anna's palm, holding the wooden bowl under her hand to collect the blood that dripped from the cut. By the time I got back to Anna, Ivy had already moved on to Adley and was doing the same to her, while Ethan watched in silent horror.

"Anna," I murmured, gently cupping her injured hand in mine. "I'm so sorry. I-I got distracted—"

"It's okay, Jessi," she whispered. "I told you, just *trust me*."

I then watched Ivy intently as she pulled Kyle's hand out from underneath him and sliced a line across his palm. The pain seemed to jolt him fully awake, and he let out a cry, his blue eyes wide and panicked, begging for help that we couldn't give.

Once Ivy finished collecting the blood from Kyle's cut, she took a few small stones from a box that she pulled from her huge tote bag and dipped them in the blood mixture, then dropped them around the circumference of the pentagram. Afterward, she poured the rest of the blood, outlining the star in the middle of the pentagram, while Kyle squirmed uselessly.

"Quit it," Ivy snarled, slapping him across the face and leaving a bloody handprint on his cheek. "Or I'll knock you out again. *Understood?*" Kyle nodded shakily, tears streaming down his cheeks.

"You're psychopaths!" I yelled, making Ivy, Nate, and Damion turn to look at me. "You've *killed* people on *multiple* occasions!"

"Shut the fuck *up*!" Ivy looked at me, her poison-green eyes boring into mine. "Accept it: you've *lost*."

I opened my mouth to retort, but Anna squeezed my hand, shaking her head and giving up. Huffing out an angry breath, I looked away, keeping quiet. Glancing back at the pentagram, I saw Ivy and Nate standing around it, hands held together and eyes closed before they began to chant.

Magic forces
black and white,
reaching out through
space and light.
Be they far or
be they near,
summon the creatures
and make the line disappear.

The flames of the black candles shot up three inches, engulfing the pentagram in a wall of flames. I jumped back, feeling the intense heat lick my skin, and I saw Ethan do the same. I heard Kyle cry out, probably ten times more frightened than we were, but Damion, Ivy, Nate, Adley, and Anna all seemed unfazed.

Ivy and Nate stepped back from the pentagram, staring at the dark side of the bridge expectantly as the flames slowly died down. I tensed, noticing everyone do the same, all surely expecting some sort of grand reaction.

But nothing happened.

"What the *fuck*? This makes no sense!" Ivy stormed over to the pentagram, inspecting it meticulously.

"Maybe it's a delayed reaction?" Nate proposed.

"That's the *stupidest* excuse I've ever heard! Did you say the spell right, idiot?"

"Of course, I did! Maybe it's just—"

Before Nate could finish his sentence, the bridge began to shake violently as if there was an earthquake happening. The flames of the candles leaped back up and burned brighter as the salt-and-blood pentagram began to break apart. Everyone gripped the railings of the bridge for support, trying to stay upright as the ground shook.

I could hear Ivy screaming at Nate, but even she was struggling to stay upright. "Why is this happening? We did *everything* right!"

"No, you *didn't*," Anna and Adley stated at the same time, sharing a look of victory.

"*What?*" Ivy roared, and my body filled with hope.

"Your virgin witch *wasn't* a virgin witch," Anna remarked as a crack ran down one of the light planks of wood that we were standing on. I then realized why Anna hadn't wanted me to panic – they'd had a plan this entire time. "He performed a spell without you knowing. Checkmate, *bitch*."

Ivy stared at Anna, her mouth open in shock. I wasn't sure what Anna was saying, but I was on board with it, based on how Ivy was reacting.

"*You...*" Ivy sneered, her voice low and menacing. "You ruined *everything*!" Ivy then lunged at Anna, sending them both toppling onto the dark wood side of the bridge.

"*Anna!*" I cried, running over to the fight. "Ivy, let her *go*!"

Ivy didn't acknowledge my presence, shouting at Anna and aiming a punch at her face. Before I could think better of it, I jumped at Ivy, and the extra jittery energy that was running through my veins gave me a boost. I managed to pull Ivy off Anna, though the two of us tumbled, only stopping when we crashed into the splintering railing.

"*Jessi,*" Ivy snarled, baring her teeth menacingly as she shakily stood up. "You bitch! You've ruined so much for me." The bridge beneath our feet fractured violently, sending wood chips flying. "So, now, I'll ruin everything for *you*." Ivy pulled out the bloodstained knife from where she'd tucked it into her pocket.

Then, in an instant, she wielded it over her head and leaped at Anna–

Everything seemed to happen in slow motion.

I couldn't hear anything besides my racing heart and heavy breathing. I zeroed in on Ivy like a hawk, and just as I started sprinting at her, the piece of wood I was standing on snapped. I then jumped in between Ivy and Anna, grabbing onto Ivy's shoulders. Using the momentum that I had from running, I flung Ivy against the railing. Just as her crazed green eyes met mine, though, I felt a deep, stabbing pain in my ribcage and cried out, letting Ivy go.

As I toppled back onto the bridge, the railing shattered into a thousand pieces, sending her collapsing into the dark, angry water below.

And just as Damion was about to charge toward me, everything exploded.

The first thing I noticed was the awful, high-pitched ringing in my ears. I felt a horrible burning pain in my ribcage as if fire was crawling across my chest. I was lying on my back on the forest floor, so I tried to sit up to see what was wrong. However, I found that I couldn't sit since, when I moved even the slightest, the pain took away my ability to breathe.

As the buzzing in my ears faded, I could hear voices shouting in the distance, though I couldn't understand what they were saying – both because they were too far and there were too many people talking at once.

I attempted to sit up again but gave up as the pain in my chest sharpened, making stars dance in front of my eyes. Gingerly, I touched a hand against my ribs, then froze, feeling something warm and wet coat my palm.

I wanted to scream at my blood-covered fingers but couldn't through the agonizing pain that was consuming me.

Anxious shouts arose from the forest, still unintelligible. As they came closer, though, I started to hear my name being called. *"Jessi? Jessi, where are you?"*

I wanted to reply, but the pain had stolen my capacity to talk. A moan escaped my lips instead.

"Guys!" Ethan shouted, and out of the corner of my eye, I spotted him running toward me. "I see her!"

I heard quick footsteps coming closer to me, and seconds later, four battered faces were hovering above me, all sharing the same, stunned expression.

"Oh, God," Ethan whispered, his voice shaking. "Jessi?"

I stared back up at them, panic crashing over me in waves. My head was now propped up on Ethan's lap, and Anna was pressing her hands hard against my ribcage. Kyle, now untied, seemed to be frozen in shock, and I couldn't see Adley.

"Stop... Stop it, Anna," I choked, feeling tears pour down my cheeks. "Stop, you're... *hurting* me."

"Shh," Anna soothed, but her voice was breaking. "It's okay. You're gonna be okay."

"What's... *happening*?" I asked weakly, the burning sensation spreading farther up my ribcage.

"You... You're just a little hurt," Ethan answered, but he was crying. "You're going to be okay, Jess."

"Where's Damion?" I croaked, afraid that he would soon hurt one of them next.

"He burned in the fire that consumed the bridge," Adley responded, and I spotted her staring out at the large flames. "Ivy died too when she was thrown over the bridge."

"We need to call for help," Anna told the group. I could tell that she was trying to be the strong one, but when her eyes met mine, I saw a tear slip down her cheek.

"Anna, they can't save her."

"Wh-what?" Anna inhaled sharply, glaring back at Adley. "What are you *talking* about? Fuck, someone call 9-1-1–"

"Anna!" Adley placed her hand on Anna's shoulder. "Jessi was stabbed with... with a *bronze* knife–"

"Shut up," Anna murmured, shaking next to me. "She... she can't..."

Everything was sinking in slowly, and it was only then that I realized what was going on.

Oh, shit.

"She... *stabbed* me?"

No one replied, but the sob that escaped Ethan's lips was enough.

My eyes still open slightly, I watched as Anna stood up, then went over to the water's edge and aggressively flung the knife into the rapids below. "*Fuck!*" she screamed, her voice breaking. Soon, Anna was back at my side, her soft hand cupping my face, though it was wet with what smelled like blood.

My blood.

"No," I gasped. "*No.* I-I'm *not*... I *can't*..."

In an instant, everything hit me.

I'm going to die.

I'm going to die.

I tasted blood in my mouth. I felt it escape my lips and drip down my chin.

"I *can't* leave you," I whispered, desperately trying to breathe against the pressure squeezing my rib cage. "Please, *help me.*"

"Shh, Jessi," Anna whispered shakily. "I've got you."

"*Please.* I can't *breathe*!" I started to cough.

Ethan kept his arms wrapped around my shoulders, holding me tight against him. I felt more blood spill from my lips, and I sobbed. My eyes felt heavy again, and I couldn't see well anymore, blurry spots consuming my vision.

"*No,*" I gasped, my surroundings blurring. "Don't go."

"No one's going anywhere," Anna promised, but I knew that was a lie.

"I can't... *see* you." The burning had now engulfed my entire body.

"I'm here, Little J," Anna told me, her voice hitching. "We're all here."

"I... don't wanna... die..."

"It's okay," Anna sobbed. "You can let go."

I fought for another breath, but everything was fading away.

The pain.

The world.

Anna's voice.

"I love you, Jess–"

Chapter 33
Ethan
Nate Tucker Must Die

I love you, Jessi." Anna reached out and touched Jessi's face softly, then planted a kiss on her lips.

I had a strong feeling that Jessi hadn't felt it at all. She had stopped struggling a few seconds before, going limp in my arms. Her eyes were now half-open.

"Jess," I choked, staring down at her expressionless face. "Wake up. *Please*." My begging, of course, made no difference, and that made another wave of pain slam into me. An ugly sob escaped my mouth, and I pitched forward, feeling like I was being crushed by a landslide.

She's gone.

"I-I can't believe it," Adley mumbled, staring at Jessi's body with fear written all over her face. "She's…"

"*Fuck off*, Adley! Like you ever gave a damn about her," Anna cried, shedding more tears as Adley jumped back, startled by Anna's response.

"I know that my relationship with Jessi is-*was* complicated. But I-I know how important she is-*was* to you."

Adley looked from Anna to me, a shaky smile on her face. "I know how much you loved her." For the first time, I then watched as tears ran down Adley's face like a waterfall – over Jessi, of all people. She sniffled, wiping the tears away hastily. "She never deserved this."

I looked again at Jessi, who was unmoving, pale, and had blood drying on her lips and chin. Her forest-green dress was soaked in red, and blood had pooled on the gravel beneath her.

I wanted to scream, but all that I could manage was a choked cry. I brushed back a strand of Jessi's hair with a shaking hand, and her cheek was cold to the touch. "Y-You promised you wouldn't leave me. You *promised*."

"Jessi," Anna whispered, shivering. "I'm so sorry. If-if only I had been strong enough to fight Ivy."

Anna and I looked up at each other, the two of us covered in Jessi's blood and crying uncontrollably. Slowly, we both let go of her, laying her head gently on the ground. I passed a hand over her face and closed her eyes.

She's gone.

Anna shakily made her way over to me. Then, we hugged one another tightly, sitting on the ground and crying into each other's shoulders.

"This is all my fault," Anna sniffled. "If I had just–"

"It's *not* your fault," I told her.

The metallic smell of blood wafting off the both of us was overwhelming, and it made me feel ten times more nauseous, but I couldn't bear to let go of my sister.

A few minutes later, Kyle came stumbling out of the forest, and he could barely look in the direction of Jessi's body. "G-Guys, I'm really sorry about Jessi," he sniffled, wiping his eyes with a hand before covering his mouth with it in shock. But then his eyes widened in alarm. "Shit, Nate! He—"

Before Kyle could finish his sentence, I caught Nate barging out from behind a tree before shoving Kyle to the ground. Anna and I quickly stood, backing up as far as we could without toppling into the water.

"*You*," Nate snarled, but he didn't seem to be addressing a specific person. "You *killed* Ivy."

"Ivy was a *murderer*," Anna growled back. "Don't expect me to feel any pity for *her*."

Nate began to tremble, but it seemed to be more out of anger than out of fear. He then reached into the pocket of his dress pants, and before I could see what he had in his hand, he let out a savage cry and leaped at us.

By the time I realized what was going on, I hit the ground hard, smacking the back of my head against the gravel. Black spots danced in front of my eyes, and I felt as if all the air had been sucked from my lungs. Despite my obscured vision, I could see Nate above me, and I felt him pinning my arms to the ground.

A shout escaped my mouth, and I tried to flee from Nate's grip, kicking my legs out and attempting to bite his arm, but nothing worked. He hoisted me upright and dragged me toward the forest. Just as I aimed another kick at his leg, though, I felt something cold and sharp press against my throat.

I grabbed Nate's arm, clawing at it desperately as I felt a knife's blade dig into the skin on my neck, drawing blood.

"Ethan!" Adley cried, her expression twisted in terror before glaring at Nate. "Let him *go*!" Both she and Anna then ran forward.

But Nate quickly pulled me back, holding the knife tighter against my neck. "Take one step closer, and I'll cut his fucking throat and watch him bleed out!"

I felt fresh tears pour down my cheeks. I choked out a sob, still grasping Nate's knife-wielding arm as if that would stop him from killing me. "Don't," I wheezed, feeling blood drip down onto my collarbone. "*Please*."

"Don't *you* tell me what to do," Nate hissed as I spotted Kyle, watching in horror from the ground. He looked as if he wanted to help but had no idea what to do.

I don't want to die.

I can't die.

I can't–

A wave of determination and adrenaline swept over me, and I elbowed Nate hard in the ribs. I then kicked him in the shin, making him howl in pain. He didn't let go of me, but his grip did loosen. I used that opportunity to get my hand in between the knife and my neck.

"You think you're so *good*, don't you, Landers?" Nate sneered, pressing the blade against my knuckles. "Well, the good ones always die." Nate dug the knife into my hand, and I screamed, blood pouring down my arm. I kicked out again desperately, but I couldn't hit anything.

No, no, no–

"Fuck you, Nate!" I heard Adley shout before I was suddenly hurtling backward, the wind whistling in my ears–

I landed sideways, rolling a few times before I stopped, half of my body dangling precariously over the edge of the small cliff that led to the rapids. Letting out a shout, I scrambled away from the water.

When I looked above, however, I saw Nate dangling in midair — right above where Ember's Bridge had been before it had been blown into rubble. Adley's hands were wrapped around his neck tightly, and he was gasping for air as his face turned bright red.

"Nate Tucker," Adley stated in a flat tone while glaring at Nate with hatred-filled eyes. "You think you can mess with us and *win*?" She laughed without humor, baring her teeth. "You've always been dumb, haven't you?"

At the question, Adley let go of Nate, dropping him into the screaming water below.

It scared me how I had almost done that to myself only a few weeks ago.

Everyone went silent, staring at Adley, whose harsh expression hadn't softened. There was a wild look on her face, her hair was tangled, and her mahogany-laced dress was torn at the hem.

She looked *powerful.*

And, for the first time, I felt *afraid* of her.

But then, her face abruptly changed, shifting to worry as she, along with Anna and Kyle, ran over to me. I had my bleeding hand in my lap, and my other hand was pressed against my throat.

I'm not bleeding that *much… Am I?*

"Oh, shit, Ethan," Adley cried, laying a hand on my shoulder. "Are you—"

"Don't touch me," I murmured, flinching away from her hand. Then, Nate's words from earlier echoed through my brain.

You really want to save your sister's killer, *don't you, E?*

"Wh-What?" Adley stammered, seeming baffled by my reaction.

"You… You *killed* Anna," I stated, standing up and swaying on my feet. "*You* even said so… You said you did it."

My vision was dimming, black creeping in on all sides.

Am I dying?

I can't die…

"You're a murderer! Get away," I slurred before the world tilted sideways, and the darkness took over.

When I opened my eyes, everything was blurry, though I could tell that I was moving. I blinked hard, then realized that I was in Adley's arms and that she was sprinting while carrying me. Not far behind us, I could see Anna and Kyle following, the two of them sharing the same terrified expression.

"What's going on?" I cried, startling Adley and making her stop running.

"E!" she exclaimed, a smile appearing on her face. "You're awake!"

She set me down on the ground, but I immediately toppled over, my head still spinning. Everyone crouched in front of me, but though they were talking, I could hardly understand what they were saying.

"Where *are* we?" I asked, looking around frantically.

"Where's Jessi?"

"We had to run, E," Adley told me gently. "You passed out after Nate died, so I carried you down the path. We're still at GV."

"Where's Jessi?" I questioned again, more urgently this time.

"We… We had to leave her," Anna choked, unable to look at me.

"No!" I shouted, attempting to stand up in protest but falling back down. "We have to go back! We can't just *leave* her!"

"Ethan," Adley said sternly. "We can't carry around a… a *body*."

"But-but then someone will just *find* her there – like how I found *you* in the graveyard!"

Adley flinched, her eyes full of tears. "I know. I'm sorry, but this is the way it has to be."

"No, no, *no*…" I murmured, covering my face with my hands as if that would erase the entire night.

My best friend is dead.

She's gone, and she's never coming back.

"Guys, we have to keep going," Anna cried, and I nodded even though I didn't want to.

Taking a deep breath, I then stood up with the help of Adley, as afraid as I still was of her.

I guessed that this was just going to have to be the new normal.

We continued running down the gravel paths of the park as Adley told us every so often where to turn – she knew the park's layout by heart. The cut on my hand was still throbbing, but thankfully, like the shallower cut on my neck, the bleeding had slowed.

As we reached a clearing, we all came to a stop, gasping for air. I bent forward, placing my hands on my knees, and I stared at the ground, willing myself not to pass out again.

"Where are we even going?" Kyle asked, panting just as much as I was.

Adley sighed, combing a hand through her matted hair. "Our best bet is probably Crystal Lake."

My eyebrows shot up in surprise. I'd heard bits and pieces about the neighboring town before, but from what I knew, it had been mostly abandoned for over a decade. I wasn't even sure if they printed it on maps anymore.

Maybe that was a good thing for now, though.

"Wait," I gasped as everything registered in my mind. "We're *leaving*?"

"We have no other choice," Adley responded, sighing. "We can't exactly stay here anymore."

"How are we going to explain that we all just *disappeared*?" Kyle asked, shaking uncontrollably. "I know nobody knows that Anna and Adley are alive, but Ethan and I still have lives."

"Everyone will probably assume we're dead. We left the dance to hang out at the park, and a small fire turned into an uncontrollable one, killing us and burning our bodies."

"*What*?" I cried, staring at Adley as if she had two heads. "We *can't* do that!"

"We *have* to." Adley's expression softened as she looked me in the eye. "I'm sorry, E. It's that or you and Kyle go back to living your normal lives while lying to everyone forever about what happened tonight. Anna and I would either have to keep living as different people or... we'd have to leave for good."

"There *has* to be another option," I prompted, unable to accept the outcome.

"Maybe there is one, but what if Ivy, Nate, or Damion *aren't* dead like we thought? What if Ivy's mother or other creatures come after us next?" Adley questioned, and we all nodded slowly, understanding her point. "We're risking our lives living here no matter what."

"Okay," I whispered, glancing around at the only three people I had left. "As long as we have each other."

It was hard to feel grateful when I had just learned that everyone had been lying to me about *everything*.

It was hard to feel grateful when I had just watched someone that I loved *die*.

It was hard to feel grateful when all I felt was *empty*.

As I ran, I felt the small amount of motivation that I'd had fade away, and I stumbled, nearly bringing myself to the ground. My head hurt, the dizziness hadn't vanished, and the smell of the blood caked on my clothes was threatening to make me sick. I just wanted to drop to the ground and stay there *forever*–

No, I told myself, finally picking up my pace. *You can't quit.*

For *Kyle*, who needed a friend to stick by his side.

For *Anna*, who needed a brother to care for her.

For *Adley*, who needed a partner who wouldn't judge her actions.

For *Jessi*, who no longer had the chance to keep going.

For *myself*, who knew deep down that maybe things can get better.

I couldn't give up.

Not *then*. Not *there*. Not *ever*.

June 23rd, 2019 – 2:45 PM

I t's graduation day!" Anna cheered, smiling far much more than she should have been.

"That stupid stop sign prevented me from going farther," I moaned, rolling my eyes at the forest-green car.

"At least you can start having Paydays," Ethan reminded me, then grabbed the first three cards from the College Career stack and handed them to me. "What are you choosing?"

Of course, I was stuck with the usual, shitty salary cards, such as a fashion designer, a teacher, and a secret agent.

My salary in *real* life – away from The Game of Life that we were attempting to play on the kitchen table – wasn't the best either, but at least I got to say that I was officially an author.

After deciding to show off my writing skills to the rest of the world two years ago, posting *my* updated version of *Romeo and Juliet* – which I titled, *Raven and Josie: Take Two* – on Wattpad, I decided to self-publish. From there, my novel became a hit, and I eventually started selling paperback copies at Barnes & Noble.

Now, in a few days, I was going to fly to LA to help write the screenplay for the novel's Hulu movie adaptation.

Over the past three years since Jessi's death and the battle on Ember's Bridge, a lot had happened. Nothing had been quite the same, but I couldn't lie and say that the fresh start wasn't something we had all needed. With the help of my mind control abilities, we had been able to get on a Greyhound bus and move to Indiana, where we bought a nice Victorian house. With changed names and fake IDs, nobody had recognized us – even when it was announced on the news that not only was Jessi Alvarez found dead, but Jenna Adams, Kyle Meester, Aurora Dickinson, and Ethan Landers were pronounced missing – and hadn't been found since.

I selected the secret agent card and spun the colorful wheel, then advanced six spaces and landed exactly on the Payday space. "You owe me 100K," I remarked, sticking my hand out across the table to Kyle, who was rifling through the paper money.

These days, Kyle stayed home to cook and keep the house clean, while Anna and Ethan worked at the 7/11 down the road, and I stayed locked in my bedroom and wrote as much as I could. Moments where we all sat in the same room and smiled, however, happened more often by the month since we were finally moving on with our lives.

After Kyle handed the cash to me, Anna spun the wheel next and advanced six squares, landing on the Getting Married stop sign. The table fell silent as she closed her eyes and stuck two fingers into the plastic peg bag. When she opened her eyes to see that it was pink, I could tell that something had come over her since her wide smile had become sad.

Anna had found it the hardest to recover after Jessi's death. After all, she had fallen in love with Jessi, and watching her die on the bridge had scarred her the most. We had attempted the month after Jessi died to visit Ember falls for her funeral, but we had only been able to lurk in the shadows and watch from afar to avoid being spotted.

It had been hard for Anna to accept the fact that Jessi could never be resurrected like we had been, but there was no loophole – Fallen couldn't be brought back to life.

Anna placed the new peg in her hot-pink car's passenger seat before she spun the wheel for gifts. We each gave her 100K before she spun another six and landed on a Payday square, where she got 100K for being a scientist. She grabbed it herself before pushing the board closer to Kyle for his turn.

As he spun, Kyle closed his eyes and crossed his fingers. "Please land on a five. Please, give me a *five*!" When the spinner slowed, though, it landed on a four. "Come on!" he remarked, advancing his yellow car to an action spot. "I wanted to get a vacation. Paris would have been nice–"

"Stop whining and pick up the damn action card," I remarked, passing him the top card of the deck. When he picked it up, he chuckled at its sight. "What?" I asked, knowing that everyone was wondering the same question.

"It's a Spin-the-Wheel card. This one's for a treasure hunt… I used to always pick Dylan to be my opponent for this card," Kyle recounted, smiling at the memory. "It's weird not having him and Calvin around all the time."

"I know, but this is how it has to be," Ethan reminded

Kyle, his eyes full of sadness. "At least we can still talk with them."

After the night on the bridge, Dylan had texted Kyle to see how the dance had gone since they hadn't talked since. Luckily, that had prompted Kyle to invite Dylan and Calvin to Indiana since both Kyle and Ethan wanted to admit the truth to them about everything. Though they didn't always see each other, the boys still Skyped, and Calvin and Dylan visited every once in a while, promising to keep our secret.

"Please, no tears," Anna cried, and we all laughed. "Your turn to spin, E." At the command, Ethan spun a nine, landing on the twin space.

"Damn, have things gotten heated between you and Adley?" Kyle teased, and I felt my face burn. I looked to my side to see Ethan's face to be just as red.

"Shut up," Ethan laughed, shoving Kyle's arm playfully, though he didn't seem to mind the callout.

Ethan and I had eventually found a way to get close again. Nothing was perfect, of course, but we loved each other so much that we decided to put our pasts behind us. Our only fear was what the future held since, after all, I was still a demon, while he was a human.

"All right, what are their names?" Anna asked with a smile, looking from me to Ethan. I did the honor of pulling out the two pegs, then placing one pink and one blue in the second row of Ethan's car.

"I mean, I've never thought about names," Ethan stated, combing a hand through his golden curls. "But, I don't know, I'd like to name the boy Jack."

My heart stopped for a quick second as I realized what Ethan had just said.

He wanted to name one of his children after my father.

I stupidly felt a warm tear trickle down my face. "Ethan," I laughed tearfully, smiling and holding his hands in mine. "I love that. And, I was thinking, I'd like to name the girl Jessica."

"After *Jessi*?" Anna gasped, and I turned to look at her, then noticed a smile consuming her face. "You know she always hated it when you called her that, right?"

"It'd be a way to preserve the memory," I reminded Anna, chuckling at the thought. "We'd always have a piece of Jessi with us."

We were all then teary-eyed, and the silence that fell over our table next didn't feel uncomfortable – it felt *necessary*.

"Guys, you know you haven't even *had* these babies yet," Kyle pointed out. "And Adley, you aren't even sharing the babies in this game–"

"Stop ruining the moment!" we all cried, breaking into laughter again.

It was odd not worrying about what was going to happen next since we had finally come to the end of our story. The villains were dead as we knew, and we were safely hidden from any dangers. Though we had lost a few people along the journey, we learned that we could survive just about anything – from heartbreaks to deaths, and from resurrections to battles against evil.

Together, we had never lost hope.

Maybe that was the biggest accomplishment of all.

Author's Note

Each day, so many people attempt suicide, and the worst thing is that most of these people show clear warning signs. If you know someone who is struggling, you can help them. Just asking someone about how their day is going can change a lot.

A few warning signs that may also help you realize if a friend or family member is at risk include: experiencing a loss of appetite, a loss of interest in activities, a withdrawal from others, energy loss, sleeping too much or too little, substance abuse and/or self-harm, a large personality change, talking about killing themselves, and saying that they have no reason to live.

If you are having suicidal thoughts, please know that you are not alone, and there are people who would miss you deeply. There are also so many people who can help. It is not weak to admit that you are struggling.

If you or someone that you know have had suicidal thoughts or may show one or more of the warnings signs above, don't hesitate to reach out. Contact Talk Suicide Canada at 1-833-456-4566 (45645) or the National Suicide

Prevention Lifeline at 1-800-273-TALK (8255). You can also learn more at www.988lifeline.org

Acknowledgments

It breaks my heart when I realize that this is the end of a story that I've spent five years with. Writing has been what has carried me through the difficult moments in my life, and it has been such a pleasure getting to dive deeper into the characters in this book and share with you their different sides. Saying goodbye hurts, but there are times when an author knows that the story can't go any further and that it is time to write *The End.*

This story has been such a journey, and I couldn't have done it without you. Readers play such huge roles, and no matter how you did it – either you helped me create ideas or read and supported me – you inspired me to keep writing. So, as I always like to do, I have to start by thanking *you*, who chose to read this story and take the time out of your life to dive into mine.

Secondly, I have to thank Mom and Dad for being the most supportive parents that an author could ever wish for. Thank you for listening and understanding when I would freak out over the slightest things such as typos and plot holes. Your love has carried me through this journey, and without you, I wouldn't be here today, writing my *second* acknowledgment page. I also have to thank my family, as always, for being so loving and supportive no matter the cause.

Thirdly, I must thank my amazing friends for being there for me and keeping me sane – especially my very close ones who always put up with my crazy ideas and rants about books. You have been a great inspiration (even if you don't know it), and your love has made a huge impact on my life. I'll forever be grateful for your support and help with this project. This also includes all my first readers who helped me expand my ideas, develop my characters, and improve this piece more than I ever could – especially my online friends, either from Wattpad or social media, such as Minoo, who have stuck with me throughout the years and still help correct the grammar mistakes I make that Word never seems to catch.

This duology will always be a part of me, and it has been such a joy to create and write these characters and storylines. Without you all, this book wouldn't have been possible. So, *thank you* for loving these characters and the town of Ember Falls just as much as I do.

About the Author

Enya Clancy is an author of dark dramas and murder mysteries, including *The Immortal Bloodlines* duology. When she isn't writing, she could be found reading a good thriller or listening to music. She lives in Canada and enjoys binge-watching horror movies, writing poetry, and capturing moments through photograph